SHE WAS MESMERIZED BY HIS EYES

Cordelia felt his gaze travel slowly down her cheek, linger for several agonizing seconds on the pulse throbbing in her throat, and come to rest on her breasts. Her skin burned with heat, and a sensation that was something between terror and yearning erupted within her. Without conscious awareness she reached out her hand toward the count, and he took it into his clasp and stroked her fingertips with his thumb, tracing circles around her knuckles.

Suddenly a kaleidoscope of new sensations burst inside her, overwhelming her with their intensity. Cordelia wanted him to carry her hand to his lips and press a passionate kiss into her palm. She wanted him to stroke every inch of her flesh. She wanted to bare her throat to his caress. She wanted what she had never before dreamed of wanting. . . .

Prince of
the Night

Jasmine Cresswell

A TOPAZ BOOK

TOPAZ
Published by the Penguin Group
Penguin Books USA Inc., 375 Hudson Street,
New York, New York 10014, U.S.A.
Penguin Books Ltd, 27 Wrights Lane,
London W8 5TZ, England
Penguin Books Australia Ltd, Ringwood,
Victoria, Australia
Penguin Books Canada Ltd, 10 Alcorn Avenue,
Toronto, Ontario, Canada M4V 3B2
Penguin Books (N.Z.) Ltd, 182–190 Wairau Road,
Auckland 10, New Zealand

Penguin Books Ltd, Registered Offices:
Harmondsworth, Middlesex, England

First published by Topaz, an imprint of Dutton Signet,
a division of Penguin Books USA Inc.

First Printing, July, 1995
10 9 8 7 6 5 4 3 2 1

 REGISTERED TRADEMARK—MARCA REGISTRADA

Printed in the United States of America

To Malcolm,
even though he doesn't believe in vampires

Prologue

☾

The Duchy of Modena, November 1836

He had chosen her weeks earlier, at the time of the grape harvest. She was sturdy of limb and solid of body, and went about her tasks with the slow-moving grace typical of her peasant ancestry. Last week he had learned that she was called Maria, the most common of all the names given to female infants born in the duchy.

Dakon studied her from afar, always from the protection of the shadows, trying to decide if her character was as phlegmatic as her appearance. The last thing he needed was a woman possessed of too much imagination, and he was vastly relieved when he detected no hint of undue sensitivity in her makeup. He wasn't sure how much longer he would be able to control his impulse to mate. Even so, despite the cresting urgency of his need, he was unwilling to slake his thirst for sexual release at the risk of almost certain death for his partner.

Once the decision was made that Maria would be

the one, he found himself praying to a deity he believed in only intermittently. The words poured from him unbidden as he prepared for sleep. Please God, he whispered in the cruel, blinding light of dawn. Let her survive the mating. Let her accept me and live.

If he had dared, he would have prayed for her to survive the birth that would inevitably follow, but Dakon's deity—if he existed—was a harsh one, not given to granting extravagant wishes. Dakon resigned himself to accepting the limits of possibility, and contented himself with praying for Maria's temporary survival. He would not think of the day, eleven months from the mating, when his son would be born, and Maria would die.

Her parents accepted his offer and surrendered their daughter willingly enough to his charge, declaring themselves honored by the prospect of service to their lord. Their questions about the precise role Maria would play in his household were stilled by the pathetically few silver coins Dakon had paid. He would willingly have tendered more, except that his generosity would have caused comment, and his father had warned him to avoid arousing anyone's interest or suspicions at the time of his cresting. For Maria's sake, he felt a moment of anger that she should have been abandoned so readily by those whose role it was to protect her, but the anger soon passed, drowned in the increasing urgency of his need to mate.

He had no cause to feel surprise at the behavior of Maria's parents. Dakon had learned early in life that dire poverty and strict morality could rarely coexist. Hunger quieted even the most active conscience, and his education had trained him to take advantage of this human weakness. The Vam-pyr survived in large part because of human frailty.

He salved his own conscience with a week of further close observation after Maria took up residence in the villa. To his unutterable relief, she adapted to her surroundings with the unflappable calm of those who entirely lack imagination, performing her new domestic chores with the same animal grace she had previously shown when working in the fields. In short, he concluded, she was an ideal candidate for a successful mating. He chose the night of their joining with care, waiting for the moon to wane, and a spate of thunderstorms to pass. For some reason, it seemed that the electricity generated by a gathering storm increased the violence inherent in the act of penetration, and Dakon was determined to take every possible precaution. He looked forward to the moment when he could notify the Council Elders that he had mated again— and that the human female had survived. He knew such an experience was rare, and he anticipated boasting of his achievement at the next regional gathering of the Vam-pyr.

The night appointed for their joining arrived with agonizing slowness. Maria came to him shortly before the midnight hour, bathed and clothed by his housekeeper in a traditional green silk robe, dyed the color of the Vam-pyr sun.

She had protested the scrubbing with soap and the submersion in hot water far more than the prospect of losing her virginity to a master she scarcely knew. Dakon's sensitive ears, made more sensitive by the hormones flowing in preparation for the mating, had heard her screams as the water was poured over her head, washing lice and a year's worth of olive oil from her hair. Horrifyingly, her screams excited him, and he felt the tingle of desire explode in the sensitive sacs already beginning to bulge in the roof of his mouth.

Dakon willed himself to calm. He reminded himself that he was disciplined, caring, honorable. He had spent the past year training himself for this moment, expiating for the death of the last female he had mounted. There would be no mishaps tonight, he had sworn it to himself on numerous occasions. He would prove that humans who mated with the Vam-pyr could survive.

The candles flickered in a draft of air blowing in through a crack in the casement window of his bedroom. Maria shifted nervously from foot to foot as she stared at Dakon. Even after bathing, her skin was still dark from years of exposure to the powerful sun of Earth. Dakon visualized her darkness against his pallor and again he felt the powerful—delicious—promise of impending ecstasy.

"Do not be frightened," he said, trying to speak softly, and not sure if he succeeded. He moistened his dry lips, wondering if she could hear his heart banging against his ribs. "Come closer, my dear. I promise that I will be very gentle with you." Even to his own ears, the promise sounded false, although he made it in total sincerity.

Obediently she edged toward him, her bare feet silent on the tile floor. He realized as she approached that she was shivering, her teeth chattering, her body convulsing. He hoped it was from the cold. God, how he hoped it was from the cold and not from fear. Surely she was too stolid, too ignorant, to be so fearful? Had he not spent weeks determining that of all the young females within a hundred-league radius, she was the one least likely to be overcome by irrational fears?

He drew her to him, running his hands over her face, pressing his erection against the softness of her belly. Desire seeped into every pore of his skin and every cell of his body. The saliva gathered in his mouth, bathing the buds that shielded his fangs in the fluid of sexuality. He felt the sacs swell with an exquisite premonition of urgency. He swallowed, forcing himself back under control.

He realized that he was trembling, just like Maria. The knowledge soothed him. Perhaps, like him, she was shivering with the onset of desire. Human females were capable of feeling desire, a study conducted by Hakylm last century had proven it conclusively, showing that they had a particular attraction for the Vampyr. It was another human trait that Dakon had been trained to take advantage of.

But Dakon didn't want to take advantage of Maria. He wanted to mate with her, that was all. "Why are you shivering?" he asked. "Are you cold?"

"No, lord." Her voice cracked with fear, and Dakon felt a surge of rage. What was she frightened of? Why did she tremble? He hadn't done anything to her yet. Nothing, that is, save stroke her cheek with gentle fingers.

If she was determined to wallow in irrational fears, there was little point in delaying further. Better to proceed and permit her to see that those fears were without foundation. He carried her over to the bed and laid her against the pillows, stroking her hair from her dark eyes with tender fingers. He was proud of his self-control, proud of the fact that he was able to resist the growing urge to lie down on top of her and sink his fangs deep into the gloriously tempting column of her throat. Reining in his rampant desire, he ran his hands across her breasts, parting the pale green mating robe, baring the sturdy outline of her body to his heated gaze.

"Lord, I am a virgin," Maria whispered. "You will not hurt me?"

"Of course not," he snapped, irritated that she had spoken, annoyed that she had interrupted the exquisite fantasy building in his mind. He had known she was a virgin, of course, otherwise he would not have chosen her. Centuries of trial and error had proven that matings only resulted in offspring if the human females were virgin.

The moment of irritation broke the hold he had maintained over his state of arousal. In a single surge of overwhelming force, his fangs expanded and broke through the sacs containing them, just as he felt the pressure of his erection build to a level that demanded immediate release.

Maria saw his fangs at the same moment she felt him press against the barrier of her virginity. She screamed in terror, a mindless cry that echoed and reechoed throughout his bedchamber. He felt her fear, absorbed it into himself through every one of his senses, vaguely aware that he no longer resented her fright, but actually welcomed it. The smell of her terror was the most potent aphrodisiac he had ever known, beyond anything he could have dreamed of in his most erotic youthful fantasy. He was swamped with the need to possess, to penetrate, to procreate.

Dakon thrust himself deep into Maria's body, holding her hands high above her head and falling upon her neck with a hunger that could not have been equaled by a lifetime of fasting. His fangs pierced the skin of her throat and slipped into the smooth cartilage of her jugular. Ahh, what ecstasy! What blissful release from years of arid, tormented waiting! Her blood flowed warm, sweet, and ambrosial over his tongue. He swallowed the exquisite nectar, drinking in her fragile essence as he thrust into her body, filling her with his seed. How wonderful it was that such delight should also produce the happiness of a son, an heir, a Vam-pyr child that Dakon would love and cherish, the grandson ZArymp had craved for so many years.

The spasms of ecstasy slowly ended, the ripples of his release convulsing him over and over again. The joining complete, he collapsed panting onto the limp body of his mate. Although she was no more than an uneducated peasant, he felt a great tenderness toward her, a deep gratitude that she had allowed him to slake his desire at the same time she became the receptacle for the seed of his son. Mindful of his weight, he rolled away from her, drawing in great lungfuls of refreshing air.

Still spent from the force of his mating, he made her a silent promise. During the next eleven months, he would see that she was afforded every possible kindness and luxury. He would tend to her needs, humor her slightest whim, shower her family with money. He owed her at least that much. As for the birth, he would not think of it.

"Maria," he said softly, staring into the comforting darkness. "Maria, I am indebted to you for the gift of your body. Ask for what reward you wish, and I will try to give it to you...."

She didn't reply. Overwhelmed by a sudden dreadful premonition, he rolled over and gazed down at the woman who had been his mate.

As soon as he turned, he saw the hideous wounds in her neck, the gaping slashes around which blood was already congealing in pathetic patches of sticky red. The euphoria of his mating dissipated into an icy sensation of dread.

"Maria!" Her name rasped in his throat as he worked frantically to repair the damage wrought equally by his fangs and his mindless lust. He willed her to wake up, to survive the depredations he had wrought upon her reluctant and terrified body. He tried to release his fangs again so that he could pour the life-restoring fluid of sexual mating into her body, in exchange for the ·blood that he had sucked from her with such reckless abandon. But his fangs had shriveled and retracted inside their protective sacs, and he knew it would be days, perhaps weeks, before they regenerated.

Still, he could not bring himself to acknowledge the fatal finality of what he had done. He worked on her lifeless body for hours, striving with every art known to humankind and to the Vam-pyr to return life to her lifeless body. In the end, as the sun rose and infiltrated the sanctuary of his bedchamber, he was forced to admit the truth. He had murdered Maria. Worse yet, in his heart of hearts, he had always known that the inevitable result of his mating would be precisely this: a human female, offered no meaningful choice, surrendering her life to assuage the sexual needs of an arrogant Vam-pyr.

He had been a crass, conceited fool, Dakon decided. He was still young, barely a century old, and it usually took three. or four hundred matings before a Vam-pyr could control his lust sufficiently to mate successfully. Even then, accidents were frequent, and the rate of impregnation unreliable. Still, Dakon could not forgive himself. His youth and sexual inexperience might partly explain, but could never excuse, the willful arrogance of his behavior. Maria had not deserved to die, even in the noble cause of creating a new generation of Vam-pyr. Her life had a worth and value he was not at liberty to ignore.

In his efforts to revive Maria, he had sewn up the jagged wounds in her throat, bathing the ripped flesh in his own blood to speed the creation of new tissue. He had not been able to bring her back to life, but so great was the regenerative power of Vam-pyr blood, that the raveled edges of her skin had knit together, hiding the evidence of the death he had caused. It would be quite easy to explain away her death, which meant that he wouldn't have to leave the Duchy. For that, he was glad. He had grown fond of the villa, and proud of his accomplishments in turning neglected land into profitable vineyards. In the future, there would be no need for him to move, no need to cut the roots he had begun to put down, because no more humans would meet their deaths at his hands.

Touching the almost invisible scars on Maria's neck, Dakon vowed that he would never again subject a human female to the dangers of his Vam-pyr lust. Tonight, he had mated for the last time. He had murdered his last human female. Placing his hand on Maria's silent heart, Dakon swore it.

Chapter One

(

Duchy of Modena, March 1859

Miss Cordelia Hope prided herself on possessing more than her fair share of British fortitude, and a sanguine disposition that inclined her always to look upon the brighter side of life. But this afternoon, finally, both fortitude and good cheer had deserted her.

The rain had been falling without letup for the past sixteen hours, and the donkey tracks that the locals laughably insisted upon calling roads had long since degenerated into quagmires of oozing mud. From experience, she knew that the sullen gray light would soon give way to impenetrable darkness, making travel hazardous to the point of folly.

Worst of all, a few minutes ago, the driver hired to take them to the Villa of the Three Fountains had suddenly stopped the carriage in the filthy courtyard of a wayside inn, and refused to drive any further. Cordelia tried to protest, but the driver simply unhitched the horses and disappeared into the fetid darkness of a ramshackle hut behind the inn. Despite all her pleas, he refused to come out, and the three exhausted travelers had been forced to seek refuge in the tavern.

Shepherding her companions ahead of her, Cordelia looked around the squalid taproom, met the hostile gaze of the innkeeper, and tried her best not to feel terrified. She would not surrender to hysterics just because she and her party were hopelessly lost, stranded in a hovel that barely deserved the name of inn, abandoned in a remote region of Italy hovering on the brink of war.

She knew she could look for no help from her traveling companions, the Lady Mary May Stanwyck, only daughter of the Sixth Earl of Stanwyck, and Ellen Harding, her ladyship's elderly maid. Ellen had been a bundle of nerves ever since they boarded the ferry to cross the English Channel, and she'd spent the past week in imminent expectation of being murdered by brigands. Hunched on a stool in the corner of the tavern, she alternately emitted little moans of despair and sobbed into her sodden handkerchief.

As for Lady Mary, she at least refrained from tears, although not out of any desire to be obliging. Lady Mary knew from years of careful observation that she was unable to cry without making the tip of her exquisite nose quite red, so she cried only in situations where absolutely no other method of achieving her goals existed. Seating herself on the room's only chair, nostrils pinched in disapproval of her squalid surroundings, she occupied herself in complaining about Cordelia's inadequacy as a travel guide.

"My constitution is too refined to endure the rigors of any more of your muddles," she said, glowering at Cordelia. "I am faint with fatigue."

"Then rest while you have the chance," Cordelia said, clinging to her fast-vanishing supply of patience.

Her calm response infuriated Lady Mary, who liked her social inferiors to show a proper degree of fear. "The earl gave me into your charge, Cordelia, and if you fail to return me safely to his care, you may be sure that he will seek *dire* retribution."

"I do not doubt it," Cordelia said wearily, well aware that the Earl of Stanwyck was not a man to accept failure from his minions, even if those minions happened to be cousins of the family, like Cordelia.

"I don't understand why you insisted on setting out from Piacenza this morning," Lady Mary said, her voice cracking with a hint of genuine fear. "You should never have left the safety of the town without my father's man of business to escort us. You may rest assured, Cordelia, that the earl will hear from me how recklessly you behaved."

"We waited in Piacenza for more than a week," Cordelia pointed out, stung into an attempt at self-defense. "*Signor* Pesante never arrived at our appointed meeting place, and nobody could tell us how to get a message to him. For a lawyer who has supposedly worked all his life in this region, *Signor* Pesante seems mysteriously unknown."

"The people you asked were all ignorant dolts," Lady Mary said. "All Italians are ignorant dolts."

"In which case, it hardly matters that we have left Piacenza, does it?" Cordelia murmured. "We are merely exchanging one set of dolts for another."

Lady Mary tossed her curls, which were drying in a golden halo around the exquisite oval of her face. "I'm sure Mr. Peasant has arrived in Piacenza by now, and it's your fault that we have left. I begged you to show a little forbearance and follow my father's instructions to the letter."

In fact, Lady Mary had sworn that she would throw

herself from the balcony of her bedroom if they did not leave Piacenza at once, but Cordelia didn't bother to remind her of this fact. She knew when to save her breath. Lady Mary's threats and complaints had long since become tedious from daily repetition, but this afternoon she looked so pale and fine-drawn that Cordelia was afraid that the stresses of the journey might have serious consequences for her cousin's health.

The innkeeper had been watching them in calculating silence as they shook the worst of the rain from their cloaks and hoods and settled in the taproom. He now inched out from behind the counter and bowed very low, his manner a strange mixture of hostility and obsequious courtesy.

"Most gracious ladies, how may I be of service?" he asked in thick dialect.

"We need to hire a new carriage driver for a short journey," Cordelia answered in standard Italian, hoping he would understand.

The innkeeper's eyes gleamed. He rubbed his hands. "Most honored and excellent *signora*, I am at your service. . . ." His voice tailed away and he looked pointedly at her purse.

Cordelia sighed. They had very little money left now that *Signor* Pesante had failed to arrive with fresh funds, but she was becoming desperate. She pulled a crown from the tiny travel pouch hidden at her waist, and held it up.

The innkeeper snatched at the coin, and she moved it just out of his reach, aware that she'd taken a grave risk by letting him see that she carried money on her person. The poverty they had witnessed during the past week had been so appalling that she had lived in daily expectation of being murdered for their money.

She was shaking inside, but she forced herself to

show no fear. "To earn this crown you must tell me how to reach the Villa of the Three Fountains. You must also provide me with a driver who can take us there."

If she had not been watching so closely to make sure that he understood her Italian, she might not have noticed the tiny shudder, and the flicker of his eyelids at the mention of the villa. Then his expression shuttered, and he bowed, shaking his head regretfully.

"Most excellent *signora*, it is my wish to be of service to you. Alas, I do not know how to drive a carriage myself, and there is nobody else here, save my son, who . . ." He broke off abruptly. "We cannot take you to the villa, *signora*."

She was surprised by his response, but not as surprised as she would have been if she hadn't already met the same sort of evasion many times this week from the townsfolk in Piacenza. Her staunch British soul rebelled at the prospect of outright bribery, but she could see no alternative. With extreme reluctance, she reached into her pouch and extracted a golden guinea.

The innkeeper's eyes bulged at the sight of the shiny coin. His hands clenched at his sides, and he licked his lips. "Is that really gold, *signora*?"

"Yes, it's a British golden guinea, and it can be yours. To earn it, you have simply to drive me and my two companions to the Villa of the Three Fountains."

A bead of sweat popped on the innkeeper's forehead. Then he turned away, closing his eyes, as if he could scarcely bear to look at the gleaming gold. "I cannot drive," he repeated. "I am sorry, *signora*. I cannot help you."

His words were simple, but Cordelia could hardly believe she'd understood the Italian correctly. For a golden guinea—probably the equivalent of at least three months' income—she had expected the innkeeper to vault into the driver's seat before she could finish speaking.

"What!" she exclaimed. "Of course you can take us there!"

He didn't turn around. "No, *signora*. I cannot drive. I cannot take you to the Villa of the Three Fountains." Almost to himself he muttered, "I must protect my sons."

Cordelia felt her self-control begin to fray around the edges. "If you are not willing to drive, then find us someone in the village who can," she insisted.

"Alas, I cannot help you, *signora*. There is nobody in the village who will drive your carriage."

Cordelia bit her lip, ready to scream in frustration. Ever since they had arrived in Piacenza, they had been met with a conspiracy of evasion and silence. Quite apart from the failure of the earl's man of business to keep his appointment, what was it about the Villa of the Three Fountains that had all the locals shifting uneasily in their shoes?

"What does the tavern keeper say?" Lady Mary demanded. "Lud, I swear, if we do not get to this wretched villa soon, there will be no need to continue your search, for I shall be dead of neglect and fatigue."

It was quite typical of Lady Mary to consider that once she was dead, the two remaining members of her party would no longer have any need for shelter. Cordelia accepted the implication without any particular rancor, having grown accustomed to her cousin's selfishness.

"Would it help you to feel better if I asked the innkeeper for a glass of cordial?" she suggested.

Lady Mary did not deign to reply. Her silent shudder at the prospect of touching her lips to any drinking vessel in this establishment was answer enough.

Cordelia knew from experience that there was no point in attempting to persuade Lady Mary to change her mind, so she turned her attention back to the problem of finding an escort to the villa. Determined not to accept defeat, she spread the Earl of Stanwyck's ancient map on the counter and pointed to the intersection of two small roads.

"That crossroads lies no more than half a mile to the north of this tavern," she informed the innkeeper. "And here, no more than six miles to the south, is an estate named the Villa of the Three Fountains. It must be very close to us. Why is no one willing to drive us there?"

The innkeeper barely glanced at her faded map. "Most excellent *signora*, I believe that you would be wiser to spend the night here. We have a bedroom in the loft. I could make it comfortable for you."

"What is he saying now?" Lady Mary demanded. "Goodness, gracious me, Cordelia, I cannot believe that we are still hanging about in this filthy taproom. Why are you taking so long to make such simple arrangements?"

Cordelia translated the innkeeper's offer of a bed in his loft, and Lady Mary let out a shriek of pure, unadulterated horror. "Lud, Cordelia, have you taken leave of your mind? You surely do not expect me to share an attic with you and Ellen? *Three* of us in one bed?" She flapped her kid-gloved hand in front of her face. "Heavens, I shall faint, I know it."

"Please don't," Cordelia said, reaching for her smelling salts and wafting them under Lady Mary's quivering nose. "I realize now that I was foolish even to suggest spending the night here."

Lady Mary decided not to faint. 'Thank God," she said, pushing the smelling salts away. She opened her eyes just in time to see two horsemen ride into the muddy courtyard in front of the inn. "Oh look!" she said. "Soldiers. Thank heaven for their arrival! They will be able to help us."

An ominous rumble of thunder was followed by a flash of lightning and a momentary lull in the lashing downpour of rain. The two soldiers dismounted quickly, their full cloaks dragging with the weight of accumulated rainwater.

Austrians, Cordelia thought. For once she was in complete agreement with her cousin. Thank God for their arrival! They, of all people, would know how to find the Villa of the Three Fountains, and they might even be willing to provide an escort. Thank God, she thought again, recognizing now that help was at hand just how close she'd come to real panic.

The Austrian soldiers strode into the dingy tavern, pulling water-logged scarlet shakos from their heads and dripping streams of water from their riding capes. "Bring us wine!" one of them shouted.

The innkeeper complied in silence and the taller of the two soldiers tossed a couple of copper coins toward him before striding into the taproom. Suddenly realizing that they were in the presence of three women, they stopped abruptly in the middle of the room, setting their mugs onto the rickety wooden mantel and tugging at their jackets. Cordelia noted with rueful resignation that the younger officer needed only one glance at Lady Mary before he started preening.

The older officer, a tall man with weathered features, was made of sterner stuff than his junior. After a single awestruck glance at Lady Mary, he was able to recover his wits sufficiently to incline his head in a polite nod of acknowledgment to all three women.

"If I may make so bold, ladies, I beg leave to introduce myself and my colleague. I am Captain Hesse of His Imperial Majesty's Fourth Hussars and this is Lieutenant Waldheim." He spoke in French, the language of diplomacy and international affairs, although his native tongue was presumably German.

Neither Ellen nor Lady Mary understood what had been said, so Cordelia stepped forward. "How do you do?" she replied, also in French. She said nothing more, since etiquette taught that ladies did not impart their names and business to perfect strangers.

Captain Hesse clicked his heels, setting his spurs jangling. "I beg to know if there is some way in which we could be of assistance." He hesitated for a moment, then added, "It is unconventional, I know, but would you honor my colleague and me with your names? If I may be so bold, this is no place for three ladies to find themselves unescorted by a gentleman."

Cordelia was so entirely in agreement that she debated for no more than a few seconds before deciding to trust the soldiers with an introduction. "My name is Miss Cordelia Hope, and I am traveling as a companion to Mrs. Frederick Ford, who is my cousin."

Mrs. Ford was the name under which it had been agreed that Lady Mary would spend the next several months. The mythical Mr. Ford was supposedly a member of the British government in India, posted to a station where it was too unhealthy for his wife to accompany him.

Cordelia completed her introductions. "We also have with us Ellen Harding, who is Mrs. Ford's maid, and as you may have guessed, we are visitors from England."

The two officers acknowledged the introductions with elaborate bows and the welcome information that they both spoke English. Lady Mary and Ellen were deeply impressed. Cheered by the sight of two English-speaking gentlemen with such splendid sets of whiskers, Ellen finally stopped sniveling. She stood up and bobbed a curtsy.

Lady Mary, equally partial to mustaches, and similarly revived by the mere presence of two handsome males, bestirred herself enough to twist in her chair, allowing the officers a glimpse of her ravishing profile and glowing violet eyes.

"How fortunate that you should chance to be in this benighted region just when we need you," she said.

The lieutenant's uniform buttons almost popped, he stood up so straight and threw out his chest so far. "Officers of ze Emperor are always eager to be of service to fair ladies," he said.

"But why are Austrian soldiers stationed in Italy?" Lady Mary asked, wrinkling her brow in a charming admission of puzzlement. Her lack of knowledge about the history and politics of the Italian peninsula was spectacular in its totality, and until now, she had expressed not the slightest interest in learning who held ultimate power in the Duchy of Modena, despite the fact that they had been watching Austrian troops muster and drill for most of the week.

Both the officers were stunned into momentary silence, but Lady Mary's infallible effect on all human males had taken hold, and the lieutenant instantly forgave her ignorance. "We serve his Majesty ze Emperor Franz Josef of ze House of Hapsburg," he said, his tone of voice reverent. "Zis area of the Italian peninsula forms an important part of our empire."

"How splendid," Lady Mary said, and probably meant it. Ideals of democracy and national independence were of no importance to her. She smiled sweetly at the soldiers, an innocent child apologizing for not quite having learned her lessons. "There are so many emperors in Europe these days that I simply can't keep them all straight. They come and go with such speed, don't they?"

The captain looked stupefied, as well he might, and even the lieutenant swallowed hard. The House of Hapsburg had ruled in central Europe for over five hundred years, and Austrian pride in their heritage was matched only by their stubborn refusal to see that the era of imperial domination was ending.

Before the officers succumbed to apoplexy, Cordelia decided that it would be wise to change the subject. "We would be very grateful if you could help us hire a driver for our carriage," she said. "We have been having so much trouble finding someone reliable to take us to our destination. The driver who abandoned us here didn't even wait to be paid he was so anxious to be off about his own pursuits."

"Now that is certainly an extraordinary tale!" the captain said, chuckling. "In my experience, these Italians are a grasping set of knaves, always out to snatch a coin or two."

"They do seem to live very close to starvation," Cordelia said.

"And whose fault is that?" Lady Mary demanded. "If they worked harder, they wouldn't be so poor." She spoke with the fervent conviction of a woman who had never performed even five seconds of gainful labor.

"Very true." The captain smiled benevolently. "We have, over the years, found it impossible to instill any sense of loyalty or discipline into the local peasants. However, that is neither here nor there. Do, please, tell me how we can be of help to you lovely ladies. Where is it precisely that you wish to go? Tell us, and we shall personally drive you to your destination."

"How kind." Lady Mary rewarded the hussar with one of the ravishing smiles she normally reserved for dukes and princes of the blood royal. "We wish to find a place called the Villa of the Three Fountains. I do hope it isn't too far away, since I am most desperately fatigued."

The two soldiers exchanged a startled look. "The Villa of the Three Fountains?" Captain Hesse repeated. "What an odd coincidence, Mrs. Ford. That is the very place to which my lieutenant and I are headed."

"You are? How simply splendid! Then you can take us there." No one had ever accused Mary of being needle-witted, and she found nothing strange in the fact that two officers in the Austrian Imperial Army had business to conduct in a villa that belonged to the Earl of Stanwyck and was occupied—as far as Cordelia knew—only by one elderly manservant and his equally ancient wife.

The captain's expression became wary. He coughed, cleared his throat several times, and fiddled nervously with the shiny gold braid on his jacket. "Is the Count of Albion expecting you?" he asked finally. "The count is not ... that is to say, I have not found him to be a man who receives many visitors."

Cordelia blinked and Lady Mary looked puzzled. "The Count of Who?" she asked.

"Ze Count of Albion," Lieutenant Waldheim repeated. "Did you not say that you vish to be escorted to the Villa of the Three Fountains?"

"Well, yes, but the villa belongs to my fa—"

"I'm sorry, but we are not acquainted with the Count of Albion," Cordelia cut in ruthlessly, not allowing Lady Mary to finish her sentence. Given the circumstances of their journey, the fewer mentions they made of the earl's name, the better. "Who is he, may I inquire?"

The atmosphere in the taproom cooled noticeably. "He is the Italian nobleman who owns the Villa of the Three Fountains," Captain Hesse said, his friendly smile turning to a hard, assessing stare.

"Of course he doesn't own the villa!" Lady Mary protested. "My fath—"

"There must be some mistake," Cordelia said, giving her cousin's arm a warning squeeze. "Our destination is the Villa of the Three Fountains, but we are not familiar with anyone called the Count of Albion."

"But I can assure you ze Count of Albion owns ze villa," Lieutenant Waldheim said. "He owns all ze land for miles around. You might say zat he is ze grand seigneur of the region."

Cordelia's stomach lurched with a premonition of disaster. "Then we must be seeking a different villa with the same name," she said. "The villa we seek is a modest establishment, with very little surrounding land, and it was deeded to ... er ... to Mrs. Ford's ancestors over a hundred and fifty years ago."

Captain Hesse shook his head. "You may take my word for it, Miss Hope. There is only one Villa of the Three Fountains in this area, and the estate is quite definitely owned by the Count of Albion."

"The villa we seek has been in the hands of caretakers for over a hundred years," Cordelia said. "Perhaps

the Count of Albion has rented the villa along with
the farmland ..."

The two officers stared at her in silent incredulity.
"Ze Count of Albion is not a caretaker," Lieutenant
Waldheim assured her. "Ze villa belonged to ze
count's father and his grandfather before zat. It is a
place of most great prosperity, or so I haf been told."

Cordelia unfolded her faded map, spreading it out
for the Austrians to see. "I would have sworn that the
villa we're searching for is no more than six or seven
miles from this tavern."

Captain Hesse bent over the map. "The place you
have marked is beyond question the Count of Albion's
villa," he said, straightening. "Am I to understand that
you have reason to believe the estate belongs to
your family?"

"I have documents to prove it," Cordelia said. "The
villa once belonged to the Ossoli family—" She broke
off abruptly. In light of Lady Mary's circumstances, it
was imperative that no whisper should ever leak out
of her true identity.

"I am astonished to hear of this." The captain
frowned, lost in thought. Then he bowed, heels click-
ing. "Clearly, this is a puzzle that cannot be solved
without the assistance of the count himself. The lieutenant and I will escort you to the villa." His voice
faded into uncertainty. "I am sure that, in the circumstances, the Count of Albion will be willing to receive you."

Lieutenant Waldheim cast an adoring glance in
Lady Mary's direction. "No man could refuse shelter
to a lady as luffly as you."

The captain looked more cheerful at this thought
and, in truth, the lieutenant's logic was impeccable. If
the count was like every other male member of the

human race, as soon as he clapped eyes on Lady Mary, an invitation to stay was guaranteed.

"I am loath to impose on a stranger's hospitality," Cordelia said to the captain. "But I believe we have no choice at the moment."

"Then let us be on our way," Captain Hesse said. "If you are ready, ladies, we will depart at once. If the rain gets no worse, we should be at the home of the Count of Albion within the hour, two hours at most."

Lady Mary rose, energy renewed. She shook out her skirts and twirled toward the officers in a rainbow of ruffles and a midnight blue cloak. "Tell me, this Count of Albion, does he have a wife by any chance?"

"No," the captain said, walking her toward the inn door. "The Count of Albion is considered a confirmed bachelor."

"I haf never met him," the lieutenant confided to Cordelia. "He has a reputation as something of a recluse." The lieutenant lowered his voice to a conspiratorial whisper. "It is rumored zat ze count is not entirely—normal—in his habits."

"What does that mean?" Cordelia asked.

The lieutenant cast her a speaking glance. "Alas, he has no interest in the ladies. His servants, you understand, are all young boys, except for one elderly housekeeper."

Cordelia couldn't imagine why anyone would choose such an odd way to staff their household. "All boys, you say? How very strange."

"Yes, indeed. He has dozens of young boys serving him. And very good-looking, all of them."

Captain Hesse spoke sharply. "That's quite enough gossip, Lieutenant. You had better make haste to get the horses."

"Yes, sir." The lieutenant saluted. "Certainly, sir. At once."

Captain Hesse ushered Lady Mary to the rickety shelter of the tavern porch, and Ellen followed her mistress outside, waiting for the lieutenant to drive the horses out from their rough, lean-to shelter. When Cordelia attempted to join them, the innkeeper stepped out from behind his counter and intercepted her.

"*Signora*, I could not understand what was agreed between you and the Austrians. Are the soldiers taking you to the Count of Albion's villa?"

"Yes, they are."

"Have a care," the innkeeper whispered. "The villa, it is not a good place for honest people."

Cordelia felt an unexpected shiver of fear. "Why not?" she asked. Captain Hesse turned around at that moment, and the innkeeper ran behind his counter, polishing busily with a filthy rag. "No reason," he said. "I meant nothing of importance, *signora*."

The captain went outside again and Cordelia turned back to the innkeeper. "We shall have the protection of Captain Hesse and his lieutenant," she pointed out.

The innkeeper spat. "Bah!" he said. "Austrians."

He obviously believed those two words said it all.

Cordelia hoped—fervently—that he was wrong.

Chapter Two

(☾

The thunder and lightning started again when they had been traveling southeast for less than an hour. The light failed rapidly as the heavy clouds spilled torrents of soaking rain, and their carriage rocked and slipped at every bend in the muddy, unsurfaced road. Cordelia was greatly relieved when a drenched Captain Hesse tapped on the window to inform them that they had finally arrived at the boundary of the Count of Albion's property.

"The villa is straight ahead of you," he shouted as they rounded yet another sharp curve. A large house came into view. "There it is! The Villa of the Three Fountains!"

Cordelia's first impression of the villa was not favorable. Set atop the crest of a low hill, its stucco exterior washed in gray, the shuttered windows seemed to stare sightlessly into the lashing curtain of rain. As the horses toiled toward the massive entrance gates, and her view became clearer, Cordelia decided that the layout of the house created the bleak impression that it was disconnected from the surrounding countryside, a lonely fortress set in a sea of fallow brown fields. She wondered if the present count was responsible for the unhappy effect, or if he merely had to live with the architectural mistakes of his forebears.

The carriage rocked with more force than usual as it bumped over a deceptively deep puddle in the driveway. Lady Mary turned ashen and slumped deeper into her pillows, pressing one hand to her brow, and the other to her stomach.

"Dear God, I cannot endure many more minutes of this. I swear, every bone in my body aches, and I do not have an inch of skin that is not bruised."

"It's been a horrible day," Ellen agreed, clutching the leather hand strap and trying simultaneously to adjust a pillow in the small of Lady Mary's back. "A horrible two weeks, in fact. I wish they had trains over here, like they do in England."

"Do you feel sick, Mary?" Cordelia asked, worried by the pallor of her cousin's complexion and the sheen of sweat on her forehead. "Would it help to eat a dry biscuit?"

"No," Mary snapped, pressing a handkerchief to her mouth. "Stop pestering me, Cordelia. I cannot abide these constant inquisitions into the state of my health."

Cordelia drew in a deep breath, counted to ten, and managed to hold on to her temper. If Mary refused to face up to the reality of her state of health, then Cordelia was prepared to humor her. At least for another week or two.

The driveway from the gate up to the villa ended in a large, but deserted courtyard, paved in slabs of gray stone. Through the downpour of rain, the prospect on all sides appeared unrelievedly dreary. Cordelia could see no sign of the three fountains that gave the estate its name, nor of any shrubs or flowers that might have softened the grim angularity of the house. Worst of all, the front door remained closed although the sounds of their approach must have been audible for several minutes. What would they do if the Count of Albion refused them hospitality? Would her cousin survive a night spent sleeping in the carriage?

The captain nudged his weary horse toward the portico and dismounted, looping the reins over the painted balustrade. He knocked loudly, several times, but the only response was silence. He knocked again. The door was finally flung open. An old woman, clad in the black dress of an upper servant, stared out at the captain with unconcealed hostility.

"Oh, it's you," she said in Italian, only faintly accented by the local dialect. "My master has been expecting you any time this past hour."

"Hello, Anna," Captain Hesse replied in his halting Italian. "I trust the count is keeping well?"

"He's middling, no more. He works too hard, that's his trouble."

"I shall try not to add to his burden of work."

The old woman shrugged. "But you will. You always do. Come on in then, if you must."

"My horse is wet and hungry...." Captain Hesse gestured to his mount.

"The stable boys will take care of your horse, just like always. Here they come."

Three good-looking youths ran into the courtyard. All of them were wearing sturdy leather shoes, an amazing luxury for this part of the world, and all of them looked well fed. The count went up a couple of notches in Cordelia's estimation. He might live in a dreary house, and have a strong aversion to visitors, but at least it seemed that he made adequate provision for feeding and clothing his servants.

"Who else have you brought with you, Captain?" Anna asked, nodding toward the carriage. "Must be one of your generals at least to ride in such a fancy vehicle."

"Not the general, alas. He is very much preoccupied at the moment with preparations for quelling—" Captain Hesse broke off in midsentence. "That is to say, the carriage belongs to two English ladies and their maidservant—"

"English women?" Anna exclaimed. "*Three* of them? And you've brought them here?" She sounded astonished, as if the captain had admitted to bringing along a menagerie of Borneo tigers and Indian cobras to sit at the count's dinner table.

Captain Hesse clicked his heels. "Yes, that is correct—"

Anna shook her head. "Sorry, Captain, but you know they'll have to leave right away. I can't have women on the premises."

"I understand the count's rules," Captain Hesse said, looking more and more uneasy. "However, these ladies have been stranded in the area through no fault of their own. They are travel-weary and in urgent need of a place to stay for the night. There is no need to introduce them to the count if he wishes to avoid their company. The villa must have a dozen bedchambers, probably more. Surely the count would not refuse to let them occupy just one of those rooms when their need is so desperate."

For the first time, the old woman sounded a touch uneasy. "Rules are rules," she said. "They can't stay here and you know that as well as I do. They're females, and the count will never allow them to sleep in the house. Especially now. This isn't a good time." She stopped abruptly, as if regretting having said as much.

Cordelia found the conversation so extraordinary, she wondered if she'd misunderstood Anna's Italian, although the woman spoke with the clearness and grammatical accuracy of an educated upper servant. She couldn't believe that, even in this benighted part of the world, the Count of Albion was so old-fashioned that he forbade all women to enter his house. Straining to catch every word, she let down the window to its fullest extent, ignoring Lady Mary's complaints about the damp and the blowing rain.

She saw Anna shake her head. "You know better, Captain. No women. Never. Not anywhere in the house, unless the count has given express permission. In advance."

"I am aware of the count's ... customs," Captain Hesse said. "But what is to become of these poor ladies? Where are they to go? They are foreigners, and the country is about to tumble into civil war!"

Anna shrugged. "They shouldn't have left England and you shouldn't have brought them here, that's all I know. But as a gesture of goodwill, I'll tell the stable lads to provide them with fresh horses. There's nothing more I can do for them." She turned to go.

Cordelia couldn't bear to see the housekeeper disappearing into the cavernous darkness of the hallway, taking with her all hope of a warm bath, a hot drink, and a clean bed. She pushed open the carriage door and jumped down the steps.

"Wait! Please wait, *signora*! I must talk to you!" Cordelia raced up the slippery steps, skirts hitched indecorously high above her ankles. To her relief, the elderly servant paused and swung around, scrutinizing her without a trace of expression on her wizened face.

"Yes, *signorina*?"

"Please reconsider your decision," Cordelia said, trying to tuck a strand of wet hair behind her ear and wishing she possessed even half of Lady Mary's capacity for looking ravishing under any and all circumstances. "My companions and I have been traveling for over three weeks, and we are in urgent need of the count's help."

"How so?" Anna asked. "How can you need his help? I'm sure he's never met you."

What with one thing and another, Cordelia's supply of tact was almost exhausted, but somehow she managed to grit her teeth and force a smile.

"We've been searching for several days for a villa where we're expected as guests. We have reason to believe that the count, your master, could help us to find this villa. Nobody else seems to know where it's located."

"Not even your fine Austrian friends?" the old woman asked, swiveling just far enough sideways to shoot a scornful glance toward the captain and his lieutenant. "Those Hapsburg tax collectors can usually find every jar of pickled olives in the district. Seems to me, a fancy villa shouldn't be too much of a challenge for their hunting skills."

Whatever business her master might have with the Austrian soldiers, Anna herself obviously cherished no tender feelings toward them, or toward the army of occupation that they served.

Cordelia thought swiftly. Somehow, she had to win the cooperation of the housekeeper without offending the two Austrians, who might yet prove to be her only resource for finding a bed for the night.

"We met Captain Hesse and Lieutenant Waldheim by chance," she explained. "I'm most grateful to them for escorting us here, but they are not friends of ours, and they have no more idea than we do as to where we can find the Villa of the Three Fountains."

"What?" She had finally caught the housekeeper's attention. "What nonsense is that, *signorina*? This is the Villa of the Three Fountains, as you must be aware."

"I am indeed aware," Cordelia said, deciding to be bold. "My dilemma is this. You believe that the villa belongs to the Count of Albion. I have documents that state quite otherwise. The villa belongs to my family, and the income of the property has been deeded to me. To all intents and purposes, for my lifetime, I own the Villa of the Three Fountains."

The captain gave a little harrumph of disquiet, and Anna's gaze became hooded. "That can't be right," she said at last. "My master was born here, and his father and grandfather before him. You should reexamine your documents, *signorina*. They are not in order."

Cordelia shook her head. "Whatever the explanation for this muddle, you may be sure that my documents are in perfect legal order." The Earl of Stanwyck had many faults, but he would never have ordered his daughter to the Villa of the Three Fountains without impeccable documentation to support her right to stay there. From his point of view, far too much was at stake to risk such unnecessary problems.

"Who sent you here?" Anna asked finally. "Why have you come?"

Two simple questions, Cordelia thought wryly. She wished she could answer either of them honestly.

"We come on important family business," she said finally. "In connection with the estate."

"Family business?" Anna demanded. "Which family? What is the name of this family that supposedly owns my master's villa?"

"I would prefer to discuss that with your master."

"Quite right," Captain Hesse said, stepping forward. "Anna, the *signorina* has said more than enough to convince me that she indeed has business to discuss with the count. You know very well that you are dealing with a lady of quality, so please treat her with the respect she deserves."

The old woman's gaze rested briefly on the captain, and her eyes narrowed in scorn. "Is that why you brought her here?" she said. "So that she could make trouble for my master?"

"Don't be absurd," Captain Hesse said angrily. "Your master and I are partners, not enemies. Enough of this ridiculous delay, Anna. Inform the count that I am here, with my lieutenant and three English ladies who have business to conduct with him."

"And if I refuse?" the housekeeper asked.

"You would not be wise to make such a mistake." Captain Hesse placed his hand over the hilt of his sword, although he didn't draw it. "I am here on official business of the Emperor, and I can tolerate no interference in the execution of my duties. Stand aside, Anna. In the name of His Imperial Majesty Franz Josef, I demand entrance for myself and these ladies."

Anna hesitated for a split second. Then, in a gesture of utter contempt for his threats, she turned her back on him and walked away. But she left the door open, and the captain gestured to indicate that Cordelia should make haste to go inside.

"Go!" he ordered. "Follow the housekeeper. I will see to Mrs. Ford and her maid."

Lifting her muddied skirts, Cordelia followed the retreating servant into the dim interior of the hallway. Once inside, her first impression was of cool, filtered light and the delicate scent of fresh-cut flowers. Her second impression was of emptiness. In contrast to the clutter of carpets, furniture, ornaments, photographs, and heavy draperies so common in English houses, the vestibule of the count's home was almost devoid of furnishings, its gray marble floor quite bare, its high walls color-washed in a shade of pale lavender that Cordelia had never before seen on a wall.

Her third impression was that they were being watched, although she couldn't see any servants, not even Anna, who seemed to have disappeared through a door set almost invisibly in the stucco plaster wall.

The hallway was lit by two oil lamps, turned very low. She peered into the dusky recesses of the hallway, searching for the source of her sensation. She saw nothing out of the ordinary, and yet the impression of being watched grew stronger, despite the fact that in the spacious emptiness of the hallway, she couldn't imagine anywhere that an observer could be concealed.

Lady Mary and Ellen, escorted by the two officers, soon joined her in the echoing hallway. Anna reappeared almost at the same instant, walking briskly down the corridor toward them.

"My master has been informed of your arrival. Please, *Signor Capitano,* instruct your companions to leave their wet cloaks here in the hallway, then come this way. The count has agreed that the women are permitted to spend the night here. They are to wait in the drawing room while their bedchambers are made ready. No doubt you and the lieutenant will wish to wait with them and greet the count."

She bobbed another minimal curtsy and gestured to indicate that the visitors should proceed through a high, arched doorway into a room furnished—albeit sparsely by English standards—as a traditional drawing room.

"I will arrange for refreshments," she said as they trooped into the room. She nodded toward Mary. "It would be better if your maid stayed with you, *signora*. There's no place for her in my kitchens. Now, if you will all take seats, ladies and gentlemen, I will inform my master that you are here." Grimly, she added, "It seems he is planning to meet with you. In person." She made the pronouncement through lips pinched tight with disapproval.

Cordelia translated the housekeeper's remarks, and they all sat down. "Anna is being more difficult than usual," Captain Hesse said as soon as she had left the room. "I have no idea why the count puts up with her sour ways."

"Servants need to be properly disciplined or they run out of control," Mary said. "What a strange woman Anna is, to be sure."

The lieutenant gave a short laugh. "Then from everything I haf heard, she is ideally suited to work for her master. Can you imagine a household run by thirty young boys and an old crone like Anna?"

"The painting above the mantel is most interesting," Cordelia interjected, thinking that it might be wise to refrain from insulting their host in his own drawing room—particularly since she couldn't rid herself of the sensation that they were being watched. "The style is unlike any with which I'm familiar. Can you suggest where it might have originated, Captain?"

Captain Hesse shook his head. "Indeed not. A most curious style. What is your guess, Waldheim?"

A low voice spoke in Italian from the doorway. "It comes from the Kingdom of Siam, *signorina*. My . . . father brought it home from his travels. Do you like it?"

Cordelia swung around, instinctively rising to her feet. "Yes, yes I do."

"It was a gift from the King of Siam himself, and I have always admired it. He has forty wives and more than a hundred children. When I stayed with him, I couldn't decide whether such a life represented absolute bliss or the ultimate torment. Keeping the peace in such a large household cannot be easy, even for a tyrant. One can only chop off so many heads, after all."

The man who had spoken leaned against the jamb of the doorway, his face cast somewhat in shadow by the mahogany doors. Cordelia knew, instantly and without rational justification, that this was the man whose presence she had sensed earlier. She couldn't make out the features of his face with any clarity, and certainly she couldn't detect the slightest trace of a smile, and yet she had the oddest impression that he found them all mildly amusing—like a grandfather, watching the antics of a baby trying to walk.

He was tall and broad-shouldered, the cut of his tailcoat unexpectedly elegant for a man living in such a remote country district. But then, if his father had traveled to Siam, the count and his family were hardly country bumpkins. Cordelia wasn't sure if his hair was truly raven black, or whether the shadows cast by the lamplight created the illusion of gleaming, blue-black luster. It was definitely not a trick of the light that made his skin appear unusually pale, and the absence of a beard or mustache merely emphasized his pallor. Perhaps Anna had not been lying when she claimed her master had been feeling indisposed. Cordelia wondered if the count's indolent leaning posture against the pillars of the door frame indicated physical weakness rather than casual disinterest in his visitors.

The count's eyes met with hers for the briefest of instants, and Cordelia thought she saw his jaw clench, as if the mere sight of her set his teeth on edge. Why, she wondered? What could she possibly have done to provoke such a reaction?

As if mesmerized, she found herself unable to look away when he walked forward into the drawing room. His steps were light, soundless, almost fluid, and she was struck by the frivolous thought that he would look wonderful on the dance floor. To her acute embarrassment, she realized that her gaze was fixed with most unladylike intensity on the movement of his hips, and she hastily jerked her eyes upward, toward some more decorous spot.

Her gaze landed on his face and she saw that his features were strongly defined. His cheekbones stood out with particular prominence, their height and sharp angles underlined by a flush of hectic color that suggested a fever. Perhaps she had misinterpreted the clenching of his jaw when he looked at her earlier.

Poor man, she thought, seized by an odd flash of sympathy. *I do believe he is in a considerable amount of pain.*

He bowed to them all, then took his position directly in front of the fire, his booted foot resting comfortably on the fender. "Ladies, welcome to my home," he said in slow and careful English. "I am the Count of Albion. I believe you wish to speak with me. I hope you will tell me how I may be of service?"

Chapter Three

The count straightened from his introductory bow. His eyes were so dark that he appeared to have no pupils, making it hard to judge the precise direction of his gaze. For a split second, Cordelia had the impression that he inspected each one of them with a swift, razor-sharp intelligence and that his eyes rested longest on her. Then the illusion broke. His mouth relaxed and his gaze drifted toward the Austrians.

"Captain Hesse, I have been expecting you," he said in fluent, but heavily accented English.

The captain clicked his heels smartly. "Excellency, it is good to see you again. It's been too long since our last meeting."

"I understand you have brought one of your colleagues with you?"

"Yes, indeed. May I present my lieutenant, Heinrich Waldheim, of His Majesty's Imperial Guard."

Lieutenant Waldheim executed one of his elaborate, button-popping salutes. "Excellency," he barked. "I am honored."

"The honor is certainly all mine," the count murmured. "It is always a pleasure to meet a loyal servant of the Emperor."

He was fiddling with his watch chain as he spoke and didn't appear to be looking at any one of them in particular, but Cordelia couldn't shake the odd impression that his attention was in reality directed toward her with mesmeric force. The room was cool, almost chill, and yet she felt a sheen of sweat break out on her forehead. Acutely uncomfortable, she stared down at the toes of her shoes, determined to destroy the link that somehow seemed to have been established between herself and the count.

Apparently she didn't succeed because a moment later, he stood at her side. "Allow me, *signorina*." He pressed a handkerchief into her hand. "I think you need this."

It was difficult to breathe, impossible to think. "Thank you," Cordelia murmured, accepting the handkerchief. She had already pressed it to her brow before she stopped to wonder how he knew that she needed one. How embarrassing if she had been visibly sweating!

Horses sweat, men perspire, ladies merely glow. Her glowing had clearly exceeded acceptable limits.

Unwilling to look at him, she folded his handkerchief into a neat white linen square and tucked it beneath her folded hands. The count didn't speak, nor did he move away. She knew, beyond a shadow of doubt, that his eyes were fixed on her face, although she refused to look up and confirm her conviction. She felt his gaze travel slowly down her cheek, linger for several agonizing seconds on the pulse throbbing in her throat, and come to rest on her breasts.

Wherever his gaze touched, her skin burned with

heat. The effort of keeping her eyes averted caused her physical pain, and her stomach churned with a sensation that teetered somewhere between terror and intense yearning.

The yearning grew, swamping the fear, until the urge to reach out and take his hand became almost irresistible. She shut her eyes, fighting off the compulsion to seek his touch. As soon as her eyes closed, she was assailed by the shocking image of the count lying next to her, his head resting against her naked breast, his mouth moving to suckle at her breast . . .

Cordelia snapped open her eyes and shot up ramrod straight in her chair. Appalled by the indecent train of her own imaginings, she realized too late that she had already acted upon one of them. Without conscious awareness, it seemed that she had reached out her hand toward the count and he had taken it into his clasp. He was now gently stroking her fingertips with his thumb, tracing caressing circles around her knuckles.

A kaleidoscope of sensations burst inside her, all of them new, all of them overwhelming in their intensity. She wanted him to carry her hand to his lips and press a passionate kiss into her palm. She wanted him to stroke not just the tips of her fingers, but every inch of her flesh. She wanted to unfasten the buttons of her blouse and bare her throat to his caress. She wanted . . . so many things she had never before dreamed of wanting.

By the exercise of more willpower than she had known she possessed, Cordelia managed not to faint. Feverishly, she grabbed the count's handkerchief from her lap and thrust it at him, hoping he might believe that was why she'd reached out to him in the first place.

The count's fingers stilled, then closed around the handkerchief.

"Excellency, pray release my hand," Cordelia murmured, her voice hoarse.

For a split second, she thought he would ignore her request. Then he let her hand drop. He shut his eyes, pressing the handkerchief against his mouth as if to assuage a sudden burst of pain.

Cordelia winced in sympathy. "My lord, is there anything I can do to help?" she asked in a low voice.

"No, nothing." The count opened his eyes again, and acknowledged her presence with a slight nod of his head. "I thank you for the return of my handkerchief, *signorina.*"

"Thank you for lending it to me, Excellency."

"You have the most beautiful hands. Did anyone ever tell you that?"

"No, Excellency." Cordelia looked away, striving for composure. The warm glow of desire began to spread over her again.

The count muttered something she couldn't quite hear. Cordelia thought it might have been "I mustn't do this." Do what? she wondered.

The strange longings she had been experiencing stopped as abruptly as they had begun. She drew in a shaky breath, and the beat of her heart gradually slowed to normal. When she finally felt courageous enough to look at the count again, she discovered that he was once more standing by the fireplace, his booted foot resting casually on the brass hearth rail, his attention fixed on his watch chain. Of his white linen pocket handkerchief, there was no sign, nor did his calm, abstracted manner betray any hint of what had passed between them.

Cordelia sneaked a surreptitious glance at the other

occupants of the room. As far as she could tell from their expressions, nobody had noticed her shocking conduct, or the count's surprising attentions to her. On the contrary, they all seemed blissfully unaware that anything untoward had occurred. Nobody gave the slightest sign of having heard their highly improper conversation.

Ellen finally turned and caught Cordelia's eye. Cordelia felt her cheeks turn crimson, but the maid gave her a cheery smile and a little bob of the head. From the way she was fussing with her skirts, it seemed almost as if the maid had just that instant settled down onto the sofa. And yet, she had been making precisely the same movements when Cordelia last looked toward her, before the incident with the count. How could that be? Surely Mary would never put up with her maid squirming and wriggling for several minutes at a stretch, especially since they were seated so close together.

Cordelia swallowed over a throat turned suddenly dry. Nobody was paying her the least bit of attention, and yet surely somebody would be looking at her askance if she'd really offered her hand to the count, and he'd gazed down at her, caressing her fingertips with slow, provocative strokes, while murmuring that she had beautiful hands.

Panic washed over her. Dear God, had she finally been overwhelmed by the manifold stresses of the journey? Was it possible that she'd imagined the entire episode with the Count of Albion?

She laced her fingers tightly together, determined to get a better grip on herself. *So much for my much vaunted common sense,* she thought wryly. *Clearly I am overtired and overwrought. I should consider this*

*a timely lesson in the value of humility. Mary and Ellen
are both handling this situation much better than I am.*

The count smiled benignly at the assembled group,
his gaze coming to rest on the soldiers. "Captain
Hesse, we are neglecting the ladies," he said. "I would
be most obliged if you would be so kind as to introduce me to your traveling companions."

"It will be my pleasure, Excellency." The captain
stepped forward and gestured to Mary. "Mrs. Ford, I
make you known to His Excellency, the Count of Albion. Excellency, I present to you, Mrs. Frederick
Ford, a visitor from England."

The count might have a reputation as a misogynist,
but it seemed that he was just like any other man
when confronted with the vision of Mary's beauty. His
pale face aglow with admiration, he swept into a bow
that would have done credit to the Emperor's drawing
room at the Imperial Court in Vienna.

Cordelia couldn't imagine how she had ever persuaded herself that the count's attention had been
fixed on her. He seemed enraptured by the bouncing
gold of Mary's curls, and the dazzling blue of her eyes.

"What a happy chance, ma'am, that of all the doors
in the Duchy, you should come to mine. Welcome,
welcome! We are delighted to have you here."

Mary, ever willing to be gracious to a man who
admired her, stood up from the sofa and sank into
one of her most elegant curtsys. "A happy chance
indeed, Excellency. I thank you for your hospitality."

She waited, head bowed and her skirts billowed into
a dark blue pool of the finest quality wool gabardine.
The count beamed in approval of the pretty sight. "A
nymph from the sea," he murmured, extending his
hand with panache. "Permit me to assist you to your
feet, dear lady."

Blushing and fluttering, Mary placed her hand—as tiny and exquisite as the rest of her—on his silk sleeve. The count raised her up with a grand flourish.

"Thank you, Excellency." Mary rewarded him with a dazzling smile. "May I now make known to you Miss Cordelia Hope, my companion, and Ellen Harding, my maid."

The count acknowledged the maid's presence with a smile and a nod. Then he bowed courteously toward Cordelia. She dipped into a slight answering curtsy, relieved beyond reason that he chose not to come any closer. When she straightened, she realized that she was trembling so hard she could barely stand. The count's dark, unfathomable gaze pulled away from her, and she sank down onto her chair, wondering how she would have survived if the count had walked across the room and offered to shake her hand.

She didn't need to worry about that possibility, since his attention seemed fixed exclusively on Mary. "There are some advantages to rank," he said, smiling at her. "With your permission, madam, I shall claim a seat next to you on the sofa. It is too many years since this house has enjoyed the pleasure of such a charming feminine presence."

"Thank you, Excellency, I am delighted to be here." Mary accepted his praise with a gratified toss of her curls, and a prattle of drawing room chatter. The count had a title, handsome features, and, by all appearances, plenty of money. As far as she was concerned, that meant that his compliments were to be treasured, whatever his other attributes might or might not be.

Bored with inanities she had heard too many times before, Cordelia stopped listening to her cousin's conversation with the count. Her relief at not being the focus of his attention was great, and yet some small part of her couldn't help but feel regret that the count was proving himself to be so very much like other men.

Outside, the dusk had settled into full darkness, plunging the drawing room into heavy shadow, but the count—caught up in his flirtation with Mary—seemed unaware of the inadequacy of the lamps burning weakly in the far corners of the room, and he made no move to call for a servant to bring more lights.

Still, the room wasn't exactly gloomy, despite the pools of shadow. The decor was muted pastel, the draperies straw-colored satin, and the furniture all delicate antiques from the eighteenth century. Together, they created an ambiance that seemed pleasantly restful after the crimson, gilt, and dark mahogany so favored by the hotels where Cordelia and her companions had spent the last two weeks.

She looked around sleepily. Exhausted by the demands of their journey, and lulled by the comfort of her upholstered armchair, she felt her eyelids growing heavy. How nice it would be if they could cut the idle chitchat and go straight to their rooms, she thought.

Thirsty as she was, bed seemed even more appealing than refreshments. Goodness, but she was tired! She yawned discreetly behind her hand and wished she could excuse herself from the drawing room. She visualized herself released from the discomfort of her corset and petticoats, slipping into a clean nightgown, and lying down on the smooth linen sheets of her bed. Instantly, the count came and lay down beside her, his hair dramatically dark against the white embroidered pillow, his hands cool against her heated flesh. She reached out to stroke his silky hair and felt his body press against hers, warm and comforting. She sighed with sleepy pleasure.

Despite the darkness of their room, she could see that he was smiling, his teeth gleaming strong and white in the glow of a single candle. Sleepiness gave way to desire and she shivered with anticipation as his mouth lowered toward her breasts. His lips brushed her shoulders in a tender caress. She moaned with pleasure. Her skin began to burn as she felt the count's heated flesh press ever more closely against her. His mouth trailed kisses in a slow path leading toward her throat, and she ripped at the pale blue satin ribbons of her nightgown, tearing them open, baring her neck to his pleasure. His lips touched the pulse beating at the base of her neck and he pressed his mouth hard against her flesh.

For a moment, she was bathed in a peace more complete than anything she had ever known. Then, horrifyingly, she felt the slash of a knife blade slicing into her neck. Heat and blood drained from the wound that she suddenly realized the count had inflicted. In an instant, she was deathly cold. Her teeth chattered with the cold. Dear God, she was dying!

She tried to tell the count that he was hurting her—killing her—that he must stop what he was doing, but her throat was paralyzed and she could make no sound at all. Her hands reached up, clawing at her neck, pushing the count away. The blood gushed from her wounded neck, and a dark curtain started to fall in front of her eyes. Just before the curtain cut out all sight and sound, the paralysis of her throat muscles relaxed for a fraction of a second and Cordelia screamed: a high, keening scream of pure terror.

Captain Hesse was at her side in an instant. "My

dear Miss Hope, what is wrong? In God's name, what happened?"

Cordelia blinked, then rubbed her eyes, feeling dazed and totally disoriented. Where was she? Surely to goodness she hadn't really been in bed with the Count of Albion? She looked around and realized to her mortification that she was in the drawing room, that Ellen was patting her hand in a vain attempt to soothe, and even Mary had sprung to her feet, looking worried. Everyone in the room was gaping at her. Everyone, that is, except the count, who had walked over to one of the windows and seemed to be staring out into the gardens.

For a frightening moment as she looked at the rigid line of the count's shoulders, her vision blurred and she saw again the bed with its lacy linen pillows and their heads resting in close proximity. She fought hard for control, and the debilitating vision disappeared.

Lieutenant Waldheim eyed her with evident concern. "You are most flushed, Miss Hope. Do you haf discomfort? An ache in the head, perhaps?"

"No, thank you, it was but a passing moment of weakness. . . . I'm sorry, terribly sorry." She searched for some acceptable excuse to explain her scream. "I do apologize to everyone. I thought I saw a mouse. It was foolish of me to make such a fuss about something so trivial."

She could feel the collective sigh of relief that everyone produced when she gave her explanation. Except for the count, who continued to stare out of his window.

"A mouse, eh?" Captain Hesse smiled indulgently. "I know that many ladies find the little creatures most alarming. However, they are not harmful, you know.

I am sure he was even more frightened of you than you were of him."

"Undoubtedly," Lieutenant Waldheim said, nodding sagely. "Alas, at zis time of year field mice can become a problem. The supply of their food increases, you see, and so do zey!"

"Listen!" The count spoke abruptly. "Do you hear Anna's footsteps? I think she must be coming with your refreshments. If you will excuse me, ladies and gentlemen, I will leave you to enjoy your cake and coffee."

"Oh no, Count, please don't go," Mary protested. She patted the cushion next to her, her smile at once commanding and flirtatious. "Do sit down, dear sir. I hoped you would honor us with your company at least a little longer. We were having such an enjoyable conversation until Cordelia frightened us all."

As if she were connected to his innermost emotions, Cordelia felt the count's rejection of Mary's overtures as clearly as if the emotion were her own. Then, abruptly, the sensation cut off.

"Alas," the count said. "Your invitation is tempting, Mrs. Ford, but I am engaged elsewhere." He bowed. "*Signori e signore,* I wish you all a pleasant evening and a night of restful sleep."

Mary was not in the habit of having her whims refused. She pouted. "You cannot desert us now, Excellency. My cousin hasn't even asked you how we are to find the Villa of the Three Fountains."

The count didn't even glance toward Cordelia. "Tomorrow," he said, his voice sounding strained. "I shall be at your service tomorrow."

Before Mary could say anything more, Anna entered the drawing room, pushing a serving trolley ahead of her. She paused in the doorway, looking none too pleased to see her master.

The count returned her stare, his stance oddly defiant as he met the fulminating gaze of his housekeeper. Cordelia felt the strangest mixture of emotions humming between them. Anxiety, affection, mutual respect, and mutual irritation, underlined by some other emotion—darker and more intense—that she couldn't identify. What an extraordinary combination, she thought..

Cordelia had lived such a quiet life with her father in Cambridge that, until he died and the Earl of Stanwyck summoned her to London, she hadn't realized that her skill in reading other people's feelings was quite out of the ordinary. Once she was taken into the earl's busy household, she had soon learned that such sensitivity could be more of a curse than a blessing, and nowadays she tried hard to shield herself from the assault of other people's emotions. Only strong feelings could breach the protective walls she had learned to build around herself, but so powerful was the tension flowing between Anna and the count that she felt literally buffeted by its force.

She had another ability that she thought might be linked in some way to her intuitive grasp of other people's feelings; a skill for understanding foreign languages that was almost uncanny. Living in Cambridge, surrounded by scholars of every stripe, it had seemed easy and natural for her to study the great works of Italian literature with Professor Richardson, England's foremost authority on the works of Dante Alighieri, and she had spent many happy hours chatting with his housekeeper, a treasure from Milan whom the professor was wise enough to acknowledge as his most valuable Italian discovery.

Despite this, when Anna directed a volley of swift questions toward the count, Cordelia was surprised to find that she could understand much of what they said, especially since both master and servant chose to speak in low voices and in a dialect that they undoubtedly considered different enough from Italian to be incomprehensible to their listeners.

"What are you doing here still?" Anna demanded of the count, rearranging the cream jug and the coffeepot with a lot more force than was necessary. "You must have heard me coming. You promised me you wouldn't stay for more than a minute or two."

"The blond one is very demanding," he said. "And I would prefer not to arouse their suspicions if that is possible."

Anna snorted. "The food will make you ill, the state you're in. *That* will make them suspicious for sure."

"I have no intention of eating."

"Ha! What has that to say to anything? I can see the smell of these cakes is already turning your stomach. You are exhausted. You need rest. Look at you, running a fever and trying to handle these pushy visitors—" Anna broke off abruptly. "How are you coping with the women? Will it be a problem tonight?"

"I'm coping . . . just. Fortunately, only one of them is a virgin."

"*Only* one. Ha! Just our luck that one of them had to be a virgin. Which one is the virgin? Not the blonde presumably."

"No, the one with brown hair and beautiful gray eyes."

Anna looked at him sharply. "It would be that one. She's more your type than the blonde. Are you in pain, lord?"

"I will survive. Don't fuss, Anna."

The housekeeper relit a small burner under the coffeepot. "What do they want, the Austrians? Why have they brought these women here? Is it a plot?"

"I believe not. These women really are stranded travelers. Nothing more, I'm sure of it."

Anna snapped a linen napkin open and tossed it over her arm. "You believe the best of everyone. That's your problem."

He smiled. "I have so many problems, according to you."

"You're too trusting. The Austrians are a danger to us," Anna said. "I'm sure they brought the women to test you. Get rid of them. I don't like that lieutenant."

"The Austrians will be taken care of, and to our advantage. You know that."

"What about the women? How will you handle them?"

"Anna," the count said. "Enough. They, too, will be taken care of."

He turned to his visitors, and spoke in English, as if translating on behalf of his servant. "I apologize for keeping you all waiting. My housekeeper could not find any tea in our kitchen supplies. She is very worried. She says English ladies always drink tea and she hopes that her coffee will prove an adequate substitute."

Cordelia held herself very still, determined not to betray the dangerous fact that she knew the count was lying. Should she tell everyone what Anna and the count had really said? What would happen if she did? What had the count meant when he said that his visitors would be *taken care of*? The phrase sounded ominous, and yet she supposed there could be any number of innocent interpretations of the words.

But that wasn't the only puzzle. What in the world had Anna meant by her question about virgins?

Only one of them is a virgin, the count had replied. How could he possibly know? Had she misunderstood the dialect word they both used? She must have, Cordelia decided. No other explanation made sense. Perhaps the word she had translated as *virgin* simply meant *spinster.* Since Mary was supposedly married, and Ellen was widowed—although how would the count know that?—the count might have been telling his servant that only one of the female visitors was unmarried. But why would he bother to pass on such an irrelevant piece of information?

The harder Cordelia tried to find explanations, the more mysterious the count's exchange with Anna began to seem.

Cordelia looked at Captain Hesse, hoping against hope that he might have understood something of what had been said. Unfortunately, it seemed he had not. Both the Austrians spoke excellent French and English, but neither of them had much command of Italian, and they seemed to have no interest at all in learning the dialect of the local peasantry. Which meant that Cordelia bore the responsibility for being the only one of the visitors who knew the count was lying.

She hesitated a fraction of a second too long without speaking up, and Mary broke into the silence. "No tea, Excellency?" She sighed, then managed a brave smile. "Well, never mind. After the dreadful brews we have been drinking for the past few days, I have no doubt that Anna's refreshments will taste delicious, tea or no tea. I can see from here that the cake looks simply wonderful."

The count inclined his head. "I am confident you

will find Anna's coffee excellent and her baking superb." He turned to his housekeeper and spoke in slow, classical Italian. Presumably this time he wanted to be sure Cordelia and the soldiers understood what he was saying.

"If you will cut the cake, Anna, I will serve it to our guests, and perhaps Mrs. Ford will be kind enough to pour the coffee."

For a moment Cordelia thought that the housekeeper was actually going to disobey her master. But after an ominous delay, she cut into the bright yellow cake, heavily powdered with sugar. Then she wheeled the cart over to the sofa, bobbed into a curtsy and pointed from Mary to the coffeepot.

"*Café*," she said. "*Signora.*" She mimed to indicate that Mary should serve the coffee.

In the usual way of things, Mary enjoyed taking her time to pour tea and coffee, since it gave her a splendid chance to display her delicate wrists and tiny hands to advantage. But she was so hungry and the coffee smelled so good that she didn't bother to waste time rearranging the implements on the tray and fussing with the lumps of brown sugar. She poured the coffee with more speed than elegance, handing out cups while the count passed around delicate porcelain plates, each graced with a generous slice of cake and a heavy silver fork.

"Count!" Mary exclaimed when everyone else was served. "Come, pray do not hang back! Take a cup of coffee and a slice of your cook's excellent cake."

"Thank you, but I stayed only long enough to see you all served," the count said. Cordelia had the impression that he could barely restrain himself from running out of the room. "I must leave you now for my next engagement. Excuse me, ladies and gentlemen."

Mary could be more stubborn than an entire stable of mules when she failed to get her own way. She smiled roguishly at the count. "Excellency, I am famous in London for refusing to take no for an answer. Come, what can be so pressing that you cannot eat a sliver of cake and drink a sip or two of Anna's wonderful coffee? We are all so delighted to have made your acquaintance and have a dozen questions still to ask you. Here, taste this coffee. Have I added sufficient cream?"

She held out a cup of steaming and aromatic coffee, but Anna snatched it from her, forcibly preventing the count from accepting it.

She glowered at him, every bit as stubborn as Mary. "Don't you dare eat or drink anything from that trolley," she muttered, reverting to dialect. "You know what it will do to you."

"Right," the count said, his voice shaky, but laced with mockery. "It will be the death of me."

His words fell on Cordelia's ears with the force of a thunderclap. All her suspicion and uneasiness coalesced into a single blinding realization. How could she have been so stupid not to understand the significance of the housekeeper's repeated warnings to her master? The coffee and cake were poisoned!

"Heaven help us!" she gasped. "He's trying to kill us!" Cordelia sprang to her feet, lunging for the piece of cake that her cousin was about to put into her mouth, and simultaneously snatching Ellen's fork.

"Don't eat that," she panted, scarcely noticing that in her panic she had knocked over the coffeepot. "Captain! Lieutenant! Everybody—stop eating and drinking *now*!"

"Cordelia, are you run mad?" Mary demanded, using her napkin to mop up pools of spilled coffee. "Look what you've done to my dress! It's ruined."

"The cake is poisoned!" Cordelia said. "None of you eat it, please!"

"Good God!" Captain Hesse and Lieutenant Waldheim sprang to their feet in unison. "Poisoned?" the captain exclaimed, his hand going automatically to the hilt of his sword.

The lieutenant set his coffee cup on a side table and backed across the room until he was standing shoulder to shoulder with his captain. He scowled ferociously at all of them, not sure whether to rebuke Cordelia for hysteria, or the Count of Albion for treachery, but quite certain that he ought to be doing something vigorous.

"I feel sick," Ellen said. "I ate all my cake already. Oops." She clapped her hand over her mouth and promptly collapsed in a swoon.

Mary gave a shriek of genuine terror. "Oh, dear heaven, my maid is dead, and I have ingested poison! What will become of me? I am doomed."

"No, you're not," the count said, sounding more exasperated than guilty. He glared at Cordelia as he strode across the room and scooped Ellen into his arms. "Of course you're not doomed, or dying, or anything else. Neither is your maid. The cake is harmless. A simple Madeira recipe, you have my word on it."

"Release the servant," Captain Hesse demanded, his sword weaving threateningly.

"With pleasure," the count snapped. "She's not a light weight, you know." He placed her carefully on a chaise near the window and stepped back. "Does anyone have smelling salts?" he asked.

"I have smelling salts," Cordelia said, rummaging

in her reticule, and wondering why the count was pretending to be so helpful. She waved the salts under Ellen's nose, and the maid regained consciousness almost immediately. The count, she noticed, turned deathly white and walked quickly to the opposite end of the sofa.

"Oh, miss," Ellen groaned when she saw Cordelia. "I ate me piece of cake in three bites. Now me whole stomach is a-churning. Am I going to die?"

"Only of panic and indigestion," the count said brusquely. He handed the maid a glass of water, and added a curt instruction that she should sip it slowly.

Brows drawn together in a furious frown, he turned to confront Cordelia. "I must repeat the question asked by your cousin. Have you taken leave of your senses, *signorina*? In God's name, why do you believe the cake is poisoned? I have never heard anything so ridiculous."

"Then why won't you eat it?" Cordelia demanded. "I distinctly heard Anna warn you not to touch it."

The count was silent for a second too long. "I have a tiresome digestive problem," he said at last, sounding oddly weary. "The cake is likely to make me quite ill, but it will have no adverse effects on anyone in your party, I can assure you."

His explanation sounded reasonable, so reasonable in fact that Captain Hesse returned his sword to its scabbard and Mary—after a fulminating glare at Cordelia—returned to dabbing angrily at the coffee stain spreading over the skirts of her favorite traveling gown.

"Goodness me, Cordelia, I wish you would be more careful before you make such wild accusations," she said. "The coffee may never wash out of this gown, not to mention the fact that you nearly gave me an attack of the vapors. First screaming and terrifying us all because you saw a mouse. Now this absurd accusation against the count. Really, I don't know where your wits are hiding themselves these days."

Cordelia knew that she ought to apologize, but the words wouldn't come. Instead she turned to the housekeeper who had watched the entire turn of events in stony silence.

"If the cake is not harmful, Anna, why don't you eat a piece?"

The housekeeper gave her a look that was withering in its scorn. "I will eat a piece of cake with pleasure, *signorina.*" She glanced up at the count, speaking in normal Italian, not dialect, so that Cordelia and the Austrians could all understand. "With your permission, lord, I will eat a slice of the visitors' cake."

He shrugged and replied in the same language. "Of course, if you feel you must."

To Cordelia's surprise, Anna ate methodically through a large slice of cake, and washed it down with the cup of coffee Mary had poured for the count. When she had finished, she carefully wiped her fingers on a spare napkin and turned blank-faced toward Cordelia.

"I trust you are satisfied, *signorina.* As you see, the cake has done me no harm whatsoever, nor the coffee either. You have nothing to fear from my cooking. The kitchen of the villa is well known in the region for the fine quality of the ingredients we use."

Cordelia knew that she ought to be reassured, but somehow she couldn't escape the feeling that they had just watched a conjurer and his assistant pull off a clever trick. Still, neither Ellen, nor Anna, nor anyone else seemed to be suffering the slightest harm, and she couldn't continue to make accusations based on nothing but her translation of a conversation conducted in a dialect she didn't really understand. Thinking back over the count's exchange with Anna, she could remember nothing that contradicted his claim that he had a severe digestive problem.

Reluctantly, Cordelia concluded that she had made quite enough of a fool of herself for one evening and that she had no choice other than to make the apology everyone in the drawing room seemed to be waiting for.

"I see that I have made a most mortifying mistake," she said. "I apologize, Anna, and to you, Excellency, for doubting the motives behind your hospitality."

The housekeeper shrugged and turned away, still offended. The count inclined his head in bare acknowledgment, his hands clenched at his side, and his shoulders rigid with tension.

"My reputation is not one of great amiability," he said in English. "But I had not realized that people arrive here at the villa expecting me to poison them under the guise of offering them refreshment."

"I'm sure they do not," Cordelia said, swallowing another stiff dose of pride. "The fault was entirely mine, Excellency. I can only apologize for my suspicions and beg that you will not punish my traveling companions for my rudeness."

"How do you expect me to punish them?" the count asked.

"By refusing them hospitality for the night. But I beg you will be generous. They . . . we . . . are all very weary and Mrs. Ford is especially in need of rest."

"Of course you can all stay," the count said carelessly.

"You are very generous—"

"It's easy for me to be generous," he said, interrupting her thanks. "My house is large, and I don't need to see you again."

Cordelia didn't attempt to dispute his statement, although she knew he was wrong. They would have to meet again to discuss the problem of who owned the Villa of the Three Fountains. However, neither she nor the count seemed to be in any fit state at the moment to resolve whatever hideous muddle of the Italian legal system had produced the confusion in ownership. Cordelia decided this was a time to eat large quantities of humble pie, not to demand proof that the Count of Albion had valid title to his villa.

She dropped a small curtsy. "I thank you for your willingness to overlook my mistakes, Excellency. As I said before, you are most generous."

The count smiled sardonically. "Oh yes, I'm a very generous fellow. It is one of my more outstanding characteristics." He moved to the door, taking care to give Cordelia a wide berth. Then he turned and bowed. "Excuse me, please, ladies and gentlemen. I will once again wish you a restful night in my home."

In Italian he added, "Anna, if you would come with me, please." He left the room without waiting for their replies, Anna following hard on his heels.

Mary broke the uncomfortable silence that ensued. "Well, Cordelia, you certainly made a total fool of yourself in front of the count and everyone else."

"I'm sorry," Cordelia said, aware that the rebuke was well deserved and yet still far from confident that they were safe and that she'd imagined all the danger. She tried to explain. "The conversation between Anna and the count was so extraordinary that I became suspicious of their motives toward us all."

"How was it extraordinary?" Captain Hesse demanded. "What did they talk about? Did they mention me or the lieutenant?"

"Yes, they did," Cordelia said. "Anna wanted to know why you are here. She seemed to suspect your motives in bringing us here, but the count assured her that we are harmless."

Mary tossed her sodden napkin onto the trolley with an impatient exclamation. "Really, Cordelia, how can you be sure what the two of them said to each other? After that humiliating episode with the cake, it should be crystal clear that you don't understand the local dialect sufficiently to make any claims about their discussion whatsoever."

"That's not quite true," Cordelia pointed out. "I heard Anna warn her master not to eat the cake, and she also ordered him not to drink any coffee. And, if you recall, the count didn't deny that his servant had issued such a warning. He simply said that I'd misunderstood the reason *behind* the warning. He has a digestive problem, he claims, which was why Anna insisted he shouldn't eat cake or drink coffee."

"You still sound troubled, Miss Hope." Captain Hesse smiled a touch patronizingly. "Perhaps I can set your mind at rest. The count has mentioned the troublesome weakness of his digestive system in the past. In fact, when we have been together on previous occasions, he has always eaten most sparingly. I have remarked upon it and he has explained how carefully he must choose his food."

Cordelia saw that it would be wiser to keep her doubts to herself, since nobody was willing to share them. Gathering the remnants of her dignity, she responded briskly to the captain. "In that case, it does seem that I may have been leaping to a great many wrong conclusions. Perhaps it is time for me to retire to my room for the night before I make any other gaffes."

Mary sniffed. "And when the servants bring us our dinner, pray refrain from knocking the trays onto the floor and shouting *poison.* I, for one, am feeling quite hungry."

"I am sure Miss Hope will put her worries into proper perspective once she has a chance to rest," Captain Hesse said. "No doubt we shall all feel much more lively in the morning. Traveling is exhausting, especially on these bad roads and in this appalling weather."

Nothing could have seemed more desirable to Cordelia at this point than the privacy of her own bedroom. "I'm sure you are right, Captain," she said. "Is there a bell to summon a servant to show us to our appointed rooms?"

"Over here," the lieutenant said, giving a hearty tug to an embroidered pull by the fireplace. A youth, probably not more than twelve years old, answered their summons within moments.

He bowed politely to all of them, but his gaze slid from the spilled coffeepot toward Cordelia and she had the distinct impression he barely managed to hide a grin. "*Signori e signore,* my name is Guido. How may I help you?" he asked in careful Italian.

"We wish to be shown to our rooms," the captain replied.

"Certainly. If you will follow me, Donna Anna has prepared sleeping chambers for all of you in the west wing. The count has instructed me to say that he hopes you will be comfortable, and that he trusts you will find the supper that has been prepared for you acceptable. We were not expecting so many visitors, you understand, and it has been prepared in haste."

Cordelia translated for the benefit of Mary and Ellen. She tried to keep her voice strictly neutral, but some of her residual doubts must have shown in her face because Mary spoke with unusual tartness. "The count sends that message because he is a courteous host, Cordelia, and not because he wishes us to ingest large servings of poisoned food."

Cordelia winced, knowing she deserved the reproof. "I will bear that in mind," she said.

"Thank goodness for small mercies," Mary said. "Mayhap if you can avoid regaling us with your Gothic fancies, we shall survive dinner without Ellen fainting or you screaming. Lord knows, I am ever the optimist."

She turned to Guido, indifferent to the fact that the lad spoke no English. She belonged to the school of traveler who assumed that any foreign servant could understand an instruction if it was given loudly enough and repeated often enough.

"Take us to our rooms," she commanded, gesturing to the door. "Our bedrooms," she said more loudly. "Our sleeping chambers," she shouted, pointed her finger in the direction of the ceiling.

"*Sí, signora.*" Guido bowed and mimed to indicate that they should follow him.

Captain Hesse offered Mary his arm. With considerable reluctance, Lieutenant Waldheim offered Cordelia the same courtesy. They walked in silence up the staircase, and he gave her only the smallest of bows at the door to her bedroom. Clearly, the lieutenant did not approve of her.

"I trust the world vill seem a less ... threatening ... place after a good night's sleep, Miss Hope."

"I trust so, too, Lieutenant."

He clicked his heels. "I bid you good night."

"Good night." She nodded a dismissal to Guido and walked into the bedroom, sighing with relief to be rid of both her charges, and the Austrians, in one fell swoop. She came to a precipitous halt when she saw Anna, hands folded in front of her apron, waiting at the side of the bed.

The housekeeper nodded a greeting. "Good evening, *signorina*. I have come to sleep with you tonight."

Cordelia felt her pulse accelerate. "Thank you, but I would really prefer to sleep alone—"

"I regret, *signorina*, that it is not a matter of choice. Tonight, I shall sleep in this room with you."

"I see," Cordelia said quietly. "And if I wish to leave the room for any reason?"

"Tonight, *signorina*, that will not be permitted. I regret the inconvenience."

"How about tomorrow?"

Anna smiled grimly. "Tomorrow, *signorina*, there will be nobody more anxious to see you out of this bedroom and off the premises than me. But that is tomorrow. And for tonight, it will be better for everyone if you hurry up and get to bed." She walked over to the door and sat down on the chair she had already drawn up beside it. "Hot water and fresh towels are behind the screen, *signorina*, together with the usual necessities. You will see that bread and preserved fruit and hot milk have been served for your supper. It's a simple meal, but the food is tastily prepared and quite safe."

Cordelia looked around the room. "My valise?" she questioned. "Has any of our luggage been brought upstairs?"

"It seemed easier to leave all your bags and trunks strapped in place," Anna said. "I have provided everything you might need for the night and for the other two women as well." She gestured toward the dressing table. "As you can see, *signorina,* a brush and comb await you, and also some scented toilet waters that I hope you will find agreeable. As for your nightgown . . ." She turned and pointed to the bed. "I have provided you with a nightgown from the trousseau of the count's own mother."

Cordelia glanced toward the bed. She blinked. Chilled by a foreboding more powerful than it was rational, she hurried across the room to inspect the gown more closely. She discovered that laid out against the lacy pillows was a nightdress she recognized all too well. From the blue satin ribbon at the throat, to the delicate Meissen lace at the wrists, it was identical in every tiny detail to the nightdress she had been wearing in the vision that had overtaken her in the count's drawing room. Seized by the calm that precedes disaster, Cordelia swung around and confronted the housekeeper.

"Am I a prisoner here?" she asked.

Anna didn't looked surprised by the question, but her answering smile was sad. "No, *signorina,*" she replied. "You are not a prisoner. In this villa, only the count is a prisoner."

Chapter Four

(

Cordelia would have liked to ask Anna probing questions about the nightgown, but she couldn't think of any way to raise the subject without making herself look ridiculous, or worse, mentally unbalanced. Hot with embarrassment, she edged around the bed, keeping her gaze averted from the offending garment.

She tried to convince herself that she was making too much of a minor coincidence. Nightgowns were invariably white, after all, and most of them were decorated with lace and satin ribbons. It could only be chance that this particular nightgown looked just like one she had imagined during a very embarrassing daydream.

Chiefly because she didn't know what else to do, she decided to take advantage of the hot water and towels that Anna had provided. Prisoner or not, she might as well be clean, and the lump of perfumed soap was very tempting.

By the time she'd washed from head to toe, combed the road dust from her hair, and dabbed toilet water behind her ears, her travel-weary body felt considerably fresher, and her muscles had stopped aching. Her nerves still jangled uneasily, and the similarity of the two nightgowns continued to trouble her, but for a traveler who was being held a virtual captive, she decided she was coping quite well.

When she emerged from behind the screen, Anna was waiting for her with smiles and kind words. "Come and sit by the fire," she said, sounding surprisingly friendly. Apparently she had decided that if she was to act as jailer, she would play the role with good cheer. "There is a chill to the air tonight and the fire will warm you while you eat. A terrible wet spring we've had this year. Never known another spring like it, not in all my born years."

Cordelia was tired, cold, hungry, and thirsty, but she was neither addled nor weary enough to trust Anna's sudden burst of hospitality. She'd already noted that there was no bellpull in the room to summon other servants, and she had only Anna's word that she would be allowed to leave the next morning. In view of what had gone before, Cordelia planned to treat all the housekeeper's offers of friendship with extreme caution.

Resisting Anna's blandishments, she seated herself at the little table drawn up before the fire, stretched out her hands to the blaze, and tried not to smell the heady aroma of hot coffee.

"Would you like me to serve you, *signorina*?" Anna held up the silver coffeepot.

Cordelia sighed. "Thank you, but I'm not thirsty."

"Then I will serve myself," Anna said. "With your permission, of course, *signorina*."

Cordelia nodded, staring longingly as Anna filled a small cup with coffee. Then she cut a thin slice of bread and spread it with sweetened preserved peaches. Still standing, she ate the bread and drank the coffee, draining the cup. When she'd finished, she dabbed her mouth with the corner of her apron and cast Cordelia a look that was more sympathetic than anything else.

"Would you care to reconsider your refusal, *signorina*? The coffee is very good, and it is still hot. The count brought these special chafing stands back with him from one of his journeys in the Levant. We have found them a great blessing when serving hot food, since the kitchens in this villa are far from the dining room."

"How amazingly thoughtful of him."

Anna ignored Cordelia's sarcasm. "Yes, indeed, *signorina*. My master has a real concern for those who serve him. Now, do you wish for a nice hot drink after your long day of travel?"

The housekeeper was positively falling over herself to be amiable, Cordelia thought as she debated her options. She was very hungry, and parched with thirst, and it seemed unlikely that the food was poisoned if Anna was willing to partake of it. On the other hand, the fact that the housekeeper hadn't instantly collapsed didn't prove the food was safe to eat. There were plenty of slow-acting poisons, and a dozen tricks for lulling potential victims into swallowing them. But Anna would surely have no reason to resort to elaborate poisoning schemes in order to commit murder? If killing were on her mind, Cordelia could be disposed of by a single swift blow to the head, or a quick thrust with a sharpened knife. Given the turmoil of threatened war, and the feudal backwardness of the Duchy, the Count of Albion's word was probably law in the region around the villa.

Whatever the potential dangers of trusting Anna, Cordelia's thirst was fast overcoming her fears. She could have withstood the offer of food all night, but a drink was well nigh irresistible.

"Some coffee would be agreeable," she admitted at last, deciding that she could permit herself a couple of sips, just to wet her parched throat. Two sips couldn't kill her, could they?

Anna filled a big cup almost to overflowing, adding a spoonful of thick yellow cream. "Do you care for sugar, *signorina*?"

Anna hadn't taken sugar, Cordelia remembered, so she shook her head, mocking herself for the feeble precaution. "No, thank you. No sugar."

The housekeeper cut two slices of bread and spread them generously with preserves. "Enjoy your supper," she said, unfolding a linen napkin across Cordelia's lap and setting the cup of coffee and plate of food in front of her before returning to her straight-backed chair by the door.

Cordelia took a tiny sip of coffee—and then another, and another. Heaven! Rarely had a hot drink tasted so wonderful. The cup was soon empty. Cordelia stared longingly at the bread heaped with fresh preserves. Since she'd drunk the coffee, she decided she might as well eat the food, too. She could only die once, she reflected wryly, so why die hungry?

She'd already eaten both pieces of bread and was in the midst of savoring a second cup of wonderful creamy coffee when a knock sounded at the door.

Scrambling to her feet, Anna pressed herself against the door, plump body visibly tensing. "Who is it?" she asked brusquely.

" 'Tis I, Albion. Let me in."

Anna shot an anxious glance toward Cordelia and

then quickly turned her back, so that her face couldn't be seen. To Cordelia's amazement, the servant still didn't open the door, but spoke to the count through the panels.

"No, master, you cannot come in. You know that I will not permit you to enter this bedchamber."

The count's response was low and soft, but to Cordelia, his voice seemed laden with the threat of violence. "Anna, I am your master. You will obey me. *Open the door.*"

"No, lord." Anna's voice trembled. "I'm very sorry, lord, but you must go back to your room. You promised me you would not leave your bedchamber tonight."

Silence fell, thick and heavy with tension. Finally the count spoke again, his voice racked with anguish. "Anna ... I cannot ... bear it ... any ... more."

"Yes, you can, lord. You are strong." Anna spread her hands against the panels of the door, almost as if she wished she could touch her master through the wood. She spoke gently, soothingly. "Where is Guido, lord? Why has he left you alone?"

A second long silence ensued. "Guido is— sleeping."

Anna drew in a sharp, frightened breath. She shot another nervous look over her shoulder toward Cordelia, then leaned even closer to the door. This time, she spoke so quietly that Cordelia could scarcely hear the question. "Are you sure Guido is sleeping, lord?"

"Yes. I am sure. He sleeps, that's all. Nothing more, I swear it."

"When he wakes up, what will he remember, lord?"

"Nothing," the count snapped as if he resented being questioned. "There is nothing for him to re-

member," he added more temperately. "After all
these years, Anna, you should know that there is nothing to fear with the boys."

Anna shot a nervous glance over her shoulder,
flushing when her gaze locked with Cordelia's. She
turned back again, speaking through the panels of the
door. "Go back to your bedchamber," she said.
"Please, lord, do as I say and no harm will be done
this night."

"Will you come to me? Help me stay away from
her?"

"Yes, lord, I will come to you."

"Anna . . . I am sorry. Tonight, the pain is almost
more than I can bear . . ."

"There is naught to be sorry for, lord."

"I should have heeded your advice and sent the
women away."

"Do not trouble yourself, lord. I shall come to you.
Go now, and speak to no one. Hurry back to your
room! Lock the door, I have the key to let myself in."

"Yes. I will do that. I am going now, Anna."

Cordelia listened in disbelieving silence as the
count's stumbling footsteps faded into the distance.
The earlier conversation she'd overheard between the
count and his housekeeper had seemed strange, but
this one passed all bounds of the rational. Her stomach churned with the sick realization that the count,
for all his good looks and dashing airs, must be of
unsound mind. He had demanded entrance to Cordelia's bedchamber like a grand seigneur from the oppressive days before the French Revolution. A minute
later, he had pleaded with Anna like a child seeking
comfort from a nightmare.

And what in the world had happened to Guido, the
serving lad? What did it mean when the count stressed

repeatedly that he was *sleeping*? Nothing good, Cordelia was quite sure. It sounded as if the count involved his serving lads in some horrible perversion—Lieutenant Waldheim had hinted as much—but her knowledge of such matters was too slight to guess what that perversion might be.

She didn't have many seconds to mull over what she'd heard. Anna swung around, her face flushed, her gaze distracted. "Well," she said, her manner almost defiant. "So now you know the truth. My master is not well."

Cordelia stared at the servant in blank astonishment. If there was one thing she was quite sure of, it was that she didn't have the faintest inkling of "the truth" concerning the Count of Albion.

She cleared her throat. "Actually, Anna, I don't believe I do know the truth. It seems that the count suffers from ... um ... from a mental indisposition." That sounded less rude than saying the count was crazy.

Anna's gaze became hooded, but she seemed almost relieved by Cordelia's interpretation of events. "As you say, *signorina,* the count suffers from a most unfortunate ... mental indisposition. That is all, nothing more." She continued quickly, before Cordelia could interrupt with a question. "Alas, when my master succumbs to one of his spells, he cannot be trusted to behave himself as a gentleman should when in the presence of a young lady. Now you know why I felt it necessary to keep watch over you tonight, to protect you."

"Er, yes. Thank you for your concern." Cordelia wasn't at all sure what Anna was hinting at. Was she trying to say that the count, when seized by his illness, roamed the corridors of his villa, seeking to ravish his female houseguests? If so, why was Anna protecting her rather than the divinely beautiful Lady Mary, who was surely far more at risk? Or was the servant hinting at some darker secret? Cordelia tried, and failed, to imagine some secret vice even more terrible than a predilection for despoiling one's houseguests.

It seemed that Anna was indeed suggesting that the count was of a lecherous disposition. She lowered her voice confidingly. "As a young man, my master had a reputation for taking advantage of many an innocent girl. Now he is trying to reform his libertine ways. But you know how hard that can be for a gentleman who has never been taught restraint. Unfortunately, the count's mother died when he was born, so he had no woman to raise him and teach him self-control."

"Quite," Cordelia said, as if she understood exactly what the housekeeper was talking about. In truth, having been brought up by an elderly father who found the behavior of star nebulae vastly more interesting than the behavior of people, her acquaintance with the proclivities of libertine males was limited, to say the least.

"The count sounded as if he was in great pain," she added, surprised to find herself feeling an odd sympathy for him.

"He is in pain," Anna answered distractedly. "However, you need not worry, *signorina,* his bouts of sickness last no more than a couple of days."

"Do you wish to leave me and go to him?" Cordelia asked.

Anna's face flooded with relief. "I think that would be for the best, *signorina,* if you don't mind."

"Not at all," Cordelia replied, deciding not to remind the housekeeper that she had appointed herself as Cordelia's guardian, not the other way around.

Anna opened the bedroom door a scant few inches, and peered into the corridor. After a few seconds, she closed the door again. "All's well so far," she said. "But I must go to him. Now, *signorina*, bolt the door after me and you will be quite safe. Whatever you do, admit no one to your room except me. Is that understood? No one must go out or come in. You do understand, don't you? Don't go out, and let no one in. No one except me."

"Yes," Cordelia said. "I understand your instructions, Anna. Completely."

The servant was too worried about her master to realize that Cordelia had merely confirmed that she understood Anna's instructions, and had made no promise to remain inside her room.

"Good, good," Anna murmured, slipping into the corridor. She stuck her head around the door. "I won't be gone many minutes. Remember, *signorina*, bolt the door. I shall wait outside the room to hear you do it."

Cordelia obligingly crossed the room, shut the door, and shot the bolt home. "It's done, Anna," she called out. "As you can hear, I am safely locked in."

"Very good, *signorina*. Enjoy another cup of coffee or another slice of fresh bread, and I shall return in but a few minutes."

Cordelia waited until the sound of the housekeeper's hurried footsteps faded into silence, and then she grabbed her cloak and reticule, unfastened the bolt, and opened the bedroom door. Thank goodness she hadn't undressed for bed! She needed to find Mary and Ellen and awaken them with all possible speed. They didn't have much time to make good their escape if Anna really planned to return within a few minutes.

Breath coming fast and shallow, Cordelia threw her cloak over her shoulders and stepped out into the upstairs hallway. The single lamp was turned so low that the light it cast seemed to emphasize the length of the shadows rather than dispel the darkness. The count, doubtless for some nefarious reason, didn't seem to like bright lights.

Feeling her way along the wall, for she certainly couldn't see her way, Cordelia searched for the entrance to the room shared by Mary and the maid. She'd noted the room's location when they came upstairs, on the right of the hallway, second door down from her own.

She knew the Austrians each had a room three or four doors further down the corridor, but they could fend for themselves, she decided. By his own admission, Captain Hesse had visited here several times previously, and he had survived to tell the tale. Besides, for all she knew to the contrary, he might be working hand in glove with the demented count. She knew nothing about the Austrians except what they had told her.

Cordelia passed the first door, and was relieved when her fingers encountered the latch of the second. Thank God! In the dark, distances seemed endless. She was going to have a hard time persuading Mary to leave the villa at this hour of the night, but clearly they were putting their lives in jeopardy if they stayed. As far as Cordelia was concerned, the innkeeper with his bed in the loft was looking better by the minute. Rascal he might be, but at least he had seemed an honest rascal. Or if worst came to worst, they could spend the night in their carriage. Somewhere not too far from here there must be a respectable inn where they could stay while they sent an urgent message to the elusive *Signor* Pesante.

She turned the knob on Mary's door, breathing a sigh of relief when she found it unlocked. She crept inside. Anna and the count might be safely tucked away in a room on the other side of the corridor, but a knock could easily bring them out to check on who was roaming the hallways. If they were going to make good their escape, she couldn't afford to attract their attention.

On tiptoe, she crept further into the bedroom. "Mary? Ellen?" she whispered, gliding toward the bed, her hands stretched out in front of her to feel for obstacles.

There was no reply. Mary didn't much like the dark and usually kept a light of some sort burning all night, but tonight the lamp on the dresser had been turned down even lower than the one in the corridor, and the drapes were closed tight, shutting out the moonlight. However hard she strained, Cordelia could see nothing beyond a few indistinct shapes and shadows.

At last the bed loomed in front of her, a curtained monstrosity from an earlier century. For no good reason, she was suddenly sweating with fear. She wished she could see better, or that she could hear the comforting buzz of Ellen's snores, or that her cousin would wake up. Any sound that broke the oppressive silence would surely relieve the heart-stopping impression that she had just walked into terrible danger.

"Mary?" she repeated, her voice sounding unnaturally loud. She drew back the bed curtains with some force, glad to hear the reassuring rattle of the brass rings. "Mary, wake up! We have to leave. There is something very wrong with the situation here."

A strong masculine hand reached out and grasped her wrist, holding her in a grip that was at once caressing and imprisoning. Cordelia went very still, then wondered fleetingly why she didn't scream.

"I knew that you would come," the count said, his voice low and husky, rich with satisfaction. "I knew that you would find me before Anna did. She thinks I went back to my room, but you knew better."

Cordelia was shaking with fear, and some other emotion that sent the blood racing through her veins with feverish speed. "I did not come to you," she said, her voice as low and husky as the count's. "I didn't intend to enter your room. I was looking for my cousin . . ."

She couldn't see his smile, but she felt it, clear through to her bones. "No, Cordelia, you were not looking for your cousin. You know quite well that her room is on the other side of the hallway.

"I didn't know any such thing! It was dark and I was disoriented!" Her denial was impassioned. It was also a lie, she realized. Dear God, the count was right! She *had* been looking for him.

"I have waited twenty-five years," the count said. "A quarter of a century. Is that not long enough to expiate my sins?"

Cordelia swallowed hard. "I don't understand what you're talking about, Excellency."

"It is of no consequence." He stood up, and she saw the outline of his body as a darker shadow against the duskiness of the room. "You are here now, and that is all that matters. Oh God, let me touch you."

Still holding her wrist, he reached out with his other hand, and Cordelia saw that he trembled. She knew, with an instinct that went beyond reason, that he shook with the intensity of his longing for her.

"Excellency, you must not do this ..."

"On the contrary, I must. Forgive me, Cordelia." He drew her closer, but he didn't enfold her in his arms, or crush her mouth with kisses. Instead, with infinite gentleness, he traced the outline of her cheek, drew his finger down over the point of her chin and along her throat. His fingers paused at the pulse throbbing at the base of her neck, and she felt a yearning emanate from him—a yearning so intense she feared for a moment that she might swoon under its force.

"You feel what I feel," the count whispered. "It has never been like this before. I can see inside your mind as if you were Vam-pyr."

As if she was what? A shudder convulsed her body, but it was a shudder of longing, not of loathing. Her skin tingled with sensitivity, each tiny grain of flesh exploding with sensations a hundred times more intense, a thousand times more compelling, than any she had known before. Her breasts ached, throbbing with a need that was entirely new to her. She stared at the count in mute supplication, pleading with him to explain what was happening to her.

He didn't answer her with words, just cupped her face in his hands and stared deep into her eyes. "You are ready for me, aren't you?" he murmured. "Without touching you, without any drugs or potions, your mind has opened to me. God in heaven, it is a miracle that you came here at the time of my cresting. I burn for you, Cordelia."

She was a virtuous woman, raised to have high moral principles. She didn't understand all that he was saying, but she knew she should turn her back on him and run screaming from the room. And yet she did not. Rather, she reached up and returned his caress, running the tips of her fingers over his hauntingly beautiful face and feeling her entire body thrum with the pleasure and excitement of touching him.

Deep in her womb, she felt an ache of bitter emptiness, a longing for fulfillment so intense that her senses spun. Beneath her fingers, she felt his cheeks distend and grow harder. She brushed her thumbs over the smooth bumps, fascinated by their pulsating tumescence. Standing on tiptoe, she pressed her lips against the strange swelling.

For a split second, for an infinite moment out of time, she felt his joy, shared in his ecstasy. Then, with a terrible cry, he flung her from him with a force great enough to carry her halfway across the room.

"No!" he roared. "No, I swore never again!" Holding his head in his hands, gagging as if he could barely keep from vomiting, he strode over to the window, pushing it open and drawing in great heaving gulps of air.

"Get out!" he ordered Cordelia, without turning around. His voice cracked on the command. He swayed, shoulders trembling, and his hands clenched around the drapes with a force that threatened to pull them from their moorings.

"Get out," he repeated, his voice tormented. "If you value your life, leave me. *Now*."

Paralyzed by grief and longing, Cordelia couldn't move. She wanted to touch him, to reassure him, to feel again the urgent throbbing of his swollen skin beneath her fingertips, and yet some sixth sense warned her that to do so was to court the most violent and deadly of dangers. Even as she hesitated, the door burst open and Anna ran into the room, her expression wild, and her hair spilling from its pins.

Panting, shoulders heaving, the housekeeper cast

one swift glance from the count to Cordelia and back again.

"Take her away," the count said, his words thick and slurred. "Lock her up. *Don't leave her alone, not even for a second.*"

Anna didn't reply. In frantic, panic-filled silence, she took Cordelia's arm and literally dragged her from the room. She pushed her out into the hallway and shut the door, but she didn't come out of the room herself. Cordelia heard the bolt slam into place, and the heavy key turn in the lock. The murmur of Anna's voice drifted into the corridor, but Cordelia was way beyond making sense of what was said inside the count's darkened bedroom.

She'd been handed another chance to escape from the villa, but she didn't take it. She leaned against the wall, too weary to move. Her body felt enervated, so completely drained that even thought seemed to require impossible quantities of energy. Her limbs numb, her mind a blank, and her senses deadened, she slid down the wall and collapsed into an exhausted huddle on the wooden floor.

She had no idea how long she had been lying there when Anna came out of the count's bedroom. Cordelia was aware of the housekeeper's presence, but it required too much effort to react to that presence, so she simply lay where she had collapsed, wrapped in her cloak, her head resting on her hand.

With unexpected gentleness, Anna knelt beside her and slipped her arm around Cordelia's shoulders. "Can you stand up, *signorina*?" she asked softly.

"No." The one-word reply depleted every last ounce of Cordelia's resources.

"Wait there," Anna said. "I will return in but a moment."

Cordelia felt not the slightest inclination to disobey. She waited with perfect docility until the housekeeper returned carrying a glass of cordial. "This will help you to feel stronger," Anna said. "Drink, *signorina.*"

After all her precautions and suspicions about the housekeeper's previous offerings of food and drink, Cordelia took the glass with barely a qualm. She noted with abstract interest that her hand shook as she carried it to her mouth. She sipped the cordial, which was some sort of sweet, fortified wine, and felt an almost imperceptible lightening of her lethargy. When she'd finished drinking, she put the glass on the floor and leaned against the wall, eyes drifting closed.

The housekeeper knelt beside her again. "*Signorina,* you must try to walk," she said. "You will rest more comfortably in your bed."

Cordelia made a token effort to stand. That was enough for Anna. The housekeeper grabbed her by the waist, and forced her to her feet. Taking most of Cordelia's weight onto her plump shoulders, she spoke quietly into the darkness. "Come, *signorina.* You need the comforts of your bed and a good night's sleep."

Cordelia shuffled along the corridor like a hundred-year-old woman. She made no protest when Anna started to undress her, but when the housekeeper tried to clothe her in the nightgown that had once belonged to the count's mother, she was filled with a burst of energizing terror.

"No! I won't wear it!" She struggled fretfully, flailing her arms and pushing the gown away, until Anna caught her hands and held them captive.

"Very well, *signorina.* No nightgown. You shall sleep in your shift if that is your wish."

Cordelia didn't care what she slept in so long as it wasn't the nightgown. Too sluggish to bother with a reply, she slid between the lavender-scented sheets of the bed and closed her eyes.

When she opened them again, it was morning. The sun streamed through a crack in the curtains, setting dust motes dancing. Of Anna there was no sign.

She was just preparing to get out of bed, when a light tap sounded at the door and a young masculine voice spoke cheerfully in Italian. "*Signorina,* breakfast is served in the morning room, if you would care to partake of it. Your friends are already awake and eating."

Moving carefully, because she still felt stiff and uncoordinated, Cordelia sat up in the bed. "*Grazie,*" she replied. "*Vengo subito.*"

"*Prego, signorina.*" The boy walked away, his footsteps quickly fading into silence.

Cordelia swung her legs to the floor and stood up, wrapping herself in the starched linen bedcover since she had no dressing gown. To her relief, she found that her legs felt steady enough, despite her wooziness. It was only her head that still felt thick and heavy, so that forming each thought required an effort akin to swimming through treacle. Hoping that fresh air would blow away the lingering cobwebs, she staggered over to the windows, drew back the draperies, and flung wide the casement.

The rains of the previous day had finally ceased, although the skies remained sullen with the threat of another storm. Drawing in a gulp of reviving, rain-scented air, Cordelia stepped out onto a small balcony, enclosed by an unusual stone and wood balustrade instead of the more typical wrought-iron railing.

The room where she had slept overlooked a rear courtyard that was apparently close to the stables. She could hear the stomp of horses' hooves and the jingle of harnesses floating up to her on the morning breeze, along with the faint, pungent smells of hay, horse sweat, and manure.

Still trying to cast off the lingering tendrils of sleep, she leaned against the balustrade, watching the pale sun attempt to break through a stubborn covering of cloud. The rattle of wooden wheels on paving stones drew her attention to the scene below just in time to see one of the stable lads drive a small cart, something like an English pony trap, into the courtyard.

Because of the way the stable lad happened to have drawn up the cart, Cordelia could see clearly into its interior. She watched, more out of idleness than curiosity, as a door to the house opened, and Anna came out. Two youthful servants followed, their hands crossed and held in such a way as to provide a rough-and-ready chair for the young serving lad supported between them.

Cordelia's interest quickened when she recognized the boy they were carrying: Guido! Guido was the servant who had shown them to their room the night before, the servant about whom Anna had made such anxious inquiries.

Her heart began to thump faster and she leaned over the balcony, suddenly eager to get a better view of what was happening. Unaware of her audience, Anna gestured impatiently, urging the trio of serving lads forward. She held open the door of the carriage and helped the two young boys to bring Guido inside. His head lolled onto his chest, and for a horrifying moment Cordelia thought he was dead. Then she heard him give a snort, and he wriggled around, nestling his head against the blanket that had been folded along the back of the wooden seat. No, he wasn't dead, just sleeping.

Satisfied that Guido was settled, Anna hurried back inside the house and returned carrying a rough-hewn box, fastened with a sturdy leather strap. From the way she puffed and panted, Cordelia concluded that the box was heavy. She set it at Guido's feet, wedging it between the seat and the cart wall, then slammed the door.

"All right. Take him home!" she called to the stable lad driving the cart. "And remember, tell his family the count has paid off their debts. With the extra money Guido has earned, they should be able to buy themselves a pig, or maybe two. They will be set up for life."

The stable boy whipped up the mule, and the cart lumbered out of the courtyard. One of the other serving lads said something to Anna, his words inaudible beneath the rumble of the departing cart. Whatever he said didn't please Anna. She made to cuff him around the ears, and he ducked, obviously an expert at avoiding her blows. Then he ran into the house, his friend at his heels. Anna followed, shaking her fist, but making no real effort to catch them. In truth, much as Cordelia wanted to see Anna as a villain, she had a suspicion that both boys were giggling.

Cordelia returned to her room, wondering exactly what it was that she had just seen. A servant being sent home to his family, that was certain. But why? And how sick had the lad been?

One thing was certain, Cordelia decided, as she splashed cold water on her face. She and her companions would be leaving the Villa of the Three Fountains this morning, as soon as fresh horses could be harnessed to their carriage.

In view of what she'd seen and heard over the past twelve hours, she suspected that their lives depended on getting away from the villa.

Chapter Five

After three weeks of escorting her cousin through Europe, Cordelia should have known better than to assume Mary would agree to leave the villa just because Cordelia wanted her to. In fact, Mary refused even to consider taking to the road again. She had slept wonderfully well, undisturbed by the count's nocturnal prowling. She had thoroughly enjoyed her breakfast of sweet rolls and a drink made from the juice of preserved apricots. Basking in the flirtatious attentions of Lieutenant Waldheim, she had no intention of returning her aching limbs to the torment of another day shut up in a bumpy carriage. Cordelia's suggestion that they might be in danger from the count was met with incredulous laughter. Her requests to leave the villa fell on stubbornly deaf ears.

Anna, who would presumably have championed Cordelia's plea, was unavailable to lend her support.

"She is with the master," one of the serving boys informed them. "Nobody is allowed to speak with

Anna today unless she sends for them. That is the rule, *signorina.*"

"Why would you want to see a sour-faced old biddy like Anna?" Mary demanded, helping herself to another sweet roll, although she'd already finished one breakfast. Since none of the serving boys spoke English, she saw no reason to be discreet in her comments. "And why on earth does her opinion matter to you? She is the housekeeper for heaven's sake! A *servant.*"

"And the only woman in the entire household," Cordelia pointed out. "She urged me last night to leave here as soon as possible."

Mary frowned, then hastily smoothed out the wrinkles before they could take hold and leave a permanent mark. "She probably wants to avoid extra work, but why should we care about that? Our rooms are comfortable, the cooking is excellent, and the company is delightful, particularly Lieutenant Waldheim's. Since my father has seen fit to banish us to this godforsaken part of the world for the next five months, we may as well stay here as anywhere else."

"There's a minor problem with your logic," Cordelia said. "This is almost certainly not the villa where your father ordered us to stay."

"You cannot be certain of that." Mary's temper flashed. "Goodness, gracious, Cordelia, I don't understand you. We have been searching for the Villa of the Three Fountains for more than a week. Now we have found the wretched place, and you want us to leave again! Really, there's no pleasing you."

Cordelia sighed and decided to take a different tack. "We need money," she reminded her cousin. "I'm down to the last ten pounds your father allotted me for the journey."

"Papa has made arrangements for us to receive an allowance," Mary said.

"Yes, through *Signor* Pesante, his Italian lawyer, who has so far been conspicuous only by his absence."

"I'm sure he will turn up any day now."

"And how do you suppose *Signor* Pesante will find us if it turns out that there are two estates with the same name, and we're staying at the wrong one?"

For the first time, Mary looked seriously worried. Talk of money always had the power to concentrate her mind. Then she shrugged. "If there are two estates with the same name in this region, then Mr. Pesante must know about both of them. If he doesn't find us in one place, surely he will move on to the other? And in the meantime, we can remain comfortably situated here at the villa instead of racketing about the countryside in that monster of a coach."

Cordelia's face must have shown her frustration, because Mary made an unexpected attempt at conciliation. "Cordelia, I understand your worries, but before we go jouncing off into the Italian wilderness, we need to speak with the count. For all we know, *his* ancestors may have reached some agreement with *our* ancestors about renting the villa. Papa was not in a communicative mood when we left England, if you recall. Lord knows, he didn't exactly inundate us with helpful details about our journey, or about what we would find when we got here."

Cordelia had to admit the truth of that statement. The earl had been so furious with his daughter that Mary's most artful displays of contrition had been barely sufficient to win her his grudging promise of continued financial support.

"The earl described the estate to me as a modest place in the care of an elderly couple," Cordelia said.

"By no stretch of the imagination could this estate be called modest. The income from her must be significant by any standard."

Mary dipped her fingers into the verbena-scented fingerbowl. "Then you should be pleased with the way things have turned out, shouldn't you? After all, Papa has deeded the income from the estate to you, so if it's hugely profitable, you will have far more money than you expected—"

"The estate is only in trust to me," Cordelia reminded her quickly. "Remember that I am to use the income from the estate to care for your—"

"I know the arrangements!" Mary snapped, flicking open a napkin and drying her fingers. "God knows Aunt Louise spent long enough drumming them into my ears! In between prosing on and on at me, she kept saying how fortunate I was to have you with me to take care of all the practical details. So why don't you take care of them, instead of harassing me?"

"That's what I'm trying to do—"

"With remarkably little success," Mary said tightly. "The point is that Papa has forbidden us to communicate directly with him and you haven't been able to find Mr. Pesant, who is supposed to communicate for us. Therefore, it seems to me there is nobody left to answer your questions except the count himself, who is temporarily unavailable. So it is quite absurd to talk about leaving here when we have nowhere else to go and nobody to turn to. And that's the end of the matter, Cordelia. I won't discuss it further."

Unfortunately for Cordelia's peace of mind, Mary's arguments were eminently reasonable. Against them, Cordelia could set nothing except her own fears and fantasies. If she insisted on leaving, she wouldn't even know if she should direct the carriage driver to turn north or south, east or west. In the circumstances, how could she justify leaving the comfort of the count's villa?

Acknowledging defeat, Cordelia accompanied Mary into the drawing room. Lieutenant Waldheim greeted Mary with delighted smiles, and Cordelia with a cool bow. Apparently, he still hadn't forgiven her for what he considered her foolish behavior the day before. Still, his general mood was oppressively cheerful. As far as he was concerned, the count's illness was a blessing, since it left him free to spend the day flirting with Mary, an activity at which he showed himself to be almost as well skilled as she.

Captain Hesse, on the other hand, could barely contain his impatience at their enforced idleness and Mary's beauty seemed only a modest compensation prize. By midafternoon, he was so tense that he was pacing the drawing room like a caged cheetah. When a watery sun broke through the afternoon clouds, he leaped at the chance to escort Cordelia on a tour of the villa's gardens.

"I had not expected our stay here to exceed a single night," he admitted as they crossed the terrace and took a meandering pathway which led to a walled enclosure, surrounded by hazel trees. "These are troubled times in the Duchy of Modena, and it's most inconvenient that I cannot conclude my business with the count promptly. As you can imagine, there are many other tasks to which I should be giving my attention."

"The Italian revolutionaries have managed to win a great deal of support from other European governments," Cordelia murmured. "The situation must be difficult for your government."

The captain snorted his contempt. "The King of

Piedmont and that wretched prime minister of his have manipulated international opinions with their lies. They are jumped-up nobodies, but they're determined to cause trouble for my emperor. As for Mazzini and Garibaldi with all their nonsense about freedom and democracy. . . . Well, words fail me."

Cordelia's sympathies lay entirely with Prime Minister Cavour and the Italian rebels who were struggling to win their independence from the Austrian imperial government, but she was far too polite to say so. She could certainly sympathize with the captain's frazzled nerves. For a man of action, enforced idleness was always hard to endure.

"I heard rumors when I was in Piacenza that the Austrian army of occupation had still not received precise orders from Vienna," she said. "That must make your situation all the more difficult."

"I would ask who is spreading such rumors if I didn't know already that they are all over the Duchy," the captain said, sounding weary. "As a result, while the politicians in Vienna argue among themselves, the Italians are flocking to Giuseppe Garibaldi's banner in ever greater numbers. The longer we delay in taking firm action, the more difficult our task of restoring order becomes."

"You sound certain that this struggle will come to war," Cordelia said. "When we left England, the newspapers still talked of a negotiated settlement."

"Lombardy and Modena have been part of the Hapsburg Empire for generations," Captain Hesse said. "Our emperor will never hand over his inheritance to revolutionaries, and the King of Piedmont can never satisfy his desire to be king of all Italy without Lombardy and Modena as the jewels in his crown.

There is little room for negotiation in such conflicting desires."

"Perhaps not, but we can hope the calmer voices will prevail, so that people of goodwill can work to find a peaceful compromise," Cordelia said.

"The emperor prefers to settle his arguments on the battlefield," Captain Hesse said.

"Yes, I'd heard that," Cordelia said. The warlike attitude of the Hapsburgs didn't sit well with the rest of Europe, nor was it considered certain that the Austrian armies would win if they were actually forced into a fight. Still, Cordelia wanted to avoid quarreling with the captain if she could. "In England, you know, General Garibaldi is considered a hero with an almost mythical ability to rally his troops. He has won some amazing victories in the past."

Captain Hesse looked grim. "If the Italians fight hard, the battle will be long and bloody instead of mercifully swift, but the outcome will be the same."

"Are the Austrian armies so sure of victory?" Cordelia asked as gently as she could.

Captain Hesse hesitated for a betraying second. "Yes," he said at last. "But I wish I could dismiss Garibaldi's skills as lightly as some of my superiors. Our troops are better armed and better trained, no question. But in battle, soldiers need more than guns and bayonets if they are to win. They need good leaders, and a conviction that their cause is just. The Italian army is a collection of ragtag, fire-eating rebels, but Giuseppe Garibaldi inspires such devotion among his men that I am afraid we Austrians will take heavy losses before our superior weapons and training carry the day."

Cordelia was surprised that Captain Hesse could be so reflective about Garibaldi's appeal to the Italian

revolutionaries, but before she could make any comment, the captain seemed to realize how indiscreet
he'd been, and hastily changed the subject.

"I'm taking you to see the garden that gives this
estate its name," he said, shepherding her through the
arbor of hazel trees. "The famous Villa d'Este near
Rome has many more fountains, but I believe the garden the count's father established here is truly the
most beautiful in all of Italy."

As he spoke, he opened a white wooden gate set
into the stucco wall. The sound of splashing water
filled the air and, as if to show off the garden at its
very best, the sun broke through the clouds, bathing
the terra-cotta pots of mimosa that flanked the entrance in vibrant, golden light. Cordelia caught her
breath on a tiny exclamation of sheer delight.

A giant chestnut tree grew in the exact center of
the circular garden, framed by a triangle of three tall
fountains. The pedestals were fashioned of glittering
blue-black stone, and the fountain spray spumed out
of golden spigots, designed in the shape of rosebuds,
before cascading into a series of mosaic-tiled bowls.
Sunlight refracted through the water droplets in irides-
cent crystals, capturing the colors of the multihued
tiles, and reflecting them with such dazzling brilliance
that, for one magical moment, Cordelia had the impression that the fountains had turned into a single
shimmering rainbow of color, swirling around the
huge tree.

At this time of year, after so much rain, the predom-
inant color in the garden was green, with budding
leaves on the chestnut tree fluttering in the breeze,
and with a scattering of spring flowers bordering neat
squares of thick spring grass. She could visualize how
colorful the garden must look in high summer, and

how welcoming the cool splash of water would be as the fierce Italian sun scorched the surrounding countryside.

"It's truly lovely," she said, pulling off her glove to allow the water from the spray to splash over her outstretched hand. The droplets were icy cold, but the water felt clean and pleasantly soft on her skin. The damp smell of new leaves filled her nose, so that unconsciously she breathed deeper, drawing in the fresh scents of the garden. "This is truly heavenly," she said.

"I think you are beginning to understand why the villa has such a reputation for beauty," the captain said, smiling at her with obvious pleasure.

"Indeed," Cordelia replied, thinking that beneath his pomposity, the captain was rather a nice man. "The layout of the gardens and fountains is very unusual, isn't it?"

"Very unusual," Captain Hesse agreed. "Perhaps that's part of its appeal. Even the most jaundiced visitor finds something fresh to admire. I discover new beauty each time I come here."

Cordelia sidestepped a marble bench, placed to give a view of the fountains framed by the drooping branches of the chestnut tree. "Do you know who originally designed this garden?" she asked. "It must have been here for several centuries."

Captain Hesse nodded. "There have been fountains here for more than three hundred years. The originals were built during the sixteenth century by a Venetian trader returning from the East."

"The mosaics are unlike anything I've ever seen before." Cordelia stared in fascination at the designs worked into the fountains. Each bowl seemed to depict a different aspect of the sky, although nothing she had ever seen through her father's telescope remotely resembled the fanciful sky captured in the mosaics. In one bowl, a dark, yellowish green sun rose in a sky tinged with purple, circled by two moons and a trail of pink stars. In another, the same strange sun was shown in a more distant perspective, surrounded by fifteen objects that Cordelia thought might be planets. In the final bowl, the sky was shown as darkening toward night, with the moons faded to pale silver crescents and the stars eerie green pinpoints of light, scattered in random configurations that bore no relationship to the familiar constellations Cordelia had known since childhood.

Captain Hesse peered over her shoulder. "Whenever I look at those designs, I wonder why an artist would want to portray a sky that has no reality," he said.

"It's almost as if he's drawn a picture of another world," Cordelia said, feeling her stomach knot in an oddly intense response to the strange sun and its alien string of planets.

The captain laughed. "Now that is an intriguing notion, Miss Hope."

She cast a final look at the mysterious green sun, wavering beneath its veil of water. "I'm surprised that the mosaics have remained so colorful after all these years," she said.

"They aren't original. The count brought in craftsmen from Portugal to effect repairs to the mosaics. He rescued the garden from virtual wilderness, and rebuilt the fountains from scratch about fifteen years ago."

"He certainly did a magnificent job," Cordelia said.

The captain nodded his agreement. "And not only on this garden. He is a keen horticulturist, and if you tour the estate, you will see that in contrast to most

Italian landowners, the count employs many advanced farming techniques."

"Do you know exactly how long the count's family has lived here at the villa?" Cordelia asked.

"His family has lived here for three generations," the captain said. "I understand that when the count's grandfather bought the estate, the villa and the surrounding land had been allowed to run down almost to the point of ruin."

"That often happens where there are absentee owners, and caretakers who have neither the financial resources nor the energy to care for the property," Cordelia said, then shivered at the truth of her own words. Is that what had happened with the Stanwyck estate? Had some previous earl grown weary of attempting to care for a distant estate, and seized the chance to sell it when a buyer came along? She felt physically sick when she contemplated the disastrous consequences for Mary if the Count of Albion had legal title to the estate where the Earl of Stanwyck had ordered his daughter to stay hidden.

"You don't happen to know who the absentee owners of this estate were, do you?" she asked the captain. She tried to make her question sound casual, but from the captain's sudden scrutiny, she knew she hadn't succeeded.

"I'm afraid not," he said, looking at her thoughtfully. "I don't believe the count ever mentioned the names of the original owners, but I do recall his making a couple of oblique references that made me think they must have been English."

The beauty of the garden was no longer enough to prevent a heavy sinking feeling in the pit of Cordelia's stomach. It was surely stretching the long arm of coincidence beyond the breaking point to assume that there were two estates with the same name, both owned by absentee English landlords, and situated so close to each other that their location on the map was shown by the identical dot.

If an ancestor of the Earl of Stanwyck had sold the Ossoli dowry lands to the count of Albion's grandfather, the action would have been illegal, since entailed lands couldn't be sold. But the precise legalities of the situation scarcely mattered. The Count of Albion had all the resources to fight his case in the Italian courts, whereas she didn't even have the money to rent a cottage for the next five months. How in the world was she going to take care of Mary and Ellen? Her ready cash amounted to ten pounds sterling, and employment prospects in this poverty-stricken region didn't seem rosy.

The garden benches were too wet to sit on, so she and the captain continued walking until they had toured the entire garden. Captain Hesse offered her his arm as they turned back toward the villa. "You look troubled, Miss Hope. I trust nothing I've said has alarmed you?"

"You have merely put my own fears into words," Cordelia admitted. "At first I was quite sure that the Count of Albion must be a trespasser. Now I am beginning to fear that we are the trespassers."

"You said that you had documents proving your ownership of this estate." Captain Hesse didn't exactly ask a question. Instead, he allowed his comment to hang delicately in midair.

"I do. But what if there has been a hideous muddle in paperwork and the estate I believe is mine was, in fact, sold years and years ago to the Albion family? From what I have learned over the past twenty-four hours, I cannot discount such a possibility, despite my impeccable documentation."

Captain Hesse cleared his throat. "Presumably you would then return to England . . . ?"

Cordelia gathered her wits quickly, before she could betray Mary's secrets. "Yes, yes, of course that is what we would do. However, I am probably seeing problems where none exist. How could my documents be faulty? We have received income from the estate on a regular basis, and wages have been paid each year to the caretakers. If the Count of Albion's grandfather bought the estate almost a hundred years ago, why do we have no documents to show that the sale took place? Why do we continue to receive income from the estate?"

"I wish I could answer you," the captain said. "Unfortunately, it seems to me that only the count can provide the information you need to resolve this matter."

"You're right, of course, and I should never have bothered you with the details of our situation—"

Captain Hesse clicked his heels and carried her hand to his lips. "My dear Miss Hope, you haven't bothered me at all. On the contrary, your charming presence has made a tedious delay very much more bearable for me."

The captain was undoubtedly flirting with her. In normal circumstances, Cordelia might have been flattered—after all, he seemed a sensible man and he did have a pair of truly splendid whiskers—but she had too much on her mind to allow for the luxury of flirting, even with a handsome soldier in a dashing uniform. Returning his smile, she removed her hand from his clasp and changed the subject.

"I think it's going to rain again," she said, indicating

the dark clouds gathering on the horizon. "We'd better get back to the villa."

A few spots of rain began to fall almost as she was speaking. Cordelia and Captain Hesse both increased their pace. The light shower of rain turned rapidly into a downpour, and they both ran the final few yards to the house.

Just as she arrived at the door, Cordelia paused for a moment and looked up, not even sure why she did so.

The count stood at a window high up on the third floor of the villa. She knew that he was looking down at them. At her. The rain sheeting against the panes distorted her vision, so that it seemed to Cordelia that his hands clawed frantically at the glass and his mouth appeared twisted into a rictus of agony. Then, as she watched, Anna came and stood beside him, interspersing herself between his body and the window. With slow, deliberate movements, the housekeeper closed the drapes.

"Miss Hope, come inside!" Captain Hesse called. "You are getting soaked!"

"Coming," she said, but she waited until the drapes cut off all sight of the count before she stepped into the hallway, and once she was safely inside, she found that her face was wet with tears, as well as with rain.

The agonized scream exploded inside Cordelia's head, jerking her upright in the bed. Her heart pounded and sweat dampened her skin, but gradually—thank God—the terrible screaming faded into silence. She held her breath, waiting for another scream, but the villa seemed silent except for the normal creaks and sighs of a sleeping household.

The silence bothered her. Why was nobody rushing

to investigate? Was she the only person who'd heard the dreadful cry? She was sure she hadn't been dreaming—could have sworn the sound was real—and yet it seemed strange that nobody else was stirring.

Shaking off the last remnants of sleep, Cordelia pulled on her robe and slippers, then lit her candle from the night-light standing on the dressing table. Opening the door of her bedroom, she peered out into the deserted corridor. Nothing moved. No sound disturbed the quiet, not even the rumble of a snore.

She must have been dreaming, Cordelia decided. In the normal run of events, she wasn't in the least prone to nightmares, but these past few days had not been normal in any sense of the word.

She waited for a few minutes, peering into the semi-darkness, her stomach knotted with tension, her whole body taut with the expectation of hearing another scream. Nothing happened. The night remained drowsy and peaceful..

Cordelia let out a breath she hadn't even realized she was holding. Best to return to bed, she decided. After her experience with the count the night before, she had no intention of roaming the hallways searching for the source of the noise. Some things were better left unknown and unexplored.

She had her hand on the latch of her door, when the scream came again, a cry of such profound and tormented yearning that she covered her ears to block out the sound. The scream continued, echoing and re-echoing in her mind until she shrieked herself in shared agony, shoving her hands against her ears to cut out the noise, and doubling over with the pain.

Almost immediately, the door across the hallway was flung open. Captain Hesse, resplendent in a tasseled nightcap, and still tying the sash of his silk robe, burst into the corridor.

"Miss Hope, calm yourself! What is it? What has happened?" The captain marched to her side, all spry military efficiency and male authority despite the informality of his appearance.

He took her hand and chafed it briskly. "My dear Miss Hope, you must tell me what is wrong. You will do yourself an injury if you continue to scream so hysterically."

Abruptly, the scream inside her head stopped. Her throat unclenched, and she regained control of her voice. Clinging to the captain's arm, Cordelia slowly straightened. She leaned against the wall, fighting to draw breath. She realized that other doors had now opened. Ellen, gray hair pinned into sausage curls, rushed into the corridor wrapped in the counterpane from her bed. The maid hobbled across the hall to Cordelia's side, clucking anxiously. Even Mary, blue eyes blurred with sleep, peered around the edge of the door, golden curls tumbling about her shoulders in glorious disarray, mouth open in surprise.

"Cordelia!" she exclaimed. "Whatever is wrong?"

Emerging from his room, Lieutenant Waldheim seemed momentarily rooted to the spot by this forbidden glimpse of Mary's beauty. He recovered himself quickly, however, and averted his gaze from the swell of her bosom. Then he strode down the hallway to join the captain, trying to fasten his frogged uniform jacket over the bulk of his nightshirt.

"Miss Hope! Good heafens! What has happened?" He peered into the murky reaches of the hallway, searching for villains. "Haf you been attacked? Robbed? Violated?"

Only by a scream inside my head, she thought wryly, managing—just barely—to shake her head.

"Miss Hope, you must tell us what is wrong," Captain Hesse said gently.

She saw the circle of faces staring at her, waiting for an explanation, and she realized that there was absolutely nothing she could say that was truthful, and wouldn't sound crazy.

"I had a nightmare," she said finally, blushing at the feeble excuse. "I apologize most sincerely for having disturbed all of you."

The captain tried to look sympathetic, but Lieutenant Waldheim merely looked impatient. He tapped the side of his head, discreetly indicating to the captain that he had no great faith in her sanity.

Captain Hesse frowned, but he patted Cordelia on the arm with betraying condescension. If he didn't share Lieutenant Waldheim's opinion, he clearly considered her overendowed with hysterical imagination.

He held her hand, stroking soothingly, as if she were a frightened animal. Or the village idiot. "My dear Miss Hope, there is nothing for you to fear, but I know how sensitive you ladies can be." He smiled encouragingly. "If you would like to have an extra lamp in your room, I'd be happy to lend you mine. Brighter lights often help to assuage irrational fears."

"Thank you," she replied stiffly. "I won't need any extra lights. My nightmare is unlikely to recur."

"I should hope not!" Mary exclaimed. "Really, Cordelia, I don't know what's come over you these past few days!" She tossed her curls angrily, then decided to show the Austrians that she was as sweet-natured as she was beautiful.

She smoothed her frowns into smiles and softened her voice until it was creamy as whipped butter. "If you're frightened, you can sleep with me, Cordelia dearest. I daresay the strain of the journey has been greater than you realized, but with adequate rest you will soon be your old cheerful self."

Cordelia adjusted her face into a smile and held it there, despite the fact that she was afraid her skin might crack. "Thank you, Mary, but I shall do very well in my own room."

"As you wish, dearest." Mary yawned, the picture of normal, healthy sleepiness in contrast to Cordelia's neurotic, wakeful tension. "Come back to bed, Ellen, and we will do our best to snatch another couple of hours of sleep."

With another charming smile for the officers, she held out her hand to the maid. "I'm sure you need your rest even more than I do, Ellen. You've worked so hard today."

"Not really, my la—, I mean, ma'am. Just ironed a few dresses and such like. But I am sleepy, when all's said and done." Ellen clutched the counterpane around her neck and scuttled back to her room.

The lieutenant marched off as soon as Mary closed her bedroom door, but Captain Hesse insisted on waiting outside Cordelia's door until she was safely back in bed.

"Now, you are to tell me when you are tucked in," he said from outside her door. "I shall be standing right here, on guard, so to speak."

It was difficult to guard against screams that took place only inside her head, Cordelia thought, walking back to her bed. "I'm under the covers," she called out dutifully, a few moments later. "Thank you, Captain Hesse, for your concern. I assure you that I won't awaken the household again."

"Very well, Miss Hope. Good night. Remember that

you have nothing to fear here at the villa, nothing at all. You are surrounded by friends."

"Yes, of course."

The captain's footsteps retreated the short distance down the hallway to his own room.

There was scarcely time for Cordelia to hear the thud of his door closing when the scream erupted inside her head for a third time. She buried her face in her pillow, pounding her fists into the mattress in the desperation of her efforts to keep herself from crying out in response.

Eventually, what seemed like hours later but probably was only minutes, the scream faded into a deadly silence that was almost more horrible than the cry itself. Where her head had reverberated with the scream, now it pounded with the agony of silence, the frantic need for contact to fill the void.

Cordelia got out of bed again. Her hands were shaking so violently that she muffed several attempts to fasten the ribbons at the neck of her robe. Giving up on the hopeless task, she snatched her candle from the dresser and crept out into the hallway.

Where had the scream come from? She knew, with a certainty that went beyond logic, that it was the count she had heard. Last night, he had been sleeping in a room that was situated close to her own bedroom. But today the servants had indicated that his rooms were in the west wing of the house, and this afternoon, after her walk, when she had glimpsed the count, he had been standing at the window of a room on the third floor.

Cordelia walked steadily down the dark and silent hallway toward the rear of the house. Oddly enough, now that she had decided to seek out the count, her trembling had stopped. At the juncture of the central portion of the villa with the small west wing, she discovered a stairway that went both down and up. If she walked downstairs, she guessed that she would emerge in the kitchens, or perhaps the pantry or stillroom. If she walked upstairs, no doubt she would find the servants' sleeping quarters.

And, perhaps, the room or rooms where the count waited out his "bad spells"?

As she hesitated, wondering what the consequences might be if she insisted on speaking with the count, she saw a serving lad coming up the stairs. He was slightly older than the general run of youths who served the count, but still more boy than man, and Cordelia was sure she had never seen him before. He carried a tray, set with a crystal carafe and two polished glasses.

He stopped abruptly when he saw Cordelia. He nodded at her, glancing around uncertainly as if unsure whether to continue upstairs or retreat to the kitchens.

"Good evening," Cordelia said in Italian, as if it were the most natural thing in the world for houseguests to be found wandering the back hallways of the villa clad only in their nightclothes.

The boy nodded, relieved to have Cordelia set the tone. "Good evening to you, *signorina*. How are you?"

"Well, thank you."

The two of them stared at each other, neither one quite sure what to say next. The serving lad cleared his throat. "His Excellency is waiting for me to serve his brandy, *signorina*."

"Then certainly I must not delay you," Cordelia said, smiling. "Please, go ahead. Lead the way."

"Thank you, *signorina*." The lad made a wide circle

around Cordelia, then started to climb the stairs to the third floor, looking back nervously over his shoulder to see if she was following.

She was most definitely following. As if she had every right to do so, Cordelia climbed the stairs behind the servant, trying to look like a guest who'd been invited to visit the count's quarters.

"It's dark on these back stairs, isn't it?" she said, holding her nightstick high. "I expect you are glad for some extra light."

"Truth to tell, I'm used to the dark," the serving lad said. "The master, he doesn't much care for bright lights. Hurts his eyes, so he says."

"A troublesome affliction, but he copes so admirably," Cordelia murmured, trying to sound as if she knew exactly what they were talking about.

The servant wasn't convinced, or else he was intelligent enough to stick to the main point at issue. He looked at her doubtfully. "Does my master know that you are here?" he asked. "Coming to his room, I mean?"

"Why of course," Cordelia said, flashing a bright smile. Her reply wasn't entirely a lie, she reassured herself. She had a suspicion that the count knew more about her movements than could be accounted for rationally. How else could she explain the extraordinary tug of attraction that had drawn her to his room last night, against all reason, and against every precept of behavior she'd ever been taught? How else could she explain the screams that only she had heard?

The serving lad hesitated for another second or two. Then he tapped softly on the panels of a door situated at the furthermost reaches of the third-floor hallway.

It was opened at once by another boy that Cordelia didn't recognize. "Come in," he said. "Anna says you're . . ." His voice faded into horrified silence. "My God, Pietro! What are you thinking of? Why have you brought *her* up here?"

Pietro shuffled his feet and held out the tray with the brandy, almost as if it were a peace offering. "She says she is expected. Here. Take this."

"Expected?" The servant stared in amazed disbelief from Pietro to Cordelia and back again. "That's not possible. *Signorina*, please, return to your chamber at once."

A door set into the paneling of the room flew open and Anna called out to the servants. "Where is that brandy? He needs you in there right away. Both of you! Come! This will be your night to serve the count."

She stepped aside just long enough to shoo the pair of serving lads ahead of her. Those few seconds were all Cordelia needed to get a glimpse of the inner sanctum, and the sight that met her eyes was so horrific that she gasped and followed Pietro into the anteroom, entirely forgetting that she had neither right nor reason to be there.

The sparsely furnished inner room was dominated by a heavy, four-poster bed, bolted to the floor. The Count of Albion, clad only in breeches and an open shirt, stood at the end of the bed, clinging to one of the posts, his head drooping, his face hidden by the thickness of the pillar.

Anna swung around at the sound of Cordelia's smothered exclamation. Her face crumpled into an expression of appalled surprise. "Madonna and all the saints, *signorina*, are you determined to cause trouble? Get out of here before the count sees you."

"It . . . is . . . too . . . late," the count said, his voice

low and threaded with pain. "I know . . . she has come
. . . to me."

Belatedly, Cordelia realized that the count wasn't
simply standing by the bedpost, clinging to it for support. He was lashed to the bed by rope and leather
thongs, held immobile by knots that looked viciously
tight. Dear God, he was a prisoner in his own home!
What did that mean? Was Anna keeping him captive?

Cordelia swallowed over a burgeoning fear, and
managed to find her voice. "My God, Anna, release
him! Have you run mad? Why have you tied him up
like that?"

"Get away from him, *signorina.* Do not approach
the bed." Anna didn't look in the least guilty, merely
frantic with worry. "Do not question what you do not
understand, *signorina.* I beg that you will return to
your own room and speak to no one of what you
have seen."

"But this is an outrage. Anna, I cannot permit
you—"

"Tell her she must leave!" The count's voice
reached her, low and throbbing with pain. "Anna, I
cannot hold out much longer. The bonds will break."

Cordelia saw that his hands were tugging at the
cords, pulling frantically in an effort to release the
knots. The muscles bunched and corded on his neck
and forearms, and the leather thongs creaked as they
stretched and loosened.

With a thrill of shock, Cordelia realized that the
count wasn't fighting to break free of his bonds. Instead, he was struggling to hold on to the bedpost,
clinging to the wooden pillar with all his strength. Far
from trying to tear himself loose, he *wanted* to be held
captive. She stared in horrified fascination, sickened
and yet unable to look away.

"Get out," Anna said to Cordelia, no longer bothering to be polite. She pushed Cordelia toward the outer door, yelling to the serving lads as she did so. "You, Carlo, get over to your master. Here, Pietro, give me one of those glasses."

She continued propelling Cordelia toward the door while she simultaneously fumbled in her apron pocket and pulled out a small packet of powder. When Pietro held out his tray, she tipped half the powder into each wineglass.

Pietro seemed to know what was expected of him. Looking a little frightened, he splashed brandy into the glasses and swirled the mixture around until the powder dissolved.

"Is this for my master?" Pietro asked, and his voice cracked on the question, squeaking up into the high register of the boy he still was.

"No," Anna said. "It's for you. Drink it. When you wake up, you will be on your way home and several gold pieces richer. No harm done."

Pietro viewed the brandy glass with evident reluctance. Carlo walked over to his side with a slight swagger. "Here, give me a glass. I've already volunteered."

Cordelia and Anna had reached the outer door. Anna grabbed hold of Cordelia's arms and shoved her into the corridor. "Go," she ordered. "I don't have time for you now. Your presence here in the house is bad enough, without having you right on top of my poor master. You are making him sicker than I have ever known him."

Cordelia made no further protests. She fled back downstairs, her stomach churning with revulsion. God in heaven, what had she seen? While she'd been living at the earl's house in London, she had heard vague rumors—none of which she'd really understood—

about noblemen whose perversions kept them excluded from polite society. In her wildest flights of fantasy, it had never occurred to her that she would one day witness someone acting out what surely must be one of those dreadful perversions. How truly appalling that the count should involve ignorant young peasant boys in his own sick fantasies. Presumably, when he was finished with them—and she couldn't bear to imagine what that meant—he paid them off and sent them back to their families. Cordelia began to understand why she hadn't been able to find anyone in Piacenza willing to drive their carriage. And no wonder the innkeeper had refused to allow his young son to act as a messenger! Rumors about the count's unnatural customs must be rampant all over the countryside. Was it possible that Captain Hesse and Lieutenant Waldheim hadn't heard them?

Cordelia crawled under the covers of her bed, telling herself that the Count of Albion's behavior was not only obscene, but also grotesque, and a barbaric exploitation of the youths he employed.

Lying in bed, her body stiff with the tension of unresolved questions, she wondered what weakness in her own character caused her to view such a monster with feelings that were far closer to sympathy than to anything else.

Despite everything that she had seen, Cordelia had the uncomfortable feeling that if anyone at the villa was in danger, it wasn't the serving lads, or even her. It was the Count of Albion himself.

Chapter Six

( )

The torment of his cresting had never before been so long or so terrible, and Dakon knew that it was the presence of the human female, Cordelia Hope, that intensified his pain to such agonizing levels.

For some reason—perhaps the mere coincidence of her arrival right at the moment when his body entered the climax of its cycle—he had been drawn to her with a fascination greater than any he'd ever experienced for a human female. True, his experience of human females in recent years had been limited, but in his youth, before Maria, there had been many flirtations, many efforts to experience the emotion that humans called love.

Of course, he had always failed, just as his father had predicted he would fail. With human females, the Vam-pyr seemed unable to achieve that meeting of the minds that underpinned every worthwhile relationship. And without mental intimacy, Dakon wondered, how could humans claim that there was love?

As soon as he reached maturity and left the protection of his father's home, Dakon had been forced to learn how to live in an unnatural state of mental solitude. Even with Anna, despite all that he owed her, he could share only a blurred, formless affection. So when Cordelia Hope arrived on his doorstep, his mental probes had been careless, nothing more than a reflexive, automatic gesture.

He had been stunned by her response. The moment he touched her mind, he had been overwhelmed by the force and power of their mental connection. And the link between the two of them, entered into so casually, had proven almost impossible to break. The erotic images they created together took on an addictive life of their own.

Given the limited self-control he had available during the turmoil of his cresting, Dakon was powerless to stop the seductive pleasure of their mutual fantasies. Cordelia's mind hummed with activity. Her emotions were soft, swirling clouds that wrapped themselves around his soul, drawing him in, offering him a comfort and a delight he'd scarcely known how to resist.

But in the end, he *had* resisted. Summoning every last ounce of his willpower, he forced himself to erect an impenetrable mind barrier, knowing that to indulge in mental foreplay would lead inevitably to disaster. Because, in the end, Cordelia would reject him, just as every human female rejected mating with the Vampyr. And he would be forced by the imperatives of his nature to overcome her rejection.

Overcome her rejection. What a pretty euphemism for a brutal act, Dakon thought acidly. In plain words, he would rape her. And he had sworn never again to walk down that twisted path, for at the end of it he would find damnation.

There were moments during the three hellish days

that followed his first encounter with Cordelia when Dakon wondered if he would survive the torment of his unfulfilled need, tantalized as he was by her nearness. Resting, exhausted, between bouts of uncontrollable tremors, he told himself that he had finally found a way to cut the lifespan of the Vam-pyr to more human lengths. Iron and garlic merely caused skin allergies, he reflected wryly as Anna wiped the sweat from his forehead with a cool cloth. Abstinence from mating was guaranteed to provoke an allergic reaction of the entire Vam-pyr system.

Anna watched him, her eyes dark with sympathy. She ran her gnarled fingers over his swollen cheeks, and he clenched his jaw, wincing at the instant throbbing of the tender sacs that protected his fangs.

"Only a few more hours, lord, and then it will be over." Anna kept her voice low, knowing how all his senses were painfully magnified during the time of his cresting.

"I ... hope ... so." He refused to calculate how many more hours remained before his sacs burst. The pain of waiting would be unendurable if he started counting off minutes and seconds. Last night he'd fallen into that trap, and the silent screams of his despair had brought Cordelia straight to his side—only to witness the degradation of his suffering. By giving in to weakness, he had subjected himself to shame.

Dakon swallowed, moistening his sacs, and for a split second, the pain throbbing in his fangs abated. "Where ... is ... she?" he asked Anna.

"Gone out with Captain Hesse, lord." Anna didn't need to ask who *she* was. She cleared her throat. "They have driven to the village of Ponte Nuova. I told them that I thought *Signor* Pesante had offices there."

Shivers rocked him. Dakon waited for them to stop

sufficiently for him to reply. "Why would you tell her something so nonsensical?"

Anna shrugged. "It is better for you if she is out of the house."

"So you sent her off on a wild-goose chase?"

"If I had my way, she would never have been let in the house." Anna showed not the slightest sign of remorse. "When she is gone, you feel better. This is the first time you have been able to hold a conversation in twelve hours. And it will do her no harm to look for *Signor* Pesante, just because you and I both know she will never find him. The day is dry and not too chilly, and I offered them the use of your new phaeton. She and the Austrian will have nothing to complain about."

Dakon would have scolded her if he'd had the energy. "I am going to have to deal with that situation, Anna. After all, we cannot push aside her questions forever. Legally, this may well be her house."

"True, but you do not have to deal with her until you're feeling stronger. Nor with that interfering captain, either."

"Are both the Austrians still here?" Dakon asked.

Anna shook her head. "Not the lieutenant. Captain Hesse sent him off about his business, back to the regiment, but the captain looks like he's willing to wait a month." She sniffed. "I don't know why he has to hang around, sticking his long Austrian nose where it doesn't belong."

"Possibly because I am assisting his cause?" Dakon suggested mildly. "You do remember that I am a declared ally of the Austrian imperial government?"

"Right." Anna snorted. She wrung out the cloth and returned it to his forehead. "Let the captain dance attendance on your English virgin and perhaps he'll forget about Italian troop movements for a few hours."

"*My* English virgin?" Dakon said ruefully. "Dear God, Anna, how I wish she were!" He said nothing more, because his body convulsed, his stomach clenching in dry, heaving gasps of need. Anna soothed him with a thimbleful of blood saved from Carlo's donation, but Dakon knew that his heart must eventually give out under the stress he was imposing on it. He would probably survive the multiple stresses of abstinence this time. But next time? And the one after that?

For three thousand years, Vam-pyr scientists had tried to find an artificial stimulant that would mimic the effect of female blood, sucked into the Vam-pyrs' system during the shattering culmination to a mating. All their attempts had failed, and Dakon realized that each year—each cresting—his own makeshift remedy became less successful. Ten years ago, a cup of blood from one young serving lad had been enough to precipitate a rupture of his mating sacs, sending the life-nourishing fluid streaming into his system. Two years ago, his need had increased and it had taken two cups. This time, he had already drawn blood from three serving lads—and it hadn't been enough. Another young boy would have to be mesmerized while Dakon drew blood from the veins in his wrist and sipped slowly, without pleasure, praying for release from the brutal pain that preceded culmination.

He didn't dare contemplate what would happen when the time came that nothing would appease his starving body other than the real blood of a female virgin, drawn warm and pulsing into his mouth.

Dakon forced his eyes open, trying to shatter the forbidden images crowding into his mind. But even with his eyes open, he saw Cordelia, her throat bared to his touch, and her hands stroking his cheeks in a delicate, erotic caress. The longing that seized him was tinged with unbearable sadness because such tempting images could never have any foundation in reality.

Don't think of her, he warned himself. Contemplate the great philosophical truths of the universe.

Think about the Vam-pyr, your fellow exiles.

Yes, he would think about the Vam-pyr, his own kind. Not surprisingly, his regimen of self-imposed abstinence was not popular with most of the Vam-pyr community and ZArymp, his father, was infuriated by Dakon's willful indifference to the survival of the Vam-pyr race.

You have a duty to your own people! ZArymp had thundered when they met at the midcentury gathering of the Vam-pyr in Bucharest. *Mate! Propagate! Survive! That is your obligation as a Vam-pyr! As my only living son.*

Dakon winced. "Do we not also have a duty toward the humans whose world we share?" he asked mildly.

He should have known better than to make such a suggestion to his father. ZArymp exploded into an impassioned account of all the reasons why the Vampyr had every right to kill a few humans in order to guarantee the survival of their own species. ZArymp was a conservative, very much of the old school. In his heart of hearts he saw no difference between human beings and the rest of the wildlife that inhabited Earth. If oxen could be harnessed to the plough, and pigs slaughtered for pork chops, why was it immoral to use human females to insure the survival of the Vam-pyr? Besides, human society was so innately barbaric, it didn't deserve to survive. The Vam-pyr were doing the other races in the universe a favor by culling the numbers of humans before they learned to journey among the stars.

Dakon had always found an irony to the Vam-pyr view that because *humans* were so violent, the Vampyr had a moral right to slaughter them. ZArymp, of course, could see no irony in his viewpoint at all.

"Tomorrow the Rescue!" ZArymp bellowed, waving his clenched fist toward the night sky, and chanting the article of faith that was drummed into every Vampyr from early childhood. "And remember, Dakon, when the ship comes for us, you must have a son to take home with you! So is it written."

The Book of the Vam-pyr contained many lessons whose meaning had been lost in the four thousand years of exile, and there was constant debate as to exactly how much could be known about the real Vam-pyr civilization. On one subject, however, there was no debate. The Book of the Vam-pyr, written by the Captain of the Founding Fathers, made it quite clear that six hundred Vam-pyr had been trapped on the third planet of the solar system by an accident that destroyed their skyship. It was also clear that the original Vam-pyr had lived in daily expectation of rescue. Most modern Vam-pyr descendants clung to the same elusive hope. After three thousand years of silence from the home world, Dakon found such faith willfully naive.

"Why do you doubt that a rescue ship is on its way?" ZArymp had asked at their last meeting, just as he asked every time they met. "Remember, my son, that to complete a journey through the stars requires many centuries."

"Our would-be rescuers have already had forty centuries," Dakon pointed out. "How long does it take to equip one starship and point it toward Earth?"

"I cannot answer your question, as you very well know," ZArymp said. "We have no idea how long it takes to prepare for such a journey. We have lost the knowledge that permitted our ancestors to sail among the stars."

Dakon covered his eyes in the Vam-pyr gesture of deference to one of greater rank. "Most honored father, I do not believe that the Vam-pyr of the home world know that our ancestors survived, or that we exist. Can you not accept that we will never return to our own world?"

"Of course I do not accept your blasphemy." ZArymp scowled at his son across the room, darkened to the perfect level of comfort for the Vam-pyr eye. He took his son's hand, and laid it gently on the table. "But what you say, if it is true, merely provides greater reason for you to mate with a human female. If we must survive here, on this insignificant planet, then we will do it. We are Vam-pyr! We are strong! But you deny your nature and your heritage when you refuse to give life to a son."

ZArymp's gruff voice quivered. His father was beginning to show the first signs of old age, Dakon realized with a pang. ZArymp, in fact, was three hundred and thirty-four years old by human reckoning, and well into late middle age by the standards of the Vampyr. But he still continued to mate three times a year, just as he had for the past two and a half centuries. Dakon's mother, and one other human female, had survived the mating process and become pregnant with ZArymp's seed. Dakon's mother had survived the pregnancy, but died in giving Dakon life. The other female had died six months into the pregnancy, taking her frail, partially formed Vam-pyr son with her into death. Out of ZArymp's seven hundred and

fifty matings, Dakon was the sole living offspring.
Which meant, Dakon thought bitterly, that seven hundred and fifty human females had surrendered their
lives in order that ZArymp might procreate a son.

Dakon found the price of his existence an intolerable burden, and he had no intention of adding his own
trail of murdered women to the sacrificial pile created
by his ancestors. A half dozen of the younger Vam-
pyr agreed with him, and it was a sad fact that at the
Bucharest Council the total number of Vam-pyr had
once again decreased, this time from four hundred and
sixty-three to a mere four hundred and fifty. There
were no successful births to report from the previous
decade.

Dakon's thoughts faded into incoherence as the culmination to his cresting came ever closer. Mercifully,
in the final moments before his sacs burst, he lost
consciousness and came to only when the soothing
balm of their fluid poured over his fangs and dripped
slowly down his throat, easing the parched, brittle dryness. The release was nothing at all like the ecstatic
climax to a mating, but his starving body seized on
the life-giving trickle of liquid and gradually began
to revive.

By three o'clock in the afternoon, five days after the
arrival of Miss Cordelia Hope and her companions, his
spring cresting was over. Dakon was able to swallow
a glass of sweet red wine, and eat a few mouthfuls of
dry roasted pork. Meat was always the easiest thing
for the Vam-pyr digestive system to handle, and pork
the easiest of all meats to keep down in the wake of
a cresting. By four, he was able to bathe and wash his
hair without screaming at the touch of hot water
against his scalp. By five, such were the astonishing

recuperative powers of the Vam-pyr body, he was ready to rejoin the world.

"Send a message to our guests," he said to Anna. "Tell them I shall join them tonight for dinner. We don't want Captain Hesse to speculate longer than he must on the nature of my *indisposition*."

Anna was well used to the febrile surge of energy that always overtook him in the wake of a cresting, and she had long ago stopped trying to scold him into resting for a period of convalescence. Dakon was surprised that tonight she reverted to old habits.

"Master, it has been a difficult few days. You would be well advised to remain quietly in your room at least for tonight."

His sense of well-being, not quite as perfect as usual, was nevertheless profound. He simply laughed at her excessive caution, and hugged her with easy affection. "Anna, old friend, the cresting is over. I am safe. Hale and hearty for another three months."

"Are you, lord? You have never before been forced to deal with a young and susceptible virgin on the very night of the culmination."

"Anna, she is no longer a threat to me," Dakon said. "My need and desire for her are both gone. On the other hand, my need for some decent food and pleasant company are both overwhelming. I have been staring at the bedposts in my torture chamber for too long. Come, Anna, be a good soul and, for once, refrain from arguing with me. Tell our guests that I will join them at dinner tonight."

Mary refused absolutely to loosen the stays on her silk moiré evening gown, and nothing either Ellen or Cordelia said would convince her to change her mind. The news that the Count of Albion was joining them for dinner had sent Mary on a giddy whirl of preparation. She was humming beneath her breath, at peace with herself and the world, until she made the fatal discovery that her favorite dress would not close around her expanding waistline.

Ellen, ordered to achieve the impossible or lose her job, struggled until the steel bones of her mistress's corset crushed and squeezed the thickening flesh into the requisite twenty-two inches.

Eating, it was clear, would be completely impossible, but Mary was accustomed to attending dinners at which she consumed nothing except a spoonful of sorbet, and a sip of consommé. Ladies were supposed to have fairylike appetites, and Mary rarely ate more than a mouthful or two in public.

Tonight she would eat nothing at all, but she was adept at moving the food around her plate and appearing to swallow.

When Cordelia tried to protest, Mary simply threatened to break into hysterics, a tactic she had always found extremely effective. Once again it worked perfectly. Cordelia was silenced not because she lacked the courage to stand up to one of her cousin's tantrums, but because she feared for Mary's health.

"Mary, have done with these childish threats," she said sharply. "You shall wear your gown laced that tightly if you insist upon such foolishness."

Mary's pouts vanished with magical swiftness. "It's all very well for you to prose on and on," she said, her voice even more breathless than usual because of the pressure of her internal organs squeezing against her lungs. "But I have no idea what you expect me to wear, Cordelia, if not this dress. Since my father did not see fit to provide us with the funds for any new clothes, perforce I must wear what I have."

"Ellen is skilled with her needle," Cordelia said. "You must give her time tomorrow to spend some hours sewing. No doubt she will be able to alter your favorite gowns to accommodate your needs as time goes on."

"Alter them!" Mary's face grew scarlet with frustration, and a bead of sweat popped out on her forehead. "Alter them! Why not suggest a pinafore across my middle and have done with it? You cannot think that I ... *the only daughter of the Earl of Stanwyck* ... would consider going out in public in a dress that has had the seams let out!"

"Upon reflection, I can see that you would not dream of doing such a thing," Cordelia said with perfect truth. She decided this was one argument she had no need to win right away. Reality would soon dictate the inevitable solution, and even Mary would not be able to avoid it, because there was no money for new clothes. Besides, her cousin's social calendar was unlikely to have any entries over the next few months and so the question of what she would wear to formal dinners was moot.

The stays, however, were obviously causing her cousin considerable discomfort. "Mary, are you sure you feel well? You look ..." Cordelia chose her words carefully. "You look ... constrained."

"I don't feel constrained. I feel splendid." Mary tapped her foot, anticipation of an evening spent flirting with the count restoring her good humor to the point that she almost forgot the pain of her cinched waist and crushed belly. "Come along, Cordelia, the hour is growing late. We should not keep the count waiting. I'm sure he's longing for some cheerful conversation after all those days shut in his rooms with nobody but Anna for company."

If only her cousin knew what the count had really been up to, Cordelia thought grimly. The images of what she had seen in the count's private sanctuary remained far too clear in her mind for comfort.

Given all that she knew, she couldn't understand why she felt this secret, bubbling excitement at the prospect of seeing him again. To punish herself for being so foolish, she was wearing the dowdiest evening dress in her wardrobe, a shabby hand-me-down of gray silk. She reminded herself that the Count of Albion was a ruthless debaucher of young boys. It was hideous, perverted even, that she should nurture this yearning for his company.

A vision in soft rose pink, Mary glided out into the hallway, refusing Ellen's offer of a helping hand, and pushing Cordelia to the side. To Mary's delight, her timing in leaving her bedroom was ideal. The Count of Albion chanced to be crossing the far side of the downstairs hallway just as she reached the top of the staircase. He was thus at the perfect observation point for admiring the graceful vision of Mary descending the stairs.

The count stopped and bowed as soon as he caught sight of them. "Ladies, what a delightful surprise! I bid you good evening."

Mary gave the count a sunny smile and rewarded him with a laughing toss of her curls. Cordelia gave him a curt nod, then turned her gaze and kept it fixed rigidly between her cousin's shoulder blades. She tried not to notice that the count looked almost indecently handsome in formal evening dress, and she ignored the little ripple of warmth that washed over her, as if the count had sent her a private, intimate greeting.

Mary floated down the stairs, her hand barely touching the banisters, her chin tilted with teasing provocation, her great balloon of a skirt the picture of opulent richness in contrast to the delicate slimness of her waist.

The overall effect was delightful, a vision of feminine charm, but Cordelia felt a flash of sympathetic anger on her cousin's behalf. Women—*ladies*—paid a heavy price for the illusion of fragile beauty that society forced upon them, she thought. How many hundreds of hours had Mary been drilled by her dancing instructors and governesses simply in order to achieve that illusion of effortless, graceful femininity? What would the Count of Albion say if he knew Mary had achieved her slender waistline by literally crushing her flesh and bone between fortified steel bands?

Cordelia heard her cousin moan, and a split second later, she saw her stumble.

"Oh dear God! She's fainted!" She grabbed for her cousin, her reflexes quick and agile, but she was four or five steps behind Mary on the staircase and her hands plucked only at air. For an endless moment she watched as Mary toppled into a headlong plunge for the bottom of the staircase.

Bundling her skirts over her arm, Cordelia raced down the stairs, sickly aware that she had no hope of reaching Mary in time to prevent disaster.

She saw a blur of movement, felt the stirring of disturbed air, and then—miraculously—the Count of Albion was standing on the stairs, with Mary in his arms.

"Oh, thank God! How in the world did you manage to catch her? You were even further away than I was!" Cordelia panted.

"I saw her toe catch on the edge of a stair," the count said. "I was moving to catch her almost before she started to fall."

There was no other credible explanation, and yet Cordelia could have sworn the count started to move after she did, and he'd been much further away. He looked at her, his extraordinarily dark eyes impossible to read. "Shall I take your cousin upstairs?" he asked. "I believe she should be in her bed."

"Yes, thank you. If you can carry her so far, it would be best to do that."

"She is too tightly laced," the count said, climbing the stairs as if the burden in his arms were a feather pillow rather than a full-grown woman. "The circulation of blood to her brain has been diminished to a dangerous degree. She will do herself a permanent injury if she doesn't loosen her stays."

Cordelia blushed. Stays and corsets were the sort of female garment that gentlemen were not supposed to mention in polite company. She cleared her throat. "Mrs. Ford's room is the second door on the left at the head of the stairs."

"Yes, I remember."

Ellen greeted them with cries of alarm, and much hand-wringing. The count laid Mary on the bed.

"Get scissors," Cordelia said to the servant, already unfastening the buttons on her cousin's gown. "Otherwise we'll never be able to unfasten those knots you tied earlier in the laces of her ..." She felt the count's gaze on the back of her neck and stumbled to a halt. "Please get me some scissors," she said. "Hurry, Ellen!"

"Yes, miss. I'll be back in a trice. They're in my sewing case in the dressing room."

Cordelia jumped when she felt the swift, light touch of the count's fingers on the nape of her neck. "You were losing your hairpins," he said softly. "Your hair is very thick, isn't it?"

"Yes. It's almost unmanageable."

"It's beautiful," he said simply. "Like your hands."

Cordelia fixed her gaze on the tiny pearl buttons of her cousin's gown. Her hands shook and she clasped them firmly in front of her, determined not to let her gaze drift around toward the count.

"Damn stupid dress," the count muttered. "Idiotic corsets. Why in the world did the silly woman torture herself like that?"

Cordelia bit her lip, but she didn't say anything. The awful truth was that she couldn't be entirely sure the count had spoken aloud. She pressed her hand to her cheek, and realized she was burning hot. Was she feverish? Hallucinating? Hearing voices and imagining that she was in communication with the count? She bent her head, keeping her gaze fixed rigidly on Mary's buttons. She'd already made enough of a fool of herself where the Count of Albion was concerned. She wasn't going to say a single word that betrayed her inner turmoil.

When the count finally spoke, his words could hardly have been more conventional. "If there is no further way in which I can be of help, Miss Hope, I shall leave Mrs. Ford in your most capable hands."

Cordelia pulled the counterpane modestly high around Mary's neck. "Thank you, Excellency, there is nothing you can do. But I know my cousin would want to express her thanks. You moved so quickly to save her. Without you, she would have suffered a nasty fall."

"I'm glad I happened to be near," the count said. "But if we are to prevent more such unfortunate incidents, you must persuade Mrs. Ford to wear the loose clothing that is more suited to her condition. Pregnancy and corsets do not go well together."

Cordelia forgot all about not looking at the count. Her head jerked up. "P-pregnancy?" she stuttered. "What do you mean?"

"You are perfectly well aware of what I mean. Your cousin is with child. All being well, she will give birth about five months from now."

"H-how could you possibly know that?"

"You told me, Miss Hope."

"Of course I did not! It is almost the last thing in the world I would have told you."

The count's dark eyes gleamed ruefully. "I do not mean that you told me in so many words, Cordelia."

"I do not believe that I have given you permission to use my Christian name, Excellency."

He sighed, and she felt his hesitation before he decided to humor her. "As you wish, Miss Hope. However, I believe it is too late for either of us to resort to convenient social prevarications, since we both know far more than we should of each other's secrets. So I will speak frankly. Your cousin will harm the son she carries if she does not pay better attention to her health. You know it, and I know it. Now we must endeavor to see that Mrs. Ford learns the same truth."

Cordelia stroked Mary's forehead, worried that she hadn't regained consciousness. "How do you know that my cousin is carrying a son?" she asked, not attempting to deny the validity of his other assertions.

"You must allow me to keep some of my secrets," he said quietly. His eyes met hers, and for a perilous moment she felt again the warm sensation of intimacy flow between the two of them. Against all common sense, she found herself wishing that she could let her guard down and talk with him freely—

She blinked and drew in a hard, deep breath. "In an earlier century, you would have been accused of being in league with the devil," she said, her voice all the sharper because of her insidious wish to confide in him.

"You are quite right," he said. "Several of my ancestors were accused of exactly that."

They both heard the sounds of Ellen returning and he bowed, his expression returning to one of cool, impersonal courtesy. "I apologize, Miss Hope, for any misunderstanding that may have occurred between us. Believe me, I am as disconcerted as you are by our mutual urge to exchange confidences."

Ellen bustled back into the room. "Here's the scissors, miss, I had to look for a strong pair. And I brought the smelling salts, in case we needed them."

"Thank you, Ellen." Under the guise of shifting Mary into a different position, Cordelia turned her back on the count. She felt marginally less vulnerable when she could keep her face hidden from him. Over the snipping of her scissors, she heard the light tread of his footsteps retreating toward the door.

"I'm sure you will not wish to come downstairs tonight for dinner, Miss Hope, so I shall instruct the servants to send supper here, to Mrs. Ford's room. If there is any other way that I can be of assistance, I trust you will inform me."

"Thank you, Excellency. You are most kind." She felt as if she and the count were actors in a play, with Ellen for the audience, and the real drama being played out in a silent exchange heard only by the two of them. Although what that silent drama might mean, she had no idea.

The bedroom door opened, then quietly closed. Cordelia wondered why she felt suddenly depleted, as if the light and energy had been drained from the room.

She wondered how the count had known that she wanted to eat dinner in Mary's room.

She was almost afraid she knew the answer to that question.

She cut through the final snarled knot of Mary's laces.

"There!" Ellen exclaimed. "You've done it, miss! Now we can take off her stays."

Cordelia pulled apart the offending corset, and gently massaged the bruised and dented flesh of Mary's rib cage. Her cousin stirred, her eyelids fluttered, but then she became alarmingly still again, despite the fact that there was no longer any obstruction to her breathing.

"We must try the smelling salts," Cordelia said to Ellen. "She's still much too pale."

"Like that count," Ellen said, wafting the crystal bottle beneath Mary's nose. "White as a ghost, he is."

"Yes, but for him it's a natural condition," Cordelia said.

"Is it, miss? Is that what he told you?"

Cordelia swallowed hard. "Er . . . yes," she said. "In a way." She quickly changed the subject. "Look, my cousin is regaining her senses, thank goodness!"

Mary drew in a ragged breath and her eyelids fluttered, then opened. She gagged, pushing feebly at Ellen's hands. "Take those foul salts away!" she gasped. "Oh God, I shall be sick!"

"Not if you lie still," Cordelia said. "Don't move, Mary." She touched her hand to her cousin's forehead, worried when she found it cold and clammy. "Here, drink a little of this. A sip of water will help, I promise. Do you have a headache?"

Mary took a single sip of water, then struggled to sit up. "I'm all right. Stop fussing."

"I'm glad you're feeling better." Cordelia put down the glass. "Heavens, Mary, you frightened us all. If the count hadn't managed to catch you . . ."

"I must thank him," Mary said. "Wasn't he splendid? I think I may decide to fall in love with him. It would relieve the boredom of this godforsaken place."

Cordelia set the glass down on the bedside table, pleased to observe that her fingers were quite steady. "Would you like to change into something more comfortable to eat your supper?" she asked Mary. "After a good night's sleep, I expect you will feel more the thing."

Mary swatted Cordelia's hand away. Her voice rose ominously. "I don't want to change into something more comfortable. I want to have dinner with the count!"

"Oh no, my lad—I mean, ma'am." Ellen was appalled. "You cannot go downstairs, my lady, not when you just fainted and gave us all such a fright."

"Go away, Ellen. If I wanted your opinion, I'd have asked for it." Pushing her maid to one side, Mary sat up and swung her legs to the floor, but they buckled under her when she tried to stand, and she collapsed back onto the bed, sobbing in frustration.

"Damn! Damn! Damn!" Tears streamed down her face, and she dashed them away with the back of her hand. "Oh God, I *hate* being pregnant," she said. "I hate this stupid baby, and I hate Gerv—" She stopped abruptly.

She wiped her eyes on a corner of the sheet and continued more calmly. "I'm not going to have this baby. I've decided to ask Anna if she knows how I can get rid of it."

Ellen gasped. "Oh no, my lady! You cannot! 'Tis a mortal sin to kill a babe in the womb."

Mary's smile was tinged with bitterness. "The only sin I committed was one of stupidity. I should have found someone in London to take care of the problem instead of confessing my fall from virtue to Papa. What an idiot I was!"

"You did the right thing," Cordelia said quietly. "If you had tried to rid yourself of the baby, you could easily have died yourself. It's a very dangerous procedure to induce an abortion."

"How would you know, Miss Goody-goody? I don't suppose you even know what a man does to a woman in order to get her with child, much less how to get rid of the damn thing."

"I have some idea," Cordelia said quietly, although in truth her information on the subject was rudimentary, to say the least. "I know that the vicar's wife in Cambridge established a refuge for fallen women, and many of them came to her injured and bleeding when they had resorted to corrupt midwives in an effort to abort their babies. The death rate for those poor women was fearful, however carefully they were nursed. They contracted fevers, and died in short order."

"That was no more than they deserved." Ellen pursed her lips. "I expect it was God's judgment on them," she said.

Mary stared unseeingly ahead. "Perhaps they died because they didn't care to live," she said. "Sometimes I wonder . . ." Her voice faded away, and her gaze dropped to the starched linen counterpane. She plucked aimlessly at a loose thread, her face showing signs of almost unbearable weariness.

Cordelia felt a surge of fear. She had seen her cousin excited, flirtatious, and happy. She'd seen her angry, sulking, petulant, and arrogant. She had never before seen her despairing. She put her arm around her cousin's shoulders, risking a rebuke that never came. That was even more frightening. Mary rarely appreciated gestures of affection from her inferiors.

"You have everything in the world to live for," Cordelia said. "You won't forget that, will you, Mary?"

Her cousin gave a small, harsh laugh that ended in a sob. "Oh certainly I have everything to live for. I am just the bride every English nobleman is looking to find. The mother of a bastard. What could be more ideal?"

"You are not yet twenty," Cordelia said. "Your life is ahead of you, and your past mistakes can be overcome. I'm sure when you return to London the earl will be so pleased to see you that the reasons we are here will be forgotten. And nobody else in London will ever know what has happened."

Mary said nothing, and Cordelia took her hand, squeezing it comfortingly. "That is why we are here, Mary, so that you can resume your life without being ruined by a single mistake."

"And what about you?" Mary's eyes finally focused, and she looked at Cordelia, her emotions visibly teetering between resentment and fear. "Will you be happy to spend the rest of your life taking care of my *mistake*?"

"Yes," Cordelia said. "For I have always wanted a home and child of my own, and that is exactly what I will have."

Mary turned away. "Well, at least one of us will be happy, it seems."

"I'm confident that, in time, all of us will be happy," Cordelia said. "You will go on to have other children, Mary, and you can be sure that I will love your baby, and care for him as diligently as you would wish."

"You are always the optimist, aren't you?" Mary
flopped against the pillows. "However, it seems to me
that there is a rather large and putrid fly in this jar of
honey you're describing."

"What is that?" Cordelia asked, relieved to see a
trace of color creep back into her cousin's cheeks.

"We can't find the house that my father deeded to
you, nor can we find Mr. Peasant. So you and my little
mistake have nowhere to live, and no source of income
to keep you both fed and clothed."

"You're quite right, and if the baby were due to be
born next week, I would be very worried." Cordelia
tried to inject a convincing note of confidence into her
voice. "Fortunately, we have almost five months before the baby will arrive, and since the Count of Albion is now recovered, I shall be able to speak with
him first thing tomorrow morning. I believe that he is
the key to solving all our problems."

"You are such a relentless optimist that you exhaust
me," Mary said, closing her eyes. "Haven't you realized yet that the count isn't the answer to our problems, he is the cause of them?"

"What do you mean?" Cordelia asked.

Mary shrugged, without bothering to open her eyes.
"There is only one Villa of the Three Fountains, and
the Count of Albion is living in it."

Mary tended to view the world in simplistic black-
and-white terms, but this time she'd cut straight to the
heart of their problem. Whatever the true legal position, the chances were nil that any law officer in the
Duchy would evict the count from his estate on the
basis of musty English documents. True, the Earl of
Stanwyck was a powerful man who had the resources
and the influence to clarify the situation in a minute.
But the earl would never come to Modena, would

never acknowledge that his daughter was staying there. That was the whole point of the exercise: Mary's stay at the villa was to be kept a permanent secret.

Cordelia was saved from having to find something cheerful to say by the arrival of the servants carrying trays loaded with varieties of cold meats, bread, and preserved fruits. The food, as usual, looked delicious. Ellen ate with gusto, and even Mary managed to swallow tastes from several different dishes.

Cordelia discovered that she'd lost her appetite. If the Count of Albion was living in their villa, how would they survive for the next five months? How would she find the money to provide food and adequate shelter?

They were excellent questions. Unfortunately, Cordelia had no answers.

Chapter Seven

❨

Mary was finally asleep. Cordelia returned to her room and collapsed into bed. Unfortunately, her worries about the future bred and multiplied in the silence of the night, and she finally gave up her attempt to sleep. Crossing to the window, she opened the heavy drapes just wide enough to peek at the outside world. To reassure herself that it was still there? she wondered wryly. Ever since they arrived at the villa, her grasp on reality seemed to have been slipping.

She couldn't see the Garden of the Three Fountains from her room, so she had to content herself with admiring the neat layout of the grounds immediately surrounding the villa.

On the horizon, olive groves and vineyards loomed, almost invisible in the darkness. In the foreground, trees framed her view, black sentinels in the fitful moonlight, their fragile young leaves trembling in the breeze.

It was a peaceful scene, more evocative of the verdant English countryside than the barren, sun-scorched hills she'd expected to find in this part of Italy.

Cordelia pressed her forehead against the cool windowpane and watched the clouds make patterns of shifting shadows on the paths. As she watched, some of the tension that had been keeping her wakeful began to ease. Perhaps if she returned to bed, she would be able to sleep after all.

At the very edge of her vision, one of the shadows moved, darker and more defined than the rest. She peered intently, and the shadow split in half, resolving itself into two men wearing long dark cloaks, huddled against the trunk of a tree, deep in conversation.

The scudding clouds cleared from the face of the moon, and the two men were briefly exposed in a shaft of bright moonlight. Cordelia stared in grim fascination.

One of the men was the Count of Albion. The other was the coach driver who had abandoned her at the wayside inn.

Instinctively, Cordelia jumped back, hiding behind the thick draperies so that she could observe the men without being seen. Too late, she realized that she should have stayed still. Her movement caught the attention of the count, just as his movement a few seconds earlier had caught her eye. He looked up, his gaze traveling straight toward her window. Although it was ridiculous to imagine that she could read his expression across a hundred feet of darkness, she could have sworn she saw both resignation and rueful amusement flicker across his face.

She met his gaze with an emotion that felt oddly akin to a challenge, and her cheeks were burning when he finally looked away. Despite the fact that he now knew she was watching, he didn't attempt to conceal his acquaintance with her errant coach driver. On the contrary, he put his arm around the man's shoulder and bent low to whisper a confidence in his ear. She saw the carriage driver hand over a small bundle of papers, which the count slipped into a pocket in the folds of his cape. The two men shook hands.

She shouldn't be surprised to discover that the Count of Albion was on intimate terms with the driver who'd abandoned her, Cordelia reflected acidly. Hadn't she suspected almost everyone of duplicity from the moment she arrived in Piacenza? There was no reason to feel a sense of betrayal when everything she knew about the count suggested that he was a man of degenerate habits, steeped in deception.

After a few more moments of conversation, her sometime coach driver pulled the hood of his cloak over his head and disappeared into the thicket of trees. The darkness instantly swallowed him.

The count looked up toward Cordelia's window again, and touched his hand to his forehead in a mocking salute. Then he swept into a formal bow, his cape billowing around him in a swirl of black wool and brilliant scarlet silk lining.

Wait for me. The words filled Cordelia's mind. *I must talk with you. It's important.*

The count straightened from his bow and Cordelia closed the drapes with a furious snap. She was hallucinating again. Obviously she couldn't hear what a man said to her over yards of empty space. Of course she couldn't!

The count hadn't spoken, and she hadn't heard him. Even if he came to her room, she had no desire to listen to him, no desire to be his audience while he spun another web of elaborate lies.

She scurried back to bed, pulling the covers up to

her chin, and willing herself to fall asleep. Not surprisingly, she grew more wakeful by the minute. Why did the count need to prowl his own gardens at the dead of night? If he wanted to meet someone—even a dishonest coachman—why would he not simply invite him to the villa during the daytime?

The obvious answer was that the Count of Albion was plotting something deeply nefarious, something so terrible that he couldn't let even his own servants know what he was up to.

Cordelia tossed and turned on a pillow that suddenly felt as if it were stuffed with gravel, painfully aware of just how vulnerable she and her two charges were. In truth, the count could murder all three of them and it would be months before anybody realized they were missing. And if someone had warned the count that Cordelia was claiming the Villa of the Three Fountains as her own property, he would certainly have reason to be rid of her.

A soft tap came at her door. She sat up in the bed, heart hammering. "Wh-who is it?" she asked, as if she didn't know the answer quite well.

The count's voice came low, and oddly tender. "It is I, Albion. I need to talk with you."

"I'm n-not dressed. I'm in bed."

"Definitely an added attraction, Miss Hope. Please let me in."

She resisted the dangerous impulse to fling the door wide. What was it about this man's voice that dissolved her common sense into instant mush? Why did she have this insane urge to trust a man whose every action warned that he was not to be trusted? Perhaps that was the secret of Bluebeard's success, she thought wildly. He didn't capture his victims and drag them screaming to their doom, rather they walked willingly into his lair.

"You c-cannot come in, Excellency. It would not be . . . proper."

"I did not realize that propriety was so high on your list of values, Miss Hope." She could hear amusement in his voice, and she could picture his face as clearly as if he'd been standing beside her. His mouth would be held in a firm, straight line, but his impossibly dark eyes would gleam with tantalizing laughter. She pushed the image aside. Her willpower was already about as sturdy as gossamer and she needed no beguiling mental pictures to distract her.

"English ladies do not receive gentlemen in their bedrooms," she said primly.

"I am sure you are correct, Miss Hope." Laughter lingered in his voice. "However, that poses no problem for us. Allow me to reassure you: I am not a gentleman."

She conquered a disastrous desire to laugh, and replied as sternly as she could. "If true, that would make it even less proper for me to receive you, Excellency."

"Possibly. But I feel constrained to point out that, although it is several years since I was last in England, and I am no longer current with the standards of polite society, I believe I can state with confidence that *nothing* about our relationship is even remotely proper."

"Then it is time for us to change our conduct." She congratulated herself on sounding firm—until she realized that she was halfway toward the door, and her hand was stretched out ready to turn the knob and let him in. She ran back to bed and jumped under the covers as if the sheets and counterpane would protect her from her own folly.

"Go away," she said. Her breath caught on a sob. "Please, Excellency, go away."

The laughter vanished from his voice. "Miss Hope, I cannot leave until we have talked. Lives are at stake, perhaps many hundreds of lives. Do not refuse to hear me, I beg."

"Hundreds of lives?" she said, her voice heavy with sarcasm. "Surely you exaggerate your own importance, Excellency. Certainly you exaggerate mine. Nothing that has passed between us could possibly affect the destiny of anyone save ourselves."

"You mistake the matter, Cordelia. I need to explain what you have seen this night, so that you do not unwittingly cause a tragedy."

Cordelia. It was outrageous that he should address her so intimately when they were mere acquaintances, and yet she loved the lilt in his voice when he said her name. She realized she was out of bed again and on her way to the door.

She sat down on the edge of the mattress, back ramrod straight, trying to get a grip on her flabby willpower. "Once again, I must remind you that I have not given you permission to use my Christian name, Excellency."

"I apologize most humbly, but please let me in. I must explain--"

"Explanations aren't necessary, Excellency. I know what I saw. You were talking to that rogue of a carriage driver who tricked us into leaving Piacenza—"

"Poor Giancarlo," the count sighed. "I was afraid you'd recognized him. Now it's *really* important for me to speak with you. I am confident you have misinterpreted the significance of my dealings with Giancarlo."

Poor Giancarlo indeed! And she was quite sure she

hadn't misinterpreted anything! Cordelia seethed in silent indignation. "I'm sure it was most inconvenient of me to recognize him. No doubt that makes it difficult for you to invent convincing lies—"

"Cordelia, I'm coming in," the count said with sudden urgency.

"No, don't you dare open the door!" She stared at her naked toes and wondered why she wasn't running across the room and slamming home the bolt.

"I must get out of the hallway, Cordelia. We've woken Captain Hesse, which was the very thing I wished to avoid." The count stepped inside her room as he spoke, bringing with him the cool scents of night, rain showers and fresh air.

He shut the door and leaned against it, gaze fixed on her in silent appeal. "I beg you, Cordelia, don't scream."

In truth, she hadn't even thought of screaming until he mentioned it. She drew in a shaky breath. "If you leave, Excellency, I shall have no cause for screaming."

He shook his head impatiently. "You're not genuinely frightened and this isn't the time to play missish Victorian virgin."

"Why not? I *am* a vir—" Cordelia flushed, horrified at how the count could lead her into indiscretion within seconds of their being together.

"I am all too aware of the fact that you are a virgin, Cordelia." The count's smile was edged with tension. "It is a fact that has caused me considerable grief over the past several days."

She almost asked him how her virginity could possibly cause him grief. She stopped herself just in time. The man was a lying rogue who had somehow found a way to excite her most base emotions and prurient interests. Ladies and gentlemen definitely did *not* discuss the subject of virginity after a mere five days of acquaintance. In fact, she doubted if it was a subject that could ever be addressed with propriety, even between husband and wife.

With difficulty, Cordelia dragged her thoughts back to the practical matter at hand. "How could we have woken Captain Hesse?" she asked. "You spoke barely above a whisper."

"A whisper was all it took. The captain sleeps like the seasoned soldier he is, with one ear and one eye always open. Inevitably, we disturbed him. It was careless of me to conduct my conversation with you through a closed door. Unfortunately, where you are concerned, I find that I am too often careless."

Cordelia ignored that comment. "I don't hear anyone moving in the corridor," she said. "How can you know that Captain Hesse is awake?"

"I heard him get out of bed a few minutes ago." The count frowned and cocked his head to one side, appearing to concentrate. "He's gone back to sleep now," he said, as if it were quite possible to hear through the thickness of several walls and detect whether or not the captain slumbered. "For the moment at least, we are safe from his curiosity."

"I believe I was never at much risk from Captain Hesse," Cordelia said tartly.

"Not you personally, perhaps, but others were—are—very much at risk. From his actions, and those of his government." The count walked toward her, the scarlet silk lining of his cloak flashing with each step. "Cordelia, we have a great deal to talk about," he said, unfastening the frogs of his cloak and tossing it onto the bed.

She turned away, wrapping her arms around her

waist, terrified not that the count might touch her, but that she would not resist his touch. She was all too aware of her bare feet, and her unbound hair, tumbling over her shoulders in a thick, unruly cascade. She acknowledged the shocking fact that she felt no shame at the impropriety of her appearance and that she had no desire to find her dressing robe and put it on. If she was totally honest with herself, what she felt was not embarrassment, but a hot yearning ache to be held in the count's arms.

He stopped a scant few inches behind her, but she sensed his presence as acutely as if he'd taken her in his arms. "Cordelia, will you not look at me?" he asked.

The huskiness in his voice sent heat shimmering through her like the zap of a lightning bolt. Her fingernails dug into the flesh of her arms, but somehow she managed to keep her voice cool and uninflected. "Excellency, the ... intimacy ... of this situation is inappropriate for both of us. Please make your explanations quickly and leave."

"Sometimes it is not easy or quick to explain the truth," he said. "Have you not found that lies are often much more readily convincing?"

"I believe I shall be able to detect the difference on this occasion."

"I hope so. I could make it so." He hesitated for a moment. "I *shall* make it so."

She felt the touch of the count's hands on her shoulders, and instantly her vision blurred. The floor rocked beneath her feet and the world blacked out. From within the blackness, she felt the count steady her.

"Are you all right now?" he asked.

"Yes." It was a lie. Her head swam, her limbs felt

leaden, and her insides fizzed with delight, definitely not symptoms of being "all right."

The count lifted the heavy weight of hair from her shoulders, combing his fingers through the smooth silky strands. She felt the brush of his lips against the side of her neck, and the simultaneous caress of his hands on her body. When he stroked the tiny half moons her fingernails had made in her arms, the pain vanished and the little wounds healed.

"Cordelia." He whispered her name, and the sound became another form of caress, echoing inside her mind with the lilt of music. The tune became plaintive. "Dear God, Cordelia, I never intended this bond to grow so strong between us. What are we going to do now that we both know it exists?"

"I . . . cannot . . . imagine."

"Neither can I." His voice was rueful. "Now that we have tasted the forbidden fruit, how can we be content without it?"

"Are we really speaking to each other?" The bizarre question seemed quite easy to ask with his arms holding her, and the warm darkness wrapping them securely in its embrace.

"Yes, but not with words. When I touched you, your mind opened to mine. That is why we feel so close, so much in harmony."

"Whenever you hold me, this is what happens," she said.

It was a statement, not a question, but he answered her anyway. "Yes—unless I deliberately seal off my thoughts."

It seemed entirely rational to accept that they were conversing without the need for words. Cordelia had no difficulty in believing that as soon as the count touched her, their minds were able to link. "Your feelings toward me are tender," she said, wonder flooding her at the realization. "Gentle and caring."

"It is amazing that you can sense my emotions so readily," he said. "Sometimes even my father can't do that." He rubbed his cheek against her hair. "Since you can sense the truth of my feelings, you know that I have never felt this way before toward any human."

A curious image took shape in her mind, one she couldn't comprehend, almost as if the count considered human beings an alien species, and women a frightening subspecies. The image faded as swiftly as it had formed, to be replaced by a vision of water splashing into the fountains of the villa's garden on a hot summer evening. Cordelia realized that the count was picturing the two of them in the Garden of the Three Fountains, and she leaned back, resting her head against his chest and sharing his vision. Unthinkingly, she reached behind her to draw his hands more tightly around her waist.

"The garden is beautiful, isn't it?" she said.

"My favorite place in the world. It would give me great pleasure to spend an evening there with you."

"That would be nice. I like ... being ... with you. We could have a picnic."

He chuckled softly. "You have no skill as a mind-deceiver, Cordelia. You weren't thinking about picnics. You were thinking that you would like me to hold you more closely."

She realized it was useless to deny the truth, and he drew her more intimately against him, nuzzling her hair, and splaying his hands over the flat plane of her stomach. "You have no need to guard your thoughts from me, sweetheart. Trust me, you do not like caressing me anywhere near as much as I like to caress you."

She had a sudden vivid image of exactly where the

count wanted to touch her, and she felt her entire body blush. "Is your touch just in my mind, too?" she asked.

"No, it's very real. See?" With seductive slowness, he traced a winding path across her rib cage. His hands cupped the weight of her breasts and squeezed lightly. Through her nightgown, his thumbs traced circles around her nipples and her skin tingled with exhilarating fire. The heat built, cresting inside, until her body melted with joy at the prospect of their union.

She turned so that they faced each other, reaching up to link her hands behind his neck, pulling his mouth down toward hers. She wanted him to kiss her and it seemed pointless to try to disguise her desire. Even more than a kiss, she wanted, quite desperately, to feel again those mysterious bumps of swollen flesh that had throbbed beneath her fingertips. The mere thought of feeling them grow at her touch sent chills racing up and down her spine—

Dear God, we cannot do this. I will endanger her. My sacs are reforming!

His anguished thought cut through the misty haze of her longing. Abruptly, the count disentangled himself from her embrace, shoving her away with a violence that made her stagger. Cordelia toppled against the bedpost, clutching it to prevent herself from falling. For a moment, her mind blanked, and she teetered on the edge of fainting.

She managed to steady herself, and when she looked up, saw the count standing by the window, gazing out into the garden. His profile was serene, his expression impassive, and his demeanor gave not the slightest hint that seconds earlier she had been locked in his arms, begging him to kiss her. Instead of having some mystical link with his mind, she felt totally distanced from him, and when she tried to read what he was feeling, she could sense nothing at all. A wax statue would have conveyed more emotion.

With a shudder of despair, Cordelia realized she must have been fantasizing again. What was it about the Count of Albion that provoked such shameful imaginings? Why was it that in his presence she visualized activities that she would have considered depraved and demented only days earlier? If this was what it felt like to desire a man, she reflected ruefully, no wonder there were so many fallen women. She'd never understood why Mary had been prepared to risk her entire future for the sake of an illicit liaison with a man she knew was already married. Finally, she comprehended something of what her cousin must have felt.

The count gave no sign that he had any clue about her erotic imaginings, which was a minor salve to Cordelia's pride. On the contrary, when he turned to speak with her, he appeared as remote and formal as the strictest chaperon could have wished.

"Thank you for allowing me into the privacy of your bedroom," he said. "I need to speak with you about Captain Hesse. I must warn you, Miss Hope, that the captain is a danger to us."

Miss Hope. Strange how much she missed the soft lilt of the count speaking her given name. Struggling to regain control over herself, she spoke more sharply than she intended. "How could Captain Hesse be a danger to *us*, Excellency? There is no *us*. We are involved in no cooperative enterprise."

"That is so," the count agreed equably. "However, I persuaded myself that you would view the plight of the Italian Nationalists in the same light as I do. Was I wrong?" He looked at her, and for an instant she thought she saw tenderness and longing in his gaze. Then the shutters returned.

"I am arrogant enough to believe that I am not mistaken, Miss Hope. I feel sure you are a passionate believer in the right of the Italians to govern their own country."

She refused to be beguiled. "I'm a visitor to the Duchy of Modena, which is a province of the Austro-Hungarian Empire. It's inappropriate for me to take sides in what is essentially a personal conflict between the Emperor Franz Josef and the King of Piedmont."

"A prudent response," the count said. "I, on the other hand, am going to show no such caution. I put my life in your hands, Miss Hope, by declaring that I am an ardent supporter of the cause of Italian freedom. I believe it is time Italy threw off the yoke of foreign oppression and became a unified nation. To that end, I have spent the past five years actively working for the overthrow of Hapsburg rule in Modena. As I'm sure you are aware, those are treasonous statements for a citizen of this duchy."

Cordelia's heart pounded hard and fast. "You must forgive me if I find your protestations somewhat hard to believe, Excellency. It is widely known that you are an ally of the Austrian occupying forces in Italy. You have said so yourself. Your servants all know that you are sympathetic to the imperial cause. And Captain Hesse has spoken with enthusiasm about your faithful cooperation with the Austrian government."

"In real life, as opposed to the realm of mathematics, a straight line is not always the shortest distance between two points."

"It is too late at night for riddles," she said. "And my father was the mathematician, not I."

"Then let me speak with crystal clarity, with no

pretty metaphors to hide the unpleasant truth. In order to further a cause one admires, it is sometimes necessary to consort with the enemy. The Austrians are my enemy, although they believe they are my friends. I invite them into my home. I offer them hospitality—and then I betray them."

She flinched at the razor sharp edge to his words, knowing instinctively that his betrayal of the Austrians did not sit comfortably with his conscience. She felt compelled to offer him consolation. "Sometimes, in a noble cause, we must resort to methods that trouble us."

"The ends justifies the means?" he murmured. "It is more than fourteen hundred years since Saint Jerome warned Christians to avoid falling into that enticing moral trap."

Cordelia clicked her tongue impatiently. "The trouble with philosophers is that they forget we aren't making our choices in a perfect world."

He looked amused. "Would you care to clarify that caustic comment?"

"The world is full of thorns and briars," Cordelia said. "Quite often, there is no *good* choice for us to make. However much we struggle, sometimes we can only take the path that promises to inflict least harm."

"Can betrayal of friendship ever be the path of least harm?"

She hesitated before answering because in her experience, men very rarely cared to hear women's opinions on matters of ethics. But the count's expression conveyed no hint of scorn or condescension, so she risked giving him an honest opinion. "Austrians and Italians are currently on a collision course, so in order to prevent a war, you may be forced to pretend a friendship for Captain Hesse that isn't real—an unfortunate means to a desirable end. Surely even Saint Jerome would understand and approve."

The count shook his head. "You credit me with far too much power. I have no hope that my actions can prevent a war. The Italians demand freedom, and the Austrians intend to slaughter them back into servitude. My aim is merely to limit the killing on both sides by ensuring that the Italians win an early victory."

"You think war is inevitable, then?"

"Inevitable and imminent. Alas."

Cordelia sighed. "It's such a pity that the Emperor Franz Josef believes he has a divine right to rule. In studying history, I've often thought that there is nothing more ruinous to good judgment than the conviction that God is on one's side."

The count smiled. "Except, perhaps, the belief that one is God, a view which is excessively popular among emperors in the East."

"You are lucky to have traveled so much," Cordelia said wistfully. "It is something I have always wished I could do."

The count looked at her in silence for a moment, then he turned away, massaging his cheek as if he'd experienced a sudden and unexpected toothache.

"Excellency, are you in pain?" Cordelia asked when he hadn't spoken for almost a full minute.

His gaze, dark and totally unreadable, locked with hers. "My name is Dakon," he said. "I find that I have a highly unwise urge to hear you say it."

Her pulse beat faster, but she didn't look away. "Dakon," she said softly. "It is an unusual name."

"Unusual to you, perhaps, but it is much used in my . . . family."

"Your forebears weren't originally from this part of Italy, then?"

"No," he said after a momentary pause. "No, my family does not originate in this part of the world." He pressed his fingers against his jaw, rubbing without seeming to realize what he was doing.

"Dakon," she said. "Are you quite sure you're not in pain?"

He hesitated. "A little," he acknowledged finally. "The discomfort is . . . unexpected . . . at this time."

"Is there something I can do to help? I would be most willing."

She sensed the violence of the struggle waging within him, although on the surface he showed not the slightest trace of emotion. "No," he said at last. "There is nothing you can do to help."

"If I can't help, perhaps I should send for the housekeeper?"

"For Anna?" He closed his eyes, and when he opened them again, Cordelia saw the familiar gleam of self-mockery. "Please let's keep Anna out of this. She would scold me and say I told you so. And as always, of course, she would be quite right."

Despair lurked just below the surface of his self-mockery, and Cordelia sensed that he was troubled by something more profound even than his betrayal of Captain Hesse and the Austrians. Acting on instinct rather than thought, she crossed the room and pressed her hand against his cheek, right over the spot he'd been massaging.

Instantly, she felt the flesh swell and grow hard beneath her palm. The sensation of swelling, far from repelling her, caused an acute twist of pleasure deep inside her body.

"Dakon, is this what causes you pain?" she asked,

brushing the tip of her forefinger over the slight protuberance.

"Pain is not quite the right word." He covered her hand with his own and rubbed his cheek against her palm. His eyes drifted closed, and she was suffused by sensations of ease and pleasure. Dakon's pleasure, she realized suddenly. As soon as she'd touched him, the link between them had been reestablished. She hadn't been imagining their earlier intimacy, after all. However much Dakon wanted to pretend indifference, he *had* caressed her. He *had* held her and longed to kiss her. Their minds *could* link.

With a strangled gasp, he flung her hand away and strode to the other side of the room, positioning himself so that she could see only his back.

"Enough!" he said. "No more of this dangerous foreplay."

Cordelia was stung. "I'm sorr—"

Dakon was breathing hard. "You have not the slightest reason to apologize, Cordelia, the fault is entirely mine. You have no idea of the horrible dangers you run. I, however, am all too aware of the risks."

"I don't understand—"

He swung around, his expression forbidding. "It is not necessary for you to understand. It is only necessary that you should heed my warning. Do not touch me again, Cordelia. Do not touch me, for it seems I cannot vouch for the consequences if you do."

"Perhaps I would be willing to face those consequences if you explained them to me."

"The consequence is death," he said harshly. "A somewhat permanent penalty for indulging in a few moments of pleasure."

Her throat constricted. "Death? Wh-what do you mean? Whose death?"

"Yours, certainly, and perhaps mine, too, for if I harmed you, I would have no wish to live." Dakon's head bowed wearily. "Enough of this, Cordelia. Forgive me, but we should not talk of this anymore."

"But I must know—"

"No, enough! For both our sakes, it would be better if I returned to my original purpose in coming here tonight. I need to explain to you why I was meeting with Giancarlo—"

She almost laughed at the incongruity of interjecting Giancarlo's name into a conversation that had tossed about such huge themes and wild improbabilities, but she sensed the glass-brittle tension within him and found herself anxious to ease it. "Giancarlo—do you mean our carriage driver?" she asked.

"Yes, indeed. I'm sure you consider him an unreliable fellow who had no excuse for abandoning you, but he meant you no real harm."

"He did not behave well toward us, that is certain. If Captain Hesse had not chanced to ride by when Giancarlo deserted us, we should have been in severe straits."

"Take pity on him, Cordelia. Giancarlo, poor man, has been in an agony of indecision ever since you and your traveling companions arrived in Piacenza."

She sensed the gradual lightening of Dakon's mood, although she also sensed that he was holding himself on the tightest of emotional leashes. She thought that one day soon she might be tempted to see what would happen if she tried to make that leash snap. But not tonight. She still wasn't quite ready to trust that she had sorted truth from illusion in the chaotic swirl of their relationship.

"I can't imagine why Giancarlo was so troubled by our arrival in Piacenza," she said. "We offered him a fair price to drive us here, and he was free either to accept or to decline. He chose to accept, then failed to honor his bargain."

"His choice was far more complicated than you know." Dakon leaned forward, hand outstretched. A hair's breadth away from touching her, he snatched back his hand, as if he'd just remembered his own warning about the potential dangers of intimacy.

"It is one thing to trust you with *my* life," he said. "It is quite another to trust you with the lives of others. Promise me, Cordelia, that you won't reveal what I'm telling you here tonight. If Giancarlo is identified to the Austrians as an Italian rebel, his life won't be worth the price of a hot dinner."

"You have my word that Giancarlo's secrets are safe with me," Cordelia said. "I have no wish to send any Italian into the clutches of the Austrian secret police, not even a carriage driver who abandoned me at the worst inn this side of Turkey."

"Cordelia, my love, such words merely reveal your innocence as a traveler. There are many inns this side of Turkey that would make you long for the cleanliness and sophistication of our friend Rafael's establishment."

Dakon smiled at her, and Cordelia was quite sure he had no awareness of what he had said. *My love.* Somehow, she didn't think those were words that he had used with any frequency. She hugged the sound of them to her.

"Why did Giancarlo abandon us?" she asked. "What in the world was his purpose?"

Dakon tried to look solemn. "He decided you were too dangerous to transport any further. He was planning to contact me and ask my advice as to what should be done with you."

"He thought we were dangerous? How nonsensical! The only danger we presented was the possibility that my cousin might suffer an attack of travel sickness."

"It is clear that you have no idea how much curiosity you and your two traveling companions have aroused over the past couple of weeks. The three of you have caused more gossip among the Italian freedom fighters than any other topic save the date and place at which the Austrian Army will launch its opening attack."

"We have caused gossip among the Italian rebels?" Cordelia stared at the count in openmouthed astonishment. "I can't have understood you aright. What possible interest could they have in three English ladies, whose behavior was so proper that we barely stirred from our hotel rooms?"

"A great deal." Dakon's dark eyes gleamed with suppressed laughter. "It was generally concluded that you and your cousin were not English at all, but Austrian spies, sent to bewitch honest Italians with your beauty."

"You cannot be serious! Nothing we did could possibly justify such a wildly improbable conclusion."

"Not improbable at all," Dakon said. "Not only are you and your cousin both exceptionally beautiful, you were also traveling unescorted save for an elderly maid, in itself a most suspicious circumstance. Moreover, Captain Hesse and his lieutenant returned from a week's foray into Lombardy, and were reported galloping at full speed toward Piacenza. What's more, they followed you to Rafael's inn the instant it became clear that none of the locals would drive you to the Villa of the Three Fountains."

"Since we had no idea Giancarlo would abandon us

at the inn, we couldn't possibly have arranged for the captain to meet us there."

"We decided that the Austrians had been secretly following you, and only provided a public escort when Giancarlo refused to drive you any further."

"*We* decided?" Cordelia said. "Am I to understand that these extraordinary suspicions were shared by you as well as Giancarlo and his friends in Piacenza?"

"To a certain extent," Dakon said. "I had already arranged a meeting with Captain Hesse, of course, so I didn't find his presence in the area surprising. But I did wonder if he had become suspicious of my loyalties. I thought perhaps he wanted you or your cousin to seduce me, in the hope that I might say something indiscreet during the course of a night of passion."

Cordelia tried not to blush at this casual mention of seduction and nights of passion. "I would have thought that a conspirator such as yourself would have learned to keep your own counsel. It is hard to imagine a woman successfully tempting you to indiscretion."

The look he gave her was both incredulous and tinged with irony. "Since you are a virgin, you probably don't realize that men can be persuaded to reveal all sorts of things they shouldn't when they are in the throes of sexual desire. A trained courtesan can be one of the most valuable weapons in a spy's arsenal."

Cordelia laced her fingers in her lap and examined them intently. "You're blushing," Dakon said. "What are you thinking?"

She cleared her throat. "Lieutenant Waldheim hinted that your tastes . . ." She tried again. "The lieutenant seemed to think that you were not very interested in women, however beautiful."

"Ah, I see." Dakon's gaze remained steady. "You

have just confirmed my opinion that the lieutenant is nowhere near as astute as his captain."

"Then the lieutenant is wrong?" Cordelia asked, scarcely able to believe her own ears when she heard herself asking questions about such a forbidden topic.

"It is widely known that I employ only young men to serve me," Dakon said. "But whatever the lieutenant may have believed, I am sure Captain Hesse has long since conducted his own investigations, and has learned that of all the young men who have left my employ, none has ever served as my lover. The captain undoubtedly finds that information puzzling, and he would very much like to know the precise nature of my sexual tastes."

"And so you wondered if he had sent my cousin to tempt you?"

"It seemed possible," Dakon said. "Two beautiful women arrived in the duchy, demanding escort to the Villa of the Three Fountains. It was only prudent to consider the possibility that the captain had sent you to tempt me. A choice of blonde or brunette, whichever might be my fancy."

"And were you tempted?" The question popped out before she could control it.

"You know that I have been tempted beyond reason."

She looked deep into his dark eyes. "If I am a spy for the Austrians, you have told me much that is dangerous."

"That is true, but I have always been arrogant in my belief that I cannot be deceived by a mere human. If I am wrong in your case, then God help me, for good men will die."

"Why do you always have that strange intonation in your voice when you say 'humans'?"

"What?" He looked at her, clearly startled by the sudden twist in their conversation. "I am unaware of any special inflection to my voice. What sort of intonation do you mean?"

Cordelia tried to articulate something that was almost indefinable. "When you say the word *human,* an image forms in your mind as if you are identifying a different species, one that you don't quite belong to."

Dakon appeared stunned by her explanation. After a moment's silence, he chuckled. To Cordelia, the sound of his laughter seemed forced. "I must have been hiding here in the villa too long," he said. "I hadn't realized my taste for solitude had become so pronounced, and so readily discernible."

What she had sensed in Dakon wasn't a desire for solitude, but almost the opposite—a despairing awareness that however hard he tried, he would never entirely fit in. But she had no right to probe so deeply into his most private and personal fears, so she allowed his explanation to pass unchallenged.

Dakon's gaze fixed on her lips with mesmerizing intensity. "In war, it is wiser always to expect betrayal. Except that with you . . ."

"Yes?" she prompted.

"With you, I do not care about the rules," Dakon said.

She didn't know what would happen if she touched him, so she spoke quickly, to dispel her overwhelming urge to take his hand. "You can trust me, Dakon. I will not betray you."

"When you look at me so, I find myself thinking that I could share with you the deepest and darkest secrets of my soul and that you would understand and accept me." He leaned toward her, then looked quickly away. When he turned around again, he reclined against the cushions of the chair, deliberately increasing the space between them and lowering their building tension.

"Do you not wish to hear the other reasons why my fellow revolutionaries found you and your companions so suspicious?" he asked.

"I most certainly do. It still seems to me that you all leaped to amazing conclusions on the basis of very little evidence."

"I have not listed the whole indictment against you," Dakon said, smiling wryly. "Your beauty and unconventional travel arrangements were not the only sources of speculation. Even more damning was the fact that you spent an entire week scouring the town of Piacenza, trying to find someone who would take you to the offices of *Signor* Pesante."

Cordelia stared at him in blank astonishment. "To ask the whereabouts of an Italian lawyer is scarcely an activity that justifies the conclusion that we are Austrian spies," she said.

"True. Except for one trivial fact. *Signor* Pesante is the code name the local revolutionaries have given to General Garibaldi's headquarters."

"Good heavens!" Cordelia exclaimed. "So while I was searching for my lawyer, the rebels all thought I was trying to discover their secret encampment. What an incredible coincidence!"

Dakon looked embarrassed. "Not precisely a coincidence, I suspect. You see, I suggested the code name of *Signor* Pesante to the local Nationalists."

"Do you know him, then?" Cordelia asked. "If so, you seem to be the only person in the entire duchy who has ever conducted business with him."

Dakon did not respond directly. "The truth is, Cordelia, I fear you have been the victim of my perverse sense of humor. When I chose the name *Signor* Pesante as a password, I was well aware that he was supposedly the Earl of Stanwyck's man of business in the Duchy of Modena."

Cordelia felt the blood drain from her face. If Dakon knew enough to link the names of the Earl of Stanwyck and *Signor* Pesante then it seemed likely that her worst fears were realized: the Earl of Stanwyck didn't have clear title to the Villa of the Three Fountains. Some previous earl had probably needed to raise ready cash, and had sold his Italian estate to Dakon's ancestors.

Of course the sale of entailed lands was illegal. Knowing that, the impoverished earl must have taken steps to hide his wrongdoing. Hence the current Earl of Stanwyck had no idea that the villa wasn't available to serve as a refuge for Mary.

Cordelia tried not to let her panic show. "Since you know that *Signor* Pesante acts as the Earl of Stanwyck's man of business in this area, I assume you are acquainted with him. I would appreciate it, if you would ask him to contact me as soon as possible."

"I would help you if I could, Cordelia, but there is, alas, no way for me to put you in touch with *Signor* Pesante."

"I don't understand . . ."

"The lawyer, *Signor* Pesante, does not exist. I invented him."

Cordelia jumped to her feet. "You did *what*?"

"I invented *Signor* Pesante," Dakon said with infuriating calm. "I needed a lawyer who could conduct correspondence with the Earl of Stanwyck's solicitors in England. I decided that it would be far easier to invent such a fellow, rather than to employ a real lawyer."

He made it sound as if the invention of phantom lawyers at whim was entirely rational. Cordelia clung determinedly to the thread of reason. "How is it possible that *Signor* Pesante arranged to meet me in Piacenza if he is only a figment of your imagination?"

"As the one who handles all of his correspondence, I can assure you that *Signor* Pesante never agreed to meet you anywhere," Dakon said.

"Then why did the Earl of Stanwyck promise me that the arrangements with Signor Pesante were taken care of?"

"Because as far as he was concerned, they were. The Earl of Stanwyck wrote to *Signor* Pesante and commanded him to meet you in Piacenza during the first week of March. I received that letter from the earl only yesterday, much delayed in its transmission, no doubt because of the barricades and checkpoints the Austrians have erected all over the duchy."

"And you never replied to that letter?"

Dakon shook his head. "Believe me, had I received the earl's letter in time, I would have written to him and invented some excuse as to why you should not come here. If necessary, I would have told him that the villa had burned to the ground."

"But he promised me that the arrangements had been finalized and were all in order," Cordelia protested. Despite the fact that she had been anticipating just this sort of muddle for days, the magnitude of the earl's arrogance—his irresponsibility—left her floundering. "How could he claim that *Signor* Pesante was expecting to meet us when his letter hadn't been answered?"

Dakon shrugged. "From the tone of his correspondence, I conclude that the earl is a man who expects to have his orders obeyed. He wrote to *Signor* Pesante and gave him instructions. As far as the earl was concerned, the matter was taken care of."

"If *Signor* Pesante doesn't exist, then it must be you who has been forwarding quarterly payments to the Earl of Stanwyck," Cordelia said.

"Yes."

Dakon did not elaborate. She wondered how in the world to phrase her next question. How did you ask someone if he realized that he had no legal right to an estate where his family had lived for three generations, and for which Dakon's grandfather had presumably paid a substantial price? More to the point, did the precise legalities of the situation really matter? She was alone in a foreign country, with no lawyer, and almost no money. Even if she wanted to do so, her chances of evicting Dakon from the Villa of the Three Fountains were virtually nil.

"Do not look so stricken," Dakon said softly. "You may rest comfortably in the knowledge that I have too many secrets of my own to have any interest in betraying yours—or those of your cousin."

His words underscored the magnitude of Cordelia's problem. Not only were they all stranded in the Duchy of Modena with nowhere to turn for help, but Mary's secret was in imminent danger of being revealed. How much of the truth had Dakon guessed? she wondered. He already knew Mary was pregnant, and that the Earl of Stanwyck had sent them to the villa. Would he make the crucial connections between those two facts and realize she was the earl's daughter?

"It seems that we are confronted with an awkward muddle," Cordelia said with vast understatement. "You see, the Earl of Stanwyck has deeded the management and income of the villa to me. For life."

"The devil he has," Dakon said.

"I can understand that you are shocked."

"Not shocked. Merely reflecting that one's sins have a most irritating habit of coming back to haunt one."

She wasn't sure whose sins he referred to. Knowing there was no way to avoid confronting the issue of how his ancestors had come into possession of the estate, she grasped her courage in both hands and spoke up. "Dakon, there is clearly some confusion about the true ownership of this property. Do you know how you came to inherit the estate?"

There was an infinitesimal pause before he answered her. "I didn't inherit it," he said finally. "I stole it."

Chapter Eight

C

Captain Hesse paced nervously, too excited to stand still. "Your messenger came last night on schedule?" he demanded.

Dakon nodded, spreading the documents Giancarlo had delivered over the desk. "He brought just what I had been hoping for. Look for yourself."

Captain Hesse picked up the top sheet of paper and started to read. On occasions such as this, Dakon blessed the fact that the Vam-pyr features were, by human standards, essentially without emotion. After a hundred and thirty years of practice, he was pretty good at producing whatever human expression was needed to suit his purposes. He adjusted his mouth into a smile that conveyed equal measures of triumph and modesty. Then he gestured to a small packet of letters buried among the other papers.

"I believe you will find these were worth waiting for, Hesse. Speaking for myself, I was *very* well pleased with the delivery." He allowed his upper lip to curl into a faintly contemptuous sneer. "The peasant who brought them had no notion of what a price-less burden he carried. He seemed more than satisfied with the few coins I gave him as a reward."

"I don't suppose he could read," the captain said, shuffling rapidly through the bundle of papers and extracting the letters. "These Italian peasants never can, you know. They're an ignorant lot."

Dakon waited for a moment before he trusted himself to speak. "They have a passionate commitment to their revolutionary ideals nonetheless. They may be illiterate, but they can all quote verbatim from Mazzini's speeches."

Captain Hesse snorted. "They rant about freedom and democracy without any idea what the words actually mean. I can imagine the mess they would make if they were ever in charge of their own affairs."

Dakon held on to his smile. "Fortunately, since Austria controls every facet of their lives and their government, they are at liberty to devote all their attention to the task of avoiding starvation."

Dakon need not have worried that the captain would hear the sarcasm underlying his remarks. Hesse grunted his agreement and picked up the first letter, skimming it quickly. Eyes widening, his gaze rested on the signature.

"*Giuseppe Garibaldi,*" he murmured, his voice hoarse with excitement. He picked up the second letter, turning at once to the signature.

"*Count Camillo Benso Cavour,*" he read. "By God, Albion, I would like to know how you came by this correspondence!"

"With extreme difficulty, and copious dispersal of golden coins," Dakon responded, his voice dry. "Fortunately, I am blessed with friends in both Prime Minister Cavour's inner circle, and also among General

Garibaldi's most trusted advisors. Eventually I was able to persuade ... an acquaintance ... to steal the letters."

"You are certainly blessed in your friendships," Captain Hesse said, chuckling. "If only those treacherous Italian rebels knew the truth about you!"

"Indeed," Dakon murmured. "I think many who call themselves my friend would be astonished if they knew where my true loyalties lie."

The captain held a letter up to the light, straining to detect the watermark. "Can you be sure the correspondence is genuine?" he asked, his mood changing from jubilation to sudden anxiety.

"I am sure," Dakon said. "My source is entirely reliable. However, I doubt if your superiors will rely upon my word. The letters reveal such important information that the Austrian High Command would be fools to trust that the letters are genuine without careful checking."

"Very true, but fortunately we should be able to assess the authenticity of the correspondence without undue difficulty."

"How?" Dakon asked, trying to sound naively curious rather than anxious. He deepened his smile. "You can scarcely ask Cavour or Garibaldi to verify their signatures."

Captain Hesse laughed. "Alas, no! But we have intelligence experts in our camp who are familiar with the handwriting of both Prime Minister Cavour and General Garibaldi."

"Will their judgment be trusted?" Dakon asked. "This is vital information."

"Indeed it is. Fortunately I am personally acquainted with two officers who have detected very clever forgeries in the past. I shall make sure that their opinions are listened to."

That was good news, Dakon thought. It was imperative that the letters should be accepted as genuine. And since they had been written by Cavour and Garibaldi for the express purpose of deceiving the Austrian High Command, Hesse's intelligence experts should be able to give a strong endorsement of the authenticity of the handwriting.

The captain scanned the last of the letters with avid interest. "I wish to God there were more pages," he said. "The correspondence cuts off at a crucial point—"

"Yes, alas, I am aware of that." Dakon gave a carefully calculated sigh of regret. "Unfortunately, as you can see from the dates, the correspondence is ongoing. The final details of Garibaldi's plans still seem to be unsettled, although the general outline is clear. If I am able to acquire any further letters, I shall send word to you via the usual channels. The letters themselves are too valuable to entrust to a courier, don't you agree?"

"I agree completely. In the meantime, let us return to the correspondence we have in hand. It seems clear to me that Garibaldi plans to devote his major military effort to the capture of Milan."

"Yes, I reached much the same conclusion," Dakon said. It was Dakon who had insisted that the correspondence would be more convincing if it contained gaps, so that the Austrians would be forced to do a little detective work in order to deduce the exact nature of General Garibaldi's supposed battle plans. He was relieved to see that Captain Hesse, at least, was taking the carefully laid bait and swimming off rapidly in the wrong direction.

Dakon tried to bolster the intriguing hints planted in the letters. "It would be logical for Garibaldi to set his sights on capturing Milan, don't you think? After all, it is the center of Austrian power in the occupied territories. Prime Minister Cavour cannot hope to claim that his side has won a decisive victory unless they have Milan in their hands."

Captain Hesse nodded. "I am in complete agreement with you, although some of my commanding officers have tried to argue that Garibaldi would never be so foolish as to launch an all-out attack on a city he knows to be heavily fortified."

"Fortifications have never stopped Garibaldi in the past," Dakon pointed out, ironically aware that he had truth momentarily on his side. "He seems to believe that a thousand of his troops have the fire in their bellies to defeat ten thousand regular soldiers lined up against him." He shrugged so that he wouldn't appear too admiring. "Still, his luck cannot hold forever."

"You are quite right, and especially not against the superior troops of the Austrian Empire." Unconsciously, Captain Hesse drew himself up taller. "He will learn a lesson or two in humility when he faces our cavalry on the battlefield." Captain Hesse fingered the hilt of his sword. "You have been to Vienna and seen the full glory of our troops in action, Albion, so you know what I'm talking about. You know that the Austrian Army is unlike any other in the world. No other soldiers are as thoroughly trained as ours."

Dakon pretended to murmur agreement. The captain was partially right, he reflected. Austrian troops were extraordinarily well trained—in ceremonial drill. The Emperor Franz Josef was fond of designing new uniforms for his regiments and then massing the army for giant parades that were picture perfect in their

precision. However, the Emperor showed no enthusiasm for spending money on the modern weapons that
would enable his men to cope with the blood and
chaos of an actual war. During a recent trip to Vienna,
Dakon had seen for himself that some of the foot
troops were still equipped with eighteenth century
muskets. Provided Garibaldi and the Nationalists
could keep the element of surprise on their side,
Dakon had no doubts at all about who would win the
battles of the forthcoming war.

Captain Hesse renewed his study of the letters.
"Hmm, it seems Garibaldi plans to assemble his
troops at the Piedmont border, ready to launch them
into action the moment war is declared. I suppose the
provisioning is easier that way, with Victor Emmanuel's supply lines to tap into."

"Undoubtedly," Dakon agreed.

Captain Hesse twirled his mustache gleefully. "Well,
Signor Garibaldi won't be able to get away with one
of his famous sneak attacks this time! Ha!" He
slapped his thigh, barely able to contain his jubilation.
"Won't the old rogue be surprised when he finds himself having to fight for every inch of road on the way
to Milan!"

"I am quite sure the last thing Garibaldi plans is to
fight a pitched battle against the full might of the Austrian Army," Dakon agreed with absolute honesty.
"He must know that his army would be wiped out
within days. Within hours, even. I will wager he is
relying heavily on the element of surprise."

"Then perhaps we may look for his surrender without a fight when he realizes that his plans are discovered? In his favor, it must be said that he doesn't like
to squander the lives of his men." The captain seized
Dakon's hand and shook it fervently. "You promised

me a prize worth waiting for, Albion, and with these letters you have fully lived up to your share of the bargain. The Austrian Empire has reason to be grateful to you. After the war, I shall make sure that you are suitably rewarded by the emperor."

"I look forward to acquiring at least a modest estate in Hungary," Dakon murmured. "I have many good friends in the Transylvania region and would like to own some property there."

The captain smiled. "You can count on getting your estate, Albion, you have my word on it." He slipped the bundle of documents into a slim leather portfolio and tucked the case under his arm.

"I ordered your horses groomed and watered," Dakon said. "It remains only to wish you Godspeed."

"Thank you. But first, a word of warning, if I may, on a subject that has begun to trouble me greatly over the last couple of days."

Dakon inclined his head. "Certainly. Your advice is always welcome."

"It concerns your guests, the three ladies I brought here. I urge you to be rid of them, Albion, without delay."

"Rid of them?" Dakon allowed himself to look as startled as he felt.

"Send them packing. With all possible speed." The captain's mouth tightened into a harsh line. "The fact is, Albion, that I behaved with unforgivable naïveté in bringing them here. I confess to being dazzled by Mrs. Ford's good looks and Miss Hope's charming portrayal of desperation. In retrospect, I realize I should have left those three mysterious ladies exactly where I found them."

"But they were stranded travelers, in dire straits—"

"I very much doubt it. Not to put too fine a point

on it, Albion, I have concluded that the women are spies, and potentially of great danger to our cause."

"Spies!" Dakon adjusted his features into an expression of horrified surprise. "My dear Hesse, I am shocked to hear this! What reason do you have for making such an astonishing accusation?"

"Several reasons. First of all, Mrs. Ford is so ravishingly beautiful that I don't think any husband in the world would allow her to travel about Europe unescorted, especially not in a country that is preparing for war. Since she is clearly lying about her marital status, and since it is almost impossible to imagine what legitimate business she might have to conduct in the duchy, it is logical to conclude that she is a courtesan who has been sent to entrap you."

"I cannot agree," Dakon said blandly, diverted to discover that the Austrians and the Italians were both equally ready to suspect Cordelia and her companions. "Why would anybody bait such a trap for me? You forget that it is common knowledge within the duchy that I am not attracted to beautiful women."

"Er ... yes ... that is so." Hesse cleared his throat, obviously embarrassed by this reference to Dakon's reputation for ambiguous sexuality. "However, I am not sure that your—preferences—in bedroom matters are fully understood by the locals."

Or by you, Dakon thought with grim amusement.

Captain Hesse tugged at his scabbard, clearly discomfitted by the direction of their conversation. "Taking everything into account, Albion, does it not seem likely that Mrs. Ford was sent here as the ultimate test of your susceptibility to feminine wiles? Her beauty is surely stunning enough to tempt any man to indiscretion."

"It is possible, I suppose." Dakon shrugged. "If you

are right, then Mrs. Ford's masters—whoever they may be—are likely to be sorely disappointed. I find her tedious in the extreme."

"So you are not tempted in the least?" Hesse asked. "You have no interest in taking her into your bed?"

You are too curious by half, Dakon decided. *Why are you so anxious to find out if I can be seduced?* He schooled his features into a picture of bored indifference. "Contrary to certain rumors that circulate in the region, I am occasionally willing to be—entertained— by a beautiful woman," he said. "But even if Mrs. Ford is determined to share my bed, she will learn nothing from the encounter save that I am a very conventional lover with no taste for the exotic."

"It is the pillow talk after the seduction that is always so dangerous," Hesse murmured.

Dakon smiled amiably. "Even so, you may rest assured that she presents no danger to me—to us. However skilled Mrs. Ford may be as a seductress, I am entirely unlikely to indulge in any form of conversation once our coupling is over. I am much too old to be swept into indiscretion by a pretty face wrapped around an empty and boring mind." *So make of that what you will, my dear captain.*

Hesse looked as if he would very much have liked to inquire more deeply into the count's sexual tastes. After a visible struggle, he conquered his curiosity. "I will rely upon your discretion, then, in the matter of Mrs. Ford. In truth, Albion, my worries center almost as much upon Miss Hope as upon her supposed cousin."

"My dear captain, if I am not bowled over by Mrs. Ford's ravishing face and form, you can safely rely upon me to resist Miss Hope's much more modest attributes. Why would any man choose brown hair and gray eyes when he has ravishing golden curls and cerulean blue eyes at his beck and call?''

"It is not Miss Hope's powers of seduction that I fear. It is her intelligence, and her capacity for picking up small hints and clues and pasting them into a larger picture." The captain spoke flatly. "She knows much too much about Italian politics for an English woman. I am convinced she is not at all what she seems on the surface."

"Whatever secret purpose she may harbor, she is only a woman. Surely you do not believe her capable of outwitting us?" Dakon spoke calmly enough, but inside he felt anything but calm. Last night, he had been so sure that Cordelia could be trusted. This morning, in the uncomfortably bright light of morning, he wondered if he had been too quick to trust. Looking back over their conversation, he found himself cursed by the affliction of all those who deal in treachery and betrayal: he could no longer accept the simple explanation for anything. Captain Hesse's suspicions renewed all his own doubts. Was Cordelia the innocent traveler that she seemed? Or was she something much more dangerous? It was even possible that the captain himself had become suspicious of Dakon's true allegiance, and had sent the women to test him. If so, it would be very clever of him to warn Dakon against them, thus protecting himself if Dakon failed to respond to his gambit.

Dakon had found such intense pleasure in Cordelia's company that he wanted to dismiss the debilitating suspicion. He found to his dismay that he couldn't. He reminded himself that he had touched the very core of her soul during the linkage of their minds. With relentless, cold analysis, he faced the fact that, since he had never in one hundred and thirty years of existence touched minds with any other human being, let alone a human female, he had no way of knowing whether or not Cordelia could deceive him in such circumstances.

He sat down, seeking out a chair in the darkest corner of the library, and shifting so that his eyes were shielded from the morning sunlight beginning to stream through the unshuttered windows. He hadn't expected his interview with Hesse to last this long, or he would have taken better steps to protect his eyes from the light.

"Do you have more specific reasons for doubting Miss Hope's story?" he asked. "Other than the fact that her cousin is very beautiful and she is overendowed with brains?"

"Her fluency in foreign languages is highly suspicious," Captain Hesse said at once. "You must have noticed that Miss Hope speaks Italian like a native. She even understands the local dialect, which I would have sworn couldn't be learned by outsiders."

"Yes," Dakon agreed reluctantly. "The local dialect is notoriously difficult to understand—"

"The obvious conclusion is that she is not British at all. She is Italian, an Italian spy."

"My dear Hesse, do you not think you are jumping to conclusions?" Dakon said. "After all, she speaks French, too. Perhaps she is simply a gifted linguist."

"The British are never gifted linguists," the captain said with utter conviction. "They suck in the belief that English is a superior language with their mother's milk. Besides, as I mentioned before, Miss Hope is far too well informed about European politics for an English lady. She tries to hide her knowledge, but she can't quite succeed."

"But for whom is she working?" Dakon asked.

"Not for the Austrians, obviously, otherwise you would know all about her." He paused, probing the captain's feelings, but sensing nothing unexpected or out of the way.

"Of course she isn't working for us," Hesse barked. "Why would I have brought her here if she is an Austrian spy?"

Dakon decided that tact required him to leave that question unanswered. "Well, then, if she is sent by the Italians, why have I not been informed of her presence in the region? Are you forgetting that I am considered the leader of the Italian Nationalists within the duchy?"

"No, I am forgetting nothing. But your high position with the rebels may render you especially vulnerable to scrutiny." Captain Hesse looked somber. "When two nations hover on the brink of war, doubts and suspicions multiply. Perhaps the Italians sent Cordelia Hope here simply because they felt a need to reassure themselves that you are entirely trustworthy."

"In which case, I had better make sure that she is convinced that I am devoted to the Italian cause," Dakon murmured.

"If you are on your guard, she can inflict no harm," the captain said.

"True." Dakon felt a great weariness as he contemplated the layers of deceit and betrayal that made up his daily life and realized how much he had wanted to set Cordelia outside that morass of lies and trickery. "Don't worry, Hesse, I believe I shall prove more than a match for Miss Hope. I was hiding state secrets when she was still learning how to write her alphabet."

The captain permitted himself a smile. "She is four-and-twenty, I believe. You cannot be more than a dozen years her senior, Albion."

Dakon returned the smile. "At moments like this, I feel at least a hundred and thirty years old," he said.

The captain's chuckle swiftly faded. "Perhaps my visits have given rise to questions among your rebel friends," he suggested. "It may be that they no longer believe the story that I come here merely to pick up the tax revenues due to the Austrian government."

Dakon nodded. "You should not come to the villa again," he said. "With war so imminent, why take chances? If we must meet, from now on let it be in secret."

"Agreed," Captain Hesse said. "You know how I can be reached, so send word if you have need of me. I take my leave with the plea that you will exercise the greatest caution in your dealings with Miss Hope and Mrs. Ford. Whatever the temptation, however sweet the seduction, do not allow yourself to trust them. Clever women are always dangerous, and in wartime they are deadly."

"I shall keep your advice in mind." That was certainly true, Dakon decided bleakly. He would be unable to forget it. "Now, Captain, may I offer you a glass of Chianti or some other form of refreshment before you leave?"

Captain Hesse pulled on his riding gloves. "Thank you, but I must return to the town of Modena as quickly as possible. The information you have provided to me must be swiftly disseminated if it is to advance the Austrian cause."

"I couldn't agree more," Dakon said. "Travel safely, Captain, and I look forward to a speedy Austrian victory."

As soon as the captain had left, Dakon closed the curtains, relaxing as the painfully bright light stopped blazing against his sensitive retina. He sat back in the chair, momentarily swamped by the turmoil and misery of his thoughts. He almost welcomed the interruption of a light tap at the door.

"Enter," he said, annoyed with himself when he realized he was hoping the visitor might be Cordelia.

Luck had deserted him. His visitor wasn't Cordelia, but her cousin. Mrs. Ford, or whoever else she might really be, poked her exquisite head around the door, her halo of curls shimmering like a burnished crown in the morning sunlight. Her plump pink lips parted into a seductive smile when she caught Dakon's eye.

"Count!" she exclaimed, tripping across the room, the flounces of her gown fluttering alluringly as she moved. "Thank goodness you are finally alone. I have been waiting all morning to speak with you."

"How fortunate, then, that I am now available to listen to you."

She looked at him uncertainly, as if sensing his mockery, but not quite able to grasp that it might be directed toward her. If she was a spy, Dakon reflected acidly, then it was no wonder she traveled in Cordelia's company. Mrs. Ford's beauty might be dazzling enough to seduce secrets from incautious lovers, but her supply of brains seemed seriously inadequate for the task of making use of those secrets.

For whatever reason, whether her own needs or on instructions from her spymasters, it seemed that she was determined to seduce him. Her eyelashes fluttered in a pretense of shyness, but her whole body sent out subtle messages of availability.

She sat on a chair that was close enough to him that the hem of her gown covered his foot. She pretended not to notice the impropriety and sent him a smile of dazzling dimensions. "I want to thank you, Count, for your prompt action last night. You were wonderful! You saved my life!" She clasped her hands to her bosom, a second-rate actress in a very tiresome melodrama.

Dakon bowed. "I am delighted to have been of service, but you exaggerate my role, Mrs. Ford."

"You are too modest, Count." Her exquisite, pink-tipped fingers moved from her bosom to her throat. She had a less-than-perfect neck, Dakon thought abstractedly. Unlike Cordelia, whose long, swanlike neck was the stuff of Vam-pyr fantasy.

Annoyed at his inability to keep his thoughts focused, he thrust the beguiling image of Cordelia aside, and returned his attention to the woman in front of him.

Her blue eyes glistened with grateful tears. "If you had not caught me when I fell down the stairs, I believe I would be dead. You saved my life, Count, and I am forever in your debt."

"Pray think nothing of it. I beg you will not make me into a hero when I am nothing of the kind. I trust no harm has come to the babe?"

For an instant, her entire face darkened with rage. Then she deliberately smoothed out her frown and pressed her smile back into service. "Thank you. Everything is well."

Dakon reached out mentally, trying to probe her emotions. He experienced the familiar sensation of sinking into a choking, cloying fog: the standard reaction whenever he attempted to touch minds with a human female. He pulled back, shaking off the unpleasant, lingering feeling of suffocation. "I am very glad that neither you nor your expected child came to harm while you are a guest in my house."

He needed no special sensitivity to know that she loathed these reminders of her pregnancy. She quickly

changed the subject. "And that is another reason for
me to offer you my heartfelt thanks," she said. "I
understand from my cousin that you have been gracious enough to offer us the hospitality of your home
for the next several weeks. It is so frustrating that
nobody can find our lawyer, Mr. Peasant. I cannot
imagine how there came to be this amazing muddle
over the ownership of the villa."

He wondered precisely what Cordelia had told her
cousin about that muddle. Last night, she had promised to keep his illegal occupation of the villa a secret.
He had believed her, until Captain Hesse's warnings
this morning forced him to view everything that had
happened over the past week from a new and harsher
perspective. It was hard to imagine a more perfect spy
than one who could read the mind of her target. Was
Cordelia that perfect spy? Dakon rubbed his aching
eyes, feeling them sting as the sunlight grew brighter.
Dear God, how weary he was of constantly doubting
the motives and the veracity of everyone around him.
How weary he was of pretending always to be someone and something that he was not.

Mrs. Ford was at his side in an instant. "Do you
have the headache?" she asked, her voice soft and
purring. "My dear count, allow me to massage your
forehead." Her voice lowered to an even more intimate murmur. "I have been told that I have magic
fingers."

Why not let her seduce him? Dakon decided. She
seemed hell-bent on doing just that, so why attempt
to dissuade her? In the immediate aftermath of his
cresting, sexual intercourse was quite safe for him and
even, on occasion, mildly enjoyable. Perhaps in the
throes of what human beings laughably considered intimacy, he might be able to decide whether Mary's

desire to make love to him sprang out of her own personal needs, or the demands of her possible employers.

Her fingers were indeed skilled as they massaged his temples. No doubt they would perform with equal suppleness on any other section of his body. He felt a twinge of mild arousal. With no difficulty on his part—and no resistance on hers—he twisted his head slightly, so that he could drop a swift, expert kiss into the palm of her hand.

Her breath instantly quickened. She hesitated for no more than a second or two before allowing her fingers to trail down the sides of his face and slip beneath the high points of his collar. He grasped her hands, carried them to his lips, and stood up all in one fluid movement. The agility of the Vam-pyr tended to make them very popular with their human lovers. He put his arm around her waist and urged her forward, into his arms.

"My dear Mrs. Ford," he whispered, his mouth against her cheek. "I do believe you are willing to show me your gratitude in a most exciting fashion."

"Oh yes, Count." She tilted her face upward, her lips parted, her body thrusting against his. His state of arousal, far from increasing, began to disappear. She wriggled against him in blatant allure. "You know that if you weren't such a special man, I would never be doing this. But you saved my life . . ."

Her words trailed away into a sigh of satisfaction as Dakon kissed her. Every movement of her body gave the lie to her protestations of inexperience, but that didn't prove she was a spy, merely that her husband—or a previous lover—had been a skilled instructor.

Her tongue met his, duelling eagerly. He avoided kissing her throat, a Vam-pyr intimacy that seemed suddenly repugnant when he remembered the soft, passionate sweetness of his encounter last night with Cordelia. Dakon trailed kisses along the swell of Mrs. Ford's bosom, but his enthusiasm for this seduction—never more than lukewarm—had died completely, and he could barely bring himself to go through the motions.

Where was Cordelia? he wondered and instantly a picture of her flashed into his mind. She was in the hall outside his study, pacing the floor and wondering if she should knock on his door. She stopped and looked up, as if she had heard him calling to her. Shaking her head in bemusement, she turned and rapped tentatively on the door.

Dakon broke away from Mary's arms, disgusted with himself for what he had almost done. Not only would *he* have been debased by the sort of mindless coupling they had been headed toward, but Mary herself deserved more than to be used and discarded because he was feeling restless and out of sorts. And because he desperately wanted to mate with her cousin.

She stepped back, staring at him with glazed eyes. His guilt increased when he saw that her lips were swollen from his kisses, and her breasts rose and fell as she dragged in swift, panting breaths. He had found their encounter almost distasteful; she had apparently found it deeply arousing. "What is it, Count?" she asked. "Is something wrong?"

"Someone is at the door," he said. "You must not have heard the knock." He crossed the room as he spoke, and opened the door. "Ah, good morning, Miss Hope. What can I do for you?"

She looked from him to Mary. Dakon followed her gaze and cursed silently. Had Cordelia caught them in each other's arms, it could hardly have been more obvious what he and Mary had been doing. He was astonished at how badly he wanted to explain to Cordelia that their kisses had meant nothing. He was even more astonished at how guilty he felt for indulging in sexual activity that was entirely devoid of emotional meaning.

Cordelia looked up at him, her gray eyes appearing dark and bruised. "I'm sorry if I interrupted something important," she said. "I will return later." On the surface her voice sounded cool and disapproving. Dakon wasn't deceived. He easily heard the hurt lurking beneath.

"Mrs. Ford was thanking me for my promise of hospitality," he said.

I can see she was, Cordelia snarled. *How unfortunate I arrived before she could demonstrate the full range of her gratitude.*

They both stared at each other. She blushed when she realized that he'd read her mind. Dakon was amazed when her thoughts abruptly cut off, as if a curtain had dropped into place. She was quite extraordinary, he reflected, with an obscure, almost possessive, pride. Young Vam-pyr males had to practice for months before they learned how to shield their private thoughts. Cordelia was learning the technique after only days.

Unless, of course, her skills had been discovered years ago, and she had been sent into his household with the precise purpose of divining his deepest, most intimate secrets. What a priceless weapon such a spy would be, especially since neither she nor her masters could possibly have expected him to be possessed of the same amazing skill.

He found that even to suspect Cordelia of treachery

left him inwardly shattered. He took refuge behind his long-established mask of courteous indifference. He bowed both to Cordelia and to her sulking cousin. "Ladies, your presence is delightful. Too delightful, in fact, for it keeps me from examining the estate ledgers, which I have sworn to do before noon today. I must beg your indulgence and ask that we continue our conversations at a later date."

Mary curtsied, frustrated but resigned. "I shall look forward to taking up where we left off, Count."

"A delightful prospect," Dakon murmured, mentally vowing that he would be sure never again to find himself alone with Mary. Even in the cause of Italian liberation, sex with her was likely to prove more than he could stomach.

Cordelia stared straight forward, her profile a study in determined blankness. "Anna asked me to inform you that His Eminence, the Cardinal of Milan, has sent word he will be arriving sometime late this afternoon. She would like to know when you wish dinner to be served."

Hell and damnation! The cardinal was a good friend and a wonderful man, but the last thing Dakon needed to cope with today was a visit from a man whose vision was sometimes too clearsighted for comfort. However, since the cardinal was the man who had persuaded Prime Minister Cavour and General Garibaldi to concoct the correspondence which had just sent Captain Hesse chasing off in pursuit of a very false trail, it was only to be expected that he would want to find out if his efforts had been successful.

Dakon bowed again, showing none of his inner turmoil. "Thank you for the message. I will confer with Anna at once. Until this evening, ladies."

"Do you wish us to join you for dinner?" Mary

asked, her expression eager. In her current state of boredom, any diversion was better than none, even dinner with a celibate Roman Catholic dignitary. Besides, there was an added thrill of satisfaction in knowing that her father, a staunch supporter of the Church of England, would be apoplectic when he heard that his daughter had dined with a papist.

"But of course," Dakon said. "Both of you delightful ladies must attend. I am sure the cardinal will find you an intriguing addition to my household."

"It is, of course, our supreme object to be a source of entertainment for your friends," Cordelia said. "Until this evening, Count."

Dakon stared at the closed door for a full five seconds after she'd left the room. He wasn't accustomed to finding his stomach tied in knots over his relationship with a mere human. If this was what happened when humans fell in love, no wonder their poets had filled a million or so pages agonizing over the bizarre sensations.

Not that he was falling in love, of course. He'd spent a hundred and thirty years proving that the Vam-pyr weren't capable of such a muddled, human emotion.

Dakon scowled. He was delighted that Cordelia had gone away. He wished she would come back so that he could kiss her. His heart lurched. His pulses raced. His sacs tingled.

It was impossible for his sacs to refill this soon after his cresting, and yet this was the second time within the space of twenty-four hours that Dakon had felt the trickle of mating fluid seeping into the tiny pouches that protected his fangs.

Dakon was an old campaigner. He knew when it was time to retreat and regroup, and that time was now. Putting Cordelia firmly out of his mind, he stormed off to find Anna.

At this precise moment, a scolding from his housekeeper was a far more appealing prospect than another minute spent contemplating the confusion of his feelings for Cordelia.

Chapter Nine

(

His Eminence, Cardinal Walter of Milan, was a severe disappointment to Mary. Despite his intimate acquaintance with the Pope, she detected no sign that he was in league with the devil, a conspiracy which would have added a pleasant spice of wickedness to the evening. Far from being lean and sinister, her preconceived idea of how a cardinal should look, he was chubby, rosy-cheeked, had twinkling hazel eyes, and seemed so well content with his vow of celibacy that he scarcely noticed Mary's beauty.

He was accompanied to dinner by his secretary, a young priest named Father Roberto, whose handsome looks contrasted sadly with his pinched personality. Father Roberto's sour demeanor suggested that an evening of self-flagellation would have been preferable to the prospect of dining with two foreign women, one of whom was scandalously clad in a low-cut gown of ice blue satin.

His Eminence was Austrian by birth and friendly by disposition, but he spoke only fractured English, and Father Roberto spoke no English at all. Mary was therefore forced to spend the evening listening to an excruciatingly boring conversation about books, music, and the effect of the wet weather on the spring planting, all conducted in broken half sentences, liberally sprinkled with French and Italian, and even—horror of horrors—the occasional paragraph of Latin.

It did not improve her disposition to see that Cordelia seemed to be thoroughly enjoying herself and was soon embroiled in a lively discussion with the count and the cardinal about some man called Dante. Dante, as far as Mary could deduce, had written a long and dreary poem about his lover, a saintly woman named Beatrice. Since Beatrice was already dead, Mary couldn't imagine why her activities were of any interest to anyone, not even the cardinal, and especially not a forceful, vital man like the Count of Albion.

Bored almost to distraction, and unable to eat more than a mouthful or two even though Ellen had laced her stays an inch looser than normal, Mary took the earliest possible opportunity to excuse herself from the drawing room. She derived a certain malicious pleasure from the knowledge that etiquette left Cordelia no choice but to accompany her upstairs.

"Lord, what a pair of doddery bores!" she exclaimed as they mounted the stairs to their rooms. "When the cardinal was rambling on about his medieval manuscripts, I actually found myself remembering our old vicar of Stanwyck with fondness. At least the vicar could speak English and had the sense not to prose on and on about his hobbies!"

"English is Cardinal Walter's fourth language," Cordelia pointed out, to Mary's annoyance. She was sick and tired of Cordelia defending every dratted foreigner who crossed their paths. "His native tongue is

German, and he also speaks fluent French and Italian. And Father Roberto is considered a classical scholar of some note. He has written a major treatise on the philosophy of Aristotle."

Mary neither knew nor cared who Aristotle was. "No wonder they're scholars! Neither of them has anything better to do than study that dreary old stuff. Papa is quite right. It is perverted that these papists aren't permitted to marry." She pouted, upset at how the dinner had turned out. "I wish they'd never come. It would have been a great deal more diverting to spend the evening alone with the count."

"No doubt," Cordelia said.

There was just a hint of waspishness in her cousin's voice, and Mary stared at her, more entertained than she had been all night. "My, my, little cousin, do I detect a note of jealousy in your voice? Surely you aren't attracted to the count?"

"Of course not," Cordelia said, but Mary noticed the faintest trace of color on her cousin's high cheekbones. Those cheekbones always irritated her, because they added a touch of exotic interest to Cordelia's face, a face that men in any case found fascinating. Fortunately, Cordelia was such a naive country bumpkin that she had no idea of the devastating effect she could produce on a man if she only set her mind to it. Incredibly, she labored under the delusion that she was not especially attractive to the opposite sex, and Mary hadn't the slightest intention of letting her know otherwise. Even Gervaise, damn him, had cast an interested eye in Cordelia's direction. Her lover's admiration was just one of the many reasons Mary disliked her cousin so intensely.

"I recommend that you relinquish any false hopes you may cherish in regard to the Count of Albion,"

she said, seething with resentment at her pregnant
state, and all too aware that if Cordelia set out to
captivate the count, she would more than likely succeed. "Trust me, Cordelia, he is much too ... virile
... for a born spinster like you."

The color in Cordelia's cheeks deepened. Unfortunately, she gave no other sign of being disturbed.
Mary clenched her teeth, finding it intolerable to contemplate spending the next several months in the company of someone who refused to lose her temper.
Mary needed arguments, and dramatic scenes, in order
to reassure herself that she was alive. Cordelia kept
urging her to be calm, for the sake of the baby. As if
she cared about the baby! If she thought God would
listen to her, she would pray every night for a miscarriage, but God, of course, only rewarded virtuous
women with miscarriages.

Mary's grasp of theology was sketchy, but she could
picture the Almighty quite clearly. He was tall and
white-haired, like Papa, and easily enraged even when
you hadn't really meant to do anything wrong, exactly
like Papa. When he was angry, his voice thundered,
shaking the clouds, and making Mary shrivel up inside
with fear and loneliness. The prospect of heavenly re-
wards had never been enough to keep Mary on the
narrow path of virtue. She was not at all sure that she
wanted to spend eternity floating in the sky with two
such intimidating people as God and Papa.

Mary suppressed a sigh of relief when they reached
her bedroom and she saw Ellen was already waiting
for her, a dressing robe in her arms. These days, Mary
felt so tired, and so ugly, that she was glad to get back
to the privacy of her own rooms, although she could
never admit that to anyone, certainly not Cordelia,
and not even Ellen, who was only a servant. If you

let people know that you were lonely and needed help, they ripped you to pieces. Papa's behavior had taught her that lesson, over and over again and she had learned it well.

"If you have no further need of me tonight, I would like to go to my room," Cordelia said with calm courtesy. "I am rather tired."

She was always so damned prissy, Mary thought resentfully. Lord knows, Cordelia would never do anything so unladylike as finding herself pregnant and unmarried. She'd probably faint the first time she watched a man unbutton his breeches, and have a heart attack when her husband tried to mount her.

That improper thought restored some of Mary's good humor. She had nothing to say to her cousin, no desire whatsoever to spend time in her company. She didn't need anybody, not Gervaise, who'd abandoned her the second he knew she was with child, and certainly not a little country nobody like Cordelia, whose mother—born into all the glory of the Stanwyck heritage—had been stupid enough to toss her inheritance away and marry an impoverished university professor.

"Run along," she said to Cordelia, her voice impatient because that was a good way to insure that she didn't sound wistful. "Don't let me keep you from your beauty sleep, because you need all you can get."

Cordelia didn't reply and Mary laughed spitefully. "Try not to dream about the count, dear cousin. It will do you not a bit of good, you know. He's mine for the taking, if I should happen to decide that I'm interested."

Cordelia looked at her out of intimidatingly cool gray eyes. "I think the Count of Albion is a man who takes, not one who is taken," she said. "You might be wise to bear that in mind. Good night, Mary. Good night, Ellen. Sleep well."

Cordelia didn't wait for her cousin to reply. She walked into her room, closing the door and leaning against it while she drew in several deep, calming breaths. She didn't really want to murder her cousin, she told herself. In truth, Mary was more to be pitied than anything else. She had allowed herself to be seduced by one of London's most notorious rakes, and she would spend the rest of her life paying for that moment of folly. However successful the Earl of Stanwyck might be in concealing the truth from the world, the memory of giving birth would live forever in Mary's heart. She would always suffer under the knowledge that her child was growing up in a foreign land, unacquainted with his birth mother, and cared for by Cordelia. Mary might profess complete indifference to the fate of the baby she carried within her, and yet Cordelia was sure that at some profound level, her cousin was terrified by her pregnancy, and the separation from her own child that she would soon be forced to endure.

Her annoyance replaced by sympathy, albeit reluctant, Cordelia cast her fan onto the bed and began the tedious task of unbuttoning her long kid gloves. Her plea of fatigue had been no more than an excuse to escape from her cousin, and she was far too wide awake to think of sleep. Dinner had been such fun, with intelligent companions providing stimulating conversation and reminding her of many happy evenings spent with her father's colleagues in Cambridge.

She would go for a walk and dissipate some of her excess energy, she decided, tossing her gloves next to the fan. Grabbing a thick, oversized shawl from the clothespress, she wrapped herself in the warm woolen folds and ran downstairs. The side door that led to the Garden of the Three Fountains was not yet barred, and she stepped outside, taking pleasure in the chill of the breeze on her overheated skin.

She walked briskly along the path, drawing in refreshing gulps of crisp night air, and feeling the tensions of the day slowly drain away. The agreeable sound of water splashing into the tiled bowls of the fountains gradually overwhelmed the scratch and scuffle of tiny animals on the prowl, and she unlatched the gate leading into the gardens, eager to see the fountains in the silver glow of the full moon.

The garden was as beautiful by night as by day. The relatively warm and sunny weather of the past two days had thickened the leaves on the chestnut tree in the center of the garden, and moonlight wrapped the budding flowers and shrubs in a silver-tissue veil of mystery.

She wished that the Count of Albion were with her. As soon as the thought formed, Cordelia realized that she had been calling out to him mentally, silently summoning him to her side. So much for her powers of mental communication, she thought, lifting her shoulders in a rueful shrug. The count was giving not the slightest indication that he had heard her invitation. Or if he had, he was choosing not to accept it.

Mocking her own stupidity, Cordelia leaned against the trunk of the chestnut tree, breathing in the smell of night-blooming stock, and letting the garden work its magic on her senses. When she heard a long, hoarse moan, for a moment she dismissed it as the call of a hunting animal.

The moan came again, chilling in its pain and loneliness. She swallowed over a throat gone suddenly dry.

"Who is it?" she called softly in Italian. "Where are you?"

"*Aiuto! Sono qui!*"

The groan was barely distinguishable into separate words, but it was unmistakably a human voice croaking out the appeal for help. Heart pounding, knees shaking, Cordelia spun around, straining to see in the darkness.

The marble bench glowed pale and ghostly in a beam of moonlight. Huddled in a heap at the end of the bench was a man, shrouded in a black woolen cloak, his head lolling sideways onto the seat, a hat pulled low over his eyes, hiding his face.

Not the count, she thought with relief. Not Dakon, she would have recognized his call immediately.

With tentative steps, Cordelia made her way to the bench, half expecting the slouched figure to leap forward and grab her if she came too close. When she was about three feet away, sure enough, the man tried to stand. He didn't even manage to get to his knees. He collapsed again, falling backward onto the bench. His cloak fell open, revealing the slash gouged into his ribs, and the hideous bloodstains soaking his rough peasant's shirt. With a strangled moan, he toppled off the bench and pitched facedown on the ground.

"Oh dear God!" Cordelia ran to his side, rolling him over, stomach heaving when she was presented with an up-close view of the gaping wound in his chest. Teeth chattering, mind blank, she gathered the man into her arms. His hat slid off as she lifted his head, and she saw that it was Giancarlo, their coach driver from Piacenza.

Giancarlo! dear God, why had this happened to him? Who had tried to kill him? Had he been mur-

dered because of his secret work with the Italian
rebels?

"Don't move," she babbled. "You will be all right.
I will get help." She ripped at her white cambric petti-
coat, but the stitching of the seams was too strong and
she pulled off nothing but a strip of lace, so she tried
to staunch the flow of blood with her shawl. The wool
didn't absorb moisture well, and blood soaked her
hands, smeared her skirts, and splattered onto the
damp earth. She could scarcely credit that a man could
lose this much blood and still continue to breathe.

With heartbreaking effort, Giancarlo lifted his hand
and placed it over hers, stopping her feverish efforts
to tend his wounds. "Too late," he whispered in the
local dialect, his voice thick and gurgling. "I . . . am
. . . glad . . . not to die alone."

She wanted to deny what they both knew, but tears
clogged her voice, preventing her from speaking. In
the two or three seconds it took to regain command
of herself, she realized that she should not squander
Giancarlo's scant resources in a useless denial of the
truth. She would serve neither him nor anyone else
by pretending that his wound was less than mortal.

"Who did this to you?" she asked, cradling his head
in her lap and stroking his cheek, desperate to make
his last moments more comfortable. "Tell me who did
this, Giancarlo."

"Count . . . great danger . . ."

She tried to keep her voice calm. "We can keep the
count safe, Giancarlo, if you tell me who did this to
you. Do you understand what I'm asking?"

"Mmm . . . yes." For a second or two, his eyes were
bright and focused. "Monsignor . . ." he rasped, the
word sputtering out between heaves of pain. "Monsignor . . . must not trust . . ."

Giancarlo's breath rattled in his throat, then stopped in midgasp. His eyes went dim. His body slumped heavily into Cordelia's arms.

For a long moment she stared at him, paralyzed by shock and grief. Then, with infinite care, she closed his eyes. She rocked back on her heels, lifting her head toward the dark sky, and whispered a silent prayer for his passing.

The crack of a twig snapping sent her scrambling to her feet. "Who's there? What do you want?"

The only response was the rustle of the breeze, playing with the leaves in the chestnut tree. She drew in deep breaths, and told herself to stop jumping at shadows. Suddenly frantic with the need to share the knowledge of Giancarlo's death, she ran headlong toward the garden gate, cursing the cumbersome sway of her crinoline and the drag of her heavy petticoats. Her foot kicked against something on the pathway and she stumbled to an abrupt halt just a few feet away from the gate.

She glanced down, wondering what had almost tripped her, and saw a knife, its blade crusted with blood. The murder weapon? She bent quickly and picked it up by the handle, shuddering when her fingers grazed the sticky blade. It was no ordinary kitchen implement, she saw at once, but the sort of ornamental dagger some of the men in the region still wore tucked into their belts. In the darkness, it was difficult to determine more than that the handle was gold-colored, and heavily embossed with an intricate, distinctive design. Seeing the finely honed steel of the blade, and the still-wet blood, she didn't doubt for a moment that she was holding the instrument that had been used to kill Giancarlo.

All the more anxious to get back to the villa and

report what had happened now that she had what might be the murder weapon, she hurried toward the gate, the knife held out in front of her. Irrationally, although her hands and clothes were coated with Giancarlo's blood, she couldn't bear the thought of touching the bloody blade. As she started to unlatch the garden gate, an awkward process made more difficult by the need to keep a grip on the dagger, a whiff of a vaguely familiar and spicy scent wafted past her.

Almost in the same instant, she realized that she wasn't alone in the garden. Someone was creeping up behind her. She whirled around, but the gate was hidden behind a trellis covered with bougainvillea, and she could see nothing through the screen of spring leaves.

She turned back to the gate, trying frantically to unlatch it. Fingers made clumsy with fright, she dropped the knife, but at least that freed up two hands to manipulate the stiff old-fashioned lock. At last the gate swung open. Thank God! She broke into a run, but she had taken no more than a couple of steps forward when she felt a whoosh of air, followed by a blow to her head and an explosion of pain that seemed to reverberate inside her skull.

She swayed, desperately trying to keep her eyes open long enough to see her attacker, but the ground was rising to meet her and the world was blurring into a collage of formless colors.

"Dakon!" she called out despairingly, but there was no response, only a bleak, empty silence. Her attacker threw his arm around her neck from behind, dragging her to the ground. His breath felt hot and heavy in her ear, and she choked on the pungent smell that enveloped him, more a spice than a perfume.

Incense, she realized with a sudden brief flash of

coherence. Her attacker's robes were impregnated with the smell of incense.

Reason faded. Scarlet clouds erupted in front of her eyes, then pulsed and collapsed. Darkness washed over her in a giant wave.

She tumbled headlong into the black, waiting silence.

The pounding in her skull intensified, the hammer strokes of pain taking on the same rhythm as the pants of the man who was dragging her along the path. Cordelia struggled back to consciousness, fighting away the nausea that threatened to overwhelm her. What had happened? Where was she?

With a tremendous effort, she managed to open her eyes, but her own shawl was wrapped over her head and she saw only gray darkness. Memory returned swiftly, fueled by fear.

She kept her body limp, feigning unconsciousness. She wasn't strong enough to fight at this point, so the less resistance she offered, the better. There was no point in inviting a battle she was sure to lose.

Eventually her attacker gave a grunt, and the agonizing bump of her heels on the pathway stopped. He rolled her over, shoving and prodding her flaccid body into a carefully chosen position. Her arms collided with something solid and she bit back a cry of revulsion as she realized where she was.

Dear God, her attacker was posing her in a grisly embrace with Giancarlo's dead body! She fought against her instinctive desire to scream and pull away. If her attacker thought she was dead, she certainly saw no advantage in informing him she was alive.

Apparently, he wasn't quite satisfied with her position. He seemed determined to push her even closer to Giancarlo, pressing his knee into the small of her back, and using his weight to propel her forward. The shawl covering her head worked loose, and she felt the stickiness of congealed blood against her cheek. Shuddering, she realized that her attacker had positioned her head smack in the middle of Giancarlo's chest.

She gagged, unable to contain a mew of horror. She would have been wise to control her instinctive outcry. Retribution followed swiftly in the form of another blow to her head. Stars exploded in front of her eyes. For the second time, she tumbled into the deep pool of waiting darkness.

"*Fraulein! Signorina!* My dear Meez 'Ope. Pleez to open your eyez. *Ach, lieber Gott!* Meez 'Ope, can you 'ear me?"

Cordelia lay still, keeping her eyes firmly shut, although she could have opened them if she'd wanted to. She knew that it was the Cardinal of Milan who held her hand, chafing it anxiously, and pleading with her to wake up. He sounded shocked and concerned, but she was afraid of him nonetheless.

If she opened her eyes, he would realize at once that she was conscious, and that might be the signal he was waiting for.

Giancarlo's dying words had been a warning against "Monsignor," and she herself had smelled the incense clinging to her attacker's clothes. The same scent of incense that now wafted from the cardinal's scarlet robes. It seemed reasonable to conclude that the cardinal was a great danger to her, however solicitous he might sound.

"Ach, vat shall I do?" the cardinal muttered. "I

cannot see where you are hurt, Meez 'Ope. Ze blood, zere is too much.''

She was wondering how long she could lie there, feigning unconsciousness, when she heard the gate un-latch and footsteps walk briskly along the garden path. Relief flooded her when she recognized the anxious, high-pitched voice of Father Roberto. "*Monsignor? Dio mio! Che passa? Che'è successo?*"

"Father Roberto, thank God!" The cardinal ex-claimed, also in Italian. Far from sounding alarmed or guilty, his voice was rich with relief. "Get over here, my friend! You are the answer to my prayers."

"What is it? What's happened?" Father Roberto's footsteps accelerated to a run. "Monsignor, there is blood on your hands! Holy Mother of God, are you all right?"

"Yes, but alas, these two lying on the ground are not by any means all right. I discovered their bodies a few minutes ago when I came into the garden to meditate before retiring for the night. They were lying so close together that I thought they were lovers."

Cordelia heard the rustling of Father Roberto's robes as he knelt beside her. He gave a horrified gasp. "*Madonna mia!* What brutality! I've never seen so much blood." He swallowed audibly. "Are they dead? I detect no signs of life in either of them."

"The *signorina* is not dead, at least not yet. I felt the pulse in her neck and it is beating with regularity."

"But the man?"

"Alas," the cardinal said. "The man is dead, which is not surprising when you look at the viciousness of his wound."

"From his dress, it would seem he is a peasant," Father Roberto said.

"Yes. I don't recognize him, do you? He certainly isn't one of the count's servants."

"He could be one of the farm workers. It is only within the house that the count is so insistent upon employing young boys." Father Roberto was still panting, presumably from stress rather than exertion, but his disapproval of the count's domestic arrangements was plain.

The cardinal was not so distraught that he couldn't find time for a homily. "My dear Roberto, you must learn to distinguish between the appearance of sin, and the reality. As I have explained to you many times, the count employs young boys so that he can teach them to read and write, and train them for some useful occupation when they leave. There is no other work for them in this benighted duchy."

"I am sure he is a positive pattern card of virtue, Monsignor." Father Roberto sounded unconvinced. His hands probed clumsily over Cordelia's scalp, pausing only when he reached the bumps caused by the blows to her head. She winced as he poked at the torn skin and matted knots of hair, but fortunately neither of the men seemed to notice her reaction.

"She must have been struck from behind," Father Roberto said. "There is a very large lump almost on the crown of her head."

"Yes, I felt the same wound. If the blows had fallen any lower, they would probably have killed her."

"Who could possibly have aimed such a vicious blow at a defenseless woman? And for what reason?"

"First perhaps we should ask why two such unlikely people were meeting here in the garden," the cardinal said mildly. "I find that almost as curious as anything else."

"I hadn't thought of that," Father Roberto admitted. "Surely they were not . . . it cannot be that they had a romantic assignation? The man is clearly a peasant, and years older than the English woman."

"A romantic assignation does not seem likely," the cardinal agreed. "I would guess that they had business dealings."

"A local peasant and a lady from England?" Father Roberto's voice rose to an astonished squeak. "What possible business could such a pair have?"

"Not legitimate business, I would conclude, given the way their negotiations ended."

"But the *signorina* seemed a most respectable young woman—"

"Appearances can be deceptive," the cardinal reminded him. "These are troubled times in the duchy, my friend, and we can safely conclude that not every foreign traveler is here for honest purposes."

Cordelia decided that she had listened to the cardinal blacken her character for long enough. He was unlikely to murder her when his secretary was standing right next to him as a witness, and the damp from the ground was seeping through her petticoats, leaving her miserably uncomfortable. All in all, it seemed time to inform the pair of them that she was conscious. She took the risk of opening her eyes.

As she had guessed, Cardinal Walter and Father Roberto knelt on either side of her, each holding one of her hands. Father Roberto dropped her hand and moved away the moment he saw that her eyes were open. But the cardinal peered at her, his chubby face creased into incongruous lines of worry—or the pretense of worry.

"*Signorina!*" he exclaimed. "Zank God, you 'ave come back to us at last! Quick, tell us 'ow ve may assist you?"

His face danced before her, pink with sincerity. The leaves on the chestnut tree blurred into a halo around his scarlet skullcap. What a saintly chap he was, Cordelia thought with bitter mockery.

"My head," she croaked. "My head hurts ... I need water ..." She fell silent, alarmed to realize that she felt genuinely on the edge of fainting again.

"I shall get water from the fountain," Father Roberto murmured in Italian. He returned with his linen handkerchief soaking wet. He knelt down in the patch of dirt between Cordelia and Giancarlo's body, and gently squeezed water onto her face, washing away the blood.

"Thank you," she managed to reply. "You are kind, Father."

"It is my pleasure to be of service, *signorina*. Here, give me your hands, so that I may wipe them clean also. I am sorry that the water is so cold." He reached for her hands as he spoke, then pulled back with a startled exclamation. "I have cut my thumb," he said. "There is something sharp lying on the ground next to you, *signorina*. Have a care when you move, or you might do yourself an injury."

In her present state, she would hardly notice another injury, Cordelia thought ruefully. Probing carefully, Father Roberto brought out a knife that had been hidden beneath her skirts. He and the cardinal both gasped in horror at what they saw.

She blinked, staring at the knife with dazed bewilderment. From the tip to the hilt, the blade was covered in dirt and fragments of leaves that clung to sticky patches of red-brown blood. But it was the handle, not the blade, that riveted her attention. Fashioned of smooth steel, it was etched with a simple geometric design, and bore no resemblance to the dagger she'd found on the pathway seconds before she was attacked.

This was a different knife! Cordelia forced her aching brain to absorb the information. So which dagger had been the murder weapon? Or had neither of them been the murder weapon? And what had happened to the knife that she'd originally found?

"*Signorina,* take care that you do not cut yourself," Father Roberto said as she reached for the knife. "Perhaps you had better let me take care of this. The blade looks extremely sharp."

Her head still ached ferociously, and she found it difficult to hold on to a coherent train of thought, but she was sufficiently in possession of her faculties to keep quiet about the other knife she'd found by the gate. Concussion or not, it was easy to deduce that she would be a lot safer if the cardinal believed she had no memory of the events surrounding Giancarlo's murder.

"I suppose you didn't see who it was who attacked you?" the cardinal asked in a macabre coincidence with her thoughts.

Cordelia wanted to give the appearance of cooperating, so she gave a tremulous smile that she hoped appeared simultaneously brave and pathetic. "Not really," she mumbled. "Everything is such a muddle. I remember coming into the garden ... I heard a noise ..."

"Yes?" the cardinal prompted with sickly kindness. "What happened next, my dear?"

"I don't remember," she said, letting her voice shake with regret. "Everything is a blank until I woke up next to Giancarlo."

"At least we now know the name of this poor man," the cardinal said, gesturing to the body. "Giancarlo, isn't that what you called him, *signorina*? Surely somebody in the servants' hall will know him and his family."

She hadn't meant to let Giancarlo's name slip out but it was so hard to concentrate. She realized that her teeth were chattering, whether from cold or nervous reaction, she wasn't sure. The cardinal finally seemed to notice her discomfort.

"Dear me, I cannot imagine where my wits have been hiding. We need to get you back to the house at once, before you take an inflammation of the lungs. Father, do you think that between us we could manage to carry her back to the villa?"

"She is very slender," the priest said doubtfully. "And the villa is not too far distant."

"Then you think we could manage without summoning any serving lads to our aid?"

Father Roberto fingered the beads of his rosary. "If I may be forgiven the intimate physical contact with a member of the opposite sex, I believe I could support her around the waist. You could take the other side." He sounded overwhelmed by the daring of his own offer.

"You are hereby given absolution for the sin of holding a woman in your arms," the cardinal said without a moment's hesitation. His eyes twinkled with suppressed mirth, giving Cordelia the impression that he found his secretary's religious fervor somewhat exaggerated. He turned back to her, his smile creasing his plump cheeks and giving him the appearance of a good-natured cherub. He patted her hand encouragingly.

"Now, my dear *signorina*, if you will permit us to put our arms around your person, we shall raise you to your feet."

The cardinal, for all his advanced years, moved with surprising agility, and soon had his arm tucked beneath Cordelia's shoulders. Father Roberto, by contrast, seemed so determined to avoid grazing the side of her breast, or risking any glimpse of her ankles and petticoats, that he could hardly bear to look at her, and so was not much help in assisting her to her feet. The poor man would probably feel obligated to spend the next week praying for absolution for the sins of his flesh, Cordelia thought with wry amusement.

She discovered that walking was far more difficult than she'd expected, since the blows to her head induced strong feelings of nausea unless she remembered to hold her head absolutely still. Given her general state of wooziness, plotting to trick the cardinal wasn't easy. Happily, Father Roberto's inhibitions gave her the chance she needed. When they were almost at the garden gate, she swayed against him, making sure that the side of her breast thrust hard against his chest.

As she'd anticipated, he abruptly withdrew his supporting arm, and she was able to stage a convincing stumble. She collapsed onto the pathway, right by the gate. And right in the area where she'd dropped the gold-handled dagger.

"*Signorina,* I am so sorry! What inadequate rescuers we are to be sure." The cardinal knelt beside her, profuse in his apologies.

By good fortune, Father Roberto added plausibility to her ruse. He muttered a stiff apology and even in the darkness, she could see that his cheeks were flushed bright red with embarrassment. Instead of immediately bending to help her, he stared into the distance, his Adam's apple bobbing, while she pretended to rearrange her crinoline—and actually searched feverishly for the dagger.

When he finally recovered his courage and turned around again, she had managed to satisfy herself that there was no longer any gilt-handled dagger lying within ten feet of the garden gate. It seemed certain that whoever had attacked her—the cardinal?—had also hidden the knife, which was distinctive enough to be easily identified. Presumably he had planted the other dagger so that no search would be made for the real murder weapon.

Puffing and panting, the bedraggled trio finally arrived at the entrance to the villa. "Anna!" the cardinal called the moment he was inside. "Anna! Where are you?" He banged on the door that separated the servants' quarters from the rest of the house. "Anna, we need you urgently!"

Tying her apron, the housekeeper came at a run. She curtsied to the cardinal with more respect than she had shown to any of the count's other visitors. "Monsignor, how can I be—Holy Mother of God!"

"I shall consider that a prayer rather than an example of blasphemy," the cardinal said dryly. "As you can see, Anna, the English *signorina* is in need of your help. And I am in urgent need of a word with your master."

"My master is in his study," Anna said, tugging at a rope that set bells jangling loudly in the servants' quarters. "What in the world has happened to the *signorina*? Did she fall?"

Father Roberto cleared his throat. "Not exactly," he said. "We believe that she has been the victim of a dastardly attack."

"An attack?" Anna said. "You mean someone deliberately tried to hurt her?"

"Yes, we found her in the Garden of the Three Fountains, covered in blood."

"Covered in blood?" Anna repeated. Her gaze sharpened with dread and she crossed quickly to Cordelia's side. "Where are you hurt, *signorina*? It is not ... your throat?"

"No," Cordelia said, and wondered why Anna seemed so relieved by that denial. The possibility that Cordelia had been wounded in the throat seemed to have sent her to the verge of panic.

"We believe she was hit over the head by someone who attacked her from behind," Father Roberto explained. "But, alas, that is not the full extent of our bad news. A peasant has been murdered, stabbed through the heart. I believe his name is Giancarlo."

"Do you mean that Giancarlo is dead?" Anna paled. "Why? How is that possible?"

"I am sorry, Anna." The cardinal placed his hands on her shoulders, offering comfort. "The wound was mortal, but we have no idea who killed him, or why."

Anna's face, never very expressive, took on a look of stony impassivity. "I see."

Oddly enough, as far as Cordelia could tell, Anna felt grief and worry at the news that Giancarlo had been stabbed, but none of the panic that had been engendered by the possibility of Cordelia suffering from a wound to the throat. Why was that? she wondered. Not that Anna's behavior had ever made a lick of sense, so there was no reason to expect a change now.

A cluster of sleepy-eyed serving lads emerged from the kitchens in response to Anna's summons, and the cardinal took his leave of Cordelia. "*Signorina*, I trust that Anna's herbal remedies and a good night's sleep will go some way to restoring your vitality. God bless and keep you, my child. I shall look forward to speaking with you again when you are fully recovered."

Father Roberto volunteered to take the serving lads out to the garden and supervise the removal of Giancarlo's body to the stables. Cordelia's head was pounding with such ferocious intensity that she was relieved when Anna accepted his offer without demur. With Anna's assistance, she dragged herself up the stairs and collapsed onto her bed.

"You cannot lie there in your wet clothes." Anna's rough voice was oddly comforting in contrast to the cardinal's unctuous insincerity. "Come, *signorina,* allow me to assist you into your nightgown. You are in no state to be fending for yourself. First, let me take out the few pins that remain in your hair, so that I can brush it with a nice soft brush. Don't worry, I won't touch the sore places, except, perhaps, to clean the cuts with a little witch hazel."

Anna might have a dour face and a gruff voice, but she had the hands of an angel. Cordelia only realized just how wet, cold, dirty, and uncomfortable she had felt when Anna had finished helping her to wash and change into a nightgown that had been warmed in front of the fire.

"There now, *signorina.*" Anna fluffed the pillows behind Cordelia's head. "I shall brew you a pot of herbal tea, and bring it straight up to you, along with a glass of my special cordial. You will scarce know yourself when you wake up in the morning, you will feel so much better."

"You are being very kind, Anna."

The housekeeper seemed reluctant to meet Cordelia's eyes. "I hope we neither of us live to regret my kindness," she said.

Cordelia's head hurt too much for her to expend

energy interpreting cryptic comments. She closed her eyes, and was already drifting off to sleep when she heard Anna leave the room. First thing tomorrow morning, she would have to tell Dakon what Giancarlo had said. He needed to be warned that the cardinal couldn't be trusted. She wished she could summon him to her, but every time she tried to reach out in a mental probe, she encountered nothing save a high, smooth wall. Moreover, the attempt to make mental contact with him left her feeling drained and exhausted.

She didn't know how long she'd been sleeping when the door banged open with a resounding crash. She pushed away the mists of sleep, and sat up slowly in the bed.

Dakon stormed across the room, his white shirt a beacon in the surrounding darkness. He ripped the covers off the bed and stared down at her, his rage almost palpable.

"I trusted you," he said, his voice husky with anguish. "I trusted you with Giancarlo's life. And you killed him. God damn you to hell, you killed him."

Chapter Ten

(

Dakon's rage was all the greater for being largely self-directed. He had spent most of the day castigating himself for allowing the pleasures of mental intimacy with Cordelia to overcome the duty that he owed to his fellow revolutionaries. He had fought in other wars of liberation during the past century, and he was well aware of the dangers a beautiful and intelligent woman could represent. He had recruited such women to seduce secrets from enemy leaders, but he had never expected to fall victim himself. Arrogant in the security of his superior Vam-pyr powers, he had considered himself invulnerable to feminine lures. Even at the time of his cresting, women represented no threat to him—except the moral threat that his self-control would break and they would be killed.

Ironically, it was Captain Hesse who had forced him to consider what a potent weapon a woman would be if she tempted him not with the usual tricks of human sexuality, but by offering him the balm of understanding, and the forbidden excitement of mental communion.

Was Cordelia Hope such a woman? Was that why she'd been sent to the villa? And if so, who had sent her? The Austrians or some other interested party? The French, maybe? Dakon found his mind spinning as he cataloged the various possible combinations of treachery and betrayal.

His probes of her mind had found no hint of conspiracy or deception, but Dakon had lost confidence in his ability to detect treachery in Cordelia Hope. He wanted—quite desperately—to believe that she was exactly what she seemed on the surface: a traveler trapped by circumstances, who happened to have an uncanny gift for linking with the Vam-pyr mind.

But the more he wanted, the more he feared. All day, his emotions had teetered between longing for her company and doubts about his ability to resist her if she was too near. At dinner with the cardinal, he had scarcely been able to concentrate on the table talk because he had been feasting his eyes on Cordelia like a lovesick schoolboy. He was a hundred years too old to be suffering the absurd pangs of first love, he reflected ruefully. By using Vam-pyr techniques developed over centuries, Dakon had acquired a sensitivity—extraordinary by human standards—to the moods and emotions of the people with whom he came in contact. From a personal point of view, this empathy was a pallid substitute for the warmth and intimacy of a genuine mind link, but from the point of view of his work as a leader of the Italian Nationalists, his skill at judging the honesty and integrity of his fellow conspirators had been invaluable. Traitors didn't survive long in Dakon's organization.

His comforting sense of being in charge of his life had vanished the night Cordelia arrived at the villa. Since then, his desire to join with her had grown to the point that it was dangerously out of control. Worried that she might become privy to any number of menacing secrets, Dakon had thrown up the strongest possible mind barriers against her.

The cost of erecting such potent mental screens had been high. True, Cordelia could no longer probe his mind, but Dakon was hair-trigger tense from the strain of keeping his protection in place. Worse still, the barriers he had erected were so thick that they were impenetrable in both directions: Cordelia could no longer tempt him with visions of intimacy, but when she was out of sight, he no longer knew where she was or what she was doing, a deprivation that left him feeling oddly bereft.

Worst of all, he could no longer sense the mood of people around him. Fear, honesty, happiness, grief, pride, rage, were no longer precise and readily identifiable emotions. He had spent the day moving uneasily through a world that had turned gray and formless.

To a human, escape from the onslaught of other people's emotions might seem a blessing. To Dakon, shutting down his empathetic abilities was like cutting off any of his other senses. He felt like a man, newly blind, trying to grope his way through the sudden and unwelcome darkness.

His frustration was intensified because some unregenerate part of him kept whispering that his sacrifice was in vain, that he didn't need to deprive himself of the bliss of intimacy with Cordelia. Wasn't it stretching the limits of credibility to believe that a mere human female could have the ability not only to probe into his mind, but actually to deceive him with her thoughts? Surely no human could ever have developed such incredible skills.

On the verge of convincing himself that he could

risk relaxing the barriers against Cordelia, Dakon had been shattered when the cardinal came to him, bringing news of Giancarlo's death, and showing him the bloody dagger Father Roberto had discovered hidden beneath Cordelia's crinoline.

Dakon had managed—just barely—to maintain his composure while the cardinal was with him. As soon as he was alone, his rage exploded.

He had stormed upstairs to Cordelia's bedroom, encountering Anna en route. For the first time in his life, he had deceived Anna, and the guilt of that knowledge fueled the firestorm of his anger. He had used his power to mesmerize, implanting a false set of memories and imposing a distorted sense of the passage of time. Anna went back to the kitchens convinced that she had given Cordelia a glass of cordial, and that Cordelia was now sleeping peacefully. Such was his power to hypnotize that unless Dakon chose to enlighten her, Anna would never know she had been tricked.

Fighting back a fresh surge of rage, Dakon drew in a hard, shuddering breath and stared down at the woman who had caused him to break almost every rule he had developed in order to cope with a life lived among aliens. For a split second, his anger—or was it grief?—blotted out everything else, and he allowed his protective mental barrier to slip.

Instantly, Cordelia detected his weakness. She reached out to him, flooding his mind with the soft, sleepy warmth of her pleasure at seeing him. He snarled his rage and her pleasure was immediately overlaid with surprise. And fear.

He seized on the fear, fortifying himself with it long enough to slam his mental barriers back into place. As soon as he was in control again, he flung the knife onto the bed. It landed on her knees, a sordid, dirty weapon staining the pristine whiteness of her nightgown.

"I return to you your property, madam," he growled.

"My property?" Her face paled, and she touched the knife gingerly. "This isn't mine," she said. "I don't know where it came from."

He felt the flick of her touch against his mind, and he turned away so that he wouldn't be weakened by watching her as he struggled to pull his protection more securely about him. After a moment or two of silence, she spoke to him out loud, her voice threaded with melancholy.

"Dakon, how can you possibly believe that I killed Giancarlo? You know that I would not . . . could not deliberately take the life of a fellow human being, especially one who fought for ideals I share."

Dakon resisted the perilous urge to turn around. With Cordelia this close, his barriers were proving at best a frail protection. "I will tell you what I know, madam. I know that Cardinal Walter heard the sounds of a struggle in the Garden of the Three Fountains. I know that he hurried into the garden and found you collapsed beside the dead body of poor Giancarlo, with blood still wet on your hands. Most damning of all, I know that I revealed to you only last night that Giancarlo was a member of the Italian resistance, and for this I believe I will never forgive myself."

He heard the swift intake of her breath. "You believe that I killed Giancarlo because I discovered that he is working with the Italian Nationalists? How can you even consider such nonsense? Why would I want to kill him for such a reason?"

"I will turn your question back to you. What other

cause is there for his murder at this precise time and
in this precise place?" Dakon shook his head. "I don't
know how I can have been so crass as to stake his life
on my whim, on my foolish decision to trust you."

"Far from trusting me, I would say that you seem
very quick to condemn me. Did the cardinal also tell
you that I was unconscious when he found me? That
I had been struck from behind and was myself as
much a victim as Giancarlo?"

"He mentioned something of the sort," Dakon admitted. "There is, however, one great difference between your fate and that of Giancarlo's. You have
lived to tell the tale, with no more than a headache
as a reminder. He is dead."

He heard her fling back the covers and get out of
bed. She came and stood behind him. Even though he
was determined not to give her access to his thoughts
by reaching out to probe her mind, he could sense her
hesitation and knew that she was debating whether or
not to touch him.

He quickly moved to the window and stared out
into the gardens. The moon provided the perfect
amount of light for his sensitive retina, but for once
the beauty of the landscape brought him no peace. He
dared not risk turning around. If he turned, he would
touch her. And then—and then he was afraid even to
imagine what might happen.

"Dakon, I swear to you that I didn't kill Giancarlo.
Surely you can see that it's absurd for you to accuse
me of such a crime?"

"How is it absurd, madam?" God, it was sheer torture to be so close to her and yet to keep his mind
stubbornly closed. It occurred to him that he could
simply walk out of the room. He dismissed the thought
almost as it formed. The torment of being close to

Cordelia was infinitely less painful than the torment of being apart.

"I am a woman of average height and build," she said quietly. "Giancarlo was a man who earned his living by hard manual labor. Even if I was determined to murder him, how could I achieve such an impossible goal? He would have knocked the knife from my hand before I could begin to attack him." Her voice shook. "Or do you think he stood still and politely unbuckled his cloak while I slashed ... while I buried my dagger in his heart."

"Naturally I do not imagine that you slaughtered Giancarlo unaided," Dakon said coldly. "Clearly, you had an accomplice."

"Then who is my accomplice and why didn't he help me when I was attacked? We are an odd pair of villains if he kills Giancarlo, then stands by without fighting when I am hit over the head and left for dead."

He shrugged. "There is no puzzle in such a scenario, madam. Spies and traitors fall out among themselves with tedious frequency. For whatever reason, once Giancarlo was dead, your accomplice had no interest in protecting you from harm. As likely as not, he is the person who hit you over the head."

"So now I am condemned as a spy and a fool as well as a murderer?" Her tiny gasp of laughter turned into a sob. "You insult me with your wild imaginings, Dakon. Whatever else, you might at least believe me possessed of sufficient intelligence not to ally myself with someone who is ready to betray me at the first opportunity."

Her voice broke when she said his name: the name that no other human female had ever used, not even Anna. Dammit, he would not turn around. He would not look to see if she was crying. He absolutely would not allow himself to touch her.

Dakon turned around. Cordelia was crying, although she was trying not to. He reached out, noticing with abstract interest that his hand was shaking. The Vam-pyr constitution was not normally prone to shaky hands, but Cordelia seemed to overset a great many rules in regard to the functioning of the Vam-pyr physiology. Dakon wiped the tears from her cheeks and somehow managed not to wind his fingers in the tangled riot of her sherry brown hair.

Her face—so unlike the unexpressive features of a Vam-pyr—displayed a slipstream of different emotions. His heart lurched as he gazed at her, but by some miracle of self-discipline he was able to keep his mental barriers in place.

He reminded himself that this was the woman who in all probability had killed Giancarlo Bianchi, a woman who had been sent to spy on him and ferret out his secrets. He took two careful steps backward, reflecting wryly that a few feet of space was scarcely adequate to protect him from the consequences of his own folly.

The high, ruffled neckline of her nightgown was ruched with pale pink ribbon and closed in a loose bow. The ruffle framed her oval face and allowed a mere inch of her neck to show. With an effort that broke sweat on his forehead, Dakon resisted the temptation to untie the ribbons and expose her throat to his longing gaze. She looked up at him gravely, her gray eyes brilliant with the sheen of her tears. "Giancarlo was already dying when I arrived in the Garden of the Three Fountains," she said. "I wish you would believe me, Dakon."

Giancarlo had been dying, not dead? In normal circumstances, it would be so easy to test the truth of her claim, but he didn't dare to relax his guard even for such a swift, straightforward mind probe. "I suppose you saw no sign of his murderer?" he asked.

She shook her head. "I didn't see anyone, or hear anything, either. I think the killer must have attacked Giancarlo a minute or two before I arrived in the garden."

"So you have no light to shed on the manner in which he met his death?" Dakon said with heavy sarcasm. "I wonder why I am not surprised?"

"I did not say that I have no light to shed on Giancarlo's murder. I said only that I had heard and seen no sign of a struggle. But Giancarlo managed to say a few words to me before he died."

Dammit, was she lying? Dakon had never realized how devastatingly helpless he would feel when he couldn't gauge the honesty of the people he conversed with. "What did Giancarlo say?" he asked, his voice devoid of expression. No need to let her see how clumsy—how truncated—he felt with his mental barriers stubbornly in place.

"I'm not sure it would be wise to tell you," she said. "In your current mood, I find it most unlikely that you would believe me. In fact, you are more likely to take anything I tell you and twist it into another piece of evidence against me."

"Nothing you say could make me trust you less," he said curtly. "You stand only to gain by giving me cause to believe that there is any explanation for tonight's events other than the obvious one that you and one of your accomplices killed Giancarlo."

She looked at him, debating inwardly whether or not to speak. At least, that's what he thought she was doing. He'd always been so skilled at *feeling* human emotion that he'd never learned to read all the subtle signs of body language and facial expression that enabled humans to interpret each other's moods.

"I am waiting, madam," he said gruffly. "I would be interested to hear your account of my friend's dying moments."

"Very well, then. By the time I found him, Giancarlo barely had the strength to speak more than a few words," she said finally. "He warned me that you were in danger."

"It is a pity that he wasted his dying breath in stating something so obvious," Dakon said..

She flinched at his sarcasm. "I had not realized that you could be so cruel in your judgments."

"You would be wise to remember that there are many things about me that you do not know," he said with deliberate coldness.

"Yes, I'm beginning to realize that." She bit her lip, steadying a quiver, then looked up, meeting his gaze with a touch of defiance. "I don't know why I'm bothering to tell you this, except that I don't want Giancarlo to have died in vain. He seemed to feel that you're worth saving, even if I'm not sure he's right."

"Your point, madam?"

"Giancarlo couldn't manage to speak a complete sentence, but his dying words to me were '... *Must not trust ... Monsignor ...*' "

Monsignor. The correct form of address for a cardinal. Dakon was on friendly terms with only one such person. He didn't believe for a single instant that Giancarlo had wasted his dying breath uttering a warning against Cardinal Walter, and Cordelia's lie infuriated him.

"You dare to accuse Cardinal Walter of complicity

in the murder of Giancarlo? A man whose entire life is a story of unsurpassed goodness?"

"I make no accusations," she said tersely. "I'm just telling you what Giancarlo said in the last seconds before his death."

Rage overcame the tattered remnants of his self-control and he seized her arms, prepared to shake the truth out of her. "You besmirch Giancarlo's memory with your lies! I have known the cardinal for more than a decade. He is a man whose superb intellectual gifts are exceeded only by his kindness and his tolerant spirit."

If he hadn't been blinded by the tempest of his own emotions, he would have remembered that grabbing Cordelia Hope was the very last thing he should do. But he was well past the point of rational planning, had been past it almost from the moment he entered her room. He dragged her roughly toward him—and was immediately lost.

The barriers he'd so painstakingly erected crumbled into instant dust. His mind flooded with the tumbling, chaotic rush of Cordelia's feelings. His pores soaked up the turmoil of her emotions: the hurt, the confusion, the growing spark of anger, and beneath everything else, the hot, throbbing pulse of her desire for him.

He knew that he should break the physical contact and rebuild his safety barriers before disaster overtook him. He knew that the last thing on earth he should do was draw her closer. He stared deep into her eyes, feeling the pulse of her desire grow stronger. The spark of her anger flickered and died.

"Dakon?" she whispered.

"Cordelia." Her name slipped off his tongue. He had been longing all night to say it, and the sound was achingly sweet. Cursing himself as every sort of fool, Dakon bent his head slowly toward the enticing softness of her parted lips.

His mouth closed over hers. He felt the shimmer of her response, and then the soft yielding of her body within his arms. When he rested his hands in the small of her back and pulled her against the throbbing hardness of his erection, *her* pleasure inundated his mind.

He had never realized that kissing was such a delightful experience, Dakon thought. How strange that the press of one person's mouth against another person's mouth could send shivers shooting through your entire body.

Belatedly, he realized that the thought hadn't been his, but Cordelia's. God in heaven, he was losing the power to distinguish between his feelings and hers, between his experienced lust and her naive passion! The close interweaving of their thoughts set off a faint, distant alarm. This couldn't be safe for either of them. This wasn't the sort of casual sex in which he indulged from time to time in the wake of his cresting. This was something altogether more powerful, more dangerous.

In a minute, he assured himself, in a second or two, he would end their kiss.

"Don't stop," Cordelia murmured. "I don't want you to stop kissing me." She reached up, clasping her hands behind his head, pulling him closer.

With barely a token struggle, Dakon gave up his futile attempts to resist. He sank into the warmth of her embrace, relishing the hot course of her desire racing through his veins. Her need for him was intense, but entirely untutored. She wanted consummation, but she had no idea what that consummation involved.

Her naïveté provoked an odd gentleness within him,

and he carried her to the bed, telling himself that he had allowed himself to blow this encounter entirely out of proportion. Sex with a human female was just sex, nothing more. The fever of his spring cresting had broken only the day before. Cordelia would be safe. He could easily control himself.

Smiling inwardly at the pleasure ahead of them, Dakon laid her against the pillows. She gasped in disbelief as his mind sent her images of what he planned to do over the next several minutes. He laughed at her wide-eyed astonishment, his anger banished by tenderness. In the passionate inimacy of their mind link, it was impossible to believe that she could have killed Giancarlo, ludicrous to imagine that she could ever betray him.

He ran his hands over her breasts, cupping their fullness, and flicking his tongue over the thrusting points of her nipples. For a split second, her passion was dampened by fear at the strangeness of the sensations she was experiencing, but her arousal had progressed so far and so fast that the fear soon became no more than an excited subnote of expectation. Her jumble of emotions coalesced into an ardent longing for what humans considered the ultimate consummation.

She trusted him, Dakon realized with a quiver of shock. Despite everything that had passed between them, she trusted him not to hurt her.

In the same instant that he sensed her trust, he discovered that his fangs were pressing hard against the flesh of his upper jaw, waiting to break through the tiny openings in front of his eye teeth. Mating fluid was already seeping from the sacs that were normally no more than tiny protuberances guarding his fangs.

The thin, faintly sweet fluid trickled into his throat, intensifying his desire with each passing moment.

It was against every known tenet of Vam-pyr physiology for mating sacs to be fully regenerated in less than two months from the culmination of a cresting, and Dakon's own experience suggested that his sacs and fangs took almost a full four months to grow back. Incredible as it might seem, Cordelia's presence must have triggered a rapid acceleration in the natural mating cycle of his body.

Regretfully, Dakon realized that he was not going to be able to enjoy a session of what human beings considered normal sexual intercourse with Cordelia.

The pressure of his fangs and the burgeoning of his mating sacs warned him in no uncertain terms that the path he was taking was one of utter, unredeemed folly. The realization that he must draw back came a split second too late; the mating fluid exuding from his sacs changed the nature of his desire. He no longer felt a warm, lighthearted anticipation of initiating Cordelia into the pleasures of human sexual intercourse. Instead, his Vam-pyr instincts had taken command.

He no longer wanted to toy with her breasts, or persuade her to open her thighs to his teasing fingers. He craved her very essence. He craved her blood. The image of her slender throat impressed itself on his inner eye, making him shudder with longing.

Through the haze of his passion, he felt a change in Cordelia's response, as her desire became tinged with naive curiosity—and the driving urgency of his own need. For some strange reason, she showed no sign of being repulsed by the images she gleaned from his mind. Shyly, she reached up, pushing her hair out of the way, spreading it over the pillow.

Dear God in heaven, she had sensed his desire and

was deliberately baring her throat to him! *Thank you, my love, thank you!*

Dakon fell forward, burying his face in the voluptuous smoothness of Cordelia's neck. With his tongue, he marked out the path of her jugular vein. His eyes were closed, but in his mind's eye he saw the pulse of her blood, flowing blue and thick through the vein, lapping onto his tongue. The glorious picture was only precoital imagination, not reality, but his sacs swelled almost to bursting point—a culmination which in recent years had taken him five agonizing days to achieve and tonight had happened within minutes.

His fangs distended at an incredible rate, growing within his sacs in tandem with his erection. Any second now, his fangs would be sharp enough and long enough to burst through their protective covering and rip into Cordelia's throat, tearing aside the delicate layer of flesh and sinking into her jugular vein at precisely the same moment that the mating fluid gushed forth at full power. A few seconds later, he would thrust into her body and flood her with his seed. Their son would be born eleven months from now, and Dakon would love him with all the pent-up accumulation of a century of yearning.

Dakon, you're frightening me.

For a fraction of a second, the pulsing throb of scarlet ecstasy ceased and his mind cleared. He stared down at the woman lying beneath him and saw not a nameless source of blood, or even a receptacle to be filled with his seed, but Cordelia, a woman unlike any other human being he'd ever known.

She gazed up at him, her huge gray eyes misty, her skin flushed with desire. Her heart was pounding so fast that it almost beat in unison with his Vam-pyr rhythm. Because he was linked to her so closely, he knew the fast beat was caused only partly by fear. Despite everything, she still desired him.

She had no sense of self-preservation, Dakon thought dazedly. Most human females felt a fatal attraction to the males of the Vam-pyr race, but their attraction invariably changed to fear right around the moment that their Vam-pyr lover started to experience overwhelming desire.

What was he going to do? Deprived of the blood they needed, the throbbing of his fangs changed to an excruciating ache. Dakon's mind clouded. Cordelia's reaction to him had always been different from other females, he thought numbly, and since she seemed willing to accept him, why should he resist? She wasn't frightened by his lust. Well, she might be a little frightened, but she wasn't truly terrified. Perhaps he had finally found the woman who was capable of surviving a mating and giving him the Vam-pyr heir he longed for. The temptation to tilt at the windmills of fate was overwhelming.

The urge to mate with her was so strong that he actually nuzzled against her neck, seeking the perfect place to sink his fangs. At the very last moment, an infinite fraction of a second before he cut into her flesh, he realized exactly what he was doing. The tiny part of his brain that still functioned on the level of reason rather than instinct reminded him that to mate with Cordelia was to kill her.

With an agonized cry, he pulled himself away from her, tossing the sheet over her throat, hiding temptation. He staggered from the bed and dragged himself over to the window, pressing his cheeks against the panes of glass and praying for the throbbing, burning heat of his sacs to cool.

His body was still in a state of full arousal, and

images of Cordelia flooded his mind. He saw her throat, bared for his possession, and her thighs parted to receive his seed. Another cry of agony tore from his parched, laboring lungs. For a few welcome moments, he lost consciousness.

When he regained his senses, desire returned at full flood. A Vam-pyr in the throes of a cresting couldn't kill his desire by any trick as simple as passing out. Dakon tried to generate the mental barricades that would shield his mind and protect Cordelia from sharing in the bleak reality of his carnal appetites. With a shudder of despair, he realized that he had neither the physical strength nor the mental stamina to erect the mental walls that would keep his lust private—and Cordelia safe.

He leaned against the windows, shivering as the fever of his cresting mounted. Perhaps it was just as well that he could not screen his thoughts, he reflected. Once Cordelia saw the bloody reality of his lust, she would run screaming from the room, and from his life. Perhaps, for both their sakes, he needed to make sure that she saw exactly what he wanted to do to her.

Dragging himself into a more or less upright position, Dakon slowly lifted his head. His gaze met Cordelia's. With despairing bravado, he flung the barriers to his mind wide open, and invited her to walk in.

Despite everything, he experienced the now-familiar jolt of pleasure as their thoughts touched and then interlocked. The ache of his fangs changed once again to a throb of excited anticipation. He felt Cordelia's response, and conquered the danger by projecting an image guaranteed to repel her.

This is what I want to do to you, he told her, throwing his voice into her mind with a silent snarl.

Before she could reply, Dakon showed her an image of herself lying naked on the bed, trapped beneath his body, her arms lashed high over her head, and her throat exposed to his ravenous need. He demonstrated—explicitly and completely—how he would use the unique skills of his Vam-pyr heritage to caress her into a state of mindless, quivering arousal. As soon as he was satisfied that she was too full of human sexual desire to resist him, he would put his hand under her chin and tip her head back against the pillows, massaging her jugular vein with delicate, tender strokes.

At the mere thought of stroking Cordelia's throat, a rush of mating fluid dripped down his fangs. He incorporated that reality into the fantasy he was projecting to her. He showed her an image of the fluid dropping onto her neck, causing the veins beneath the surface to swell, bulging until the delicate white skin of her throat was stretched taut. Dakon shivered with ecstasy. Slowly savoring each blissful second, he showed her the image of his fangs sinking deep into her throat. He twisted his head in an instinctive mating toss, and the sharp cutting edge on the side of his fangs ripped her jugular vein wide open. In his fantasy, Cordelia's blood gushed into his mouth, soothing the burning pain at the root of his fangs. His sacs burst. The final surge of his mating fluid poured out, saturating the wounds he had inflicted on her neck. The fluid trickled deep into her jugular vein, mingling his essence with her life's blood. Their mating complete, she smiled up at him, as sated and replete as he was himself.

The perfect erotic fantasy, Dakon thought bitterly. *I mate with Cordelia, but she doesn't die.* With ruthless determination, he cut off the happy ending and showed her the brutal truth of what would really happen if he tried to assuage his needs on her body. From the deep, dark place where he kept such memories hidden, he summoned up images of the women he had murdered. To make sure that she could not fail to understand his message, he showed her poor little Maria's limp and lifeless body. He sent one last terrible picture of his useless attempts to revive her after their mating. Then he sank down into a chair and waited for her to leave him.

He should have known that Cordelia would never do what he expected. She crossed the room and stood in front of him, her shoulders squared and her head held high, although even in his feverish state he had no trouble at all in detecting her inward tremble.

"Dakon," she murmured. "For God's sake, speak to me. What did all that mean? What manner of man are you?"

He found that he had lost the strength, or even the desire, to lie. He turned to look at her, the cool neutrality of his expression masking the ravaged state of his heart. He spoke the words that he had never thought a human would hear.

"I am not a man, Cordelia. I am a Vam-pyr."

Chapter Eleven

☾

Cordelia shivered, although she wasn't cold. Dak'on seemed to be in such pain that she longed to touch him, and yet she dared not. For the first time in their relationship, she was deeply afraid of him.

"What do you mean, you're a vahmpeer?" she asked, her voice breaking on the unfamiliar word. "Is that your true nationality? If so, I have never heard of your country before."

Dakon laughed without a trace of mirth. "That is not surprising," he said. "My country lies several lifetimes distant from here."

His answers made no sense. To put it more bluntly, his answers were crazy. Cordelia wondered how many examples of his perversion and madness she would have to witness before she finally accepted that Dakon was not an honorable man, weighted with inexplicable suffering, but a madman with depraved and perverted appetites.

"Distances are not measured in lifetimes," she said at last, stating the obvious. "The most distant inhabited point on earth wouldn't take more than a few months to reach. I don't understand what you're trying to tell me, Dakon.''

He winced when she spoke his name, turning away from her and massaging his cheeks in a gesture that had become poignantly familiar over the past week. When he turned around again, she sensed an undercurrent of defiance in his attitude.

"I do not come from the planet Earth," he said. "My ancestors traveled here from a distant star in the Quadr'un Galaxy."

She gulped. "You believe your ancestors came from another star?"

"Why, yes," he said derisively, although whether that derision was directed at her or at himself she had no idea. "The mosaics you have seen in the Garden of the Three Fountains represent the star system and the planet from which my people came. They sailed in a ship of surpassing strength and speed, designed to cross the vast emptiness of space between the galaxies. But when they arrived on Earth, their starship failed them, and they could never leave. We Vam-pyr descendants have been stranded in your world ever since, attempting to eke out a living among the alien humans we encountered here."

His gaze locked with hers, his eyes gleaming with the self-mockery she had sensed churning within him from the moment of their first meeting. "Do you have any further questions about my country of origin that you would like to address to me, Miss Hope?"

His stance clearly suggested that he expected her to dismiss his story as the demented ramblings of a lunatic. She replied steadily, refusing to play the game according to his rules. "How long have your people been . . . stranded . . . here on Earth?" she asked.

"Four thousand years," Dakon replied curtly. "We have recorded twelve generations of Vam-pyr Earth history."

"In four thousand years your people would have produced far more than twelve generations," Cordelia said gently.

"We live longer than human beings."

"How long exactly?" He sounded so plausible that she kept forgetting he was talking nonsense.

He avoided her gaze. "Four hundred years is not uncommon. The oldest Vam-pyr was recorded to have died at the age of five hundred and thirteen human years. He was my great-grandfather. Some evidence suggests that our lives are becoming shorter as we continue to mate with human females."

"Then why do you mate with humans?" she asked. "Since the process involves such difficulty, why do you not mate with your own kind?"

"Because we cannot," he said flatly. "There are no female Vam-pyr."

"I don't understand—"

"The ship of our ancestors that landed here carried a crew of male Vam-pyr. There were no female Vam-pyr on board. That first generation of my ancestors, the people we call our Founding Fathers, realized that they must mate with human females or they would all die before a rescue vessel could arrive. In the twelve generations of Vam-pyr that have been born since our landing in your world, no female Vam-pyr has ever been born."

"That is quite extraordinary." His story was so bizarre she almost believed it. "There must be some reason that no girls have been born. It surely can't be coincidence?"

"No, it can't be coincidence, but our scientists disagree on the biology—" He broke off abruptly, and strode restlessly across the room, appearing oddly disoriented. "You surely do not believe my absurd stories, Miss Hope? You are a sensible woman. Are my replies not confirming your conviction that you have ventured into the home of a lunatic?"

She avoided a direct answer, because common sense dictated that she dismiss his tale as a preposterous fabrication, but she wasn't quite ready to brand him either a deluded fool or a cunning liar. "My father was a professor of mathematics at Cambridge University," she said. "His hobby was astronomy, and he was particularly interested in attempting to determine whether any of the other planets in our solar system had atmospheres that were capable of supporting life."

Dakon accepted the change of subject, perhaps sensing that it really wasn't a change at all. "Your father must have experienced a great deal of opposition from those scholars who are determined to uphold the view that God created the entire, vast universe solely for the benefit of mankind."

"My father was adept at avoiding controversy. There were, of course, many prejudiced faculty members, most of whom had never gone near a telescope, but he was so polite when conversing with them that they usually didn't notice their strictures were being ignored."

"He sounds an interesting man," Dakon said, his jaw tightening as a spasm convulsed his body. He gritted his teeth, refusing to make acknowledgment of the pain. "You must miss him," he said through clenched teeth.

"More than you can imagine." Cordelia chattered on, wanting to give Dakon a few moments to recover himself from whatever malady ailed him. "Papa was always troubled by the view that we human beings are the pinnacle of God's creative abilities. To be honest, I cannot help agreeing with him. Looking around at the senseless suffering in the world, it seems kinder to believe that we were the Almighty's first effort at creation, and that He got better at the job as time went on."

His spasm had passed, and Dakon actually looked amused. "I trust you never expressed such views to your local vicar. You would no doubt have given the poor man apoplexy."

"One of the valuable lessons my father taught me was that it isn't always necessary to inform the world of your opinions. Papa was wise enough to discuss his views only with good friends who shared his interests. I learned to do the same."

"Then perhaps you can understand why we Vampyr have decided that our lives will be a lot easier if we do not proclaim our existence from the rooftops."

Cordelia shook her head dazedly, not quite sure how she had progressed from a suspicion that Dakon was insane to a conversation about her philosophy of life in the space of less than five minutes. She still didn't really believe that Dakon's ancestors had voyaged through space from another star, but he sounded so belligerent, so sure that she would dismiss his stories as nonsensical, that she found his account of his origins perversely convincing.

"There is far more reason for your people to speak out than there was for my father," she said. "Papa was merely engaged in theoretical speculation, but if your story is true, you are compelled to lead a life of constant dissembling. I don't quite understand the Vahmpeer's need for secrecy. There must be many people who would love to know that human beings aren't the only creatures in the universe capable of rational thought and behavior."

"There are many more who would fear us if the truth were known." His eyes became bleak. "And with good cause. We are creatures to be avoided by you humans."

Cordelia's lungs suddenly seemed too tight to take in air. "Why is that, Dakon?"

He stood up, towering over her, his posture simultaneously pain-racked and menacing. "Cordelia, are you willfully blind? I have shown you the truth of my nature with more clarity than you could possibly need or want. You have seen what I am capable of doing to a human female. Do you still not realize that you are in mortal danger when you are near me? Do you still not realize what manner of being I am?"

Her heart thumped loudly in her ears. "You are a Vahmpeer," she said. "You are a Vahmpeer, a voyager from a distant star."

"Vam-pyr," he corrected her softly, his voice cracking in a strange, guttural click in the middle of the word. "That is what my people call ourselves. Human beings have several other names for us. The most polite of them is *vampire*."

Cordelia went rigid with shock. "Dakon, don't be ridiculous. Vampires are a myth invented by Slav peasants still trapped in the ignorance of the Dark Ages. How can you claim to be something that exists only in the benighted fantasies of illiterate serfs?"

"I claim it because that is what I am."

A dozen jumbled images cascaded through Cordelia's mind, most of them so exaggerated in their horror that they carried no power to frighten. Ghouls rising from their graves to suck the blood from helpless newborn babies. Female vampires enticing lusty but innocent youths to a fate worse than death. Reclusive aristocrats, living in decaying castles, surrounded by bats and cobwebs, and waking only at night in order to roam the countryside, preying on unsuspecting virgins.

As that last image came to her, Cordelia realized that she was ice cold. Dakon didn't live in a castle filled with bats and cobwebs, but he did live in an isolated villa, and his domestic arrangements were bizarre by almost any standard. She vividly remembered his strange comment to Anna when she had first arrived here with Mary and Ellen: *Fortunately, only one of them is a virgin.* At the time, she hadn't understood what he meant. Now, she was afraid to inquire.

"Your face is very expressive," Dakon said. "I gather that you have finally realized that I am not a safe person to know."

"I have always realized that there is danger in knowing you, Dakon."

"But perhaps you understand at last that you would be wise to leave my home before any irreversible harm befalls you."

Despite everything she had learned, her heart contracted with inexplicable sadness at the prospect of leaving the villa, but she didn't deny the truth of his statement. She owed an obligation to Mary and Ellen, and an even more profound one to Mary's unborn baby. The Count of Albion might or might not be a vampire—her practical soul rebelled at the absurdity of accepting such a ludicrous proposition—but if he wasn't a vampire, then he was crazy. In either circumstance, the villa was a perilous place to stay. She was entitled to take chances with her own safety, but not with that of her charges, and especially not with the life of Mary's unborn child.

"I believe you're right," she said quietly. "It would

be wisest for me and my companions to leave the villa, Excellency."

He noticed her return to the formality of his title as she had been sure he would. For a moment she thought that he would protest her use of the honorific. Then he swung away, nodding a curt acquiescence. "Very well, Miss Hope. I will see that you are given money. You need not feel that you are taking charity from a stranger. When I took possession of this villa, it was hopelessly neglected. But I was perfectly well aware that the terms of the entailment prohibited your Stanwyck ancestor from selling me the land, and certainly prohibited me from walking in and refurbishing the villa to suit my own taste. In point of fact, I owe you and your family a great deal of money."

"You didn't tell me that *you* had refurbished the villa. You said that your grandfather had done so."

"Vam-pyr children are taught early how to lie in order to disguise their longevity from their neighbors. Now I find that I am weary of lies, at least between the two of us."

"The locals believe this villa has been occupied by three successive Counts of Albion," Cordelia said. "Captain Hesse even told me that the Garden of the Three Fountains had been designed by your grandfather."

"He spoke the truth as he knew it, but the garden was my creation. If you will reflect for but a moment, you will see that it would not be safe for me to live in the same place, barely appearing to age. Every few years or so, I depart on an extended period of travel. Every fifty years, I announce that I have died abroad, and I return as my son. In fact, I am the sole bearer of the title Count of Albion. I have no son, and no brothers."

He sounded matter-of-fact and more than a little weary. The question escaped before she could consider the wisdom of continuing to play into his fantasies. "How old are you, Dakon?"

The name slipped out before she could recapture it. He gave her a long, considering look before replying. "I am a hundred and thirty-one Earth years old. My father, ZArymp, is almost three hundred and forty years old."

Dakon appeared to be no more than thirty-five. Cordelia found herself in the familiar position of those who ask questions to which they really don't want an answer: she had no idea how to react to the count's claim. If he was weaving insane fantasies, then he was coloring those fantasies with extraordinary detail, including a father with a ludicrous age and an unpronounceable name.

"You do not wish to accept that I am Vam-pyr," he said, smiling with more than a touch of bitterness. "We have discussed this before, haven't we, Miss Hope? It is a disconcerting fact of both human and Vam-pyr life that lies are often much easier to believe than the truth."

"You should take heed of your own lectures, Excellency. If you had remembered that lies often sound convincing when Cardinal Walter came to you claiming that I had murdered Gian—" She broke off, seeing his shoulders shake. "Dakon, what is it? Something is causing you great pain, isn't it?"

"No, nothing is wrong." His voice gave no hint of strain, but Cordelia was suddenly overwhelmed with a wave of such black despair, mingled with such oppressive grief, that she literally staggered under its impact.

With supreme effort, she fought her way out of the

debilitating darkness and saw that Dakon had collapsed on the bed. He was writhing in agony, his breath coming in hoarse gasps that sounded dangerously similar to Giancarlo's death rattle. Cordelia felt no surprise. She had known the second she felt it that both the despair and the pain were actually Dakon's.

She crossed the room and was kneeling beside the bed before she was consciously aware of making a decision to stay and help him. He was lying with his face buried in the pillow so that she couldn't see his face. She reached out to stroke the sweat-dampened tumble of his hair, but stopped herself just in time. She couldn't afford to risk any more of those confusing, compelling visions that swamped her every time she touched him.

"Dakon." She said his name softly, wanting to let him know that she was still there even though she didn't dare touch him. "Please tell me how I can help you."

He refused to look at her. "You . . . must . . . leave."

"I will, soon. But it cannot be necessary for you to endure this repeated torment. There must be some doctor, some medicine, that can help you. Let me send for help."

"There is no help," he said, his words muffled by the pillow. "There is nothing. Leave me."

She had never heard such total and complete despair in anyone's voice. She had never felt such brutal loneliness and isolation. Cordelia realized that she didn't care what the consequences might be. She had to touch Dakon, not only for his sake, but for her own. She was torn apart by the stress of seeing him bear such agony alone.

Hesitantly, all too aware of the danger she risked, Cordelia reached out and touched Dakon lightly on the shoulder. Nothing happened. No exotic vision claimed her. No emotion swamped her.

Emboldened, she ran her fingers through his hair. The tips of her fingers grazed the nape of his neck, and she felt the heat of the fever burning beneath his skin. Despite their continued physical contact, her mind felt nothing save swirling, pain-filled blackness.

The realization that he was unconscious was followed swiftly by the dreadful premonition that she was witnessing his death throes. Why else did she sense nothing but emptiness? Her entire being rebelled at the thought of sitting passively and watching him die.

She threw herself across his body. "Dakon, wake up!"

He didn't stir. He was drenched in sweat, boiling up with fever. She conquered the panic that threatened to paralyze her, and dragged him over onto his back, shivering when she saw the sickly gray hue of his complexion, and the bruised, sunken sockets of his eyes. His cheeks were swollen and strangely misshapen, as if two huge marbles had been placed inside his mouth and then pushed up as far as they would go.

She had seen those swellings before, although never in such an advanced state of growth. Dakon frequently rubbed his cheeks right in that spot, as if seeking to ease some nagging ache. Cordelia pressed her hands lightly against his cheeks, then massaged in a gentle circular motion, hoping to relieve his pain at the same time as she tried to assess the nature of the growth. Perhaps it was some sort of infection that could be lanced?

Dakon moaned. His hand sought hers, guiding her fingers in their massage, encouraging her to increase the pressure. Astonishingly, the massage alone seemed to bring him some relief, although Cordelia could see that the size of the swelling was actually increasing. Despite this, the dreadful grayness of his complexion faded, and his color improved to the creamy pallor that was normal for him.

Suddenly, he opened his eyes, and she saw stark terror in their depths. "Leave me," he ground out. "I implore you to leave me."

"I cannot, not when you are—"

She had no time to say anything more. Dakon grabbed her hand, and carried it to his mouth. With a cry of anguished yearning, he pressed one fevered kiss in her palm before moving his mouth down to her wrist. She felt a quick sharp stab of pain, and she cried out, more from shock than from anything else.

Dakon's head lifted for a fraction of a second. She stared in horrified, appalled fascination at the two small fangs that protruded over his lower lip. They were already stained with blood. Her blood. His eyes met hers, dark and weary with regret.

"I'm sorry, Cordelia," he whispered. "Dear God, I beg your forgiveness."

"You do not need—Dakon! What are you doing?"

He didn't reply. Silently, he dragged her down onto the bed, so that she was lying alongside him. He seized her arm, holding it immobile against the pillows, and nuzzling at the pulse beating in her wrist. Her pulse rate increased exponentially. She felt the tingle of a warm liquid against her skin, almost like alcohol on a cut, followed by the oddest sensation of swelling, as if her veins were puffing up beneath the skin.

"Dakon." She whispered his name, instinctively aware that if she could force him to look at her, she would be able to prevent whatever terrible thing was about to happen. Dakon refused to look up, but her mind filled with a sudden overwhelming sense of shame and humiliation.

Dakon's feelings, she realized. Dakon knew he would die without the infusion of her blood, and yet to take it from her was literally making his flesh creep with revulsion. Cordelia was swept by compassion.

Dakon, there's no need for you to feel this way. I give you my blood willingly.

I will not kill you, he swore to her. *If I take the blood from your wrist, my love, you will survive my assault, and there will be no risk of impregnating you with my son.*

His son. Dakon assumed that he would have a son, not a daughter. *I have no brothers,* he had said. *My father is three hundred and forty years old.* Even when he was almost out of his mind with pain, he persisted in his claim that there were no female Vam-pyr, only human females who were victims of Vam-pyr lust.

She had no time for more thoughts. Scarlet blood gushed from her wrist. Dakon swallowed it in ravenous gulps. She felt a split second of infinite joy. Then silver light exploded inside her mind, obliterating all awareness. She fainted.

When she woke up, morning sun was streaming into the room, and Dakon was gone. Without him beside her, she felt a loss of part of her own soul. She had a terrible fear he would never return. Weakness overcame her and she fell back to sleep, her cheeks wet with tears.

Rain beat a staccato tattoo against the windowpane. The curtains were drawn, but not completely closed, letting in a narrow beam of light that seemed oddly brilliant. Her wrists were bandaged, but there was no pain, only a consuming sensation of lethargy, combined with a heightened sensual awareness that was disorienting in its intensity. Beneath the pit-pat of the rain, she heard the steady rhythm of someone breathing, a sound as loud as the breaking of waves on a beach. Simultaneously, she registered a smell of mingled nutmeg, carbolic soap, and starched linen. Anna, she thought. Anna is in the room.

Slowly, listlessly, she turned her head in the direction of the sounds and smells.

The housekeeper was sitting beside the fire, staring into the empty grate. Her wrinkled face was drawn into lines of ineffable sadness. Cordelia wanted to ask what was wrong, but the effort was too great and she let her eyes drift closed again.

The bed felt lonely without the weight of Dakon's body lying beside her. She wondered where he was and how she could persuade him to come back to her. She reached out with her mind, searching for him. Nothing came back to her save hollow echoes of emptiness. She hadn't realized it was possible to feel so mentally bereft.

With extraordinary effort, she dragged herself upright against the pillows. "Anna," she croaked. "Where is the count? What happened to him?"

The housekeeper came swiftly to her side, carrying a glass of cordial. "*Signorina*, why are you sitting up? You must take care not to overexert yourself. Here, drink this."

Cordelia took the cordial without protest. She knew exactly what it was made of because she could smell each individual ingredient: brown sugar, rose hips, and chamomile, boiled together and stirred into a small dose of cognac. The drink revived her, easing the dryness of her throat.

"Anna, please, you must tell me. Where is the

count?" She waited, stomach twisting into knots, while the housekeeper considered her reply.

"He has been called away," Anna said at last.

"Called away? Where?" She clutched the housekeeper's arm. "Tell me the truth. Anna, is he dead?"

Anna shook her head. "No," she said slowly. "No, he is not dead, *signorina*. In fact, physically speaking, I would say that my master is stronger than he has been in a decade. Thanks to your blood, *signorina,* he has finally received the nourishment he so desperately needed." There was a definite hint of challenge in Anna's expression, as if she recognized that she broached a forbidden topic.

Cordelia controlled a wave of nausea. "It's true, then? The count must drink human blood in order to live?"

"Only at . . . certain times," Anna said. "For years he has tried to make do with the blood of young boys, but there is no substitute for the blood of a female virgin where my master is concerned."

"The blood of men and women is the same—"

"No, *signorina,* it cannot be, and the blood of virgins seems more potent than any other. His people have discovered that they can only produce offspring if their female partners are virgin."

"How do you know so much about him, Anna? Why has he chosen to trust you with secrets that he tells nobody else?"

Anna hesitated so long that it began to seem that she wouldn't answer. But finally she began to speak in a tumbling rush of words, as if she found relief in telling what had been hidden for so long.

"I had a sister once, many years ago," she said. "Maria was the baby of our family, and I was already a widow with two young sons when Maria was taken into service with the lord of our region. The name of her master was the Count of Albion."

Cordelia found she was holding her breath. "Dakon?" she asked.

"Yes, *signorina*. The count had chosen my sister to be the mother of his son, but instead she died." Anna's eyes misted. "She was barely sixteen years old."

"And yet you have chosen to serve the count for years—"

"For twenty-three years, *signorina*." Anna shrugged. "When I first saw the count, he had come to the home of my father, escorting the coffin that held Maria's body. He told us that she had been struck down by a fever and that he wanted to help us by taking another member of the family into his service. When he heard that I was a widow with two young sons, he chose me. I was close to starvation at the time, and it seemed an excellent bargain, even though I had heard rumors that many young women died of mysterious fevers when in the service of the count. I calculated that I might die, but my sons would have a roof over their heads and food in their bellies."

"What happened to your sons?" Cordelia asked, almost afraid of the answer.

"My eldest is an apothecary in Piacenza, and Marco is a cobbler in Milano, very prosperous, with three young boys apprenticed to him. The count has been very generous to us."

"But he killed your sister," Cordelia said.

"Yes, *signorina*, that is true. But for twenty-three years now I have watched him struggle with the forces of his own nature. I know that he endures the torment of the damned in order to insure that he will never again take the life of another woman." Anna's voice thickened with compassion. "I have watched his struggles, *signorina,* and I know that he is a good man. He killed my sister, but not with evil intent. I have decided that it is for God to judge the degree of his sin, not me, or any other busybody."

Involuntarily, Cordelia glanced down at her wrists, then looked back up at the housekeeper. "Why does he take the blood he needs from young boys, instead of from women? If he is afraid of killing the women whose blood he takes, why isn't he afraid that he will also kill the serving lads?"

"He has no desire to mate with boys," Anna said. "So there is no temptation in drawing their blood."

Cordelia shivered. "Couldn't he find a woman who doesn't tempt him?"

"It seems not, *signorina.* When his blood lust is aroused, it is my master's nature to crave total possession of any young female virgin who comes near him. After Maria died, the count acknowledged the limits of his self-control. Since the night that my sister died, he has never permitted himself to be in the company of a female virgin at the time of his need. Never, that is, until you came to the villa."

"You sound angry, Anna, but I had no way of knowing that my presence in the villa would cause him to suffer."

"That is true, but the damage has now been done. He has lost his heart, *signorina,* and for my master there is no way on earth that he can recover it."

After several silent seconds, Cordelia managed to produce a tired smile. "I have lost my heart, too, Anna."

The housekeeper stared ahead, her eyes stony, but when she replied her voice was husky. "Then you have my deepest sympathy, *signorina.* I pray to the Madonna that she may find some way to solve your problem, and that of my master."

"When will the count return?" Cordelia asked. "I would . . . like to see him."

"That would probably not be wise, *signorina*. Your hearts may ache at the separation, but you will be safer if you remain apart." Anna picked up the empty cordial glass and walked quietly back to her chair by the fire. As far as she was concerned, the conversation was at an end.

The sound of someone tapping on her door brought Cordelia awake for the third time. Mary's voice came clearly into the bedroom, peremptory but underlaid with genuine worry. "Anna, I won't take no for an answer. For two days you've been telling me that my cousin is resting. I insist upon being allowed to see her. Oh, what's the use? You don't even speak English, for heaven's sake. I'm coming in."

Mary swept into the bedroom, crinoline swaying as she drew to a startled halt beside the bed. "Dear Lord, Cordelia, whatever has happened to you? You look like death warmed over, you're so pale! Heavens above, why do you have all those bandages on your wrists! Have they been setting leeches on you, or something barbaric like that? I tried to insist upon having Ellen nurse you, but you know what these wretched foreigners are like. None of them would listen to me!"

"Hello, Mary." Cordelia yawned, then realized that two things had happened: her energy level had returned to nearly normal, and she no longer had any heightened power of sensual awareness.

Mary gave a sigh of genuine relief. "Well, at least you can speak, so I suppose that's something." She pulled up a chair and sat down, her brows pulled into a frown. It was a measure of how concerned she felt about the state of Cordelia's health that she didn't remember that frowns caused wrinkles.

"We've been very worried about you," she said. "The count informed us that you'd been struck down by fever and that we should not visit you for at least twenty-four hours."

"Did he?" Cordelia tried not to appear overly interested in this news of Dakon. "Anna told me that the count had been called away on business. Has he returned?"

"No. Apparently he must visit his ancestral estates in Transylvania or some such nonsense. He will be gone for months." Mary shrugged, a gesture of irritation rather than resignation. "It has been very tiresome for the past two days, Cordelia, with the count away and you lying up here practically at death's door. I couldn't stop worrying about what would happen to me if you died and there was nobody left to translate what all these wretched servants are saying. Not a single one of them speaks English, you know. It's a wonder that Ellen and I have managed to survive with you lying up here utterly prostrate."

Cordelia stared at her cousin, aware that her mouth had dropped open. "What do you mean, the count will be gone for months?" She dragged herself up against the pillows. "Mary, are you sure?"

"Don't worry," Mary said. "The count was a perfect gentleman. He explained all about the confusion over the legal ownership of the villa, and insisted that we should remain here as long as we needed. Apparently, Mr. Peasant has been in touch with him, although why my father's man of affairs should consult with the count, I cannot fathom. Mr. Peasant has made available five hundred pounds for our personal use." Mary flicked her curls in satisfaction. "It seems that Papa has decided to relent, after all. I was afraid that we would be ordered to survive on some niggardly allowance, but five hundred pounds is quite amazingly generous. I have given Ellen five pounds, and you shall have twenty." Mary hastily corrected herself. "Well, fifteen pounds, at any rate. You really have no great need of pin money since we are staying here at the villa."

Cordelia felt as though her mind had been taken over by a giant slug that could only move after great and careful deliberation. "The count gave you five hundred pounds?" she said dazedly.

"Golden sovereigns," Mary replied with evident satisfaction. "But the money didn't come from the count, Cordelia, you're not listening to me. Mr. Peasant arranged for the payment, on behalf of my dear Papa."

Cordelia threw back the covers and reached for the robe that someone had placed thoughtfully at the foot of the bed. She tugged on the dressing robe and, ignoring Mary's little shrieks of protest, walked across the room to where Anna was observing them in grim silence. Surprisingly, after two days in bed, she felt quite strong..

"I want the truth, Anna," she said to the housekeeper. "When is the count coming back to the villa?"

"That depends, *signorina*. It depends on how long you stay here."

"You mean ..." She swallowed over the sudden lump in her throat. "You mean that he will not return as long as I remain here?"

"He will not return," Anna agreed. "The Villa of the Three Fountains is his gift to you, *signorina*. He asks me to say that he hopes you will lead a long and happy life here."

Cordelia wasn't sure whether to laugh or to cry. In the end, she realized that she was almost paralyzed with anger. "The Count of Albion is a fool," she said.

Anna nodded. "Yes, *signorina*, the very worst sort. A noble fool. I confess that I see no solution to your dilemma, but I am praying that you will find some way to cure him of his folly."

Chapter Twelve

☾

The count's gardeners had removed all traces of Giancarlo's bloody struggle with death. The marble bench had been scrubbed, the grass raked, and violets were blooming in profusion against the shelter of the stucco wall. Unfortunately, Cordelia saw the coachman's mutilated body almost as clearly as if it still lay there, but she refused to hand the murderer—the cardinal?—an even greater victory than he'd already won. She was determined not to allow the beauty of the garden to be destroyed by the cruel violence of Giancarlo's end. If she could believe anything Dakon had told her, this garden was the result of his personal creative vision, and the incarnation of his most intimate hopes and dreams. Now that he was gone from the villa, she felt closer to him here than anywhere else.

Sitting on the marble bench, Cordelia forced herself to keep her gaze fixed on the sparkling fountains rather than the path where Giancarlo had died. The water danced into the tiled bowls, refracting the sun with almost painful brilliance. Cordelia rubbed her eyes. Ever since that final night with Dakon, she had experienced curious changes in the way the world impressed itself on her senses. She no longer felt the extraordinary heightening of her awareness that had occurred when she first regained consciousness, but each passing hour brought new evidence of a subtle difference in the way her body functioned. She found herself remembering visual details with unexpected clarity, and her energy level—always high—seemed to have increased exponentially. After five hours of sleep last night, she'd woken before dawn feeling completely refreshed. Even more puzzling, the two heavy blows to her head seemed to have caused no lasting damage. The huge, painful swellings had disappeared, and she had suffered none of the headaches she would have expected.

She couldn't begin to explain how two days of bed rest could cure the wounds inflicted by the viciously hard blows of Giancarlo's murderer, unless it was in some way connected to the fluid Dakon had injected into her wrists in exchange for her blood. If Dakon were here, she could ask him, but he was probably hundreds of miles away by now, on his way to Transylvania.

The thought of Dakon made her sigh. She kept trying to convince herself that he had taken the most honorable way out of an impossible situation. Common sense suggested that since they couldn't be near each other without provoking a physical reaction that was dangerous to both of them, one or the other of them needed to leave the villa. For the sake of Mary and the baby, she was grateful that he had left without speaking to her, thus taking the decision out of her hands. From a strictly selfish point of view, however, she wished he'd given her a choice. She would have begged him to stay and be damned to the consequences.

She was worried that Dakon had left so precipitously that he'd never heard the whole truth about what had happened the night of Giancarlo's death. In Cordelia's opinion, the fact that he refused to suspect Cardinal Walter left him acutely vulnerable. It was some consolation to know that he was traveling to the far reaches of Hungary, where the intrigues of the Italian rebels and their Austrian adversaries were unlikely to cause him serious problems. With Dakon gone, silence about Giancarlo's dying words seemed to be her best policy. Given that she was a foreigner, and Cardinal Walter was a much-loved dignitary of the Church, if she suggested that the cardinal was a murderer—an agent of the hated Austrian government—she would likely be lynched by the irate peasantry. Fortunately, with Cardinal Walter safely on his way back to Milano, she felt in no danger of a renewed attack from him.

She walked across to the fountains and studied the tiled mosaics that Dakon claimed were representations of his home world: a planet that circled a star so far distant even her father's telescope couldn't bring it into human sight. Was she crazy to believe Dakon's claim to be something other than human? She couldn't rationalize her acceptance of his claim to be a member of a strange race of beings known as the Vam-pyr—while she casually dismissed every legend and myth she had ever heard about vampires as being irrelevant to her relationship with him. Why was she, the epitome of common sense, suddenly afflicted with such rashness?

It wasn't that she had some sort of absurd death

wish, or even a desire to flirt with danger. It was more that, in her heart of hearts, she couldn't bring herself to accept that loving Dakon could cause her death. And during the past few days, it had become painfully clear that what she felt for Dakon was nothing short of love. A most tiresome emotion, she decided, that seemed to bring with it an aching sense of loneliness rather than the dreamy happiness celebrated by the poets and songwriters.

Drat and botheration, she was going to start crying! Cordelia blew her nose, retied the strings of her bonnet, and took cover beneath the shade of a hazelnut tree. The light was bothering her eyes, even though the sun was intermittently covered by wispy spring clouds.

In the distance, she heard the sound of voices and the patter of approaching footsteps on the gravel path. Not feeling in the mood for company, she was on the point of making good her escape when she realized that the voices belonged to Mary and Ellen, and they were calling her name. Sighing resignedly, she changed direction and opened the garden gate for them.

"Oh, thank goodness we've found you at last." Mary sat down on the nearest bench, fanning herself vigorously. She rarely walked anywhere if she could avoid it, and the short trip from the house had left her breathless. Or perhaps that was simply the effect of her stays, which seemed to have been laced as tightly as ever, Cordelia noticed with disapproval. Mary was over four and a half months pregnant, and only the most knowledgeable observer would be able to detect any sign of her condition. Every time Cordelia visualized the squashed state of her cousin's internal organs, her own ribs and stomach ached in sympathy.

"The most terrible thing has happened!" Mary exclaimed, catching her breath at last. "Cordelia, you must write to Papa and tell him that he must allow us to return home immediately. We are in dire peril!"

Mary's definition of *dire peril* was likely to range from the discovery of a flea in her bedroom carpet to an altercation with one of the servants. "You know that the earl has forbidden us to communicate with him, or any other member of the family," she reminded her cousin. "His secretary opens all family corresp—"

"You don't have to tell me what happens to Papa's mail!" Mary's cheeks suffused with angry color. "But when he sent us away, he didn't know what horrors I would be forced to endure! If he had even an inkling of what we are going through in this benighted country, he would find us a secluded manor house in England where we could stay until—where we could stay for the next few months. He *cannot* have meant to torture me in this fashion."

Cordelia didn't reply, because she was quite sure that the Earl of Stanwyck had intended his errant daughter to suffer as much as possible. His rage on discovering that she was pregnant had been terrible to behold. When he learned that a married man was the father of her child, Cordelia had feared that he might commit murder before he regained control of his temper.

Ellen turned to Cordelia, her hands clasped in supplication. "Please, miss, you must tell his lordship we can't stay here in foreign parts any longer." The elderly maid twisted her pocket handkerchief into a tangled lump. "The armies will march right over us and we shall all be raped and murdered. There's no hope for us, miss, not if we're forced to stay here." Ellen began to cry, quiet tears of despair that were a great deal more troubling than her usual noisy sobs.

Cordelia put her arm around Ellen's shoulders while she searched for a clean handkerchief. "Come now, Ellen, dry your tears. I know it's difficult for you here, with no servants who speak your language, and everything unfamiliar. But remember, we English are famous for being brave under the most difficult circumstances."

"Yes, miss." Ellen dabbed valiantly at her tears. "I do try to be brave, miss, but it's awful hard to rest easy when I keep wondering how long it'll be afore we're all killed in our beds."

"I doubt if there's much risk of that," Cordelia said, wondering if this fear was a belated reaction to Giancarlo's murder. "Why are you and Ellen suddenly so anxious to leave the villa?" she asked Mary. "The murder of our coachman was certainly upsetting, but it doesn't mean that we are in any personal danger, you know." She hurried on, before either of them could point out that she had been hit over the head and left for dead, a somewhat personal danger by anyone's standards. "Yesterday I thought you were pleased with the Count of Albion's offer that we should remain at the villa until the baby is born."

Mary winced at the mention of the forbidden word *baby.* "Yesterday I didn't know the Austrians and the Italians were going to declare war!" she snapped. "I have no desire to find myself giving birth in a battle zone!"

Cordelia's heart missed a beat. "War has been declared?" she asked. "Oh no! When did that happen?"

"I don't know." Mary tossed her curls. "Yesterday. Two days ago. Perhaps longer, but we only just heard the news. King Victor whatever his name is ... You know, the King of Piedmont ..."

"King Victor Emmanuel?"

"Yes, that's the name. Well, Victor Emmanuel's prime minister—"

"Count Camillo Cavour?"

"Yes." Mary sounded impatient with Cordelia's persnickety desire for facts. "Anyway, there's been another uprising in Lombardy, and the Emperor of Austria has issued an ultimatum that Victor Emmanuel is to stop causing trouble in Lombardy and Venetia or he will declare war. And Count Cavour is apparently beside himself with glee that the Emperor could be so foolish as to give him such a perfect excuse to declare war."

"And war has actually been declared?" Cordelia insisted, knowing that the two rivals had sparred and threatened for the best part of twenty years.

"Well, the ultimatum is about to expire, and far from withdrawing their troops, Victor Emmanuel has ordered new troops to the border. What's more, the French emperor has promised to send soldiers to aid the Italians, although what this silly quarrel has to do with Louis Napoleon, I cannot imagine."

"The French want to redraw their boundaries with the Kingdom of Piedmont," Cordelia explained. "I expect Louis Napoleon has promised to assist the Italian rebel forces in exchange for territorial concessions from Piedmont."

"Wonderful!" Mary exclaimed with dismal satisfaction. "So now we may expect to have three armies laying waste to the countryside, instead of just two. No doubt it will be a race among them to see who will win the privilege of murdering us first."

"Your gloom is exaggerated," Cordelia said, trying

to sound cheerful, although war really did seem to be just around the corner. King Victor Emmanuel and the Emperor of Austria had been spoiling for a fight for years. Now that the gauntlet had been thrown, any doves of peace fluttering in the neighborhood were likely to get shot down by both sides.

"An ultimatum isn't the same thing as an official declaration of war," she said, as much to reassure herself as to soothe Mary and Ellen. "Sometimes it is the most persuasive tool of diplomacy. If we are lucky, this latest quarrel may yet be resolved peacefully."

Mary looked skeptical. "We can't depend on luck, not when we're dealing with these wretched foreigners. You know they fight at the slightest provocation, or no provocation at all. Look what happened to you. You were nearly killed just because you happened to be in the wrong place at the wrong time." Mary stamped her foot. "You must inform Papa that I refuse to sit here in the midst of a battlefield, waiting to be slaughtered. Surely he will realize that, in these new circumstances, he must allow me to come home?"

She sounded so wistful beneath her surface belligerence that Cordelia felt her heart contract in reluctant sympathy. Having a father like the Earl of Stanwyck and a mother who died in childbirth, meant that Mary had been spoiled and indulged, but never loved or cherished. The fact that her stepmother had produced three sturdy sons, including the heir to the earldom, had only increased the isolation of her position. Teased unmercifully by her rambunctious half brothers, and either ignored or petted by her father, it was little wonder that her moods alternated between capricious arrogance and fretful dependence.

Cordelia reached out and put her hand on her cousin's arm. "Take heart, Mary, I understand that you're frightened—"

"Of course I'm not frightened!" Mary said, shaking off Cordelia's hand. "I am simply not willing to find myself trapped in this wretched duchy while the natives squabble over which ridiculous king is going to rule them. It is quite *preposterous* for me, the only daughter of the Earl of Stanwyck, to be put in this sort of danger."

"Well, if you are not frightened, I most certainly am," Cordelia said with perfect truth. "However, the fact is that we're as safe here at the villa as we would be anywhere in the duchy. We are certainly a lot safer remaining within the boundaries of the count's estate than we would be if we started wandering about the countryside, attempting to find our way back to England. Undoubtedly the railway lines will be taken over by one or other of the armies to prevent the movement of enemy troops, and I shudder to imagine what difficulties we might encounter if we tried to travel all the way to Calais by road. You know what a difficult time we had on the way here, and neither France nor Piedmont was at war then."

Ellen seemed impressed by Cordelia's arguments. "Mayhap Miss Cordelia has the right of it, m'lady. After all, Cardinal Walter and that priest of his got turned back from Piacenza by soldiers, for all that he's such an important gentleman, and travels with half a dozen servants in his retinue."

"The cardinal was turned back from Piacenza?" Cordelia said, filled with sudden foreboding. "Do you mean Cardinal Walter has come back here to the villa?"

"Why, yes," Mary said crossly, as if Cordelia should have heard of the cardinal's return hours ago. 'How else do you think we heard news of the Austrian emperor's ultimatum, if not from Father Roberto? It's not as if they delivered daily newspapers in this backwater."

"But why were Cardinal Walter and his party not allowed to proceed to Milan?" Cordelia asked, trying to make sense of Mary's fractured tale. "Why was he turned back from Piacenza? And by whom?"

"The whole party was captured by the Italian rebels," Ellen said. "The cardinal, his secretary, and all his retinue. It seems like they had a terrible journey. According to Father Roberto, they had to come back to the villa by mule cart."

"The cardinal's taken to his bed," Mary interjected. "Anna is afraid he's caught a chill to his liver."

"There are blockades across all the roads," Ellen elaborated, obviously torn between horror at the potential peril and a ghoulish excitement. "Father Roberto said they would still be held in the rebel encampment if the Count of Albion hadn't negotiated a deal for their release. The count couldn't get their horses released, though, not even the nag that had been hauling their baggage, and that's why they had to travel back to the villa by mule cart."

Cordelia stared blankly at the maid, her mind leapfrogging over the other information and fixing on the count's name. "What do you mean, the Count of Albion negotiated Cardinal Walter's release?"

"Good heavens, Cordelia, why are you looking so dumbfounded?" Mary demanded. "Cardinal Walter is Austrian, as you ought to know, and so the Italian rebels planned to hold him for ransom. The count probably bought them off." Mary adjusted her parasol to protect her cheeks from the sun. "Really, Cordelia, I shouldn't have to explain this to you. You're the person who is supposed to understand these dreary European politics. I think those blows to your head must have affected your brain."

Cordelia was too worried by the cardinal's return and too anxious for news of the count, to be annoyed by Mary's attitude. "I was surprised to hear that the count is in Piacenza, that's all. You yourself told me that he was traveling east, to his ancestral estate in Hungary."

Mary shrugged, bored with a discussion that had nothing to do with her fear of the imminent war, or her desire to return to England. "I daresay the count is allowed to change his mind if he wishes. All I know is that he negotiated with the rebels in Piacenza for Cardinal Walter's release."

The knowledge that Dakon was a mere thirty miles away rather than en route to the distant reaches of the Hapsburg Empire filled Cordelia with a flood of conflicting emotions. She wasn't sure whether joy or anger predominated: joy at the possibility of seeing him again in the reasonably near future; anger because she was sure Anna had deliberately misled her concerning his whereabouts, presumably on Dakon's instructions.

"I have to get back to the house," she said abruptly. "I need to speak with the housekeeper. Are you coming back, too, or would you prefer to stay out here to enjoy the fresh air?"

"I have had more than enough fresh air for one day," Mary said, getting up and smoothing out the pleats of her pale blue challis morning gown. "Wait!" she exclaimed plaintively. "What's the rush? Goodness gracious, Cordelia, you take off like a hare that's been scented by hounds."

Her cousin was scarcely exaggerating, Cordelia realized, and she slackened her pace, concealing her impatience as they walked slowly back to the villa, with Ellen remaining a discreet few paces to their rear.

Mary monopolized the conversation on the way back, holding forth in a nonstop monologue of complaint. Cordelia listened patiently, wondering why she had never understood before just how terrified her cousin was at the prospect of giving birth. She finally cut across Mary's complaint that the food at the villa was giving her a backache, and tried to make her cousin acknowledge the truth.

"Mary," she said as gently as she could. "The food at the villa is delicious. Your back aches because you are carrying a baby, and because you refuse to wear clothing that is suited to your condition."

Mary's mouth thinned into a stubborn line. "I wear the clothes I have in my wardrobe. I have no other choice."

Cordelia refused to rise to the bait. She was not going to get her head snapped off by suggesting letting out seams again. "Ellen has raised three strong, healthy children," she said. "Let her show you some of the ways to alleviate your discomfort. The birth will be easier, you know, if your body is healthy and well rested."

Mary stared mutely into the distance, and for a moment Cordelia thought she would not answer. "There is only one way for me to feel more comfortable," she said at last. "And that is for this pregnancy to end. The sooner the better. Preferably before there is a live bastard mewing its way into the world, demanding attention that nobody wants to give."

"You should try not to think that way—"

"Why not?" Mary swung around, her face flushed with defiance. "I know it shocks you when I say things like that, but I can't help it, Cordelia. I'm not like you. I never wanted to be a mother. I just fell in love with the wrong man, and was foolish enough to believe his lies. He would protect me, he said. He cherished my innocence. He would make sure that I didn't fall pregnant." Mary stopped abruptly. "Oh, what's the use," she said. "You're blushing, and putting on another one of your damned prissy-mouthed expressions."

"If I blushed, it was because I was thinking how easy it is for a woman to lull herself into believing such obvious lies," Cordelia said quietly. "I wasn't embarrassed by what you were telling me."

"I hate Gervaise," Mary said through clenched teeth. "I hate him and this nauseating spawn he's planted inside me."

Before she met Dakon, Cordelia would have felt no sympathy at all for her cousin, or at best a sort of condescension. In the simplistic view of the world she had once held, there had been no room for women who indulged in passion outside the bounds of marriage. She still thought that Mary had been wildly imprudent to surrender her virtue to a notorious rake, moreover a rake who was already married and thus incapable of being forced to the altar. But loving Dakon had increased her charity, as well as her understanding of physical passion. She realized that her own state of pristine chastity had been maintained more because she'd never been tempted than because she was a woman of iron-clad moral virtue. It was a humbling realization. She also realized that Mary spoke out of the hurt of rejection and betrayal, and possibly even the twisted remnants of love.

Tentatively, anticipating rejection, she reached out and took her cousin's hand. Mary stiffened, but for once she didn't move away. Cordelia spoke quietly, trying to convince Mary of her goodwill. "I'm only making these suggestions because I believe it will be easier for you to endure the next few months if you are in good health. Please, for your own sake, won't you consider abandoning your stays? Your baby needs room to grow, Mary, and he cannot help the fact that his father betrayed you. Ask yourself if you really wish to express your anger at Gervaise Brandon by harming your own baby."

Her cousin swallowed hard. For a moment, it seemed that she hesitated on the brink of making some new confidence. Then she shook Cordelia's hand from her arm and stared down her nose, her expression as haughty as if Cordelia had recommended that Mary appear in public in her chemise and pantaloons. "Trust me, dearest cousin, loosening my stays will not increase my health or happiness one iota. If I can't rid myself of the baby, going home to England is the only other thing that will make me feel better. Therefore, I insist that you write to the earl and request permission for us to make the journey home. I would write myself, but you know he will tear up any letter from me."

Mary's voice was brittle with anger, but her eyes shone with a mist of frightened tears. For once, Cordelia's sympathy was not tempered by any feelings of irritation toward her cousin. There was something wrong with a system that permitted a dissolute rake like Gervaise Brandon to commit adultery and emerge totally unscathed, while Mary's life lay in ruins, her relationship with her father probably destroyed forever. If it was going to bring Mary comfort to believe there was a chance she could return home to England

before the birth of her baby, then Cordelia was willing
to send a letter and risk the earl's wrath.

"I will write," she said. "Perhaps the advent of a
full-scale war will mellow your father's anger. Since
there has already been such a mix-up with our arrangements in regard to the villa, he should be made
aware of the difficulty in which we find ourselves.
After all, we are dependent on the Count of Albion's
charity for food and shelter. War or no war, the Earl
of Stanwyck cannot wish such a situation to continue."

Mary blinked several times, twirling the handle of
her parasol. "Thank you," she said gruffly.

It was the first time Cordelia could ever remember
being thanked by her cousin, and she worried in case
she had awakened unrealistic hopes. "Mary, you do
understand that there is no guarantee we'll be allowed
home? Apart from anything else, if war breaks out,
the postal service will be less than reliable. Even if
my letter arrives in England and your father decides
to reply, any response he sends may not arrive for
months."

"We have to try," Mary said urgently. "Ask Father
Roberto about the mail. He has been working on the
cardinal's correspondence all morning, so he must
have some plan for dispatching it. He's in the drawing
room. Go to him, Cordelia. Please don't delay."

"I will talk to Father Roberto if you will go upstairs
to your room, take off your stays, and put your feet
up for an hour or two."

Mary hesitated, then spoke to Ellen without directly
acknowledging Cordelia's bargain. "Come along,
Ellen, I need to change. I can rest for an hour or so
before lunch."

Cordelia watched her cousin's departure with relief.
Even this small concession on Mary's part felt like a

major victory. She went in search of Father Roberto and found him, as Mary had suggested, working at a desk set up by the drawing room window, surrounded by piles of papers.

"Father Roberto, good morning," she said in Italian. "May I trouble you for some advice?"

He stood up, looking startled. "*Signorina,* I am amazed to see you out of your sickbed. How very well you look, if I may be forgiven the personal observation."

"Thank you. The swiftness of my recovery seems to have surprised everyone. Including me."

The priest shook his head, still seeming bemused. "I saw the wounds in your head, *signorina,* that terrible night, and I must say that your recovery is little short of a miracle."

"A miracle much aided by Anna's devoted nursing."

He smiled uncertainly. "Cardinal Walter offered a Mass on your behalf, *signorina.* If it is not offensive to a Protestant to suggest such a thing, it seems that the good Lord chose to listen to Monsignor's prayers."

Monsignor. The mere word made her shudder. "I am honored that His Eminence should have me in his thoughts," Cordelia said, hoping that the lie would not choke her. Ever since Giancarlo whispered his dying warning, her feelings toward the cardinal had hovered on the edge of loathing, not least because she had earlier found him so very charming.

With considerable effort, she added, "I was sorry to hear that the cardinal is suffering from a nasty chill. I trust you yourself have taken no ill effects from your hair-raising journey back to the villa?"

"I am very well, thank you. But as far as the cardinal is concerned, the news isn't good. We must hope that he is suffering from nothing more than a chill. I regret to say, *signorina*, that His Eminence is feeling sadly under the weather after our recent encounter with Garibaldi's Revolutionary Army."

"I heard of your distressing experiences," Cordelia said. "My cousin Mrs. Ford told me that you and His Eminence were captured by rebels, and that the Count of Albion negotiated your release."

"Yes, indeed, that is quite true, and we are deeply in the count's debt for our rescue. I have been thanking God ever since last night that the count stands in such good stead with the rebels. Truly, his word with them seemed to be law."

"Is that so?" Cordelia said, trying to conceal her interest in this news of Dakon. "But perhaps it is not so surprising that the count's word is obeyed by the locals. He is, to all intents and purposes, the grand seigneur of this region."

"Very true. However, the rebels listen only to those voices that please them, of that you may be sure."

"If war breaks out, the count will find many calls upon his time. Will he stay in Piacenza, do you think, or will he return here to the villa?"

"I have no idea what the count's plans might be in the event of all-out war, *signorina*. He has business interests in Piacenza that need to be looked after, as well as the estate here. His personal supervision would probably be welcome in both places."

"War brings many problems and difficult choices," Cordelia said. "Even for those who stand on the sidelines."

"Yes, if that is where the count stands." Father Roberto cleared his throat nervously. "The truth is, *signorina*, that I find myself in a somewhat awkward position. A priest's first loyalty must be to his church, and only thereafter can he consider the demands of the world. Alas, in time of war the demands of the world press very hard and I find my loyalties torn."

"You have my sympathy, Father. I understand that these must be very difficult times for you."

"Do you really understand, *signorina*? You English have enjoyed a stable and united government for so many centuries, you surely can have little conception of what it is like for those of us in Europe who are not similarly blessed. I am a native of this duchy, and naturally my heart is with the cause of Italian independence, although I do not often dare to say as much. My Church does not favor the concept of a democratic Italy united under the rule of King Victor Emmanuel."

This was the first time she'd heard Father Roberto express anything that could even remotely be called a personal opinion, and Cordelia spoke sympathetically. "The history of Modena means that the loyalties of its citizens are apt to be painfully divided."

"Yes, and the Count of Albion represents the very heart of those divisions," Father Roberto said. "It is well known that he has a close relationship with the Hapsburg government, and that Austrian intelligence officers, such as Captain Hesse, visit him frequently. Yet after our experiences in Piacenza, it seems certain that the Italian rebels believe he is their ally. In many ways, it seemed to me that he was acting as their leader." Father Roberto shook his head in an eloquent gesture of frustration. "Somebody must be wrong, either the rebels or the Austrians. In these troubled times, the count cannot be a friend to both Italy and the Hapsburg Empire, so I wonder where his true loyalties lie?"

"I am a foreigner, newly arrived in the duchy," Cordelia said, picking her way through a conversation that suddenly seemed beset by hazards. Father Roberto was Cardinal Walter's personal secretary, and she couldn't risk trusting him just because he was from Modena and claimed to support the idea of a unified Italy. She smiled, trying to appear simultaneously well meaning and ignorant. "I am the least likely person to have information about the count's true political leanings, Father. You must realize that I have known him for no more than two weeks."

"Is that so, *signorina*? When I had the privilege of sharing a dinner table with you both the other night, I gained the distinct impression that you were each very much in tune with the other's feelings, almost like an old married couple."

Cordelia hadn't credited Father Roberto with enough worldly acumen to make such perceptive observations. "The count is a seasoned traveler," she said. "I find his company and his opinions entertaining, but we are no more than chance acquaintances. Perhaps you didn't know that my cousins and I were brought to the villa by Captain Hesse, who rescued us when we were abandoned in a local inn by Giancarlo, stranded without transportation."

"Poor Giancarlo." Father Roberto's expression became somber. "You may not have found him a reliable coachman, but he didn't deserve to meet such a frightful end." He crossed himself and bowed his head in a moment of silent prayer.

"I suppose there has been no progress in finding out who killed him?" Cordelia wasn't quite sure why she asked the question. Other than searching the estate for signs of an intruder, she knew there had been no meaningful investigation into Giancarlo's murder.

Father Roberto shook his head. "Alas, no, *signo-*

rina. It must be frustrating for you to know that the man who attacked you has escaped without punishment, but I'm afraid that the murderer may never be identified until he reaches God's judgment. That is, unless you have remembered something new that would aid the investigation?"

For a moment, Cordelia was sorely tempted to tell Father Roberto the truth about what had happened in the garden that night, and what Giancarlo had said to her before he died. Then wisdom prevailed. Father Roberto admired and trusted Cardinal Walter. At best, like Dakon, he would be infuriated that she should dare to slander such a respected man. At worst, he might report her accusations to the cardinal. And Cardinal Walter might feel so threatened by her accusations that he would take steps to silence her permanently.

Reluctantly, she made the decision to lie. "I was hit very hard from behind," she said, coating her lie with the gloss of truth. "The blows were so powerful that it would be astonishing if I remembered anything."

Father Roberto gave her a quick, intense stare. He was a Jesuit, she remembered, and had obviously been trained to recognize subtle prevarications. "It would, indeed, be astonishing, *signorina*, but then we have already agreed that your recovery was more than astonishing—it was almost miraculous. Are you quite sure you have no memory of what happened to you that night?"

How quickly one lie dragged a person down into the whirlpool of another, Cordelia thought miserably. She lifted her head and met the priest's inquiring gaze with a wide-eyed pretense of innocence. "I remember nothing at all, Father. I wish that I did. It bothers me that Giancarlo's murderer should escape retribution."

"He escapes only in this world, my child, remember that. The mills of God grind slowly, but they grind exceeding fine."

"Unfortunately, it is in this world that the murderer may go on to commit other crimes."

Father Roberto pursed his lips. "A frightening possibility, *signorina,* and one I had foolishly failed to consider." He paused to reflect for a moment. "At least you can draw some comfort from the fact that Giancarlo's murderer must be as anxious to avoid another encounter with you as you are to avoid meeting him. I do not believe that you are in any personal danger, my child."

Cordelia smiled without much conviction. "Yes, it's some consolation to know that my attacker is probably many miles from here." Yet another lie. As her father would have been only too quick to remind her, liars eventually strangle themselves in their own web of deceit.

Father Roberto was fidgeting with his papers, obviously anxious to return to his correspondence. Belatedly, she remembered why it was she'd sought him out in the first place. "I realize how busy you are, Father, but those piles of letters on your desk remind me that I stand in need of your advice. My cousin is alarmed at the prospect of an imminent outbreak of war—"

"A very natural sentiment," the priest murmured.

"Yes, and as you can imagine, she is anxious to write to her family, but we have no idea how to set about such a seemingly simple task. Could you tell me if there is likely to be any safe and quick postal service between the Duchy of Modena and England over the next few weeks?"

"I wish I could answer you, *signorina.*" Father Roberto gestured to several envelopes stacked at the corner of his desk, already sealed with the cardinal's crest. "These are the letters I was hoping to send from Piacenza yesterday," he said. "Now everything must be opened and reexamined to see if it is urgent enough for me to hire a private courier."

He picked up the top letter and the pile beneath it toppled over. With a rueful exclamation, he stacked the papers into a new pile, shuffling a heavy paper cutter to the side in order to prevent them from falling a second time.

"Short of hiring a courier to carry your correspondence into France and place it in the French mails, I believe you have little hope of sending letters to England, *signorina.* Depressing news, no doubt, but my honest opinion."

Scarcely breathing, trying desperately to show no trace of her agitation, Cordelia stepped closer to the desk. "Father Roberto, that paper cutter ... could I please ..." She gulped, flooded with so many unpleasant memories that she was almost unable to complete her sentence.

"Its design is very unusual," she managed eventually. "Do you think ... Could I see it more closely?"

"The paper cutter?" Father Roberto stared vaguely at his desk, then saw the knife he had pushed to one side under a pile of letters. "Is this what you mean?" he asked, holding it out to her.

"Yes, that's the one." She took it, hoping that her hands weren't visibly shaking.

"My dear *signorina,* you have turned quite white. Are you feeling well?"

"Perfectly well, thank you."

"In view of your recent injuries, we mustn't discount the possibility of a relapse." The priest stepped around his desk and pulled the bellrope. "Pray be seated, *signorina*, while I summon Anna to assist you. You really do look as if you are about to faint."

"I assure you there is no danger of that," she said, forcing herself to speak calmly. "This—paper knife—is a most interesting piece," she said. "Does it belong to you, Father?"

"No, it is Cardinal Walter's. His grandmother was from Spain, and I believe this formed part of her dowry. It is very handsome, is it not?"

"Very handsome." She forced the words out over bone dry lips. "It came originally from Toledo, I expect. My grandfather fought in the Peninsula campaign during the Napoleonic wars, and he brought home a sword with a hilt worked in a similar design. He told me that the Spanish craftsmen had learned the art of etching steel with gold from the Moors." She knew she was babbling, but she had to keep talking in the hopes that Father Roberto wouldn't realize why she was so interested in the dagger.

"You are correct, *signorina*. The knife is from Toledo. Cardinal Walter tells me it is one of the very finest examples of their work."

She gave what she hoped was a breezy laugh and hefted the weight of the dagger in her hand. Not only was the handle decorated with an elaborate pattern of flowers and vines, just like the one she'd stumbled across in the garden, it also felt exactly the same weight.

"Goodness me," she exclaimed, hoping Father Roberto wouldn't hear the crack in her voice. "This is a very sharp knife to use as a paper cutter."

"I agree, *signorina*, but then I don't use it." The priest gave another tug to the bellrope. "Now where are those serving lads? Gossiping about war and battles, I'll be bound, and too excited to pay attention when they are called."

Cordelia seemed to have lost the capacity to be subtle. "Do you usually take care of Cardinal Walter's knife for him?" she asked.

"Not at all. His Eminence normally carries it with him, since it is in the nature of a family heirloom. But the handle has worked a little loose, and he gave it to me before we left for Piacenza and charged me with seeing to its repair." Father Roberto looked puzzled. "Forgive me, *signorina,* but is there some special reason why you are so interested in the cardinal's dagger?"

"N-no, of course not. Just that it is a beautiful and unusual piece." Cordelia tried to sound unconcerned. Inside, she felt sick. Had the handle worked loose when the cardinal plunged the knife into Giancarlo's heart? Or perhaps when he dropped it in his headlong flight from the scene of his crime? The images were too vivid to be borne, and she had no idea what she would have said if Anna had not come running into the room at that moment, her expression distraught.

"Father Roberto, thank God. You must come at once. Monsignor has taken a turn for the worse and he wishes to give you his confession."

The priest turned pale. He crossed himself, his eyes dilating with shock. "It was all those hours in the drenching rain," he muttered. "Those cursed rebels have a lot to answer for."

"Father, we must not delay. The cardinal needs you. I should not have left his side," Anna said. Her chin wobbled. "He is such a good man. Even now, when every breath hurts, he tries to cheer me and save me trouble."

"He is one of the saints on earth," Father Roberto

said. He seemed to have forgotten all about Cordelia, and he left the room without another word to her, the housekeeper following hard on his heels, equally oblivious to her presence.

Cordelia waited until they had both gone and then, with great care, she slipped the dagger into the pocket of her morning gown and walked upstairs to her room.

Chapter Thirteen

When she got upstairs, Cordelia carefully removed the dagger from the pocket of her skirt and carried it to the window so that she could examine it in the light. Tipping it at various angles, she inspected it with meticulous attention. As she had half expected, right up close to the handle, at the point where the blade met the cross hilt, she saw a tiny red-brown smear of what was almost certainly dried blood. The small stain confirmed her conviction that this was the knife that had killed Giancarlo, and that it had been taken from the scene of the crime because its owner, Cardinal Walter, could be so readily identified.

Trembling, because her memories of that night suddenly seemed painfully vivid, she ran her fingers over the handle, tracing the raised pattern of vines and flowers. The little bumps and indentations felt familiar, as if her fingers recognized the design, and she continued her stroking movements in a rhythm that became gradually more monotonous. Her eyes drifted closed and awareness of her surroundings faded, until she could once again feel the fresh night air on her cheeks, and hear the croak of Giancarlo's dying breaths as his life trickled away in her arms.

Monsignor . . . His agonized gasp seemed as clear as the moment when she had first heard it. *Monsignor . . . must not trust* . . . His breath rattled in his throat and he choked in the final agony of his death throes.

Cordelia's eyes jerked open. Heart racing, she set the dagger down on the dressing table. She stared at it fixedly, although she actually saw nothing that was in front of her, not even the knife. What she saw was a grassy bank and a mortally wounded man. The sound of Giancarlo's dying breath echoed yet again in her ears, a horrible groan, as if he fought until the last second of life to tell her something important.

Monsignor . . . must not trust . . . Rrrr . . .

What was that final sound, she wondered. The gurgle of choked lungs, or an attempt to say one more word? A name that began with the letter *R*, perhaps?

With a thump, Cordelia sat down on her bed because her legs suddenly felt too wobbly to support her. Giancarlo had prolonged the agony of death to issue his final warning. Had she squandered his efforts by misinterpreting him? She realized, dangerously late, that under the pressure of too many intense emotions, she had mentally transposed the order of Giancarlo's dying words, imparting a subtle change to their meaning. Until this moment, she had assumed Giancarlo was cautioning her and Dakon to beware of the cardinal. Now she wondered if he had been trying to tell her that the *cardinal* was in danger, that the cardinal should not trust somebody.

Monsignor must not trust . . . Rrrr . . . RRR.

That final sound hadn't been a death rattle, she decided, but almost certainly the start of another word.

Giancarlo had been trying to tell her that Cardinal Walter must not trust somebody whose name began with the letter *R*.

Father Roberto, for example, the cardinal's confidential secretary, and a man in whom he no doubt reposed complete trust. A man who, as it happened, had shown that he enjoyed easy access to the cardinal's dagger—or perhaps even a man who had lied about the true owner of the dagger. A man who would have had real cause for worry if Cordelia had run back to the house right after the murder and identified the murder weapon. If suspicion had been cast on Father Roberto immediately after the murder, he might have been forced to answer questions that he would much prefer never to have been raised.

A sudden chill brought goose bumps to Cordelia's arms. Was she building towering mountains of suspicion out of minuscule molehills of fact? Father Roberto had been born in the Duchy of Modena. He had hinted that, like most educated Italians, he supported the cause of independence from Hapsburg rule, and she hadn't doubted him. But in the whirlpool of Italian politics, it was dangerous to make assumptions about a person's beliefs merely on the basis of where they had been born. Prime Minister Cavour, in his efforts to modernize the government of Piedmont, had banished all Jesuits, claiming that they were actively seeking to impose a religious dictatorship, with the Pope at its head.

Was it possible that Father Roberto had been among those Jesuits expelled from Piedmont? If so, it wouldn't be surprising if he had conceived a lasting dislike for the Italian Nationalists, and their dream of a united Italy, with a modern, democratic government, headed by the King of Piedmont. Could that dislike have been strong enough to send him into the arms of the Austrian enemy?

In retrospect, Cordelia recognized that her suspicions of the cardinal had always been ill founded. Cardinal Walter was a short, plump, elderly dignitary, who puffed and panted when he took a slow stroll. He would have been incapable of murdering a strong, physically active man like Giancarlo. Even if he'd had help with the murder from a group of fellow conspirators, that didn't explain how he'd managed—single-handedly—to knock her out and drag her across fifty feet of garden path. She was quite sure that her attacker had operated alone and, somewhat belatedly, she realized that the cardinal lacked the strength for such a Herculean feat.

True, she had smelled incense at the time of the attack, and again on Cardinal Walter's robes when she'd recovered consciousness, but Father Roberto was just as likely as the cardinal to smell of incense. If one of them had said Mass, the other had almost certainly been in attendance. Moreover, Father Roberto was young and strong, rather than elderly and weak like Cardinal Walter. Ruefully Cordelia acknowledged that it was no wonder Dakon had found her accusations against his old friend incredible. He had doubted her because what she claimed *was* incredible.

Cordelia didn't want to leap straight from unfounded suspicions of the cardinal to unfounded suspicions of Father Roberto, but she couldn't sit closeted in her bedroom, doing nothing, knowing that the cardinal lay close to death and that Father Roberto was with him, administering the last rites. After all, if she had finally understood Giancarlo's message aright, Father Roberto was a genuine danger to the cardinal's

safety. Thank goodness, with Anna and several servants hovering at the cardinal's bedside, Roberto
wasn't likely to risk any nefarious activity.

The thought brought far less comfort than it should.
With war literally around the corner, unthinkable acts
became all too thinkable. Cordelia hurriedly crossed
to her dresser and shoved the dagger into the top
drawer, where it nestled among her collars, mittens,
and lace-trimmed handkerchiefs, the gold-embossed
handle gleaming with obscene opulence.

She paced the room, not sure what she should do
next. Confront Father Roberto? Warn the cardinal?
She was aware of needing, quite desperately, to talk
to Dakon and ask his advice. Since that was impossible, she would have to content herself with telling
Anna that Father Roberto might be an ally of the
Austrians and that he needed to be watched. Cordelia
had no doubt that the housekeeper knew how to contact every Italian Nationalist within twenty leagues of
the villa. With a warning about him issued by Anna,
Father Roberto's power to cause harm for the Nationalists would thus be neutralized.

Deciding that she needed to speak to Anna was
one thing, intruding on the cardinal's sickroom was
another. Cordelia was debating how best to send word
to the housekeeper when she felt the silent, unmistakable brush of Dakon touching her mind.

He was coming home! She smiled, unable to contain
her happiness as she ran to the window and looked
down into the courtyard. As she watched, Dakon can-
tered into the yard. He was riding a chestnut gelding
that seemed near to foundering from sheer exhaustion.
Its sides were foam-flecked and the instant Dakon relaxed his grip on the reins, its head sank wearily onto
its chest.

Dakon sprang from the saddle and patted the horse in praise for its efforts. Then he tossed the reins to a waiting stable lad, issued a few curt instructions, and ran toward the house with a speed and energy that belied the hours he had obviously spent in the saddle.

Dakon had returned! Cordelia hugged her arms around her waist, not attempting to rationalize her happiness. Then she ran out into the hallway, her crinoline swaying with unladylike abandon. The front door was flung open, and Dakon strode inside. He glanced up and came to her immediately, taking the stairs two at a time.

His face and hair were gray with road dust, his high cheekbones almost coal black. His long riding cape and boots were heavily caked with mud, and his elegant linen shirt was ripped at the collar. In Cordelia's opinion, he looked utterly wonderful. She smiled at him, and she felt him smile back, although his face remained expressionless. He took the last three stairs in a single bound, coming to a halt less than a foot away from her.

He didn't speak, simply reached out and took both her hands, flicking back the cambric ruffles at the edge of her sleeves and exposing her inner wrists. His eyes darkening with regret, he ran his thumb lightly across the almost invisible wounds where his fangs had punctured her flesh.

I hurt you, he said, and Cordelia knew that neither of them any longer had the willpower to pull back from the forbidden pleasure of allowing their minds to join. *You carry the scars of my blood lust, and yet you welcome me home with smiles. You lack even the most basic sense of self-preservation, Cordelia.*

Her name sang with the warm, lyrical softness of his feelings for her. She closed her fingers around his hands and answered him. *The scars of your touch are already faded, but the pain of your absence would always linger.*

He sighed, and his guilt momentarily shadowed her joy. *I swore that I would stay away until Anna sent word that you had left the villa. But I am so weak-willed where you are concerned that I almost rejoiced to hear that war had finally been declared. The coming of war and the cardinal's illness meant that I had an excuse to justify breaking my sworn word.*

She rested her hand against his cheek, and his guilt vanished, drowned in the drenching, surging crest of his pleasure. *I'm glad that you broke your sworn word,* she said. *I have much to tell you, Dakon.*

Somewhere at the far end of the corridor, she heard a door open. She looked behind her, but she couldn't see anyone because of a bend in the hallway.

Gianni, one of the serving lads, has left the cardinal's room; he will see us in about forty seconds, Dakon informed her.

How can you tell that it's Gianni? You can't see him.

For a moment his mind closed to her. Then the barriers opened. *The Vam-pyr have senses that are more acute than those of human beings. I can recognize the sound of Gianni's footsteps, and even his unique scent.*

Why did you hesitate to tell me that? Surely the power of your senses is a matter for pride, not for concealment?

For a hundred and thirty-one years I have avoided telling people that I am Vam-pyr. The habit is hard to break. Even Anna, who knows me better than any other human, doesn't allow herself to acknowledge the full truth of what I am.

Cordelia realized that Gianni had turned the corner

and had seen them. Dakon released her hands and bowed with formal courtesy, creating the impression that they had only that moment encountered each other.

"Good morning, Miss Hope," Dakon said in Italian, his manner one of distant politeness. "I beg you will forgive my travel dust." ·

Cordelia dropped a small curtsy and tried to remember how to use her vocal cords. "Oh ... er ... certainly. Good morning, count."

"I am relieved to find you so well recovered from your recent indisposition. I feared that you might suffer lasting damage from the ... events ... of that terrible night." *Have I told you that you look even more beautiful this morning than you did in my memories of you?*

"Fortunately, I recovered very quickly from the blows to my head, Excellency." Her voice sounded scratchy and uncertain. She tried again. "It's good to have you back, even though the cause for your return is a sad one." *Dakon, I need to speak with you alone. I've changed my mind about what Giancarlo was trying to tell me before he died. I believe he was warning us not to trust Father Roberto.*

Why have you changed your mind? "Yes, you're right. My return was prompted by a very sad cause. I was most distressed when I received word that Cardinal Walter had been taken ill as a result of his rough treatment at the hands of the Italian Nationalists. I must go to him at once—" Dakon broke off, giving a convincing portrayal of a man who is surprised by the sight of a familiar face. "Why, Gianni, my boy, we were just talking about His Eminence. How is the cardinal? Recovering, I trust?"

"Still very weak, Excellency, but he will be pleased

to know that you have come. He has been asking for you." Gianni tried to conceal his curiosity as he looked from Dakon to Cordelia and then back again. "Donna Anna says that the worst of his fever is passed, and that we should be able to nurse him back to health within a week or so."

"That is excellent news," Dakon said. "Gianni, would you arrange for some hot water to be sent to my room at once? I must wash and change before I put in an appearance at the cardinal's bedside. So much travel dirt in a sickroom would not be welcome."

"I will see to that now, Excellency." Gianni had barely started down the stairs when the door to Mary's bedroom burst open and Ellen came running out into the corridor, hair falling out of her cap and the streamers of her apron all undone. So great was her agitation that she didn't seem to notice Dakon, much less the young servant.

"Oh, miss, miss! Come quick! Her ladyship's taken sick and I cannot stop the bleeding!" Ellen's chin wobbled, and her voice sank to a whisper. "Oh, miss, I'm afraid she's going to die! There's blood everywhere!"

For a moment, Cordelia was too shocked to speak or move. Then Dakon murmured a quiet word of encouragement, and the sickening weight of her dread lifted slightly. She took Ellen's hand, and even managed to squeeze it reassuringly. "Between us we will pull her through," she said with a great deal more confidence than she felt. "If there are any supplies that you need, ask the count for them now. I'm sure he will be kind enough to see that they are brought up to us."

Ellen was far too worried to bother with polite disclaimers. "Water," she said. "We need hot water and clean rags, Excellency, and a herbal brew to ease her discomfort, if we can get her to drink it. Aside from that, I can't think of anything that will help. Her ladyship has fainted, miss, and we had best get back to her. I shouldn't have left her. She's exhausted from the pain."

Dakon bowed. "Then I must not keep you, Ellen, or you, Miss Hope. Return to Mrs. Ford at once and I will see to it that you are supplied with all that you need." Taking Cordelia's hand, he carried it to his lips. His touch brought her solace, and restored some of her calm. "Go with Ellen," he said. "I shall come soon."

Cordelia followed the maid into Mary's bedroom. She and Ellen automatically took their places on either side of the bed. After one glance at their patient, they stared at each other in mute horror.

In a fit of pain, Mary must have tossed off the covers and she rested in a pool of bright red blood. She lay so still that for a heart-stopping moment Cordelia was sure she was dead and Ellen obviously thought the same. The maid gave a cry of mingled regret and alarm, then started to sob into her apron, heartfelt sobs of genuine grief.

"Oh, dear Lord, I shouldn't never have left her alone, and now she's gone!"

Cordelia wasn't ready to surrender the fight. Ignoring Ellen's lament, she sat down on the bed, and put her finger against the pulse in Mary's throat. A faint throb of coursing blood beat against the pad of her forefinger. Relief made her almost light-headed.

"Hush, Ellen, she's not dead. Stop crying, and get control of yourself. She needs you to help her. She needs both of us now more than ever before."

Cordelia spoke more out of a desire to calm the maid than from any real knowledge of how either of them could be helpful to Mary. She leaned over her cousin, smoothing her hand gently over her forehead and pushing away the hank of sweat-matted curls that had fallen across her face.

"Mary," she said softly, hoping against hope that her cousin might hear her, "I am here to help you. Ellen and I will make sure that you soon feel better."

Mary never stirred, and her eyelids scarcely fluttered, but for a heartening moment it seemed to Cordelia that her pulse beat a little more strongly. At least she was still alive, and holding her own. If she looked closely, Cordelia could see the shallow rise and fall of Mary's chest and hear the faint rasp of her breathing.

The sight of her cousin's ravaged beauty made Cordelia's heart ache with pity. Mary's lips were swollen, cracked, and dry. Her cheeks seemed bloodless they were so pale, and her forehead burned with the onset of fever.

What was she supposed to do to alleviate Mary's pain? Cordelia cursed the conventions of polite society that had kept her so ignorant of the processes of pregnancy and childbirth. Ellen was too panicked to give practical advice, and Cordelia had absolutely no idea what might help Mary to survive this ordeal. Even though she had volunteered her time at the shelter for fallen women in Cambridge, her status as an unmarried lady had limited her activities to helping unwed mothers find employment and feeding bottles of boiled cow's milk to the orphaned babies.

Suddenly, Mary's face contorted with pain. She moaned, but the sound was broken and breathless, as if she lacked the energy even for this small protest at the agony twisting her body. Because she had no idea what else to do, Cordelia took her cousin's hand and stroked it until the spasm passed, murmuring soothing words she doubted Mary could hear, and trying to offer comfort that seemed almost insulting in its inadequacy. She was terrified by the way Mary's hand lay limp and flaccid in her clasp, as if she had already passed beyond the point where pain could touch her.

When the spasm was over, Ellen recovered herself enough to part the folds of Mary's dressing robe, and Cordelia saw the frightening stain of fresh blood spreading over Mary's nightgown and soaking into the mattress. The maid pursed her lips, shaking her head, her tears conveying without need for words that as far as she was concerned, her mistress was as good as dead.

She'd be damned if she was going to consign her cousin to her coffin without a struggle, Cordelia decided. "We need a cool cloth for her forehead," she said. "And something warm and sweet for her to drink. And I should think a fresh towel would help to soak up some of that blood. It can't be pleasant to lie in your own blood."

She railed inwardly at the deficiency of her instructions to Ellen. Apart from the towel for the blood, she would have issued virtually the same list to aid a child with measles, or an elderly gentleman with an ague. Why did she know so ridiculously little about one of the most elemental functions of a woman's body? How was the morality and decency of society aided by keeping women ignorant of the process by which they became mothers?

"I'm sure her ladyship's not feeling anything, miss." Ellen struggled to contain her tears. "She's past the point where she's hurting. Trust me, miss, I've seen too many women in the same state. I know what I'm talking about. There's no hope for her, but she's not hurting no more, at least we have that comfort."

Cordelia wasn't about to argue the point, although it had seemed to her that Mary felt every twitch and ripple of the pain that had just gripped her. "Even so, I need a dry towel and a wet cloth," she said, continuing to stroke Mary's hand in a gentle, calming rhythm. "Since she can't speak to us, how can we be sure that she feels no pain?"

Ellen brought the towel and handed over a damp linen cloth. "Thank you," Cordelia said, trying for a note of brisk confidence that was a lifetime away from what she truly felt. "Now perhaps you'll see about a warm drink for her, Ellen. I'm sure my cousin must be weakened by lack of liquids in her system." Cordelia hoped she wasn't talking utter medical nonsense.

"Yes, miss. Shall I make a tisane, miss? The kettle's on the boil and I have some chamomile and honey." Ellen spoke politely enough, but she clearly considered the preparation of the drink a complete waste of time. Cordelia refused to accept that the maid might be right.

"Thank you, Ellen, a tisane would be just the thing." She kept her voice low and cheerful, although Mary gave no sign that anything short of a trumpet call from the angel Gabriel would bring her back to consciousness. Cordelia pressed the cloth to her cousin's forehead, and wadded the towel beneath her hips, all the while murmuring little nonsense phrases of encouragement.

Alas, her words precipitated no miracle, and when the next spasm of pain came it arched Mary's back off the mattress before she collapsed again into the same shattering stillness. Her cheeks, if that were possible, appeared even whiter than before and her lips turned blue.

"Here's the tisane you wanted, miss." Ellen carried a cup of sweet-smelling chamomile over to the bed.

Cordelia thanked God for the diversion. Anything, anything at all that might help, was better than sitting and watching her cousin die without making a move to save her.

"I'll support her head on my arm and you see if you can get her to swallow a couple of sips," she said.

"Yes, miss." Ellen, despite her doubts about Cordelia's methods, seemed relieved to follow orders. She waited until Mary's head and shoulders were settled against Cordelia's chest and then she tipped the cup against her mistress's lips. Mary didn't stir, and the warm tea trickled down her chin.

In grim silence, Cordelia wiped up the dribble. "Try again," she ordered.

"Yes, miss." Ellen tipped the cup again, her eyes welling with tears. This time Cordelia was almost sure that she saw Mary swallow, and it seemed that a fraction less of the tea dribbled out of her mouth. Even Ellen was encouraged. She tried yet again, and this time there was no doubt that Mary actually drank a sip or two of the hot tea.

It was ridiculous to ascribe healing powers to honey and an herb as commonplace as chamomile, but Cordelia was convinced that Mary's breathing became a little stronger and some of the chill seemed to leave her skin. "In a few minutes we'll try her again with some more of the tea," Cordelia said. "Every ten minutes or so, Ellen. However little she manages to swallow, it might be enough to help keep up her strength."

"Yes, miss." Ellen sounded marginally less skeptical. She even went so far as to bring a fresh cloth, wrung out in lavender water, without being asked. To Cordelia's relief, no more pains racked Mary's body for several minutes.

A light knock came at the door. "I'll get it, miss. I expect 'tis the serving lad with the hot water we asked for."

She opened the door and Cordelia heard Dakon's voice. "Here you are, Ellen. With your permission, I would like to take a look at your patient if I may. I have some experience with treating the sick and injured. I spent several years in the Ottoman Empire, and have learned some of their remedies along with the best practices of our own European doctors."

Ellen had no idea where or what the Ottoman Empire might be, but she did know that it was scandalous to consider letting a strange gentleman into the bedroom of a lady who was in the throes of a miscarriage. She stared at the count in appalled disbelief. "You can't come in here, Excellency. I'm sorry, but it wouldn't be proper. Her ladyship ... that is to say, Mrs. Ford ... is seriously indisposed. With female problems. What she needs is a midwife—"

Dakon ignored her protests and walked into the room with Ellen flapping her hands and expostulating behind him. He set down a heavy copper jug of steaming hot water and turned around so swiftly that he bumped into the maid. "I'm sorry," he said, gripping her head on either side as if to steady her. He bent down, staring into her eyes. Ellen's outraged exclamation cut off in midsqueak. To Cordelia's astonishment, when Dakon released his hold on her, the maid turned in absolute silence and went to sit on a chair in the far corner of the room, her hands neatly folded in her lap.

"What's happened? What have you done to her?" Cordelia asked, half rising from the bed.

"Nothing very terrible. I have mesmerized her, that's all. She would have been so outraged if I tried to examine your cousin that I had to do something to get her out of the way. Don't worry. She will wake up none the worse for wear in a couple of hours."

Cordelia had accepted that Dakon could talk to her without words, plant his thoughts inside her mind, and his feelings deep in her heart. For some reason, it was much more difficult to accept that he included the power to hypnotize Ellen among his unique talents. Somewhat to her chagrin, she also discovered that she shared much of Ellen's outrage at the prospect of allowing him to see her cousin in such a *female* state of distress. It was one thing to throw her own personal inhibitions to the wind, and an altogether more difficult task to cast aside the training of a lifetime on behalf of her cousin.

Mary solved the problem by giving a groan that quickly faded into a series of broken pants. Without waiting for permission, Dakon threw off his jacket, dipped his hands into the near-boiling jug of water, and sat down on the bed. In a small concession to modesty, he drew the sheet up to Mary's knees, then he outraged every convention of the civilized world by gently parting the opening of Mary's dressing robe, and massaging her lower abdomen in a downward, pressing motion.

Cordelia would have protested, but Mary gave another groan, and her eyes opened for a second or two. "Wait for the contraction of her womb to pass, and then give her something to drink," Dakon ordered, still massaging. "Her body is crying out for fluids."

Cordelia was quite sure that she shouldn't allow a

man who claimed to be a vampire to sit on Mary's bed and rub his hands over her naked belly. On the other hand, Mary was showing the first real signs of life since Cordelia had walked into the bedroom. Ever practical, she decided to let Dakon bring Mary back to health first, and express all the proper protests afterward.

"A very wise decision," Dakon murmured.

"It's rude to listen to people's thoughts," Cordelia retorted, then realized how absurd her complaint was. Flustered, she turned away and busied herself in freshening the cup of chamomile tea for Mary. Her spirits had miraculously lightened. Despite all her inhibitions about allowing a man to care for her cousin in such an intimate situation, she no longer feared for Mary's life. She didn't doubt that Dakon would manage to save her.

"She won't die, I believe, but she's lost a great deal of blood," he said, once again answering her thoughts, his gaze still fixed on Mary. "She will need careful nursing for a couple of weeks until her body is able to replenish itself naturally, but that should pose no special problems."

"Ellen will do a good job. In normal circumstances, she is a competent nurse, and she's devoted to my cousin, which is why we brought her on this journey. We didn't realize how overset she would be by the strangeness of foreign travel."

Dakon let his hands rest lightly on Mary's stomach. "There, the contraction of her womb has ended. Why don't you give her some of that tea? She's semiconscious and should be able to drink."

Cordelia held the cup to Mary's mouth and tipped carefully. Her cousin drank thirstily. Her eyelashes flickered, and her eyes opened. Her gaze drifted over

Dakon, seeming not to register his presence, and settled on Cordelia. Her cracked lips twisted into a travesty of a smile.

"No doubt ... you think ... the pain is ... a fit punishment for my ... sins." Her throat was obviously so dry and sore that the words emerged in a harsh whisper.

"I am thinking nothing of the kind," Cordelia said softly. "How good it is to have you back with us, Mary."

"I ... didn't want ... Gervaise's baby. But now I am sorry that it is lost." Her eyes closed but her voice became stronger. "Have you ever noticed that God only answers the prayers He would be wiser to ignore?"

Cordelia decided that this was not the moment to embark on a theological discussion. She took her cousin's hand and clasped it tightly. "There will be other babies for you," she said, hoping fervently that she spoke the truth. "Babies that you will love, and their father, too. Now what you need to do is rest—"

Mary screamed as another pain convulsed her body. Dakon leaned forward and grasped her head between his hands, forcing her to look at him. "Relax," he commanded her. "Mary, relax your muscles and stop fighting the pain."

Her scream died away, Cordelia couldn't tell whether because she had lost consciousness again or because she was obeying Dakon. Cordelia watched, fascinated, as he continued to massage her cousin's abdomen, his thumbs pressing over her lower belly in a downward stroking motion. She wondered what he hoped to achieve, or whether he was simply trying to alleviate the pain.

"I'm trying to help her womb expel the membranes that would have contained her baby if he had developed correctly," Dakon said. "For her to be suffering such pain, the membranes must still be attached to her womb, and each pain that she endures is widening the tear in the lining of her womb. If the wound becomes deep enough, she will bleed to death. That is why so many women die when they suffer a miscarriage. That, and the infection that sets in following the birth."

"How do you know so much about a subject that is normally a mystery to men?" Cordelia asked, gathering up the bloodstained cloths and dropping them into a basin.

"Vam-pyr babies are larger than human babies when they're born, often as much as eleven or twelve pounds in weight," Dakon said. "Even when a human female survives the mating experience with a member of my race, there is a considerable chance that she will die in the process of giving birth. Miscarriage also seems far more common, as if the human womb tries to reject the alien creature it carries within."

"But if Vam-pyrs are completely different from humans, then there would never be any successful pregnancies," Cordelia pointed out. Ignorant as she was of rules concerning human reproduction, she knew that two species needed to have some elements of their blood in common in order to reproduce, which was why sheep and goats could live for generations in the same flock without interbreeding.

"That is true, although the match between our two races is obviously far from perfect. For that reason, through the centuries, many Vam-pyr have studied with human midwives and surgeons in an effort to improve the survival rate of our infants, and to try to determine why we produce only male infants. Our knowledge of the process of human birth is great. Unfortunately, we still don't seem to have any idea how to apply that knowledge in order to save more of our own babies. Or to insure the birth of a female Vampyr, which would mean so much to my people."

Dakon took the cup from Cordelia and held it gently against Mary's lips. She took a few tiny sips, although she didn't open her eyes.

"She's sleeping," Dakon said. "She's not unconscious, not anymore."

Cordelia was still uncomfortable with allowing Dakon to act as Mary's midwife, but his competence was undeniable, and her cousin's cheeks had lost their deathly pallor. To protest his actions merely because they violated society's standards seemed ridiculous.

"Have you assisted at a birth before?" she asked.

"Several times," he said. "Rest assured, Cordelia, I shall not fail you."

"The births you attended, were they of Vam-pyr babies?"

She felt the wave of his sadness, which he quickly extinguished. "No, I have never seen the birth of a Vam-pyr baby. Such births are rare. The truth is, Cordelia, our race is dying."

"Your chances of survival as a people would be so much greater if you married Vam-pyr women instead of forcing yourselves on unwilling human females," Cordelia said.

"That thought has occurred to us," Dakon said dryly. "Alas, four thousand years of Vam-pyr history on earth have so far failed to produce a female of our own race to marry."

Cordelia shook her head. "It seems so strange. In your own world, girls must presumably have been born in equal numbers with boys, so what is it about joining with human females that causes only boys to be born?"

For a moment, Dakon didn't respond. "Our scientists have concluded that the violence inherent in the act of mating with a human determines that the offspring of the union will always be male," he said. His voice was harsh, and he obviously disliked reminding her of the brutal reality of his nature.

"Then your solution is simple," Cordelia said.

"Indeed," he said, not masking his sarcasm. "So simple that the greatest Vam-pyr minds in twelve generations have not found it."

"Perhaps they have not examined the situation from the correct point of view," Cordelia said. "But it seems to me that if you insure that the mating between a Vam-pyr and a human female is not violent, then the child resulting from that union will be a girl."

She felt the astonishment with which Dakon listened to her. Then he gave a short bitter bark of laughter. "A beguiling fantasy, Cordelia. You forget that deadly fear on the part of the human female is not only inevitable, but unavoidable. To complete the act of mating, a Vam-pyr must suck blood from the jugular vein of his victim."

"If you didn't use the word *victim,* perhaps you would remember that it isn't preordained that the woman will die after mating with you."

"Very true," he said ironically. "She has survival odds of about one in ten thousand. How foolish of her to be fearful when facing such odds!"

"But she doesn't know the odds," Cordelia said. "You are infecting her with your own fears."

"Justifiable fears," Dakon said curtly.

"In your own world, Vam-pyr women must have survived the union with their husbands, even though they gave him their blood. Otherwise there would be no Vam-pyr race."

"Perhaps our race was already dying when we left our home world," Dakon said. "The survivors of the shipwreck that stranded my ancestors on Earth were all male. I have often wondered if their voyage across the stars was prompted by a shortage of Vam-pyr women."

On the verge of pointing out that there were a hundred more likely reasons for an all-male crew, Cordelia was interrupted by a harsh, throaty cry from Mary. Another pain began, racking her cousin's body, and lasting longer than any that had gone before.

The agony of pain and blood loss, followed by increasingly brief moments of respite, continued for two hours, coming to a crescendo as the sun finally dipped behind the horizon and the room filled with shadows. Cordelia was lighting lamps and candles that Dakon didn't really need, when he called to her.

"It's over," he said, his voice husky with fatigue. "I can't guarantee that there will be no infection, but your cousin's womb is intact and the fetus has been expelled." He gestured toward the bloody sheets. "Ellen can help you to clean up as soon as I wake her."

"Thank you, Dakon, from the bottom of my heart. You know that Mary would have died without your help."

One life saved in exchange for a dozen taken.

She read the thought, but Dakon didn't speak it aloud, and made no reference to it as he stood up to leave.

"I haven't yet been to visit the cardinal, and I should do so as soon as possible," he said. "He will be worried if he doesn't find me at his bedside when he awakes."

Cordelia stood on tiptoe and kissed him swiftly on the lips. "Dakon, whatever has happened in the past, today my cousin owes you her life. I can't find the words to thank you for what you have done."

He captured her face between his hands and stared down at her, his gaze somber. Then, with studied slowness, he bent and covered her mouth with his. He kissed her until the room spun around her head and the floor tilted beneath her feet.

When he released her, his eyes were darker and bleaker than a night on the Russian steppes. "If you leave my home alive," he said, "then you will have cause to thank me."

Chapter Fourteen

❨

The dagger was gone. Cordelia felt frantically among her collars and kerchiefs, but she hadn't been mistaken: the knife was nowhere to be found. Exhausted from hours of nursing Mary, she stretched her aching shoulder muscles, rubbed her eyes, and began the tedious task of checking every drawer and chest in her room to make sure that she hadn't somehow misremembered where she'd placed the dagger.

A knock came at her bedroom door just as she was closing the lid of her leather traveling case, the last place in her bedroom where the knife might conceivably be hidden. Irritable from tiredness, she tugged open the door, barely able to adjust her expression into a smile when she saw the housekeeper waiting outside in the hallway.

"Yes, Anna?" The housekeeper looked so grim that Cordelia felt a flash of concern. "Is something wrong?" She thought of the missing knife, and her heartbeat accelerated. "The cardinal! Is he all right?"

"He is recovering, *signorina,* thanks be to God. He

is weak, but his fever has left him." Anna's dour expression didn't lighten in spite of her good news. "The master wishes to speak with you before dinner, *signorina*, on a matter of some urgency."

"Certainly. I will go to him as soon as I have had a chance to wash and change."

Anna shook her head. "There is no time for you to change, *signorina*. The count is waiting outside for you and he has instructed me to escort you to him personally. Get your cloak and let me take you to him. This is a matter which cannot be delayed, almost I would say a matter of life and death."

Cordelia's concern deepened into foreboding. "He ... the count ... isn't sick?"

"No, *signorina*. At the moment his health remains excellent. But he insists that your presence is of critical importance."

Anna clearly wasn't in the mood to be communicative, or perhaps she genuinely knew nothing more. Was it possible that the dagger had come into Dakon's possession? Or perhaps he'd uncovered some other clue as to the identity of Giancarlo's murderer? Given that her suspicions of the cardinal had proven so unfounded, Cordelia was no longer willing to assume the worst about Father Roberto.

Sighing a little because she was so bone weary—so emotionally drained—that even a meeting with Dakon couldn't outweigh the appeal of a hot bath and a few minutes relaxing by the fire, she took her cloak from the hook behind the door and followed the housekeeper to the back staircase.

Anna led the way to a side door, located near the kitchen gardens, and grabbed a thick gray shawl. Dusk was falling and the mild spring day was rapidly giving way to frigid night. Drizzle misted Cordelia's face with rain, and dampened the front of her gown. Chilled, she pulled her cloak more securely about her.

Muttering complaints about the damp and the wretched, wet spring, Anna burrowed into her shawl. "Another minute only, *signorina*. We're almost there."

"Almost where?" Cordelia asked, then realized that they had skirted the house and were approaching the buildings used to house the count's carriages. With no sun to prolong the twilight, the area appeared dark and gloomy, and she wondered why nobody had chosen to light the lamps. She reminded herself that Dakon was discomfited by the full glare of sunlight, and most at ease in a semidarkness humans tended to find oppressive.

The thought of Dakon lifted her spirits, and she walked a little faster, cheered after all by the prospect of seeing him again so soon. Eager to dispel the bleakness of the night, she opened her mind and reached out, seeking the warming touch of Dakon's presence.

She felt no hint of welcome, no comforting caress against the edges of her soul. Instead, she felt the tingle of Anna's nervousness, and a lurking sense that all was not well.

She stopped so abruptly that Anna stumbled. Cordelia grabbed the housekeeper's arm and swung her around so that the two of them were facing each other. "Why have you brought me here?" she demanded. "Where is the count? I'm going no further until you tell me."

Anna's gaze slid sideways. "The count is waiting for you, *signorina*. Come, we must hurry. Step inside the carriage house and he will be there."

Her discomfiture was so apparent that a child would have been able to detect the lie. Cordelia crossed her arms beneath the folds of her cloak and refused to move, despite the fact that her fingers were turning to ice. "For the last time, I'm going no further until you tell me what you're up to, Anna. I am quite sure you're not taking me to meet with the count, so what are you planning?"

A voice spoke out of the gloom. "As always, *signorina,* your assessment of the situation is too accurate for convenience." Father Roberto stepped out from the shelter of the carriage house door and bowed to her in a mocking parody of his normally deferential manner.

Cordelia didn't wait to ask him what he meant. She swung around, breaking into a run, but Anna blocked her way. The housekeeper grabbed her arms, holding her with wiry strength and keeping her grip just long enough for Father Roberto to cover the few feet separating them and imprison Cordelia's arms in a powerful grip. She struggled, kicking backward with her feet, but he sidestepped with agility and tightened his hold on her by circling her throat with his arm in a throttlehold that felt distressingly familiar.

The smell of incense that wafted up from the sleeve of his clerical robe was debilitating not only in its strength but also in the memories it brought back. This was without question the man who had attacked her in the Garden of the Three Fountains the night that Giancarlo died, Cordelia realized. Every pore of her body recognized his touch, and recoiled against it. She tried to say something to Anna, more out of an instinctive need to protest than out of any realistic hope of being listened to. Father Roberto simply pressed his forearm more firmly against her windpipe so that her attempts to speak amounted to nothing more than a choking cough and a series of incoherent splutters.

Anna's face crumpled with worry. "Take care you don't hurt her!" she ordered the priest, her voice sharp. "Loosen your hold! There is no need for such roughness."

"I will treat her with the respect that any child of God deserves," Father Roberto said piously. Hidden from Anna's view, he twisted Cordelia's arm so hard that she felt the muscle in her shoulder tear. For a split second, the pressure of his forearm against her windpipe slackened and she was able to croak out the start of a question.

"Why?" she asked Anna. "Why did—"

Father Roberto cut off her words, but Anna had already understood what she wanted to ask. "I must protect the master," she said. "He cannot live as he must with you under his roof, *signorina*. You are a deadly threat to his peace of mind and even to his life. Father Roberto will take you to a convent in Milano where you will be safe until the war is over. Then you may go back to wherever you came from."

"That is correct, *signorina*." Father Roberto's voice poured over her, smooth as oiled silk. "I am helping Anna by taking you to a place of safety far from the Villa of the Three Fountains." He tugged at the arm he had injured, sending an arrow of agony flying up to her shoulder. "Have no fear, my dear *signorina*, I will see that my sisters in the Church take care of your every need."

The distant cry of a kestrel on the prowl startled all three of them and when Father Roberto loosened his hold for a split second, Cordelia managed to croak out a cry for help. The priest recovered almost instantly, tightening his grip so savagely that he cut off the air to her windpipe. "You must gag her, Anna. We can't have her screaming while we load her into the carriage. You know what will happen if your master discovers what we are doing."

The housekeeper mumbled her grudging assent. With evident reluctance, she removed a soft linen napkin from the pocket of her skirts and swiftly folded it.

"One day you will thank me," she said, tying the cloth over Cordelia's mouth. "I swear to you, *signorina*, that no happiness would be possible for you with my master. You may have dreamed of marriage, but such an outcome would never have come about."

"In the end, she will thank both of us," Father Roberto said, his voice full of false smiles. "Now, I must bid you farewell, Anna, and hasten on our journey. With war imminent, the threat to travelers is great, and I must meet with my escort in the village if I am to have a realistic hope of reaching Milano any time in the near future."

Struggling every inch of the way, Cordelia was dragged into the carriage house where, with Anna's help, Father Roberto lifted her into a small pony trap and lashed her wrists to one of the interior support straps.

It was evident that Anna didn't like seeing Cordelia tied up, but she patted her arm in reassurance, her eyes moist with guilty tears. "As soon as you've traveled a few miles, you'll see the good sense of what we're doing," she said. "Then, once you've calmed down, Father Roberto will be able to untie you. It's a blessing that he was needed back in Milano so urgently that he couldn't even wait for the cardinal to recover. My master would have brought you only bitter unhappiness, *signorina*. I do this for your own good, and for my master's. I beg you to believe that I wish you no harm, none at all. You do not understand what is at stake here, and my master is so besotted by you that he can no longer be trusted to act in his own best interest."

Gagged, unable to do anything except shake her head, Cordelia glared at the housekeeper, burning up inside with frustration. If she could only speak to Anna, she would be able to explain how she was being tricked by Father Roberto. Since she could barely draw a deep breath, much less speak, she had no choice but to fulminate and seethe in silence.

When Father Roberto sprang up into the driver's seat, and whipped up the horse, Cordelia communicated in the only way left to her. She flung open the barriers to her mind and called to Dakon with every ounce of strength, determination, and passion that she could find within herself.

His name reverberated silently in the night. In her mind, she saw the ripples of her call spreading out, circles of light in the darkness, until they just touched Dakon. He was so far away that she couldn't see how he answered.

Father Roberto was in a great hurry to be gone. Cordelia called out to Dakon again as the carriage rolled over cobblestones that had been covered in straw to muffle the sounds. Anna was only a tiny figure in the distance when Cordelia heard the faint echo of Dakon's response.

Dakon! Father Roberto is abducting me!

She felt no response, only an abrupt cold blackness. Her mind pulsed with loneliness, and she wondered if she had imagined that earlier impassioned whisper of her name, spoken with Dakon's inimitable lilt.

She shivered. The hood of her cape had blown off, and she had no way to pull it back on again since her hands were bound. She huddled in a corner of the open carriage, trying to keep warm and cursing herself for her stupidity. How could she have followed Anna into the garden without asking even the most elementary questions about where they were going and why? Only her fatigue, and her worry about Mary, offered a partial excuse for her carelessness.

Now she would pay the price for her lack of caution. She didn't believe for a moment that Father Roberto planned to take her to a convent. Convents were not prisons, and escape would be far too easy. And he couldn't afford to allow her to go free because he knew that she would accuse him of murdering Giancarlo.

In fact, Father Roberto was taking her from the villa so that he could kill her.

Cordelia let the stark truth sink into her consciousness. She examined the thought carefully, but whichever way she twisted it, her conclusion remained the same. Unless she could find some way to save herself, she was going to die.

Her much vaunted common sense seemed to have been in sadly short supply over the past week or two, Cordelia reflected wryly. Too late, she realized how foolhardy it had been to remove the dagger from Father Roberto's desk. If she'd been thinking ahead, she would have realized that such an action was tantamount to informing him that she suspected him of committing murder. The trouble was, at the time she removed the dagger, she'd been so convinced Cardinal Walter was the guilty party that she hadn't stopped to think at all, much less to think through the consequences in relation to Father Roberto.

The Villa of the Three Fountains had long since disappeared from view. They had reached the open road now, and Father Roberto whipped the horse to a fast trot. Cordelia leaned forward, peering around the side panel, wanting to know where they were going, even though she couldn't imagine how the information would do her the slightest good.

She recognized the route they were taking, since she had been brought this way to the villa. They were following the main road to Piacenza and would eventually pass the inn where Giancarlo had abandoned her. She wondered if Father Roberto had been speaking the truth when he told Anna that he planned to pick up an escort in the village.

If it *was* true, who would provide the escort, Italian Nationalists or Austrian soldiers? She gave up attempting to unravel that mystery, realizing that in the bubbling cauldron of Italian politics, it was useless to speculate on the precise loyalties and alliances of anyone, particularly somebody determined to conceal them. One thing she could count on with a fair degree of certainty: if Father Roberto had arranged for an escort, the people protecting him would have no interest at all in helping her to escape.

What she needed to do was stop worrying about Father Roberto, and concentrate on how she was going to escape. Freedom was certainly a desirable goal, but it was not easy to see how she might attain it. She strained against the bonds that held her tethered to the side of the pony trap and eventually realized that the cord tied around her wrists was not as tight as it appeared. Anna—thank heaven for small mercies—had been so anxious to avoid hurting her that she'd wrapped linen pads beneath the cord to prevent chafing.

Was that tiny act of kindness going to provide enough leverage for her to break free? Cordelia twisted her wrists inside the pads and decided that she had quite a lot of movement, relatively speaking. Moreover, thanks to the linen pads, she could con-

tinue to twist and wriggle without having to suffer the
pain of rubbing her wrists raw against the cords.

Galvanized by the realization that she might not be
totally helpless, Cordelia gritted her teeth and set
about the task of freeing her hands. Despite the protection of Anna's pads, the cord rubbed painfully
against the fragile skin of her wrists, and every movement of her left arm inflicted torment on her torn
shoulder muscle, but she told herself that the pain
wasn't unendurable—she'd watched Mary suffer worse
only that afternoon—and when she was finally able to
manipulate her thumb so that her entire right hand
slipped through the cords, she gave a silent crow of
triumph. A glance at the watch pinned to her bodice
showed that it had taken less than fifteen minutes to
free herself, even though it had seemed like hours.
Thank goodness Anna had been the person to tie her
up. Father Roberto should never have entrusted such
an important task to such a reluctant ally.

Now that she had one hand free, Cordelia could
remove the gag that was cutting into her mouth and
making her feel sick. After that, it was a matter of
less than a minute to get rid of the cords tying her left
hand to a small stanchion on the inside of the carriage.

She was free! Elation plastered a silly smile onto
her face and made her euphoric for all of thirty seconds. She pulled the hood of her cloak over her head,
luxuriating in the sudden cessation of wind and rain
beating against her. Then reality set in. She had two
free hands, she was warmer, and she could breathe
without choking. However, her situation wasn't exactly what one might term desirable. The carriage was
bowling along at a fast clip, and the neat rows of olive
bushes on either side of the road hardly presented an
hospitable escape route. If she jumped out, assuming

that she didn't kill herself in the act of jumping, Father Roberto would be able to recapture her within minutes. She was agile, and reasonably fleet of foot, but her skirts were so cumbersome that no olive tree was wide enough to conceal her, and Father Roberto would have an insurmountable advantage if he gave chase.

Worse still, if she failed in her first attempt, she was unlikely to get another chance. Once Father Roberto realized she was determined to escape, he would take stringent measures to prevent her succeeding. Without Anna on hand, he wouldn't bother to waste time and effort making her bonds comfortable with linen pads. In fact, he would probably set aside whatever plan he'd devised for killing her, and get on with the job. At the very least, he would insure her cooperation by hitting her over the head and rendering her unconscious.

She had absolutely no desire to be rendered unconscious, even less desire to be dead. Her goal was simply to lead a long and happy life with Dakon. And, Lord knew, that goal was likely to prove quite challenging enough without outside complications from Father Roberto.

Lips pursed, Cordelia watched the countryside flash by as she pondered her options. Clearly she had to jump, the only question was when. If she waited for the carriage to reach the village before she made her attempt, someone might be willing to offer her sanctuary. On the other hand, they might not. Father Roberto was a local, she was a foreigner. It was a gamble with unfavorable odds, but her alternatives were even less desirable.

As for her cloak and layers of petticoats, they were both a curse and a blessing, she decided, since there was a danger that they would catch in the wheels of the pony trap. On the other hand, if she avoided that hazard, the thickness of her clothing might help to cushion the impact of her fall. Provided she didn't stun herself, she would have a few seconds advantage over Father Roberto, who would have to stop the carriage and, since the horse was both fresh and spirited, might even waste another few seconds trying to tether it. Presumably he wouldn't want to lose his transportation.

Having settled on the decision to jump somewhere in the village, Cordelia flexed her muscles, trying to keep warm and limber so as to give herself the maximum possible advantage. The straggling, ramshackle cottages of the village street came into view, darker shadows against the rain-misted night. The inn where she had been stranded was situated at the far western extremity of the village. Given the unhelpful attitude of the innkeeper on their previous encounter, there was no reason to assume that he might be any more willing to offer her protection from Father Roberto than the rest of the villagers. With no way to tell who might help and who might not, she would make her bid for freedom wherever the huts and cottages offered the best hiding place.

Cordelia braced herself against the sides of the trap and slid forward on her seat. Watching the ground speed by, she reflected that jumping was little more than a polite euphemism for throwing herself head first on the ground. Still, better to die trying to escape than to go meekly to whatever unpleasant fate Father Roberto had planned for her.

Without standing up and perhaps attracting his attention, she reached outside the pony trap and fumbled for the door handle. Her fingers closed over the latch and exerted slight downward pressure. The latch responded silently. Thank God, Dakon kept his carriages in such superb condition that a fraction more pressure would have the door swinging noiselessly open, although it seemed inconceivable that Father Roberto wouldn't feel the sway of the carriage when she jumped.

On the point of leaping into the pebble-strewn mud that passed for a main street, she remembered that toward the middle of the village the road swung quite sharply to the left. Father Roberto would most likely slow down at least a little, and the natural sway of the carriage as it rounded a corner would help to disguise what she was doing.

Stomach knotting and heart pounding, Cordelia waited for the turn in the road. Sure enough, she felt Father Roberto slow the carriage as they approached the bend.

In a single swift movement, she stood up, opened the door, lifted her skirts, and jumped.

The ground rose up to meet her, striking her sore shoulder with sickening force. Her teeth seemed to rattle in her head, and she rolled sideways, not out of any concerted plan to protect herself, but simply because her disoriented body chose to move that way.

When she stopped rolling, she gagged, trying frantically to draw breath. She was winded, and her lungs refused to open and suck in life-giving air. Finally, she managed to get her breath back and scramble to her feet.

It was already too late. She had barely taken a few frantic steps toward the sanctuary of the nearest cottage when she heard the thud of Father Roberto's footsteps behind her. She knew her quest was hopeless, but she ran until her lungs were bursting and the darkness danced before her eyes. The pounding of his footsteps grew ever nearer. If she stopped and banged on a cottage door he would catch her before she could gasp out a plea for help. If she didn't stop, he would soon catch her anyway.

She ran with the primitive instinct of the hunted, not daring to stop, too frightened to plan or think, moving forward strictly by instinct. When she stumbled over a rock in the roadway, he was right behind her. Sobbing, she tried to get up, but he threw himself on top of her, sending her facedown in the dirt that was just beginning to turn to mud.

Every inch of her skin and every muscle in her body was shrieking with pain, but she didn't faint. There were moments when she wished she had been born with a larger dose of feminine susceptibility.

Father Roberto laughed softly and rolled her over onto her back, slipping his hands beneath her cloak and running his hands over her body with revolting intimacy. And this was the man who had seemed to take his vows of celibacy with excessive seriousness, Cordelia thought bitterly. Good heavens, how easily he had tricked her! So much for her vaunted capacity to sense the true emotions of the people around her.

"My, my," he said, panting slightly as she struggled to get out from under him. "What a little spitfire you are to be sure. If it weren't so very cold and damp, I would be tempted to remain here and test just how tempestuous you can be."

Cordelia instantly became still, and he laughed again. "Don't try to play the shrinking virgin with me, *signorina*. I have seen you with the count, and if you are brave enough to contemplate serving his appetites, you could most certainly accommodate mine, which are quite modest, I do assure you. At least as far as sex is concerned. Now, power, that is another matter . . ."

He reached inside his cassock and slowly withdrew a dagger that Cordelia recognized all too plainly. She closed her eyes, discovering that it was a great deal harder to confront death than she had anticipated.

She felt the prick of the blade against her neck. "You can sit up," Father Roberto said. "Provided you obey my instructions, I don't plan to kill you just yet. There is somebody who wishes to speak with you."

Cordelia wasn't sure if she would gain anything by avoiding death simply so that Father Roberto and his associates could interrogate her. Perhaps she should fight back and provoke him into ending it here and now. For a second or two she didn't move. She felt the point of the dagger nick her skin, gouging a small hole. Blood fell in warm droplets on the back of her hand.

She realized just how badly she didn't want to die. Not now. Not yet. Not without seeing Dakon again.

"Get up," Father Roberto said, knife held threateningly against her throat. "Get up, or you will wish that you had."

"Why should I aid your plans in any way?" she asked, reluctantly coming to a sitting position.

"Because it will be so much less painful for you if you do," he said. "Among the more interesting of the historical subjects I have studied is the art of torture as practiced by the Holy Inquisition. Trust me, *signorina,* you would be wise not to annoy me by ignoring my requests."

She pulled herself to her feet, shaking off his hand, which he extended in a caricature of helpfulness. She was beginning to understand what was meant by the old saying "While there's life, there's hope."

Somehow, she couldn't just lie on the ground and willingly submit to death at Father Roberto's hand. The longer she stayed alive, the greater the chance that Dakon would come to rescue her.

"Where are we going?" she asked as the priest half pushed, half guided her back toward the village street.

"To the inn," he said. "I have arranged to meet some colleagues of mine there."

Cordelia saw that she had managed to run further than she'd realized. They were at the furthest extremity of the village, no more than fifty yards from the inn.

"Yes, we are going to Rafael's inn," Father Roberto said, as if she'd asked him a question. "It is hardly a deluxe establishment, as you know, but it serves our purpose quite well."

Cordelia didn't delude herself with the hope that the innkeeper might help her. He had been too fearful even to drive her as far as the villa, so there seemed no chance he would risk his safety by defending her against Father Roberto. And truth to tell, there was no reason why he should help her. In the turmoil of civil war, he had every right to think first of himself and his family.

On the very edge of exhaustion, she allowed Father Roberto to push her into the dank interior of the inn, past the innkeeper, who was polishing his pewter with a dirty rag, and into the taproom. She was too tired even to feel surprise when she saw who else was waiting there.

Captain Hesse stepped forward, his spurs jingling, the brass of his buttons gleaming in the light of the oil lamp. "Miss Hope," he said in English, his pleasant voice underlaid by a new note of harshness. "I am delighted to see that Father Roberto has persuaded you to join us tonight."

"Go to hell," she said.

He ignored her comment and gestured toward the murky, smoke-filled corner of the taproom, where she realized belatedly that yet another man was seated. The second man stood up, snapping his heels together in approved parade ground style. Cordelia registered the bristling whiskers and ruddy cheeks of Lieutenant Waldheim.

"You remember my lieutenant, of course," Captain Hesse said.

"I remember both of you with great clarity," Cordelia said. "I was once foolish enough to believe you were my friends."

"And I was once foolish enough to believe that you were a British tourist, stranded and helpless," Captain Hesse retorted.

"That is exactly what I was, Captain."

"Let us not waste time with such foolishness," he said. "I am well aware of your true purpose in coming to the Duchy of Modena."

"Are you?" Cordelia said wryly, thinking of Mary and the baby that now would never be born. "I doubt it, Captain."

"I am more than willing for you to enlighten me," he said sharply. "In fact, I am eager in my quest for information."

"I have none that would interest you. I would, however, appreciate your services as an escort back to the villa from which Father Roberto abducted me. You will remember that I am a British subject, and as such a neutral observer of the conflict that has broken out between Italy and Austria."

Lieutenant Waldheim strode across the room and

hit her across the face so hard that she fell to the floor. "Do not waste our time with such pitiful lies," he snarled. "Tell us who you are working for and it is just possible that I may agree not to kill you."

Chapter Fifteen

Lieutenant Waldheim had aimed his blow to inflict real hurt, and for several moments Cordelia lay on the floor, ears ringing and stomach heaving with the threat of sickness. When the red, watery blur cleared from in front of her eyes, she decided there was no point in struggling to sit up, since her captors would simply ask her questions she didn't want to answer, and would hit her again when she refused to answer. She lay on the filthy floor, tried not to think about the fleas making a meal of her, and feigned unconsciousness.

The Austrians, alas, were obviously experienced interrogators and the lieutenant quickly realized what she was up to. He grabbed her roughly by the arm and pulled her to her feet, pushing her against the wall and leaning toward her with deliberate menace.

"For whom do you spy?" he demanded. "Garibaldi? Zat pig Cavour? Ze French? Yes, maybe ze French. Louis Napoleon never could resist sticking his Corsican peasant's nose into ozzer people's business."

"I am English," she said, her voice not quite steady. "I am not a spy for anyone. The British consul in Modena will be outraged when he hears how you have threatened me."

The lieutenant gave a bark of derisive laughter. "I tremble!"

"You should. One day the war will end and you will be held accountable for your actions. Her Majesty's government doesn't view the mistreatment of her subjects lightly."

Captain Hesse gave a sharp hiss of impatience, and Father Roberto exclaimed in disgust. The lieutenant, a man of little imagination in techniques of persuasion, answered her protests by delivering another slap across her mouth. His signet ring cut her lip, and she tasted blood. His eyes gleamed when she moistened the cut with her tongue and his breath quickened. His mood was so volatile she guessed he was as likely to rape her as to beat her.

The lieutenant struck her as the sort of man who preyed on feminine weakness, so she lifted her head and forced herself to meet his gaze head-on. "I can't tell you what you want to hear, because I don't know anything," she said. "However many times you hit me, I will still know nothing."

The lieutenant grimaced in frustration, and was preparing to deliver another backhanded blow when Captain Hesse barked out a brief command in German. With obvious reluctance, the lieutenant stepped away from her, his hands falling to his sides, his brows drawn together in a fierce scowl. He and Father Roberto exchanged glances, united in their disapproval of the captain's lily-livered attitude.

Cordelia wasn't reassured by the removal of the lieutenant as her questioner. Captain Hesse might have no taste for unnecessary violence, but he was a great deal more intelligent than his lieutenant, and a professional soldier to his core. Cordelia knew that if he considered her a threat to Austrian victory, he would order her shot and walk away without a backward glance, or a moment of guilt. She tried not to flinch when he gazed at her, his expression thoughtful.

His voice was mild when he finally spoke, almost as if they were back in the drawing room at the villa, but Cordelia didn't make the mistake of allowing herself to relax. "Perhaps we should consider an alliance, Miss Hope, instead of this distressing adversarial stand that brings little benefit to either of us. Father Roberto has merely confirmed my own suspicions and it is obvious to me—somewhat late in the game, I confess—that you were sent to the Villa of the Three Fountains with instructions to discover the truth about the Count of Albion's activities. Whoever may have sent you, my interest now is identical with yours. I am in need of information about the count. You can, perhaps, supply that information. Let us negotiate a deal that benefits both of us."

On the brink of again denying any role as a spy, or the possession of any knowledge that could benefit the Hapsburg Empire, Cordelia suddenly realized the advantages of pretending to cooperate with the captain. Clearly nobody in the room was willing to believe that she was an innocent victim unfortunate enough to get caught up in the toils of a foreign country's revolutionary struggle. Since the truth was likely to see her dead in short order, she might as well select a lie likely to win her a chance of release. If her captors were determined to believe that she was spying for someone, why not provide them with a villain? Preferably a faraway villain who couldn't become a target of their reprisals. Allowing them to believe she was working for a foreign government seemed a small price to pay for the sake of saving her life.

The only question was to which government should she claim allegiance? The French, she decided, would be most credible. That would explain her ignorance of the factions within the local Italian Nationalist party. Besides, if Captain Hesse believed she was French, there would be the added advantage of protecting Mary's true identity as the Earl of Stanwyck's daughter. In her efforts to save her own skin, she couldn't entirely neglect her obligations to Mary.

"It is widely acknowledged that the count isn't susceptible to female wiles," she said, careful not to appear too eager to accept the captain's offer. "Even if I were a spy, which of course is ridiculous, why would anyone send me to seduce a man who is known to be armored against feminine attractions?"

"Pray, Miss Hope, refrain from raising nonissues," Captain Hesse said. "We both know that the count's unusual household arrangement is no more than a smokescreen for his political activities. The local authorities are so busy gossiping about the strangeness of his domestic establishment that they don't notice anything else about him. But I will stake my life on the fact that those young boys of his are employed as servants, not as sexual objects. For all I know, the count's story that he wishes to provide the youth of the district with an education may be the truth. It is ridiculous enough to be possible."

Father Roberto spoke up for the first time since dragging Cordelia into the inn. "The Princess Borghese herself has confessed that the Count of Albion was the best lover she has ever taken to her bed. And God knows, the princess is an expert witness." He

sniggered with spiteful mirth. "After listening to Her
Serene Highness's confession, I can state with confidence that the Count of Albion not only likes women,
he services them with finesse."

Lieutenant Waldheim chuckled, slapping his knee
in jovial appreciation of the priest's remarks. Cordelia
wasn't sure if she was more shocked by her own jealousy at the image of Dakon in the infamous Princess
Borghese's bed, or by the casual way in which Father
Roberto betrayed the secrets of the confessional.

Trying not to blush, she focused her thoughts on
the urgent topic of how she was going to strike a deal
with her captors. Blasé resignation seemed the most
convincing pose, she decided. A woman who was willing to climb into a man's bed on orders from her
government was unlikely to cringe from making a deal
to save her life.

Shrugging, as if acknowledging defeat in an impossible situation, she looked squarely at Captain Hesse.
"What is it, precisely, that you wish to know, Captain?"

He didn't smile, but his lips curled upward with satisfaction at her apparent capitulation. "I want to know
whether the Count of Albion continues to support
Austrian rule in the Italian peninsula, or whether he
has betrayed me to the Nationalists. He has played
Austrian against Italian for so long, I wonder if he
has forgotten where his true interests lie."

"Why is it so important for you to know something
so trivial, when battle is about to break out on all
fronts? Surely the Austrian High Command has more
pressing concerns than the precise loyalties of one individual citizen, even a wealthy aristocrat like the
Count of Albion."

The captain hesitated for a moment. "If you are the
expert spy I believe, you already know that the Count

of Albion is anything but an insignificant player in the events that are unfolding before us. On the other hand, if you truly have no precise knowledge of the role he has played in recent months, then there is no reason for me to enlighten you. Suffice it to say that you are in no position to demand explanations for my curiosity. Your life is at stake, Miss Hope. If you are wise, you will answer my questions without seeking information that might be dangerous to you."

"And in exchange for my cooperation? If I agree to help you, what promises for my safety will you make, Captain Hesse? Even more important, why should I believe those promises?"

He gave her a wintry smile. "You may believe them for either of two reasons, Miss Hope. Firstly, because I am a gentleman, and my word is my bond. Secondly, because you have no choice. My promises may be of questionable worth, but they are all that you have. You are an intelligent woman, that much I have always known. Therefore you must recognize that if you refuse to cooperate with us, I will have no interest in keeping you alive. In which case, my lieutenant, or Father Roberto, will certainly kill you. They are both of them a great deal more bloodthirsty than I."

"You offer me a splendid choice," she said. "One rich with threats to my safety."

"I have no interest in slaughtering women," he said curtly. "Not even spies. If you cooperate with me, I promise to see you out of Modena and into a place of safety."

"A place of safety in France," she said, with a careful pretense of letting slip her defenses. "Will you promise to send me back to France, Captain Hesse?"

He looked at her consideringly. "If that is where you are really from—mademoiselle."

She looked down to conceal a flash of hope. "It is where I'm from, Captain. Do you give me your word that you will arrange to have me returned there if I cooperate with you?" Once she was in France, it should be a relatively simple matter to send an express letter to the Earl of Stanwyck in England, and when Mary's needs were taken care of, she would be at liberty to return to the villa. And to Dakon.

"You have my word," Captain Hesse said smoothly.

Much too smoothly. Cordelia decided it was time he realized that her intelligence hadn't gone into hiding: she saw the risks ahead. "Father Roberto is determined to have me killed," she said. "He's afraid that I am going to identify him as the man who murdered Giancarlo. How can you afford to let me go free, knowing that I can reveal Father Roberto's allegiance to the Austrian cause the minute I reach French soil?"

Captain Hesse cut across the priest's noisy protests. "Once you are in France, mademoiselle, nobody will care who murdered Giancarlo, not even your employers. And the news that Father Roberto, an obscure Jesuit from the Duchy of Modena, once spied on behalf of the Austrian Imperial Government, will provoke nothing but tired yawns."

"Father Roberto is hardly anonymous," Cordelia pointed out. "He is the personal secretary to the Cardinal of Milan."

"A position he no longer holds," Captain Hesse said. "He is now en route to a new position in the Vatican, where he will be safe from any accusations you can make, since there is no chance that the papal authorities will allow him to face a civilian court. Therefore, you can place some reliance on my promise that I will not only send you back to France, I will also protect you from Father Roberto's distressing tendency to use his dagger first, and to think afterward."

The note of disapproval in Captain Hesse's voice was blatant. Giancarlo had certainly not met his end at the captain's orders. Unfortunately, Cordelia could see no way in which she could exploit the tensions simmering among her captors to provide herself with an escape route. Rafael, the innkeeper, was still standing behind his counter, assiduously polishing, his eyes flicking from one man to the other. When Cordelia attempted to meet his gaze, his eyes shifted sideways and a flush darkened his cheeks. He didn't approve of her being held captive, that was clear. It was equally apparent that he had no intention of making any protest on her behalf.

If she was going to escape death, it would clearly be by her own efforts. Cordelia sat down on the wooden chair occupied ten days earlier by Mary. She closed her eyes for a second, trying to create a center of inner calm that she would be able to draw on when the captain started his questioning. The instant her eyes closed, she felt the desperate, probing touch of Dakon's mind. She saw him galloping along the muddy road, his cloak flying behind him in the wind, the rain driving hard against his face. With all the power at her command, she projected an image of the inn and its occupants. She felt the briefest flash of comfort and reassurance as he grasped hold of the image and let her know that he had registered where she was.

The relief of knowing Dakon was coming to her rescue flooded through her entire being.

Captain Hesse shook her hard, destroying her fragile link with Dakon. Instantly relief turned to uncertainty. Had she really seen Dakon? Or had her vision been no more than a figment of her wishful thinking? That was the problem with her whole relationship with Dakon, she reflected ruefully. She was never sure how much of it was grounded in firm physical reality and how much of it was a chimera, a fantasy created by her own mind.

The captain spoke sharply. "Mademoiselle, your attention, please. We need to know first of all for whom you work. The truth, please. We shall know at once if you lie."

How absurd it was that she, an innocent bystander, should be forced to pretend guilt in order to save her life! But if the captain was to be convinced she would have to play her role as a spy with panache. Cordelia tried to visualize how a woman sent to seduce secrets would act when caught by the opposition. She settled on a manner somewhere between brisk acceptance and reluctant confession and poured forth her ridiculous story.

"The French Foreign Minister has established a secret liaison with Prime Minister Cavour, specifically for the purpose of monitoring Austrian military intelligence," she said, hoping that the lie was big enough to be credible.

"A liaison?" Captain Hesse demanded. "A bureau, you mean?"

"More in the nature of personal links," she said, inventing freely. "A regular exchange of information through secret couriers."

"I see," the captain said, sounding as if he really did. Cordelia was impressed by her own creativity. Captain Hesse stroked his mustache. "And where do you fit into this top level exchange of information, mademoiselle? Why were you selected for the task of seducing the Count of Albion?"

"I had performed some small services for the French security forces. When my ... work ... came to the attention of the foreign minister he saw the possibility of using my talents. He ... um ... admired some of my techniques and personally recruited me for a highly secret mission."

The lieutenant and Father Roberto leaned forward, eager to hear more. She realized to her embarrassment that she had created quite the wrong impression. Or perhaps it was the right impression, given her situation. From their expressions, she could see that her captors believed she'd slept with the French foreign minister and dazzled him with her sexual skills. Even Captain Hesse looked impressed.

The captain gave a little puffing sigh of excitement. "The foreign minister recruited you personally?" he asked. "Specifically to seduce the Count of Albion?"

"Er ... yes." Cordelia knew she'd be most easily believed if she simply confirmed the captain's suspicions, however ludicrous they might be. She thought rapidly, trying to come up with some reason why the French foreign minister would know or care about a minor count in the Duchy of Modena. "The Count of Albion has visited Paris several times," she said, guessing that might be true.

A cautious nod from Captain Hesse gave her encouragement. "On one of those visits, the count offered his services to the French foreign minister as a spy against the Austrians," she continued.

The lieutenant was nodding vigorously. Emboldened, she decided to bring her story a little closer to home. "The count has traveled a great deal and claimed to have contacts with high level Austrian intelligence officers." She smiled ingratiatingly at the captain. "I suppose he must have meant you, Captain Hesse."

"Ha!" Lieutenant Waldheim could contain himself no longer. "What did I tell you, Hesse? The man is a traitor! He has been betraying our emperor almost from the moment you first took him into your confidence."

Captain Hesse looked at Cordelia. "Is that true, mademoiselle? In your judgment, has the Count of Albion betrayed me and the noble Austrian cause for which he claimed to fight?"

She certainly didn't intend to save her own life by setting the Austrians in full hunting cry after Dakon. Cordelia shook her head. "The French foreign minister never trusted the count," she said, fabricating with a fluency that was quite shocking. It was worrisome to discover that she possessed such an inborn gift for lying. "The minister always believed Albion was a double spy, secretly working on behalf of the Austrians. However, other members of the minister's staff believed that the count was providing them with valuable information, so he was trusted by some of the ministry staff, at least to a certain extent."

Captain Hesse looked so well pleased with what she was saying that Cordelia congratulated herself on inventing a story that fitted neatly into his preconceived notions. "What was your precise mission, mademoiselle? Clarify that for us, if you please. I assume some specific event must have precipitated your arrival in the duchy."

"Indeed, yes," she said, thinking wryly of Mary's pregnancy. She cleared her throat, trying to decide how to elaborate on her basic theme. "Recently some important papers were stolen." That sounded believable. In war, secret documents were always changing hands. When the captain and Lieutenant Waldheim bandied speaking glances, Cordelia felt sure she was on the right track.

"I was sent here to the duchy with instructions to find out if the count was responsible for the theft. Suspicion had fallen on him, you understand."

"The French government considered these papers that he had supposedly stolen to be important?" Captain Hesse asked, his voice thrumming with an excitement he could no longer suppress.

"Yes," Cordelia agreed. "Very important, but that's all I know about them." With a touch of convincing bitterness, she added, "My French masters have no more desire to keep me informed than you have, Captain Hesse. I was told only to find out whether or not the Count of Albion might have stolen these important papers and passed them to the Austrians. There seemed to be a great sense of urgency about the matter."

"I do not doubt it. And what did you conclude, mademoiselle?"

It was imperative that she convince the captain that Dakon was loyal to the Austrian cause. "I concluded that he has no real affection for the Italian Nationalists, and that therefore his loyalty to the French cause is even more questionable."

"You believe, then, that the Count of Albion supports Austrian imperial rule in the Italian peninsula?"

"I'm sure he does," Cordelia said, with all the conviction she could give to the lie. "I believe that the count was responsible for arranging the theft of some very important documents, and that he passed the stolen property on to you, Captain Hesse."

"Then we can conclude the letters are genuine!" Lieutenant Waldheim exclaimed in German. "That means Garibaldi will march on Milano!"

Somehow, Cordelia managed to give no sign that she spoke just enough German to understand what the lieutenant had said.

"Quiet, you fool!" the captain ordered, and added a few rapid sentences that were beyond Cordelia's power to translate. When he turned back to Cordelia, his expression was neither angry nor inquisitive. For a moment, he actually appeared sad. Why?

Her stomach swooped in the sudden fearful realization of precisely where her cleverness had led her. Good God, what a blundering fool she'd been! She had just invented a story that as good as signed her own death warrant.

Captain Hesse's next question confirmed her worst fears. "You have not told your masters that you believe the Count of Albion is working for us, have you, mademoiselle?"

"Yes, yes, of course I have—"

"Of course you have not," he said. "There has been no opportunity for you to send word to anyone in France."

"A secret courier—"

"There have been no secret couriers," he said flatly. "That means, mademoiselle, that if you are silenced, there will be nobody to inform the French that the Count of Albion is loyal to our side. Nobody in France will know that we have been given access to Garibaldi's battle plans." He smiled tightly, unable to resist his moment of triumph.

She gulped. "General Garibaldi's battle plans?"

"Yes, mademoiselle, that is what was contained in the documents we are discussing. It was the general's battle plans that the Count of Albion passed to me."

Cordelia was quite sure that Dakon had done no such thing, but she could see why Captain Hesse was so anxious to confirm Dakon's loyalty. She stared at the captain in appalled dismay, realizing the full extent of her miscalculation. The Austrians were desperate to discover whether or not Dakon could be trusted. It was hard to imagine any intelligence more valuable than Garibaldi's plans for the approaching battle. And she had plunged blindly straight into the middle of this quagmire.

She'd been so busy weaving her elaborate lies that she hadn't seen where her story was leading her. Too late, she understood exactly what she had done. Obviously, Captain Hesse couldn't allow her to return to her supposed masters in France and report that Dakon had passed Garibaldi's battle plans to the enemy. In order for the Austrians to maintain their advantage in this world of illusions, lies, and murky half-truths, the captain would have to silence her. Permanently.

Captain Hesse looked at her with a sympathy that was far more terrifying than Lieutenant Waldheim's clumsy brutality, or Father Roberto's slithering deception. "I am sorry, mademoiselle, that it has come to this," he said, and she heard genuine regret in his voice. "I enjoyed the time we spent together in the Villa of the Three Fountains. I confess that, in many ways, you are a woman I admire."

With bitter irony, she realized that, in many ways, she returned the compliment. He was a man she could admire. Unfortunately, he fought for a cause she despised.

She debated telling him that the story she'd just invented was a pack of lies, then decided to save her breath for something more useful. She had invented a story that confirmed his own theories, and he would never believe her denials. He swung on his heel, drawing on his leather riding gloves. "Bring her outside," he ordered Lieutenant Waldheim.

"Yes, sir." The lieutenant set aside his earlier belligerence and once again offered the unquestioning obedience of the professional soldier.

Cordelia rose to her feet, appealing to the captain's sense of honor. "How can you renege on your given word?" she asked. "You promised me that I would be taken back to France if I cooperated with you."

Captain Hesse's gaze remained level. As she had anticipated, he showed not a trace of guilt for what he planned to do. "In war, mademoiselle, I regret that even a gentleman cannot always keep his word."

She forced herself to say the terrible words. "You're going to kill me."

"You will be shot," he agreed, his voice even. "However, I myself will conduct the execution and you have my word as an officer in the Imperial Austrian Army that you will feel no pain. Also, be assured, mademoiselle, and you will suffer no indignities prior to your execution. Your death will be swift, clean, and dignified."

"Somehow, I don't seem to find that the consolation that you seem to feel it should be."

"I am sorry, mademoiselle." As far as Captain Hesse was concerned, their discussion was finished. She was an enemy of Austria, and she would be executed.

"If you wish to say your confession, I am here to receive you into the true Church and to give you absolution for your past sins," Father Roberto piped up. "You will be able to leave this sorry world in a state of grace, my child, despite your grievous promiscuity."

Cordelia stared at him in stupefaction. He was quite serious, she decided. Despite everything that had hap-

pened, he appeared to believe that she would turn
to him—of all people!—for absolution from her sins.
Surely, even if she'd really been French and Catholic,
she'd have preferred to trust her soul to God's mercy
without benefit of such a polluted intermediary.

"I believe I will address my pleas for absolution
directly to God," she said dryly.

"As you wish." Captain Hesse walked out into the
dingy front courtyard. Father Roberto and the lieutenant each took hold of one of her arms and frog-
marched her toward the door. As she passed the rickety counter, where the innkeeper was still assiduously
polishing, he jerked his head in an odd sideways
motion.

Cordelia automatically glanced in the direction of
his gaze, and saw Dakon dismounting in a corner of
the muddy courtyard, where three other horses already waited beneath the uncertain protection of a
slate roof, supported by four wooden poles.

Her entire being flooded with relief. *Dakon, thank
God you are come!* She sent the message instinctively.
He gave her no answer.

Her captors noticed him mere seconds later and
Captain Hesse called out a greeting.

Dakon acknowledged the welcome with a gracious
nod. He strode swiftly toward the captain, his cape
billowing behind him, the collar turned high against
the wind. His hair gleamed with almost preternatural
luster in the moonlight, and his pale skin stood out in
stark contrast to the ebony black of his clothing and
the darkness of the night.

"Arrogant son of a bitch," Lieutenant Waldheim
muttered. "What's he doing here?"

Father Roberto shot Cordelia a malicious glance.
"Perhaps he has come to rescue you, my child. Your

skills in the bedroom must be of a very high order, for he seemed deeply attracted to you. A pity you will never have the chance to compare techniques with the Princess Borghese." He chuckled in appreciation of his own joke.

Dakon exchanged a few inaudible words with the captain, then watched their approach, his expression typically unreadable. When the threesome reached Captain Hesse's side, Dakon nodded to the lieutenant and the priest, but his gaze slid away from Cordelia.

His next words sent a thrill of shock down her spine. "I claim the privilege of executing her," he informed the captain, his voice cold. "I know how she tried to deceive me and I have ridden here for the express purpose of seeing that justice is done."

"Justice will be done, never fear," Captain Hesse said. "But the woman is a prisoner of war, and I have the duty of seeing that the execution is carried out according to official regulations."

"I, however, am the man she seduced and planned to betray," Dakon said. "Have I not earned the right to act as her executioner?"

The captain hesitated. "I understand your feelings, Albion, but I have given my word that her death will be swift, and as painless as possible. This is no job for vengeful amateurs."

"I want her dead, not tortured," Dakon said. "I fight for the Austrian Empire, not to inflict pain on women." He drew a gun from beneath his cloak as he was speaking. Cordelia didn't know much about guns, but she saw that it was a modern weapon, probably a revolver, which meant that, unlike old-fashioned pistols, it was capable of firing several shots without the need to reload, enabling a considerable increase in the potential rate of slaughter.

Lieutenant Waldheim exclaimed in admiration of the weapon, muttering something about a Webley Longspur, but Dakon didn't seem to be in a talkative mood. He stepped back several paces, and cocked the hammer with his thumb.

"I am aiming for the lieutenant's shako," he said. "The bullet will enter through the imperial medallion at the front center of the crown."

Before anybody could say anything, much less protest, he had pulled the trigger. The explosion set Cordelia's ears ringing, and the smoke from the powder made her cough. When her vision cleared, she saw the lieutenant's hat lying upside down on the ground, with a neat hole burned in the dead center of the crest.

The lieutenant didn't seem to be amused by this demonstration of Dakon's undoubted shooting prowess, perhaps because he'd lost his hat, or more likely because he would have been dead if Dakon's aim had been off.

Captain Hesse, however, gave a grunt of admiration. "You're an outstanding shot, Albion. Well done."

Dakon bowed in curt acknowledgment. "Do you concede to me the right to execute the prisoner, Hesse? There will be no errors, as you have seen."

The captain still hesitated, then finally nodded his head. "Yes, Albion, you have my permission to execute the prisoner. Waldheim! Tie her up. Father Roberto, you will please find a blindfold for mademoiselle."

Numb from the enormity of Dakon's betrayal, Cordelia was seized by a merciful sense of unreality. Dakon stood impassively in the center of the dank courtyard, watching the preparations for her death. Why was he making no effort to save her? If he was planning to attempt some daring rescue, now would certainly be a good time to put his plan into action.

She tried to project that thought to Dakon, but he continued to stare at the night sky, seemingly oblivious to the imminence of her execution. She wondered why he had cut off all mental contact with her. Because he didn't want to hear her desperate appeals for rescue— or because he was concentrating so intently that he didn't dare to risk distraction? Cordelia teetered between hope and despair. She had felt such deep intimacy with Dakon that a formal declaration of their love had seemed almost irrelevant. Yet now, with death so horribly near, she realized that Dakon had told her many times that the cause of Italian liberation was dear to his heart, but he had never once said that he loved her.

A bubble of panic swelled inside her, cutting off air and leaving her feeling limp and sick. She wasn't sure how she'd expected Dakon to overcome three men, two of them armed soldiers, but she certainly hadn't expected him to request permission to kill her and then stand gazing into space with the air of a distracted philosopher.

She tried once again to touch his mind, but all she felt was a swirling cloud, surrounding an impenetrable wall. Dakon was deliberately shutting her out of his thoughts, she decided, her stomach heaving sickly at the possibility of his betrayal. She had lied for him, endured danger for him. Above all, she had trusted him, even when the evidence suggested that she would be wiser not to. Was it possible that he was going to commit this ultimate act of treachery? That instead of bringing her to safety, he would personally send her to her death? She couldn't bear to believe it. Mistrusting Dakon was like mistrusting her own innermost self.

Dakon gave a quick, jerky shake of his head, covering his eyes for a second or two with his hand. Then he turned his back on her and seemed to become absorbed in contemplation of his gun. The captain busied himself lighting a branch of candles, presumably so that she would be an illuminated target. Lieutenant Waldheim stripped off her cloak and slung it across the slate roof of the shed. "Just so zat we can be sure ze first bullet does ze job," he explained. "Ze folds of your cloak might get in ze way. You had better hope ze count didn't get lucky with zat shot he took at my hat. In zis light, I haf no idea how he will take his aim."

Cordelia didn't answer, not out of proud defiance, but simply because her mouth was so dry with fear that she couldn't speak. She finally put up a bit of a struggle, the instinctive response of a doomed captive, but when she realized how futile her wriggling was, she stopped.

Even when she offered no resistance, the lieutenant made no effort to be gentle as he tied her hands behind her and lashed her to a hitching post. Her shoulder, injured by Father Roberto, screamed out in protest. Then she wondered why she was wasting time worrying about a torn shoulder muscle when these were her last few moments on Earth.

Father Roberto emerged from the inn, carrying a piece of old linen he had unearthed. It might have started life as a table napkin, if the inn had ever possessed such luxuries, and it smelled faintly of sour wine and garlic. When he attempted to blindfold her, Cordelia finally found her voice again.

"No!" she exclaimed, revolted at the prospect of ending her life with her eyes hidden behind a dust rag. "No! I want to see the man who takes my life."

Dakon came out of his reverie and swung around

to confront her. "Put on the blindfold," he commanded curtly. "I insist upon it. Put on the blindfold!"

The lieutenant held her still while Father Roberto
made haste to comply with Dakon's order. Last requests of condemned prisoners clearly carried no
weight in this outpost of imperialism, especially if they
ran counter to the orders of the executioner.

Even with her eyes staring into blackness, and the
sounds of the soldiers' boots squelching in and out of
the mud, Cordelia couldn't quite accept that she was
going to die—and that Dakon would be the person
who shot her. He wanted the Italian Nationalists to
win in the forthcoming war with the Austrians, she
accepted that, but surely he wasn't prepared to sacrifice her to an abstract political cause?

Dakon, it seemed, was perfectly willing to make
precisely that sacrifice. As far as Cordelia could tell
with her vision obscured, he made no protest of any
kind as Lieutenant Waldheim marched up to Captain
Hesse and snapped his heels together with a jingle of
spurs. "The prisoner is ready for sentence to be carried out, sir. As you know, she has refused the services
of a priest."

"Very good, Lieutenant." Captain Hesse's voice
came to Cordelia with chilling clarity. "Prisoner, you
have been found guilty of spying against the Austrian
Empire. The punishment for that crime is death. Judgment will now be carried out."

There was definitely a cosmic irony to be found in
her situation, Cordelia decided. Trouble was, right at
this moment she could feel nothing but fear and the
bitterness of Dakon's betrayal.

Captain Hesse spoke with heavy deliberation. "Are
you ready, Excellency?"

"Yes. I am quite ready," Dakon replied.

No, Dakon, don't do this! Let one of the others pull the trigger! Please, God, at least grant me that!

"You will shoot on my command. Excellency, take your mark. Ready! Aim! Fire!"

Cordelia heard an explosion. Almost simultaneously, she sensed the faint whistle of a bullet flying past her shoulder, so close that she could smell the singe of her burning hair. Her body jerked reflexively, then went stock still. After a few agonized seconds, she realized she was alive. Dakon hadn't killed her!

Her moment of euphoria vanished instantly. Her reprieve was only temporary. Dakon had simply missed his mark, and now she would have to endure the torment of a second shot. Dear God, she'd steeled herself to face his betrayal once, but she wasn't sure she could maintain her dignity through another attempt. How many times would Dakon have to take aim before he managed to kill her?

Silence settled around the courtyard, the hush of those who have witnessed death. Except that she wasn't dead. Oddly, Captain Hesse didn't repeat his command to fire, and no second shot came from Dakon, even though she knew he must still have three or four bullets in his gun.

Instead, to her astonishment, after a few seconds of quiet, she heard the captain's footsteps walking across the courtyard. He was making his way toward the hitching post where she was tied.

Cordelia couldn't imagine what was happening. The captain laid a sweaty finger against the pulse beating in her neck, waited a moment or two, then spoke with crisp finality.

"Well done, Albion. A straight shot to the heart. She is quite dead, of course."

The captain had pronounced her dead! Cordelia was

too shocked to disagree. Was he crazy? Blind? Losing his faculties? She wasn't dead. How could she be dead? The bullet had missed her. What's more, her shoulder still ached, and her pulse—which Captain Hesse had just felt—seemed to be beating at top speed, even though he hadn't detected it.

On the other hand, she had no firsthand experience being dead. Maybe dead people frequently labored under the delusion that they were alive. How were you supposed to tell the difference? She acknowledged that she had never devoted much thought to the problem of how dead people knew they were dead.

Since Saint Peter had failed to put in an appearance to certify her current state of being, she sucked in an experimental breath of air. As far as she could tell, her lungs expanded and contracted just as they had done for the previous three-and-twenty years of her life. What's more, she could still smell the wine and garlic of her blindfold, overlaid by the tang of sweat from her own nervous body. If this was what it felt like to be dead, it was remarkably similar to the feeling of being alive.

A new set of feet clumped across the courtyard and stopped in front of her. She recognized the carbolic soap and beer smell of Lieutenant Waldheim. He bent down and peered, as far as she could tell from behind her blindfold, in the general region of her bosom.

"A clean kill, Albion," he said with grudging approval. "Straight through ze heart. I must admit you are first-rate with a gun. I could not haf made zat shot myself, not in zis light."

"Thank you." Dakon finally spoke. He sounded modestly self-satisfied, even a little bored. "How do you plan to dispose of the body, gentlemen? Would you like me to take care of those details so that you can be on your way? I know this is a time of much activity for the Austrian Army."

"But I'm not dea—"

Don't speak. Don't move. Play dead.

Dakon's command came to her with clear, uncompromising authority, but when she tried to respond, his mind was as tightly barricaded as ever, his thoughts sealed behind a mental wall as impenetrable as the gates of a prison. She continued to probe, desperate to reach him, and she felt the corner of the barricade he had erected start to crumble. She felt a quick flash of panic that emanated from Dakon, not from her. It was the first emotion she'd sensed in him since his arrival at the inn.

Don't probe, he commanded. *Don't distract me, Cordelia, for God's sake.*

"Wait a minute!" Father Roberto spoke up. "Captain, Lieutenant, look again at this woman. I swear I saw her breathing. And the blood ... I don't understand. The blood is disappearing! I swear it's drying up!"

Cordelia hastily cut off her mental link with Dakon. As she disengaged herself, she had a brief glimpse of his mental barrier, which had become blank and smooth again.

"What are you talking about, Father?" Captain Hesse didn't trouble to disguise his impatience as he walked back to take another look at the supposed corpse. Cordelia kept still and quiet, scarcely daring to draw breath, more out of a desire to avoid distracting Dakon than out of any expectation of deceiving the captain by such a puny effort. She was quite sure that Dakon was somehow responsible for creating the illusion that she was dead, and she guessed that he was maintaining the elaborate pretense only by the exertion of incredible mental energy.

Captain Hesse took her hand and felt for the pulse in her wrist. At the same time, he pressed his ear against her mouth, listening intently. He stayed in that position for what seemed like an eternity, but was probably no more than a few seconds.

"She has a hole in her chest the size of my fist. She isn't breathing and she has no pulse," he said finally. "I don't know what you were seeing, Father Roberto, but if you take another look, you will see that she is quite dead. It defies belief that she could survive a wound such as the count has inflicted."

"I don't understand. I saw no wound a minute ago." Father Roberto poked her hard in the ribs. She bit her lip and managed to remain silent. "She seems to be dead," he said at last. "But I could have sworn that this bullet hole wasn't there a moment ago."

Lieutenant Waldheim laughed. "You've been hitting the brandy bottle too hard, Father."

"I don't drink intoxicating liquors," he snapped. "Do you forget that I am in Holy Orders?"

The captain intervened before their disagreement could escalate. "Well, at any rate, we are now agreed that she is undeniably dead. Since we all have pressing tasks to attend to, I accept your offer, Albion, to take charge of her burial."

"Very good," Dakon said. "You may rely on me to see that she is disposed of, and that no awkward questions are raised about her disappearance."

"You will get rid of the so-called cousin? Mrs. Ford, or whatever her real name is?"

"Certainly," Dakon replied. "She is as foolish as she is beautiful, and will be quite happy to return to Paris if I promise her a new dress for her troubles."

"That is settled then. The situation here is left in your capable hands, Albion." Captain Hesse sprang into the saddle. "Come, Father Roberto, there is nothing to be achieved by staring so raptly at a dead body. The hour grows late and it is time for us to head for Piacenza if we are to get any sleep this night."

For two or three minutes Cordelia listened to the bustle of the Austrians and Father Roberto preparing to depart. Finally the sounds of trotting horses and clinking harness faded into silence. When the night was once again quiet, Dakon approached.

He untied the blindfold and gazed down at her, his dark eyes full of tenderness, his entire body radiating passion. She wondered how she had ever thought, even for a moment, that his face lacked emotion. Every atom of his being spoke to her of the intensity of his feelings.

"Hello, my love," he said, bending his head in a slow, inexorable march toward her lips. "Welcome back to the ranks of the living."

Chapter Sixteen

◖

Dakon and Cordelia had been kissing each other for several long and satisfying seconds when it occurred to both of them that their activity would be even more pleasurable if Cordelia weren't tied to a post with her hands lashed behind her back and a rope wound around her middle. Regretfully, Dakon broke off their embrace.

"I have always wondered why human beings consider kissing such an entertaining pastime," he said. "I am finally beginning to discover why."

"Mmm," she said, trying to gather her scattered wits. "Do all the Vam-pyr kiss as well as you, Dakon, or are you especially talented?"

She felt his smile. "I would like to claim that I am especially talented. Honesty compels me to admit that I have no special skill, except for pleasing you."

She smiled back at him, overcome by the happiness of being alive, and being in love. "I'm very glad you didn't shoot me, Dakon."

He laughed softly. "So am I. And I shall be delighted to continue my demonstration of appreciation once I have these ropes untied and you can reciprocate." He reached into the narrow space between the post and the fence and wrestled with the knots.

"This is foolish," he said after a few minutes during which he spent swearing under his breath in a very human display of frustration. "Lieutenant Waldheim has you trussed up like a Christmas goose. We'll still be here at daybreak if I try to undo each knot by hand."

"A sharp knife might help, if you happen to have one tucked in your saddlebag."

"No, I don't. Only a hoof pick for my horse, which I don't think will do the trick."

"You're a Vam-pyr," she said teasingly. "Can't you cut through rope with the touch of your fingertips?"

"Alas, no, I need a sharp blade, just like an ordinary mortal. But Rafael must have a knife or two somewhere in his inn. I'll get one and cut you free in a trice."

"Are you sure he'll be willing to help you? He has never seemed very friendly, to say the least."

"Rafael has eleven children, including four sets of twins, and he feels that a man with such heavy responsibilities can't afford to be too friendly to anyone outside his immediate family. However, he loathes the Austrians, and will be delighted to hear that you have escaped death at their hands. I'm quite sure he will loan me a knife."

"Eleven children!" Cordelia exclaimed. "No wonder the poor man always looks so harried. Where does he put them all, and how does he keep them so quiet?"

"They don't live at the inn. In fact, his wife has moved in with her sister at the other end of the village.

She says she will live with Rafael again when he has learned how to stop planting babies in her belly two at a time."

Cordelia blushed and Dakon chuckled. "You are enchantingly easy to shock, sweet lady." He brushed a swift kiss across her parted lips. "Don't run away," he said, giving a teasing twitch to her bonds. "I will not be long."

He moved through the darkness with sure, firm strides, his eyes perfectly attuned to the moonlight. Her heart lurched with an odd little contraction that she recognized as a potent mixture of love and physical desire. She had no idea what would happen over the next few weeks, but she knew that one day she would return to the villa. And when she was finally back there, she was going to find some way to convince Dakon that they could safely spend the rest of their lives together. Just now, they had been able to kiss without any disastrous consequences. Dakon had seemed confident and fully in control of himself. Surely they would gradually be able to learn how to escalate their lovemaking without creating danger for either of them?

For no reason at all, or perhaps for every reason in the world, she flung her head back and hummed the triumphant melody that began the last movement of Beethoven's Ninth Symphony. She could only remember the first dozen bars, so when she reached the end of them, she started all over again, louder than before. She imagined the music spiraling up into the sky, traveling through space until it reached the home of Dakon's ancestors, on a planet that circled a green sun, in a galaxy thousands of millions of miles away.

"Congratulation, mademoiselle. For a dead woman, you sing quite splendidly."

Cordelia's burst of song ended in midnote. Her mouth snapped closed, then fell open again in horror when she saw Father Roberto ride across the court-yard and dismount less than three feet from her.

She couldn't run away because she was still tied to the post, and it was clearly too late to pretend she was dead. In hypnotized fascination, she watched the priest walk toward her, a mouse snared by the killing gaze of a stoat. She tried to call out to Dakon, but her mind seemed as paralyzed as her body, and she couldn't make contact with him, not even to call out a warning.

When he was still a step away from her, Father Roberto stopped, she sensed that he was actually a little scared of her, despite the bravado of his greeting. He cleared his throat nervously. "If I were a supersti-tious man, mademoiselle, I would wonder if you were a ghost. But since I am not superstitious, I wonder instead what conjuring trick you employed to create the illusion that the Count of Albion had shot you dead."

Since she was obviously alive, it was foolish to deny that her death had been an illusion. Cordelia kept silent, because there was nothing for her to say that wouldn't make her situation worse.

Father Roberto circled her, then returned to stop again directly in front of her, his gaze flickering back and forth across her chest. "I cannot imagine how you managed to make that wound in your heart appear and then disappear," he said finally. "But somehow, I knew you were nowhere near as dead as you ap-peared, so I doubled back to check on my suspicions."

Did that mean Captain Hesse and Lieutenant Wald-heim would soon be returning, too? Dear God, she and Dakon had been insanely careless to waste time kissing and laughing and joking when danger lurked so very near.

She still said nothing, and Father Roberto frowned. He reached into the pocket of his robe, pulling out the dagger that she had first seen the night Giancarlo died. He released the catch on the handle, and the blade shot out with a soft, vicious hiss. The mere sight of it was enough to turn Cordelia's knees to water, and her brains to melted blancmange.

"If you will not speak willingly, perhaps this will persuade you. Where is the count?" Father Roberto spun the knife with lethal expertise. Watching him, Cordelia remembered that he had been born in Modena's hill country, where there was a centuries-old tradition of fighting with daggers.

"I don't know where the count is," she said.

"Come, mademoiselle, you disappoint me. You can do better than that." Father Roberto inserted the point of his knife blade into the top button of her gown. With a downward slash, he ripped her dress open, leaving a thin cut in her flesh all the way from her neck to her waist.

He viewed the beads of blood welling in the cut with an expression of mild satisfaction. "I trust I have now captured your attention, mademoiselle. Your cooperation would be appreciated."

She didn't reply, and his mouth tightened irritably. He drew the knife downward again, making a second cut, parallel to the first. Almost indolently, he drew little horizontal slashes to connect the two lines, making a ladder of blood between her breasts. The pain was excruciating, although the cuts weren't deep.

"When I ask a question, mademoiselle, it would be wise of you to answer. Do I make myself clear?"

"Yes." She hated to concede him the victory of a

reply, but she had no doubt that he would continue cutting her until she either responded or lost consciousness.

"Now, we will try again to conduct a civilized dialogue. If you please, mademoiselle, where is the Count of Albion?"

"Right behind you, Father," Dakon said, his voice soft with menace. "Was there something you wished to ask me, perhaps?"

˙ The priest swung around, his face turning stark white when he saw the giant carving knife Dakon wielded in one hand—and the gun he held in the other.

"I want to kn-know h-how you made us all th-think she was d-dead!" Father Roberto stuttered.

Dakon smiled, a baneful smile that lacked any trace of mirth. "I am a vampire," he said. "I can make humans like you believe any illusion I choose."

Father Roberto gave an angry exclamation and his cheeks suffused with color. "I am not an ignorant peasant to believe such nonsense," he growled. "Curse you, Albion, what kind of a fool do you take me for?"

"The kind of fool who murdered Giancarlo Bianchi, and deceived Cardinal Walter, one of the kindest and most noble human beings on this earth."

"He is a damned democrat!" Father Roberto spat out. "He betrayed his Church, his pope, and everything he should stand for!"

"The cardinal is a democrat certainly. Damned he is almost certainly not. As for betrayals, you are a fine one to talk. You have sold out to the Austrians."

"Modena is a small state in a hostile world," he said defensively. "We need the protection of the Austrian Empire. Besides, the peasants of this duchy are too ignorant to govern themselves."

"You were once a peasant, Roberto. Are you too ignorant to make choices about your own government?" Dakon tucked the knife into his waistband and held out his hand. "You had better give me your knife, Roberto. Obviously I cannot allow you to ride out of here and report to the Austrians that Miss Hope is alive. You would spoil all the plans for the upcoming battle that the cardinal and I have prepared with such care."

"You are going to kill me!" Father Roberto almost choked on the words.

"No, I have no right to pass judgment on you. I shall hand you over to the local freedom fighters. They intend to make you stand trial in their own court of justice for the murder of Giancarlo Bianchi."

"You cannot give me to the Nationalists! That would be a sentence worse than death!" Father Roberto's protest was a squeal of undiluted terror.

"You should have considered such consequences before you murdered your fellow citizens," Dakon said.

"Do you think I intend to surrender meekly, just because you order it? Think again, Count! You shall not live to take me prisoner!"

Swifter than thought, Father Roberto's arm rose and swung back. There was a flash of gleaming metal as his dagger cut an arc through the air and landed with a gentle thud in the middle of Dakon's chest.

Instantly, even in the dark, she saw the well of scarlet blood against the whiteness of Dakon's shirtfront. He swayed, clutching the handle of the dagger, and sank to his knees.

Cordelia realized that the keening moans of grief she was hearing came from her own throat. "Oh my God, Dakon, speak to me," she pleaded, tugging frantically—and uselessly—at her bonds. "Oh God, how badly has he wounded you?"

I . . . shall . . . be . . . all right. Must rest, that's all.

His reassurance echoed shakily in her mind, belied by the evidence of her own eyes. Father Roberto was already running for his horse when Dakon pushed himself up on one elbow, took aim, and fired.

Roberto froze in a tableau of terrible stillness, then slumped and slithered down the side of the horse. The frightened beast danced and skittered, its hooves pounding Roberto's already inert body ever deeper into the muddy ground. Sickened, Cordelia looked away. Finally, the terrified neighing stopped and the pounding of hooves ceased. There was no need to look back to confirm that Father Roberto had met an end as horrible as his betrayals.

Taking aim at Father Roberto had clearly exhausted the last remnant of Dakon's strength, and he lay motionless on the muddy ground, less than a foot away from Cordelia. He was so close to her, that she could touch him with her toe. For all the good she could do him, she might as well have been a hundred miles distant.

"Rafael!" She screamed the innkeeper's name with all the force of her lungs, and kept screaming until he poked a reluctant nose into the courtyard.

"Come and untie me," Cordelia ordered, trying not to sound as frantic as she felt. Rafael didn't seem the type of man to respond well to female hysterics. "For God's sake, Rafael, the count will die if we don't get him some help quickly! You must cut me loose!"

For several moments, the innkeeper seemed undecided whether to venture forth or retreat back behind the safety of his wooden counter. She was so relieved when he stepped hesitantly into the courtyard that she burst into tears.

He gave Roberto's mangled body a wide berth and approached her with the caution of an unarmed man trying to make friends with a hungry tiger.

Once he got close enough to see that she really was just an unarmed woman, tied to a stake, he seemed to gain courage. He picked up the carving knife and slashed through the cords that tied her with surprising speed and efficiency. Her circulation had been cut off for so long that she fell when she tried to walk, stumbling into a clumsy heap alongside Dakon's inert body.

It was hopeless to examine him on the muddy ground by the light of the moon, and with hands that were filthy dirty and numb from being tied behind her for so long. "Help me carry him inside," she said. "Please, Rafael, he will die if you don't help me."

The innkeeper knelt down and put his ear to Dakon's chest. "I think he's already dead, *signorina.*"

She closed her eyes, squeezing back the agonized tears, refusing to accept such a terrible ending to a relationship that had held out the promise of so much joy.

"He's unconscious, but not dead," she said firmly, trying to make herself believe it.

The innkeeper shot her a glance that was three parts disbelief and one part pity. Nevertheless, he heaved Dakon onto his broad, squat shoulders and carried him inside. He dumped him, none too gently, on the wooden table in the taproom.

"I need water, Rafael," Cordelia said. "Preferably hot water, and some alcohol so that we can disinfect the wound. And bandages, if you have them."

"No point in disinfecting the wounds of a dead

man," the innkeeper said. "It's a waste of good brandy, *signorina*."

"But the count isn't dead," Cordelia insisted, and suddenly she knew that she spoke the truth. Dakon's breathing might be imperceptible, and his heartbeat too feeble to hear, but she was aware of the indefinable—and unmistakable—sense of his presence.

The certainty that Dakon wasn't dead gave her the energy she needed to chivy the innkeeper into action. He grumbled nonstop, but in fairly short order he produced a pail of clean hot water, a stack of relatively clean rags, and a dusty bottle of cognac. This last was delivered with a scowl, and a comment to the effect that it would cost her one of those golden guineas she'd waved about so freely on her last visit.

If he had but known, he was selling his brandy cheap. Cordelia would willingly have given him her entire stock of worldly possessions if it would have helped revive Dakon. He still showed no sign of life, but determined not to give up hope, she pillowed his head on the folds of his cape and unbuttoned his shirt, steeling herself not to faint when she saw his wound close up.

Roberto's dagger had been thrown hard and fast. It had left a deep, jagged hole in Dakon's chest, but it was nowhere near as gruesome a sight as she'd expected. As she cleaned the wound, Cordelia saw that where the blood was congealing at the edges of the cut, the flesh already seemed to be knitting together.

That might be a false hope, although she didn't think so. What was certain was that once she'd cleaned the wound no fresh blood spurted out. That was a wonderful sign if it meant the internal injuries were somehow healing themselves. It was a terrible sign if it meant that Dakon was dead.

Rafael edged into the taproom, carrying another pail of hot water. "You might need this for yourself, *signorina*." He shuffled his feet, a truly reluctant hero. "You need to tend to those cuts on your chest, or they'll turn septic." He scowled. "I don't hold with violence against women, even if you are a spy. That Roberto came from a bad family. Nothing but trouble-makers for three generations. I have to say it, even if he was a cousin of my cousin. His brothers are brigands, all of them, and he was no better. A brigand in priest's clothing."

Having delivered his verdict on Father Roberto, he plopped the bucket down next to the table where she'd been tending Dakon. Rafael stared at the dagger wound with mingled admiration and puzzlement.

"You have done a fine job in cleaning him up, *signorina*. I'd never have believed you could fix him up so quickly. His wound looks as if it's been sewn by the finest surgeon." He bent down and rested his ear against Dakon's chest, grimacing with genuine regret. "It's no use, though, *signorina*. He isn't breathing, you know."

"All he needs is rest," she said stubbornly. "And I do, too, Rafael. You once told me that you have a bed in your loft. Do you think you could carry the count up there?"

"I have a bed and a fine staircase leading to it," Rafael said, opening a door behind his counter and indicating a set of narrow, twisting wooden stairs. "And I am very strong."

Cordelia rested her hand on his arm. "Thank you, Rafael. I have no money with me, but when the count has recovered and I am able to return to the villa, I will see that you are well paid for your trouble."

"There is no need for that, *signorina*. The count

has always been good to me." The innkeeper looked horrified at what he had just said. "That is to say, you may take your time in settling your account, *signorina.* I am an excellent judge of people's character, and I am sure you are an honest woman who will remember that I have eleven children to feed."

The loft was surprisingly clean and airy, with a wooden bed covered by a cotton flock mattress. As Rafael had promised, there were two clean sheets, a thick gray blanket, and a long narrow bolster covered in an embroidered pillowcase.

"From my wife's dowry," Rafael said, gesturing to the pillowcase as he laid Dakon on the bed. "We have two of them," he said gloomily. "The finest linen. Not that she ever lets me sleep on them anymore. It's six months since I have shared her bed."

He set the candle Cordelia had carried upstairs on the niche in the plaster wall and arranged Dakon's arms in a pious crossed position over his chest. After a moment's thought, he pulled off the count's boots and stacked them neatly at the side of the bed.

This apparently concluded his devotions to the dead. "I shall be sleeping downstairs if you need me, *signorina.*" His gaze flicked from Dakon back to her. "You do not mind sharing a bed with a dead person, *signorina*?"

On the point of protesting yet again that Dakon wasn't dead, it occurred to Cordelia that the morality of the village was so strict she would never be allowed to stay with Dakon unless the innkeeper believed that he was dead, and safely beyond the lures of human temptation.

"No," she said, trying not to feel squeamish about what she was saying. "I don't mind sharing the bed with a dead person."

"Very good, *signorina*. I trust you will sleep well. In the morning, I will send one of my cousins to the villa with news of what has happened here, and we will arrange for Roberto's burial. After all, he is the cousin of my cousin so we cannot leave him in the mud."

"Thank you. I appreciate all your help."

Rafael paused for a moment in the narrow doorway. "I am sorry that I could not drive you to the villa when you first came here, *signorina*. I had been warned by the Nationalists that you were a spy."

The innkeeper went downstairs without waiting for her to reply, his wooden shoes sounding loud on the wooden stairs. Cordelia stripped off her dress and crinoline, sighing with relief as she washed and refreshed her aching muscles in the pail of hot water she'd carried upstairs. The cuts Father Roberto had inflicted stung when she washed them, but the pain had long since eased. Wearing only her shift, she slipped into the bed next to Dakon.

He was cold, his skin icy to her touch. He gave no sign of breathing, and however intently she listened, she couldn't hear the thud of his heartbeat or the throb of his pulse. And yet, each time she touched him, she felt the reassuring hum of his mental presence.

Cordelia tried to decide what might be happening to him. Roberto had definitely aimed to kill, and his dagger had sunk deep into Dakon's heart. Presumably, therefore, Dakon was truly wounded, and not creating the illusion of his own death. Could she be witnessing the Vam-pyr equivalent of a human coma? A period of deep unconsciousness during which the Vam-pyr body recuperated from serious wounds and illness? She would like to believe that, since the alternative was to accept that Dakon was truly dead.

Her optimism wasn't entirely the fancy of a lovesick woman, she assured herself. She had seen the first faint signs of healing when she dressed his wound. Surely a dead man's flesh, even the flesh of a Vam-pyr, wouldn't knit together in the appearance of healing.

There was one certain way to test her theory. Almost afraid to look, she lifted the makeshift dressing she had applied to Dakon's wound. Her breath quickened at what she saw, and her heart pounded with relief and joy. She hadn't been mistaken, after all. The process of healing had continued apace over the last half hour or so, progressing so far and so fast that the wound had already closed, and the bloody mess of torn skin and flesh had turned into a graze no more severe than the skinned knee on a schoolboy.

"Dakon, where are you? What's happening to you?" She wished she could talk to him in the silent intimacy of a mind link, but she was afraid to probe too deeply in case she disturbed the healing process. She reached out and stroked his face, letting her fingers dip into the hollows beneath his high cheekbones, and caressing the tiny swellings—imperceptible to sight, but faintly discernible to her touch—that were located above his incisors. His hair, for all its thickness, was soft and fine, so silky that there was a sensuous pleasure in letting it trickle through her fingers and over her hands.

She rolled onto her side so that she could be closer to him. He still gave no sign of drawing breath, but she thought that his skin had lost some of its previous deathly chill, although the terrible, stark pallor of his complexion remained. She rested her head on his shoulder and let her hand slide between the buttons of his shirt, so that when his heart started to beat again, she would feel it instantly.

She had been lying next to him for about an hour when, without warning, without even a second where he hovered between wakefulness and sleep, Dakon regained consciousness. His eyes flew open, his heart started to beat, and his flesh grew warm beneath her hand.

He sat up in bed, alert but wary. *Where are we?* he asked.

In the loft at the inn. Her whole body glowed with the joy of having him back with her again. *Rafael has loaned us his bed for the night. He allowed me to stay with you because he's sure you're dead.*

She felt the caressing whisper of his gratitude. *But you didn't accept that.*

No. I could always feel your presence. If you had been dead, I would not have known how to endure the loneliness of living.

His mind shuttered abruptly. He stood up and walked across the room to the tiny window, and when he spoke again, he distanced himself from her by using words, not a mind link. "The Austrians didn't return while I was unconscious?"

"No, we're quite safe. Father Roberto may have doubted my death, but I'm sure Captain Hesse and Lieutenant Waldheim had no suspicions."

"Nevertheless, you are likely to be in some danger from them, at least until the war is over."

"Then I shall rely upon you to keep me safe."

His laughter was tinged with bitterness. "I am the last person in the world whom you should trust with your safety, Cordelia."

"How odd that I should find you the person whom I can most easily trust."

She heard despair in his voice. "Cordelia, you know what I am."

"Yes, you are a Vam-pyr."

"A vampire," he corrected her acidly. "An alien being who takes the life of innocent human females."

"That may have been true once. But when I look at you now, I see only a man of great honor."

He turned to her, then, the longing in his eyes over-shadowed by the tortured knowledge of where he feared that longing would lead them.

I want you, Cordelia. His words filled her mind, and her body flooded with his desire.

I want you, too, she said.

His expression didn't change, but she felt the sad sweetness of his smile as he looked at her. He came back to where she sat on the side of the bed and cradled her cheek in his hand. When she turned and pressed a kiss into his palm, he traced the curve of her lips with fingers that weren't quite steady.

You are the mate I have dreamed all my life of finding, he said. *You are the gentle spring breeze that refreshes my soul. You are a fire that roars in my blood and consumes my heart.*

Dakon, I love you. She would never have found the courage to speak the words out loud. In the silent intimacy of their souls it was easier to acknowledge the truth.

She felt his love envelop her, but he wouldn't declare it, and she knew that he fought to prevent the words taking shape in her mind.

You must leave me, he said. *I am still weak from the healing process, and my power to resist is low. If you do not leave, I will make love to you.*

Then most certainly I shall not leave.

His eyes darkened, and she felt his despair. *If I make love to you, Cordelia, you will die.*

You cannot know that—

I know it. Leave, Cordelia, while I still have the strength to let you go.

She couldn't—wouldn't—accept that loving Dakon would cause her death. Slowly, fully aware of what she was inviting, she kissed him on the mouth.

The immediate leap of his hunger answered a craving deep inside her. For a few seconds, Dakon held himself aloof. Then, with a silent cry that echoed and reechoed inside her mind, he pulled her down on top of him, ravishing her body and soul with the passionate urgency of his kiss.

His hands tore at her shift, ripping open the ribbons that closed the gathered neck, and tugging the garment over her head. She opened her mind to him as he laid bare her body, letting him feel her passion and her love. In return, he gave her a glimpse of the driving, hammering pulse of his need.

His hands swept down her body, shaping her breasts, pressing against the curve of her hips, seeking out the innermost secrets of her body.

Her need for him was soft, liquid, molten. His need for her was hot, savage, all-consuming. She drew his feelings deep inside her, drowning in the red mist of his desire. Her pleasure twisted and curled around him until it was impossible to distinguish between his driving need and her yearning ache.

Her body was flame. His was steel. Together they had the power to create something new and wonderful. Dakon nuzzled her neck, ecstatic as he felt her jugular vein swell from the impact of the fluid dripping from his burgeoning sacs. She was moist, hot, ready for him, begging for fulfillment, for the climax she sensed hovering just beyond the horizon.

He felt her need with the same burning urgency that he felt his own, a glorious aphrodisiac, an exquisite mingling of the senses. Male, female. Hard, soft. Need, desire.

In a moment, after a second or two more of blissful anticipation, he would slip his fangs into her throat. Then, when her body was safely prepared with mating fluid, he would enter her—

Yes, she said. *I am ready.*

No, I will not permit myself to hurt you!

But, Dakon—

No! Enough! I have sufficient guilt to bear without the addition of your death. With an anguished cry, Dakon threw himself off her and staggered away from the bed, leaning against the wall as his body shuddered under the impact of a denial almost too agonizing to bear. He was already weak from the loss of blood caused by Roberto's dagger. The arousal of all his mating instincts, without any hope of appeasement, left him hovering barely on the right side of sanity.

"Get out of this room," he said hoarsely, not trusting himself to survive the intimacy of speaking without words. "Go now, Cordelia." His command was thick and slurred with the impediment of swollen sacs and distended fangs. The sound of his own voice disgusted him. He was a beast, a creature of mindless lusts, incapable of controlling the reactions of his own body. And Cordelia was in mortal danger of becoming the next victim of those hideous lusts.

He turned away, unable to bear the sight of her leaving. Moments later, he heard the sounds of her getting up from the bed, but to his horror, he realized she was coming toward him, not leaving the room. He swung around, torn between the utter humiliation of letting her see his hideous, contorted features, and the desperate need to convince her that she must flee.

When she didn't immediately run screaming from

the room, he bared his teeth in a frightening parody of the wild animal that he was. His fangs, glistening with mating fluid, protruded with pointed savagery over his lower lip.

Cordelia continued to approach him, and he felt no wave of revulsion flowing from her. Didn't she realize that his needs were bestial, appalling, consuming? That he was a monster who would tear out her throat at the first opportunity?

Even now, despite his shame, his lust was so out of control that his fangs tingled and ached with the longing to sink into the beautiful smooth flesh of her neck. His sacs swelled painfully, completing the distortion of his features. He could guess how totally, utterly repulsive he must appear.

Oddly, Cordelia looked at him without flinching, and her eyes were soft and misty, almost as if she found him desirable, although he knew that could be no more than the reflection of his own wistful fantasy. Her hair, the color of sweet sherry, tumbled around her shoulders in a thick, tempting curtain. Dakon closed his eyes, imagining that wonderful hair falling around his face in a soft cloud as he sank his fangs into her throat.

The image was too wonderful, too tempting, to be borne. Dakon clung to the last, desperate reserves of his self-control, waiting with clenched fists and pounding heart for Cordelia to come to her senses and flee from the room.

"I love you, Dakon." She spoke out loud because he still had just enough control to deny her access to his mind. As she spoke, she lifted her hair, piling it high on her head and holding it there with one hand. Then she closed the last few inches of space between them and tilted her head to one side, exposing the exquisite perfection of her neck and shoulders.

"I want you," she said. "I want us to join blood and body and soul as Vam-pyr are meant to join." Absurdly, crazily, she sounded as if she meant it.

The world spun and tilted around him. *What are you doing?* he demanded, incapable of adding sound to the question even though he dreaded the consequences of giving her access to his mind. *By all that is holy, Cordelia, have you gone mad?*

Perhaps, she said. *Mad with desire, possibly.*

Desire? Desire for what? She couldn't possibly mean that she genuinely desired him. Tolerated him, perhaps, for some crazy reason, but she could not feel desire for a creature who drowned his lust in blood. While he gulped and panted, she raised her hand and slowly pressed it against his mouth.

The ecstasy of her touch was indescribable. Dakon's eyes drifted closed and he rubbed his fangs back and forth against the palm of her hand. The points were razor sharp, ready for insertion, but she held her hand very still, so he was able to avoid injuring her. She leaned close against him, her breasts pressed against his chest. Impossible as it seemed, he felt no hint of fear when he held her, only desire.

Overwhelmed by tenderness, he caressed the delicate length of her spine and the curve of her hips, all the while nuzzling his fangs against the softness of her hands. Her love flowed back to him. Before he could stop to question how it had happened, he was in bed again, lying next to Cordelia.

And his fully distended fangs were no more than a quarter of an inch from her jugular vein.

For an endless moment he stared at the woman he had come to love and she stared back at him, her gaze clear and unafraid. He wanted to mate with her more than he wanted life itself. He wanted to drink her blood and give her the life-restoring fluid from his sacs in exchange. He wanted to ease into the virginal tightness of her body, and pour out the seed from which his son would grow. But he was a Vam-pyr and she was a human, and that meant they could never mate.

Slowly, wearily, he raised his head, turning away from temptation, striving to find the strength to move out of her bed for a second and final time. The effort to break away from her brought less physical anguish than he had expected. The sense of emotional loss was more devastating than he could have imagined in a thousand nightmares.

Finally, he managed to get his feet onto the floor and drag himself upright. Cordelia gave a little whimper of disappointment and frustration. When he tried to stand, she reached up and clasped her hands at the back of his neck, pulling him back down onto the bed.

I want you, she said. *When will you get it into your stubborn Vam-pyr head that I WANT YOU!*

She had no idea what she was saying, of course. Shaking, his body convulsing, Dakon managed to keep his head averted, shielded from any glimpse of her. But she made a small, impatient sound and grasped his head between her hands, forcing his head down toward her neck until the incredible, unforgettable moment when the points of his fangs actually slid into her jugular vein at her command.

As soon as he felt her blood against the sensitive tips of his fangs, he was lost. Desire streaked through his body in an arrow of hot, burning fire. Cordelia's desire, Dakon realized incredulously, mingled in glorious confusion with his own.

His fangs sank deeper into her throat and the warm salt taste of blood filled his mouth. Cordelia's blood. The blood of the woman he loved.

His sacs burst instantly, sending mating fluid streaming into the tiny openings he had made in Cordelia's throat. His whole body pulsed with the power of her blood, and her body thrummed with the erotic impact of his mating fluid.

Passion, need, hunger, love, washed over him in giant waves. His hunger, her need, their love.

Cordelia stirred restlessly beneath him, giving a new direction to his desire even as his fangs slowly retracted and his sacs shriveled. He fought to control the wild elation roaring through his veins so that they could prolong their pleasure, but when she arched her hips beneath him in an instinctive urge to join with him more closely, his control shattered. He plunged into her, flooding her with his seed, holding her in his arms as her body shook with the intensity of her orgasm.

The shivers of her pleasure—his pleasure—finally ceased. He withdrew from her, shoulders heaving, and turned to look at her, terrified of what he might see.

You are alive, he said in wonder. *I didn't kill you.*

Are you quite sure? I was convinced I had gone to heaven. Astonishingly, he heard laughter in her voice. She yawned, and stretched lazily. *I'm so sleepy, I think you must be right. Dead people don't feel sleepy, do they?*

She yawned again and he stared at her in disbelief. The world had turned on its axis, the stars had moved, and she was yawning? *Is that all you have to say?* he demanded. *That you are sleepy?*

Her laughter rippled over him like a warm silken covering. *I could tell you that you are a magnificent lover, that I am happier than I have ever been in my life before, that I feel totally and utterly fulfilled. But that might make you too conceited, Dakon. So I shall go to sleep instead.*

He ran the tips of his fingers over her throat. The tiny incisions where his fangs had cut into her flesh were already healed, restored by the balm of his mating fluid. *I must have hurt you*, he said. *I cut into your flesh.*

You know that you didn't hurt me in the least. You felt my feelings, just as I shared yours.

He took her into his arms, unable to believe the joy to be found in the simple act of holding his mate close to his heart. *I love you, Cordelia*, he said, amazed that it had taken him so many years to understand such a simple concept. His mouth curved unbidden into a purely human smile. *I love you, sweet Cordelia. I love you.*

She yawned. *I love you, too, Dakon.*

His euphoria was shaken by a sudden fear that was all the more terrible because it contrasted so starkly with the joy they had been feeling.

What is it? Cordelia shook off her lethargy and sat up in the bed. *For God's sake, Dakon, what's wrong?*

I've made you pregnant, he said gloomily. *Eleven months from now you will give birth to my son.*

Oh, is that all? Cordelia flopped back against the pillow. *Well, you know, I'm sorry if you feel trapped, but you would have had to marry me anyway. Rafael isn't the sort of innkeeper to allow fornication in his upstairs bedroom. As soon as he finds out you're alive, he'll be summoning Cardinal Walter and marching you off to the nearest church.*

He was exasperated by her refusal to acknowledge the danger that she faced in giving birth to a Vam-pyr baby. He focused on his exasperation, because if he allowed himself to dwell on what was ahead, he knew he would be frenzied—frantic—desperate—at the prospect of losing her during the birth.

Cordelia laid her hand against his cheek in a reas suring caress. *Don't worry so much, Dakon. You were convinced that I would die if you made love to me. Instead, I experienced greater joy than I had ever known. Can you not have faith that I will give birth to your child safely? And that we will go on to have many more of your Vam-pyr sons?*

For her sake, he wanted to believe that happiness was possible, and so he held her close and whispered the words he knew she wanted to hear. Cordelia had already brought him one miracle. Could he not allow himself to hope that she would survive the ordeal of bearing his son?

Cordelia kissed him softly, lingeringly, lovingly. *Yes,* she said. *Trust me, Dakon. You can believe in miracles because together we will make them come true.*

Epilogue

(

The Villa of the Three Fountains, January 1860

ZArymp wouldn't have admitted it for the world, but he was rather fond of the human female his son had insisted upon marrying. Now that he was getting old—well, not old precisely, but a year or two past the first glow of youth—he no longer enjoyed racing around the globe in constant search of entertainment. To be honest, he'd thoroughly enjoyed the weeks he'd spent here at the villa, pretending to be Dakon's great uncle. He'd met all the local dignitaries, whiled away many gratifying hours pontificating about the future of Italy, and had generally allowed himself to be cosseted by Dakon and Cordelia. The villa seemed an infinitely more cheerful place since she had become its mistress.

Of course, the fact that his grandson was about to be born had a great deal to do with his good mood. *Grandfather,* he thought contentedly. *Now there's a title to make a Vam-pyr start counting his blessings.* He stretched his feet out toward the fire blazing in the hearth and sighed happily as he wriggled his toes inside his slippers.

Dakon strode into the drawing room, his face twisted into one of those strange contortions that humans adopted to signify concern. ZArymp had noticed recently that Dakon was beginning to embrace more and more human customs and tricks of behavior, but the boy was a hundred and thirty-two years old, so ZArymp said nothing. He had given the lad a good education and now it was time to let him find his own pathway through the alien world they inhabited.

"Cordelia's gone into the final stage of labor," Dakon said, his voice harsh with worry. "Anna has sent me from the room."

With what he considered monumental tact, ZArymp refrained from delivering a lecture on the stupidity of awarding servants—and female servants at that!—the authority to decide which rooms their masters could and could not enter.

"Anna has children of her own," he said mildly. "She will know what to do, and I am sure she will send for you if there is any need."

Dakon paced the room, back and forth, until ZArymp's head was aching. "I felt her pain," he said. "She's only been in labor for eight hours, and already the pain was almost beyond her capacity to endure. My son was tearing her apart."

"Women suffer even when they are delivering human babies," ZArymp said, offering the best comfort that he could.

"I left her only because she said my fear was making her pain worse." Dakon turned to him, his eyes haunted. "If she dies, Father, I don't know how I shall continue to live."

A servant appeared in the doorway. "Anna requests that you come at once, Excellency. The countess is asking for you."

Dakon was out of the room and halfway to the stairs before the servant had finished speaking. ZArymp got to his feet more slowly, feeling a twinge of pain in his joints as he moved. Old age, he reflected ruefully, was not an attractive state of being.

He climbed the stairs slowly, finally admitting to himself that he was not looking forward to what he might find when he reached Cordelia's bedroom. He had attended too many Vam-pyr births that ended in tragedy and, although he prayed for the best, he was prepared for the worst.

He had stopped to catch his breath on the landing at the top of the stairs when Dakon burst out of his wife's room, his expression distraught and his hair standing on end in wild disorder.

"My child is born!" he said. "Cordelia has safely delivered our baby! She is alive and well!"

"Congratulations, my boy." ZArymp felt a most uncharacteristic lump form in his throat. "This is indeed good news. What are you going to call him?"

"I don't know." Dakon still appeared half demented, and ZArymp chuckled to himself, remembering his own elation when Dakon had been born.

"I daresay there will be plenty of time to consider names," ZArymp said. "Am I going to be allowed a glimpse of this new grandson of mine?"

"Yes, Father, certainly." Dakon's mouth suddenly broke into a huge grin. The boy really was becoming the next best thing to human, ZArymp thought grumpily, with his grins and frowns and chortles. It was all this marriage nonsense that was ruining his Vam-pyr training.

Dakon finally remembered his heritage. He stood aside and bowed, his hand over his eyes in a mark of respect. "Please, Father, go in. Cordelia is feeling quite well, all things considered."

ZArymp walked across to the bed where the mother of his grandson lay propped up against half a dozen pillows. The baby was cradled in her arms, and sleeping the peaceful sleep of the very newborn. ZArymp looked down at his grandson and saw two chubby fists, and a crumpled face topped by a shock of ebony hair.

My grandson, ZArymp thought. *Dakon's son. A new generation of my people.* The Vam-pyr never cried, but ZArymp felt a strange choking sensation at the back of his throat, which he cleared by coughing noisily. Really, these human affectations must be catching, like the grippe, or measles.

"Congratulations, my boy," he said, giving Dakon an affectionate clap on the shoulder. "And well done, my dear," he said to Cordelia. He patted her hand with awkward kindness. "We are all very proud of you."

"Thank you. I'm so glad everything went well." She smiled at him, then nuzzled the baby with her cheek, her face suffused with such radiance that ZArymp felt his staid Vam-pyr heart lurch in sympathetic joy.

Dakon sat down on the bed and put his arm around his wife and child. Apart from his hair and a certain wild gleam in his eyes, ZArymp decided that his son looked almost normal. "Well, Father, how do you like my offspring?" he asked.

"A splendid little fellow," ZArymp said. "Simply splendid. If you have no other names picked out, I would like to suggest D'azek, after my own grandfather. I have always thought D'azek a good, strong masculine name."

Cordelia and Dakon exchanged glances. ZArymp had the oddest impression that they were laughing. "It is an excellent name, Father, but there is one small problem with your suggestion."

"And what is that, may I ask?"

"Our baby is a girl," Dakon said. "Cordelia and I have produced a baby daughter."

ZArymp stared at them, his mouth opening and shutting, although no sound emerged.

Dakon smiled. "Are you speechless, Father? Well, this is certainly a day of miracles."

ZArymp finally managed to find his voice. "There must be some mistake," he said. "How can you be sure she's a girl?"

"The evidence is somewhat indisputable," Cordelia said dryly.

ZArymp shook his head in bewilderment. "Vampyr babies are always boys. For four thousand years, no Vam-pyr has ever fathered a female child."

Dakon tried to look modest, and failed completely. "It seems, Father, that Cordelia and I have achieved the impossible. Our baby is unquestionably a girl."

ZArymp discovered that his eyes were moist, although it couldn't possibly be because he was crying. "I have a granddaughter," he said, and he felt the happiness rise up inside him until it exploded in a great shout of joyous laughter. "I have a granddaughter!"

He ran from the room to spread the news, the pain in his old man's joints entirely forgotten. Dakon and Cordelia heard his voice float up the stairs.

"I—have—a—granddaughter!"

Dakon kissed Cordelia's cheek, his heart overflowing with love and gratitude. "And I have you," he said. "The mother of my child, and the other half of my soul."

Cordelia laid the tips of her fingers against his lips. *We have each other,* she said. *For the rest of our lives, we have each other.*